HOME AT LAST

Jerri Corgiat

A SIGNET ECLIPSE BOOK

SIGNET ECLIPSE
Published by New American Library, a division of
Penguin Group (USA) Inc., 375 Hudson Street,
New York, New York 10014, USA
Penguin Group (Canada), 90 Eglinton Avenue East, Suite 700, Toronto,
Ontario M4P 2Y3, Canada (a division of Pearson Penguin Canada Inc.)
Penguin Books Ltd., 80 Strand, London WC2R 0RL, England
Penguin Ireland, 25 St. Stephen's Green, Dublin 2,
Ireland (a division of Penguin Books Ltd.)
Penguin Group (Australia), 250 Camberwell Road, Camberwell, Victoria 3124,
Australia (a division of Pearson Australia Group Pty. Ltd.)
Penguin Books India Pvt. Ltd., 11 Community Centre, Panchsheel Park,
New Delhi - 110 017, India
Penguin Group (NZ), cnr Airborne and Rosedale Roads, Albany,
Auckland 1310, New Zealand (a division of Pearson New Zealand Ltd.)
Penguin Books (South Africa) (Pty.) Ltd., 24 Sturdee Avenue,
Rosebank, Johannesburg 2196, South Africa

Penguin Books Ltd., Registered Offices:
80 Strand, London WC2R 0RL, England

First published by Signet Eclipse, an imprint of New American Library,
a division of Penguin Group (USA) Inc.

First Printing, August 2005
10 9 8 7 6 5 4 3 2 1

Copyright © Jerri Corgiat, 2005
All rights reserved

To children with invisible scars and the people who work to heal them

Acknowledgments

The cast of characters populating my life have my sincere appreciation, as usual: Dear husband, family, friends—you know I couldn't keep going without you!

For their help with this book, a special thanks with hugs is offered to . . .

. . . Claire Zion who, once again, helped me dig deeper,

. . . Nancy, for her willingness to share,

. . . Meredith Hollingsworth at Ozanam Home for Boys and Girls, for her dedicated attempt to educate me and for arranging meetings with various members of Ozanam's awesome staff,

. . . and to Mac, who lent his name to the fictitious Michael who I introduced in my first novel, *Sing Me Home*, never dreaming that the make-believe five-year-old of *that* book would ever develop the troubles that his now-adolescent character possesses in *this* book. The real-life Michael and the fictitious Michael may share a name, but that's all! I love you, sweetie!

Chapter 1

Oh, joy. Returning home to Cordelia, Missouri, was just what she wanted to do. *Not*.

Jutting out her chin, Mari O'Malley clenched her fists in her lap and looked away from her two older sisters, focusing instead on the dust motes dancing in a strip of May sunshine that had somehow managed to slip inside her loft apartment. When she'd moved to midtown Kansas City the summer that she'd graduated from college—God, eight years ago?—she'd thought all these windows would provide the perfect light for painting. Truth was, hemmed in by concrete and grime, they'd hardly provided any light at all. She gave a mental shrug. Whatever. Between struggling to keep her career afloat and her love affair alive, who'd had time to wield a paintbrush?

But, as her sisters Lil and Alcea had just oh-so-annoyingly reminded her, she *now* had plenty of time to do whatever she wanted. Correction: whatever *they* wanted.

After the three of them had returned from their latest visit to the cardiac care unit at St. Luke's Hospital, she'd kicked off her Icon wedges and flopped onto the futon that dominated what she airily referred to as the conversation pit. (Like the rest of her loft, though, it was mostly just *pit*.) Lil and Alcea had taken the two chairs opposite . . . and laid out their request.

No, their demand. Which she'd find laughable if they weren't dead serious.

Picking a piece of imaginary lint off her gauze cargo pants, she glanced at them through her eyelashes. It didn't look like either one of them would cave. Neither had relaxed her spine. They both had formidable spines.

But that was okay. She had a formidable chin.

Outside, a delivery truck rumbled through the alley on the north side, accompanied by a low whoosh of traffic and a squeal of diesel brakes from the east. The building's elevator clanked, and the bass from the hip-hop music next door vibrated her molars. Somewhere below, a door slammed.

At the crack, Lil's hands fluttered up to her short blond curls like startled doves before settling back in her lap. Her silk-skirted lap. She'd dressed up for The City. "I don't know how you can stand all the noise," she murmured.

"I like it. It's *life*," Mari said, conveniently forgetting how, at three this morning, the hip-hop next door had driven her to seriously consider stomping down the hall with a sledgehammer. "You'd like it, too. Or would, if you ever stepped a foot out of Cordelia for more than a minute. Why you'd remain in that Missouri backwater is one of the great mysteries of life." *And why in blazes anyone would ever think I'd go back is a bigger one.*

"Not to me." Lil smiled gently.

They'd had this same exchange before—ad nauseum. Knowing she wouldn't convince Lil of anything, she decided for once in her life not to even try.

"Let's get back on target." Alcea crossed her long, denim-clad legs. The studied casualness of black jeans, black blouse, and hammered-silver earrings that matched a few silver strands threading through the gold hair she'd left in a tumble on her shoulders were

Alcea's statement that Kansas City didn't intimidate *her.* "It's the best solution, Mari, and you know it."

No, she didn't. Going home—however briefly—was a humongous leap off the Yellow Brick Road, and she'd already stumbled through quite a few detours. Maybe everything she'd tried had tanked, but she'd ultimately find Oz . . . and not in Cordelia.

But try to convince her sisters of that.

"Why me?" Having heard their request—no, their demand—she felt as ganged up on as she had as a kindergartner getting caught with her sisters' teenage makeup smeared across her freckled face. Exasperated, she looked from one to the other. Lil's cobalt eyes—a match of her own and their mother's—held a plea. Alcea's eyes—twins of Pop's—were hard walnut. Come to think of it, maybe Alcea's jeans weren't a statement. Very little intimidated Alcea.

"The family needs you, Mari. Mother needs you. And you—" Lil was too kind to complete the sentence.

Alcea wasn't. "—have no family, no relationships, and now no business to keep you here."

She thought of the recent phone calls from Sean. "That's only partly right." Alcea leveled her gaze on Mari, and she fumbled. "Okay, maybe mostly right." She could have Sean back if she wanted, but since she wasn't sure that she did, he probably didn't count as a relationship. Nor did she want to explain. Especially to Alcea. Her oldest sister knew her history with Sean—although not the whole of it. If she had her way, nobody would ever know the whole of it. "And it's so nice of you to remind me, Hock."

She'd christened her oldest sister with the nickname as soon as she'd learned *Alcea* was the formal name for the hollyhocks lining the fence in her mother Zinnia's backyard. Wondering who was tending her mother's flowers now and remembering how Zinnia had looked lying in her hospital bed an hour ago, tangled in a web of tubes, Mari felt something like a chicken bone catch in her throat. But she wouldn't let anxiety show on her face. She gave Alcea a haughty look.

Which Alcea gave right back. And haughty teamed with Alcea's exquisite looks made her *very* impressive.

"Don't call her Hock." Lil's frown chastised them both, although stern was at odds with her gentle beauty.

Exquisite. Beautiful. Mari muffled a snort. She herself had always been *the cute one*, or *the wild one*, or—her personal favorite—*our late, little mistake*, as her mother called her.

With fondness, of course. The chicken bone twisted.

Because by the time she'd been conceived, eleven years after Alcea and nine years after Lil, and long after their mother thought she'd retired from her diapering days, the O'Malley gene pool had grown stagnant.

Lil continued. "What Alcea means is—"

"I know what she means! But why can't one of you—or even both of you—handle things with Mom? I mean, you live there."

"And we both run businesses," Alcea pointed out, "and have families."

"Oh, c'mon, Hock. Kathleen's the only kid you have, and you said she'd be interning somewhere this summer. And you have a partner. She can take care of your diner."

"That'd be real big of me," Alcea snapped. "Without Kathleen home from college to help out with the seasonal tourist trade, the diner will be more swamped than usual. And I'm not going to dump it all on Florida. She may be my partner, but she's also a single mother. You know that. Besides, what else are you going to do except come home? You're broke."

"Now, Alcea," Lil inserted. "We don't know that. We only know she closed her business. She might have money—"

"She's broke." Alcea folded her arms. "Look at her hair."

Involuntarily, Mari's hand flew to her head, where four inches of orange curls sprang from her scalp. "What about my hair?"

Lil eyed it. "Um, it *does* look kind of funny. I understand—kind of—why you'd experiment with dying it black and putting in green streaks, but"—her nose wrinkled—"green *tips*?"

Mari sighed. When she'd learned of her mother's heart attack and that it would land her in St. Luke's last week for by-pass surgery, she shouldn't have wasted time wailing and gnashing her teeth; she should have spent it shaving her head. "It's left over from the last dye job. I haven't had time for a haircut."

"Or the money," Alcea added firmly.

Lil nodded slowly. "Alcea's right, isn't she? You're broke."

Mari's shoulders slumped. Both her sisters knew *hair* had once run second only to *clothing* in her budget, and both were close on the heels of *rent*. But after shivering through a brief cold snap without heat a month ago, she'd moved *utilities* up on her list. Ergo, no haircut. "Maybe. But that's even more reason for me to stay here, isn't it? I need to make a new start, at least find a job." *Like yesterday.* "And Cordelia is no employment mecca."

Lil frowned. "But if you were living at home—"

"What about you? Maybe Alcea's out, but you're rich! You could hire as much help as you need at your bookstores so you could play Mom's nursemaid." Lil owned several children's bookstores, not to mention that her country rock star husband had more gold than Midas. "Or if you don't want to do that, you could hire an entire staff for her. So I don't see why . . ."

Her voice trailed off as Lil's eyes filled with disappointment in her and—something else. Something sadder. Mari bit her lip. Damn Lil. Always stirring up everyone's conscience. And usually right. How could you love someone and hate them at the same time? Sean's image flitted across her brain, then was gone.

"It will be hard enough to convince Mother she needs any help at all." Lil's hands twisted in her lap, although her tone stayed mild. "But she does. And you know she won't take it from anyone except family."

Well, they had plenty of *that* to go around. "Pop could handle—"

Alcea gave her a look. "Pop's no spring chicken anymore. Seventy-one isn't ancient, but it's still too much for him."

"Then *Patsy Lee*." Patsy Lee was their brother's widow and they all still thought of her as their sister-in-law, as much a part of the family as she'd been when Henry was alive. Patsy Lee would say yes. Patsy Lee was a *saint*.

"*God*, Mari." Alcea shook her head. "Patsy Lee has her job, the night classes she's taking, and three children at home—no, make that four, once Daisy's home from college. Patsy Lee would do it if we asked. But I'm *not* going to ask."

See, a saint. But okay, a busy one. "Then . . . *Daisy*." Patsy Lee's daughter. Their college-age niece. Mari knew she was playing a joker.

Even Lil looked incredulous.

Alcea recovered her tongue. "Daisy is as much a ninny as she was in preschool."

"Now, Alcea—" Lil started.

"Which leaves *Melanie*." Lil's stepdaughter. Also college-age. But unlike Daisy of the wild eye shadow, flashy clothes, and air for brains, Melanie was calm, rational, and dependable. Mari had played her ace.

Her sisters fell silent.

Feeling she'd trumped the discussion, Mari tugged on the sleeves of her unstructured jacket—apple green gauze like the pants, and part of an outfit she'd bought back when she was still fooling herself that she could afford Neiman Marcus—crossed her arms, and sat back. There could be no possible objection.

The silence stretched. Lil's gaze had dropped to her hands. Alcea was eying Lil with more than a little concern.

Mari frowned. "For Pete's sake. What now?"

"Lil has enough on her plate right now. She can't spare Melanie."

"Why not?"

Alcea hesitated.

Mari sat forward. "What aren't you telling me?"

Lil sighed and looked up. "It's Michael."

Mari had always felt an affinity for Lil's mischief-loving fourteen-year-old stepson—no surprise, since, as a teen, she'd been very much like him. "Is he sick or something? He sounded fine when you put him on the phone in March."

He had, hadn't he? She hadn't paid a lot of attention when the Van Castles had called on her birthday. Not that her self-obsession was unusual. Since college graduation, she'd paid little attention to the home front, her sights focused on her own life. And she'd been even more myopic on her birthday. In March, she'd turned thirty and now it was official: Her clock was ticking. Biological, career-ological, everyway-ological.

"He's not sick, but . . . He's gotten into trouble lately. At school. At home."

"Are you talking about that prank he pulled with the Bronco?" A bout of joyriding in his dad's car. What was the big deal?

Lil's chin wobbled, and Alcea took over. "The whole family is seeing a therapist."

"Oh, good grief." Mari laughed. "Michael is a teenager. Teenagers are all schizoid. I did more than my share of shi—I mean, shenanigans—when I was his age, and I'll admit I probably caused Mom and Pop some sleepless nights, but they didn't clap me on some psychologist's couch. Get real."

Lil's chin hardened mid-wobble. "Don't talk about things you don't understand." The sharpness in her voice was decidedly un-Lil-like. "The fact is, when I don't have to manage my bookstores, I need to keep my time available for my family—and that includes Mel. We'll all be at the psychologist's once a week, and I'll be with Jon at therapy another night—whether you think it's necessary or not."

That pulled Mari up short. Lil and Jon's marriage was troubled? Impossible. Still frequently at home during the first tumultuous months of the Van Castles' marriage, she clearly remembered how hard they'd fought for their happiness, battling Jon's shrew of an ex-wife. She'd have thought paradise would have a longer life span than nine years.

Looking from Lil's hard face to Mari's, Alcea put herself in the unaccustomed role of peacekeeper. "Maybe it wasn't in your plans, Mari, but you heard the doctor this morning. Mother will likely be released next Friday. She'll need help around the clock at first. Lil and I can't provide it. There's nobody else, and you *are* available. You've got to go back to Cordelia."

Mari felt trapped in the crosshairs of Alcea's dark eyes. Trapped, actually, by the fact her bank account was bone dry and she wasn't coming up with a whole lot of options. Still, ignoring the shame she felt flush her face—she wanted to help her mother, sure she did, but just not *there*—she scrambled for another out. "There's no way I can be ready to leave in a week."

"Yes, there is." Lil's blue eyes gleamed with a martial light Mari recognized. She groaned. Why had she gone and set Lil's back up? It was the surest way to strengthen her sister's determination. "We'll make sure of it."

* * *

And Lil did. Over the next week, using her considerable organizational skills—and her even more considerable money—Lil had paid off a month's rent, advertised to sublet the loft, and hired movers that were arriving today at one.

Not that Mari was ready. She'd had all week to pack, but she'd frittered away the time, waiting for manna to fall from heaven and save her. But on Saturday morning, when nothing had dropped from the sky except steady rain, she acknowledged defeat, dragged herself out of bed, and opened her suitcases. She'd seen her parents and sisters off yesterday, after Zinnia had been released from the hospital. And tomorrow she'd be installed as her mother's primary caregiver.

In Cordelia.

Dragging her feet didn't *begin* to cover her mood.

Cordelia.

Mari snorted, hauled a Shelli Segal embroidered jacket off its hanger, and tossed it on her bed— actually a mattress on the floor, hidden by partitions— and wondered where she'd wear it. The Rooster Bar & Grill? Fine dining at its best. Still, she'd take the jacket anyway. What else did she have to show for eight years except a pretty decent wardrobe? She scowled and reached for some hats. Spending most of her earnings on clothing had possibly been a mistake.

Cordelia.

But returning there could be her worst.

She snagged the Tommy Bahama hat she'd bought just before Sean had taken her to the Kansas City Jazz Festival four years ago. And just before she'd broken things off. Like a good little addict, she'd kicked him cold turkey after confessing her affair to Alcea.

But then a year ago, Sean had started calling again. And still did. Irregularly, infrequently, but often enough to keep her off balance.

If she had any guts, she'd hang up. But she didn't.

Because on that first call, at the first sound of his voice, she'd felt that old craving return. So far she'd said no to his suggestions that they meet, her backbone stiffened by sheer willpower. But Sean was quietly tenacious. And she was growing weak. She'd been obsessed with him—criminy, even *without* him—for a good chunk of the last eight years.

Fingering the hat, she wandered around the loft, letting memories steamroll her. She paused at a framed photo on the wall of the first TGIF party she'd attended at Carmichael Cards. Frozen in time, the art department crowded into the break room in various shades of sobriety. Hard to miss *her,* a go-get-'em, eager-eyed summer intern with her dyed neon-red hair spiked into horns, the wild feathered hoops stuck in her ears, and that goofy, excited expression. She touched her image, leaving a fingerprint in the dust. God, she'd been so *young*. And so *stupid*.

Gaze moving over the other faces, she grimaced. She couldn't remember a single name.

Except his, of course.

Sean Reynolds: art director extraordinaire. Lover par excellence.

She'd first laid eyes on Sean when he'd interviewed her for a graphic design internship at Carmichael Cards. One of the leading greeting card companies in the country, Carmichael reached its benevolent hands out to touch a lot of people beyond those millions who bought its sentimental merchandise. The business was a key sponsor of fine arts, charities, and children's art education, as well as one of the region's major employers. Positions with Carmichael were prized. She'd wanted that internship so badly, she'd postponed a studio class just to delay graduation so she could have a chance at the three-days-a-week position. And she would have done more than that to get the job once she'd seen who she'd be working for.

Fingering her résumé at her interview, Sean Reynolds had raised his warm brown eyes to hers, she'd turned all kinds of crimson, something had zinged straight into her heart, and she'd been hooked. Drop-dead gorgeous, sophisticated at ten years her senior, brimming with ambition—and without a ring on his left hand—he could lead her right down that Yellow Brick Road to Oz. She'd just known it.

Four weeks later, when he'd called to offer her the position, she'd jumped for joy. The internships went to only the top students in a few area colleges. And when he'd invited her to accompany him to a New York design show at the start of the program, she'd almost leaped out of her skin. Out of all these people in the photo, he'd picked her. Imagine that!

Still staring at the photo, she crunched the brim of the hat beyond repair. Yeah, just imagine. She'd been an innocent idiot. He hadn't led her anywhere except along the proverbial primrose path.

That trip had launched their affair. And a need for secrecy that had made her feel like such a sneak at work that, at the end of summer, she'd allowed Sean to help her set up a business largely based on Carmichael's outsourced design work. She'd turned down the permanent position that was offered. And turned away the overtures of friendship from the people she worked with. . . .

Which left nobody here to bid farewell. She exhaled noisily. Unless you counted Molly Mackerson, which she didn't. She wouldn't have even phoned her ex-client to give her a forwarding address if Molly didn't still owe her some money for a past job.

And there was Sean. Turning her head, she eyed the telephone, looked away. So, she was chicken. So what? It wasn't like she was afraid of *him*. She was just afraid of her own impulses. That, in her book, made her wise.

She unhooked the Carmichael photo and moved on,

taking down others and stuffing them all under her arm. She stopped again at a shot of her family and friends, taken on the broad front porch of her parents' rambling old bungalow on the day she'd left for Kansas City. Relegating the rest of the photos to a box, she lifted this one off the wall and studied it. Nearly everybody she'd ever known had been at her farewell party. All except one. Because by that time, she'd already put paid to the very best friendship she'd ever had.

Wondering what Andy Eppelwaite was up to now, she shook her head and sighed. Nothing good, no doubt. She dropped the picture on top of the others, stuffed her hat in the trash, and returned to her closet, attacking it with renewed vigor.

Cordelia. She could still back out. It'd cause a fuss, but dammit, her family was the size of a small city, so you'd think they could count on *someone* else. It wasn't that she didn't love her mom or that she didn't want to help her family. She knew her sisters' arguments were reasonable (God, she hated *reasonable*), not to mention she didn't have two nickels left to rub together, but . . .

But she was afraid if she skedaddled out of town on such a low note, she'd never have the courage to return. She'd get stuck in Cordelia much the same way everyone got stuck in Cordelia—too lazy or unadventurous or something to look up over the rim of the ruts they'd dug.

And . . . She blew a piece of hair off her forehead so she wouldn't have to see its green tip. *And* . . . she'd admit she hated returning like *this*.

With no job. No boyfriend. No prospects for either. And bad hair.

A knock echoed off the high ceiling. She jumped and glanced at her watch, its broad band loose on her wrist. She'd lost weight lately, giving her what she considered a rather fascinating cadaver look. (Her sisters, of course, had tall, trim figures. She was tall, too. But *skinny*.) It was only eleven. The movers had gotten the time wrong. Well, she wasn't ready; they'd have to wait.

Brushing lint off the old *Punk'd* T-shirt she'd donned over a pair of even older capri pants—why play dress up today?—she crossed the floorboards to the door, put an eyeball to the peephole, and jerked back. *Sean*. Her thoughts flew in fifty million conflicted directions, and her hands flew to her head, her chest, and down to smooth her pants. Then she crept back and peeked out again. Definitely Sean. He looked as Harry Connick, Jr., as he always had.

While she looked like something that had crawled out from behind her refrigerator.

He knocked again. "Mari! I heard you in there."

Sighing, she undid three locks, opened the door a few inches, and walked to the center of the loft. Maybe, from a distance, she'd look less frightening. Maybe, from a distance, he'd look less wonderful. What in the *hell* was he doing here?

Sean pushed the door open and hesitated just inside. One hand swept back his dark hair, then got stuffed into a pocket of his Hugo Boss trousers. The other fingered the collar of his open-necked white dress shirt, then dropped into the opposite pocket. It was a casual look. A casual pose, even if a tad fidgety. He looked everywhere around the loft, but not at her. Which gave her time to study him.

Except in her dreams, she hadn't seen him in two years. Not since she'd severed all connection with Carmichael's. And with it, her connection to him.

But now the months fell away. His every gesture was familiar. Familiar? Criminy, she'd once had him memorized backward and forward. He looked the same except for a sprinkle of salt near his temples. And maybe his eyes were older. Even wiser? Surely not. He'd never been wise.

And neither had she.

He finally looked at her and flashed a smile—all white teeth, boyish and charming.

And, God help her, she wanted to run right over and launch herself into his arms.

Then she thought of Jo—his *wife*, Jo—and turned away.

A week after their affair had started on that New York trip, she'd learned about his marriage. She'd demanded an explanation for his unbound wedding ring finger, and he'd explained an allergy to metals. How convenient. Which was how Sean liked things: convenient. But by that time, it was already too late for her to pull back, damn her own selfish hide. She'd been hopelessly, nauseatingly, *wrongly* infatuated with the man—in love for the first time and with her whole heart—and, worse than that, always willing to let him convince her that *now* would be the week, the month, the year that he'd end things with Jo.

For four years, their relationship had yo-yoed. Up, down, on again, off again. Until she'd finally, *finally* found the willpower to dump him after she'd watched her oldest sister, Alcea, struggle with the aftermath of her ex-husband's infidelity. But she hadn't given Sean up completely. For another two years, she'd hung on to the Carmichael contracts he fed her, working largely through someone else as Sean moved up the ladder at the greeting card behemoth, but still dependent on him . . . and still speaking to him . . . and even, God help her, occasionally flirting with him again.

But that had all ceased two years ago. She'd broken off all contact with both Sean and Carmichael's. *She'd* managed to weather the withdrawal pangs, but her business hadn't. It had stumbled along on shrinking profits for another two years, but without the greeting card company contracts, Designs by Mari had finally gone bust.

"You look good. . . ." Sean's voice trailed off—maybe because she obviously *didn't*. He cleared his throat. "Why didn't you tell me you were leaving?"

Not wanting to plead cowardice, she sidestepped the question. "How did you find out?"

"I saw Molly at the Phoenix last night." Sean moved farther into the room. "Boko Maru played," he added, moving further into the room.

She culled her memory for some scintillating comment about the jazz group, but hardly remembered them at all. After they'd split, she'd avoided jazz, blues, caramel macchiatos, the River Market on Saturday mornings, *Pitch* newspaper, Westport Art Fair, the Plaza, and just about everything else he'd introduced into her life.

She reached for the radio, flipped it on, and Garth Brooks warbled about burying the hatchet, but leaving the handle sticking out. How *frigging* appropriate.

"Your cousin is a big blabbermouth." She should have known Molly Mackerson wouldn't keep her trap shut—hadn't she slyly yapped on about Sean's activities nonstop after their breakup? Neither she nor Sean had breathed a word about their relationship into Molly's ears—not wanting to see it broadcast on the evening news—but she'd always thought Molly had suspected. Still, since Molly's business helped pay her bills, she'd tolerated the woman. Until two years ago, when she'd finally told Molly to shut up already, not caring at that point if she lost her best client. In fact, she'd almost hoped that she would—Molly was her last remaining link to Sean.

She stooped to unplug her Apple computer components.

"Molly *is* that." He paused. "When are you leaving?"

Detecting a forlorn undertone, she glanced over her shoulder, but he missed her frown. His gaze was once more wandering all over the loft, lighting on everything except her. Watching him warily, she straightened, wrapped the surge protector cord around itself with a few quick snaps, and tossed it in a waiting box. "This afternoon."

"Why so fast?"

"Family emergency. Mom's recovering from bypass surgery."

"So it's not a permanent move?" The hangdog note had suddenly dropped from his voice. "From what Molly said, I thought—"

"When has Molly ever gotten anything right? Mom will need me for about a month, but—" She stopped. She didn't want to tell him that her options had pretty much boiled down to Cordelia—or the City Union Mission. She'd hardly even admitted *that* to herself. "But she might need me longer."

"What about all this?" He motioned at all her belongings.

"Lil and her husband, Jon—the famous and rich country rock star, remember?—are paying to store all my stuff, and for the rent, and for the movers." Alcea and her wanderlust writer of a husband, Dak, had probably pitched in, too. "They didn't want me to have any excuse to say no." As his gaze skimmed past hers, Mari caught and held it. "Look, Sean. Why are you here?"

"I just—well, I thought I should say good-bye. In person."

They'd never said good-bye, not really. Not unless you counted that final time together when she'd shoved open a window and dropped his razor, toothbrush, robe, change of underwear, and Crew Pomade into the street. Trite, but it had felt fulfilling. Especially when a bus had run over them.

"But now that I know you're coming back, I want to tell you . . . Ask you . . ." His voice trailed off. Not surprising. Candor was missing from Sean's DNA.

Doing a mental eye roll and ignoring her upped pulse rate, she bent again to heft the CPU out from its desk cubby. The CPU was one heavy mother. She grunted, and before she knew what was happening, Sean had gently pushed her aside and taken over. After he'd lofted it onto the desk, they were only a foot apart. He was really looking at her now, really seeing her, and . . .

"God, what happened to your hair?"

She guessed she should give him credit for not calling her outfit into question, too. She'd always made it a point—and had spent a fortune—to look as polished as he always had.

Her face heated, but she raised her nose. "It's my natural color."

He'd never seen her natural color. He'd seen black with green chunks. Black with red tips. Blond with pink streaks. And that neon red. It wasn't until she'd run out of money that she'd stopped trying to fool Mother Nature.

He reached out to touch it. "I like it, it's soft. Pretty color, apricot."

"Hunh."

"Except for the green tips." He smiled. The fingers brushing her cheek did funny things to her insides. He didn't remove his hand but let it slide alongside her face, and when he finally whispered, "Mari," she was pretty much jelly.

"Hunh," she repeated, this time on a sigh, thinking, *Here it comes*, and feeling defenseless.

"Things have changed, but not my feelings for you. The phone calls . . ." He shrugged. "I didn't want to spook you. I thought I should take things slow. But when Molly said you were leaving . . ." His expression was earnest, imploring, and she leaned a bit closer. She'd always liked his mouth. Harry Connick, Jr.'s mouth. A smile tickled its corners. "Look, both me *and* my Braun shaver know you were adamant when you called us quits. But now . . . Let's start over. Let's try again. We've had closure."

Mari snapped out of her fantasies and jerked away. Her hand-wrought brass earrings slapped her cheeks. "Closure? That's pretty damned cold."

"Wait." He caught her arm. "Before you go into a fit—"

"I don't have fits."

"Yes, you do." His dark eyes were laughing, but the laughter died when she didn't smile. He put his hands on her shoulders. Aristocratic, long-fingered hands. Their warmth spread over her skin. "Just hear me out. I was devastated when Jo died, no matter what you think. But it wasn't my fault. And it wasn't yours. For God's sake, Mari, she died two years *after* you left me."

"I know. And I want to believe . . . But calling her death *closure*?" She wanted to move away, but the warmth of his hands had spread over her skin like some kind of anesthesia. She was paralyzed. "I mean, you said she was hard to live with. You said she was moody. But never in my wildest dreams did I think—"

"Moody." Sean gave a dry laugh. "She wasn't moody. She was—" He suddenly stopped and looked away.

"She was what?"

"Like I've always told you, she was emotionally unbalanced."

Emotionally unbalanced. That's about all she'd ever gotten out of him about Jo. And she hadn't pressed him for more details. Nor had she pumped Molly—in fact, she'd even cut Molly off when the woman had broached the topic of Sean's wife. She might have lost her morals but, by golly, she still had her pride. That, and she had feared Jo would become too real to her. So real that the guilt that gnawed at her would just gobble her right up.

So she'd bitten back questions and only clucked with sympathy on the many nights when Sean arrived, distracted and harassed on her doorstep, saying only that Jo's mood swings were driving him nuts. His wife was alternately clinging and demanding, angry and distant. And whenever he brought up divorce, Jo went into a frenzy, throwing things, hitting, threatening . . .

Emotionally unbalanced. It was the reason he wanted to end his marriage. And the reason he never had.

Mari had always wondered how much of what he said about Jo was the truth and how much was excuse. After all, Sean never confronted a problem head-on if he could help it. Studying him now, though, she saw a familiar bleakness in his expression. That desolation had always lent his words truth, while at the same time it had tugged at her heartstrings. And they were being yanked all over the place again now.

He took a deep breath. "I'm not saying this right. I know everything was a big mess. I know you were hurt. *I* was hurt. And I tried to move on. Hell, I even tried again with Jo once you were gone. Tried to help her. Tried to help my marriage. But you . . . you've never been out of my head."

"You've been out of mine."

"Have I?" His face relaxed, and his smile was tender. "Molly said you haven't even dated since then."

Damn Molly's eternal quest for gossip. And damn her own penchant for yammering away without thinking.

He looked around at the half-packed boxes, then back at her. "Give me—give *us*—another chance."

Mari pulled away, not jerking this time, but needing some distance. She'd given him chances. Plenty of chances. And the result had been hell.

She moved into the kitchenette and busied herself opening and closing cabinets without really seeing their contents. He didn't move. He was patient. She was not. And he knew it. He knew *her*. At one point she'd thought they'd belonged together like a pair of shoes—Manolo Blahniks, to be precise. They'd loved each other. Really. And she'd thought they'd go places together. The stratosphere was the limit.

But there had been Jo. . . .

And now Jo was gone.

Mari placed her palms on the countertop and dropped her head. Poor Jo. Did she still owe Sean's wife? Or was Mari's four-year absence from his life, the angst, the inner turmoil that may never subside enough penance? Was she throwing Sean away simply because she couldn't face her own responsibility for the whole *mess*, as he'd called it?

Finally she returned to Sean. She stopped a few feet in front of him, out of reach.

He'd perched a hip on her desk, no longer fidgeting. "Well, what do you think?"

"I . . ." Usually she knew just what she thought, but the last half-decade had taught her a lot, including the fact that her snap decisions weren't usually very snappy. "I don't know what to think."

"But it's not 'no way'?"

She chewed her lip, studying him, thinking how he'd once represented everything she'd ever wanted—and maybe still did. She expelled a long breath. "No, it's not 'no way.'" He started to reach for her, but she backed up a step. "And it's not 'throw me down on the floor and ravish me,' either."

His mouth quirked. "Then what is it?"

"I want to think. I want time." How was that for an un-snappy decision? This time she wouldn't just leap into the deep end without a life jacket. Since Sean had started calling, she'd known she'd again face a decision about him. But she wasn't ready. Whatever she might still feel for Sean was buried under layers of guilt, shame, hurt. . . .

Sean stuffed a hand in his pocket. His keys jangled.

"Okay. Take the month you'll be with your family to decide if you want to make another go of it. I'll wait."

Gee, how magnanimous. Irritation flicked her. Sean had always led. She'd always followed. Well, not anymore. "Thanks, but I'll take the whole summer and let you know in the fall."

The keys stopped jangling. His eyes rounded a little. Then, "Fine. But let's keep in touch."

It wasn't a question, but after a brief hesitation, she nodded.

"Still the same cell number?"

"No."

She'd ditched the cell. With no friends, what was the point? She reached for a pen, scribbled her parents' phone number on a scrap of paper, and handed it off. She wondered if she'd just lost her mind.

Or had finally found it.

He pocketed the paper and straightened. "I'll call you tomorrow." His voice held the same determination that he'd used to mount the rungs at Carmichael's. *And* that he'd used to convince her every time she'd broken up with him that she had to come back.

"No."

Again she noted the barely veiled look of surprise. But this time accompanied by hurt.

Sighing, she backtracked. "At least wait until Monday."

She needed time to digest his visit. And that, paired with her arrival in Cordelia, would give her a massive case of indigestion tomorrow. Monday . . .

Monday was soon enough for another jolt to her system.

Chapter 2

On Monday, Peg O' My Heart Cafe and Bakery, on the corner of Main and Oak Haven Road in the old town square of Cordelia, was in its usual state of bedlam. Waitresses flew across its red and black tiles, crockery clanked, the grill sizzled, and the noise level mounted as the old-timers settled into the red vinyl booths for a jaw, just like they did every morning. Except Sundays, of course, when they dozed off in the pews of St. Andrew's Church across the street.

Andrew Eppelwaite gave up trying to catch his grandmother's attention. Tansy stood at the grill, as she had for the last half century, shoulder blades moving like scissors under her uniform as she alternately flipped pancakes and handed off plates to the Bartlesby twins, who gave him a twitch of their apron bows whenever they passed his stool at the counter.

With an inward grin, he touched the brim of his baseball cap, but didn't otherwise answer the come-on. At thirty, he had about a decade on both Liza and Lisa. They were too young to remember him—he hadn't been back except for a few days at a time for more than four years—but you could bet their parents did. If No-Account Andy showed up on their doorstep, Mom and Dad would give him the old heave-ho. And they'd be justified. He'd been a hide-the-good-silver and lock-up-your-daughters kind of guy back then. If he hadn't been lifting a skirt or launching a brawl, he'd been guzzling beer at the Rooster Bar & Grill. Usually the latter.

He tossed some change on the counter and eased off the stool, stomping a boot to get too-tight faded jeans back into place over his long legs. He hadn't had the time, interest—or the money, for that matter—to do much with a wardrobe since he'd gotten out of the hoosegow a few years back. "See you later, Gran," he called out.

She turned and nodded a birdlike chin. Her near-white sausage curls—a vast improvement over the gold dye job she'd once had—bobbed. "Don't you go gettin' yerself up to no good, Andy." But she cackled as she said the words. What was once a worry was now a joke between them, bless her loyal little heart.

Andy grinned back and turned to the cash register. From the stool behind it, the proprietor, Alcea O'Malley Jones, gave him a smile that could melt a man's heart. She was a looker—always had been—but of course, from her almost-eleven-years-older perspective, she'd never noticed the lanky kid with the too-long hair who had hung out with her littlest sister, Mari.

"Glad to see you're back, Andy." Alcea picked up the check he laid on the counter. "Tansy's pretty proud of you."

"So Gran tells me, oh, twenty times a day. It's about time I gave her something to be proud of."

"Aunt Alcie! Look what Mommy give me!" A slim youngster with a scraggle of dark hair and demanding blue eyes, not a toddler, but not too far from it, had materialized at Alcea's knee.

Alcea bent over, scooped the child onto her lap, and examined the Hot Wheels toy she held out. "Why, Missouri, I do believe you now have a full collection of muscle cars."

Missouri nodded sagely. "'Cept a Chevelle. But

Julius"—Julius was the old mechanic over at Cowboy's Tow and Service. The name twisted around the child's tongue, coming out more like *Yool-yus*—"said he's gonna get me that one, too!" She squirmed until Alcea set her down, then ran off, showing the car and chattering a streak to anyone who would listen.

"Cute kid," Andy commented, handing off a few bills. "Muscle cars?"

"My partner—Florida's—daughter." Alcea laughed, swiveling to work the cash register. "Julius is determined to make a mechanic out of her."

Ah, the "love child," as Gran referred to Missouri. He was glad Alcea had turned away so she couldn't see his expression go sour. As Gran told it, the little girl was the product of an affair between Florida and Alcea's ex-husband. How the wife and mistress of the same man could end up fast friends and partners, let alone how Alcea could acknowledge—and, from what he'd just seen, *love*—the product of that union was way beyond his powers of understanding. Nothing against the child, but . . . His jaw hardened, thinking of his sister Anna. He didn't think he could ever be that forgiving.

Alcea turned around to hand him his change. "Mari's in town. As of Saturday night. You should look her up."

He fumbled a quarter. Blood rushed to his head, and not just because he'd stooped to pick it up off the floor. "Might do that."

He tipped his cap and pushed through the screen door with studied casualness. He wouldn't mind seeing Mari O'Malley; in fact, he'd like nothing better. But he wasn't so sure Mari would want to see him. They'd once been best buds, but after a trip into the back of his pickup at sixteen, things had changed. His fault—and something else he'd lived to regret.

Outside, he squinted up at a robin's-egg sky, tugged

his cap down against a blustery May wind until only a hint of blond curls stuck out underneath, and surveyed the church green across the road. (Some odd historical happenstance had planted St. Andrews instead of City Hall smack in the middle of the square. A fire-and-damnation first mayor, if he recalled right. And he probably didn't, since he hadn't been much for paying attention in class.)

Crocuses and daffodils had given way to ribbons of tulips that wound along walkways between ponds of *Convallaria majalis*—lily of the valley—rippling under the still half-hearted shade of maples and sycamores. Their delicate scent mingled with the Lincoln Lilacs that brushed the stone of the tall-steepled church. In sun-splashed patches, clumps of peonies were ready to burst into bloom.

"Ladies' Auxiliary sure knows what they're doin', don't they?" Paddy O'Neill had wandered up. "Bet even with all that stuff they taught you in college, you couldn't do no better."

"Bet you're right." Andy stuck out his hand. "How're you doing, Paddy?" Longtime cronies, Paddy and his grandmother had been matching each other cackle for cackle since he could remember. They even looked alike now—both bony, both wizened—except for the hair. Paddy had three tufts: two over his elongated ears, one on top of his head, now whirligigging in the breeze. He'd bet *they* knew why a church lay in the middle of Cordelia's town square—they'd probably been here when the steeple was hoisted. The old man's grip was still strong, though.

"Arthritis botherin' me some, but you know what they say—" Paddy's eyes crinkled, adding another skein of lines over the network stretched across his face.

"What do they say?" he asked, although he'd heard the answer from Paddy's lips time and again.

"Gettin' old ain't no picnic, but the alternative is worse." Paddy barked a laugh that slid into a spasm of coughing.

Andy pounded his back. "You okay?"

Paddy nodded, wiping spittle across the back of his hand. "Right as rain, but don't you go making me chase you any, hear? No longer have much get-up in my get-up-and-go."

"I promise," Andy said solemnly, not really knowing if Paddy was serious or not, but not blaming him if he was. He'd lifted a pair of antique earrings out of O'Neill's Emporium fourteen years ago, then had led the shopkeeper on a merry dash through the alleys and streets surrounding the town square until he'd lost him on Maple Woods Drive. On the broad front porch of Mari O'Malley's bungalow, he'd given the jewelry to her as an apology for things getting out of hand in his pickup truck. But aware he'd had no money to line his pockets—damn her honesty—Mari had handed them right back. Just in time for Paddy and the sheriff to grab him by the collar. Not the first—or last—in a long line of scrapes that had grown worse when Mari was no longer around to deter him. Or to shoulder a lot of the blame.

"How long you sticking around anyways? Sure know your grandma's glad to see you."

"I'll be in town for a couple more weeks, then back and forth for a few months."

"Tansy says you got yerself a new job over toward Lake Kesibwi."

"Not new, exactly. Just an offshoot of the place where I work in Kansas City. I'll be at Kesibwi for the summer."

"Well, good luck to you, boy. You do your grandma proud. Knew there was more to you than your no-account daddy."

No-Account Senior. No-Account Andy. But not anymore. Andy watched as Paddy hitched off toward

Peg O' My Heart, then stuck his hands in his pockets and started down Main. Once was, nobody thought he'd ever amount to anything. Once was, he'd thought they were right.

Pushing regrets to the back of his brain, enjoying the sun-kissed green of the Ozark hills off in the distance, enjoying the feeling of well-being that, except for a couple of blips, was several years old and still too new to be taken for granted—if he was lucky, he would *never* take it for granted—he passed Rusty's Hardware and neared Merry-Go-Read. The shop was one of three children's bookstores Mari's middle sister, Lil, had started after she'd flummoxed the town by getting hitched to a country music superstar almost nine years back. Mari had been in college then, only visiting Cordelia now and again. And never once looking him up. She'd . . .

Like he'd conjured her up, the bookstore door snapped open on a jangle of bells, and Mari strode out, nearly knocking him down.

His heart jumped, but he acted like their first real encounter in fourteen years wasn't that big a deal. "Whoa! Hang on there, Mar." He locked onto her arm to keep her from falling.

Mari steadied herself and shrugged out of his grasp. "I swear if I ever get out—" She glanced up. Blue eyes locked on blue, and her jaw dropped. "*No-Account Andy*."

He gave her a one-sided grin. "I prefer just plain *Andy*, but good to see you anyway." And it was. More than good. Same generous mouth. Same sprinkle of freckles. Same perpetual exasperation. Same . . .

Looking at her hair, he frowned. "What's up with the do? Looks like a kid outlined your hair with green Magic Marker."

She flushed as bright as her hair, one of her hands flying up to pull at a tip. "I just haven't had time to get it cut." She glanced at his faded jeans, up to his faded plaid shirt, and into his eyes, her color returning to normal, her hand dropping, disdain lurking behind her gaze. "*Some* of us are busy."

He started back down the walk, a grin lurking behind his lips. They'd picked up squabbling right where they'd left off. "Oh, I've got places to go, people to see," he assured her.

They passed the cigar store Indian sitting out front of O'Neill's Emporium, and the grin surfaced big-time. He remembered when the two of them had roped it up and tied it to the belfry of St. Andrew's Church. Thinking he'd land in more hot water than she would when they got caught, she'd stood up tall and told her mother it was her idea, though it wasn't.

"Yeah, I'll bet." She fell in beside him, matching his steps stride for stride. A peasant-type dress in some silky material slapped around her calves above shoes two stories tall. With the doodads on her ears, she looked the part of an artist. Or, at least, she looked like she wanted to look the part of an artist. That was Mari. Trying to be anything the town wasn't. In your face. Honest to a fault. Things that had maddened him; things he'd admired. "That's why you're headed in the direction of the Rooster?"

"Which is also," he pointed out, "the direction of Beadler's Feed." The Rooster Bar & Grill lay next door to the farmers' supply store. "You going that way?"

"I'm going that way." Her voice was grim. "My sister Alcea lives next to Cowboy's." Cowboy's Tow and Service was across from Beadler's.

"She's not there. I just saw her at the diner." Swinging along beside her felt good.

"I know, but her husband, Dak, *is* home. And I need to pick up an edition of Mother Goose and Lil says he probably has one. Which *she* didn't, although you'd think a children's bookstore would have a frigging nursery rhyme book, but, *nooo*, and now I'm hotfooting it down there and will probably spend the next hour searching through shelves—Dak has a ton of damn books, and you can bet neither he nor Alcea has put them in any kind of order. Alcea and Dak don't *do* order. They say they're too busy."

He almost laughed, remembering the mess in Mari's room, her backpack, and her school locker. Open *that* up, and chances were you'd get buried alive. "Why a Mother Goose emergency?"

"Because Mom has it in her head that she needs to know the exact words of 'Humpty Dumpty'—because she and Pop were arguing whether it was 'couldn't put him together again' or 'couldn't put him *back* together again,' and *this* after I'd just dropped an egg on the floor and got a royal reaming over how hard she's always worked to keep those floors clean. Which is nothing compared to the earful I got yesterday after she asked me to weed her garden and I pulled up some—some . . ." She frowned.

"Perennials?" he offered.

"Yes. What do I know? They look like weeds to me. But it's not my job to say *no* to anything she asks me, even if she knows I have a brown thumb. It's my job—bestowed on me by my two *wonderful* sisters— to play Steppen Fetchit for the next God-knows-how-long." She paused for a breath. "And wouldn't you know Pop's computer is broken and I don't have my Mac set up yet, because it would have been a snap to look it up on the Internet."

Ah, Mari was in fine form. He realized just how much he'd missed her chatter. They passed under the green awning of Sin-Sational Ice Cream where they'd shared many a soda—no romance there, just lack of funds to buy two—and stepped off the curb onto Maple Woods Drive. Beadler's Feed was on the opposite corner.

He motioned up the street. "Your folks still live up that way?"

"They won't move out of there until they die." She threw a black look in that direction. "Which might not be too many hours from now."

"I thought you all got along." As a kid, he'd envied Mari her family. He'd had Gran, but nobody else except for a sister he'd rarely seen. His mood momentarily dipped at the thought of Anna.

They stepped up on the opposite curb.

"We *do* get along." Mari sounded unconvinced. She drew a deep breath as they paused on the corner. "But Mom just had bypass surgery. The doctor warned us she might have some emotional issues—or some temporary personality changes. I guess it does that to some people."

"Gran told me about the surgery." Without thinking, he brushed a short lock of hair back from her forehead like he used to do, but she didn't react. If she was harboring any long-held yearnings where he was concerned, she certainly hid it well. He let his hand fall. "So she's not herself."

"No. She's short-tempered and has all these *unreasonable* demands, and Pop's not used to dealing with her like that, and I . . ." Her gaze flew up to his, and he could see the worry behind her frustration. "I'm just not used to seeing her like this, Andy. She needs help with *everything*, and she looks so pale and so *small*."

The intervening years had just fallen away. She was just as confiding, and he was just as willing to listen.

"It'll get better, Mar."

"I hope so." She looked around as though just remembering where they were. Her gaze fell on his truck. "*Omigod*, you still have that old thing?"

He laughed. "Hard to believe, isn't it?"

They scraped over the graveled parking lot to his Ford pickup, sitting next to a pallet stacked with bags of sand and black soil. Once a shade of apple red, the truck was now an oxidized pink where it wasn't pure rust. She peeked into the bed, apparently not seeing the assortment of shovels and spades and gardening tools, but only the past, because when she turned around, her face matched the truck.

And when their eyes locked, he knew they were both reliving the same scene. Moonlight. Tanned hands on pale skin. A lot of fumbling and cursing and grunting.

He refused to let the number of times he'd thought about that night show in his face, and grinned instead. "I had bruises on my knees for a week. Always wondered what it had done to your backside."

"Gee, how chivalrous." Her color fading, Mari punched his arm. Hard enough that he wanted to wince, but he didn't. "My backside was just fine, thanks."

He lowered the gate, stooped to pick up a bag, settled it into the bed, and went after another. She watched him. When he glanced up, her gaze was full of speculation.

"This all yours?" She motioned at the bags and tools. When he nodded, she nodded, too. "Still doing work for old Erik, are you?"

Erik Olausson owned a lawn business. In high school, even after, the old Swede had handed Andy some odd jobs, knowing Andy would be good for them until the next paycheck. Which Andy drank away before he got back to work.

He started to answer her, but as usual she already thought she had it all figured out and was off on a run. He let her go, hoping for an opportunity to rein her in later.

"Don't suppose you have time to do some work over at the folks' house, do you?" she asked. When his brows drew together, she added, "I'd ask Erik, but Mom already said she doesn't want to spend the money on—"

She broke off, but didn't look abashed at the gaffe

she'd almost made. He knew her—her brain was spinning with how to weasel what she wanted out of him in a politically correct way.

"On someone's *professional* help?" he asked mildly, heaving up another bag.

"Well, yes. But they'd pay you . . . something. I think."

Behind her, a brand-new Mercedes pulled up in front of the Rooster. He glanced at it, then his watch.

Mari snorted, apparently misinterpreting the gesture as a need for libation. He didn't wonder at it. Time was, he'd be knocking back brews before noon.

"Seamus doesn't open up the bar until eleven." Her tone held derision.

He hid another grin. Let her have her delusions for now. He didn't have time for explanations; he needed to finish this up and get to his meeting with the Mercedes's occupants. "I have an appointment at the Rooster." He bent for another bag.

"With who? Jim Beam?" She didn't wait for an answer, but rushed on. "So, will you? Help out Mom? It would mean a lot to her to know her gardens were taken care of, and by someone who knows at least something about what he's doing. *Please?*"

He straightened and looked down at her. She raised her eyes, looking miffed at having to do so. At almost five-ten, she was no shrimp, and she'd always liked looking over everyone's heads. She'd hated that he'd grown to six-four by the time they were sixteen.

"Since when have I ever said no to anything you asked?" He gave a pointed nod at the pickup, and her face fired up again. That had *all* been her idea, even though he'd been a more than willing participant. His mind cycled through everything he needed to do over the next few days, but he didn't want to pass up this opportunity. "How about Thursday?"

"Thursday?" Her face fell. "But that's three days

from now. I was hoping you could come out today because she wants—"

"—you back out there weeding the thing this afternoon."

"Well, yes."

He did a God-grant-me-patience eye roll, knowing nothing spurred Mari on more than a hurdle in her path. "I do have a few things I need to do." He motioned at the pickup. "And in a few minutes, I have an appointment, remember?"

Her eye roll matched his. "Oh, yeah. Your *appointment*."

A few minutes after exacting a promise from him that he'd do the work she'd requested, Mari left, striding across the street toward Alcea's house. Skirt flapping, she was a Cossack out on a raid. Watching her, Andy smiled. His heart felt light, and he felt smug. He'd known the more obstinate he appeared, the harder she'd push to get her way. Hence, he'd gotten his own. He'd see her again, and as long as she was in Cordelia, he'd find ways to see her more than that. He'd never hoped for a second chance, but it looked like it had arrived on a platter.

Andy lifted the bill of his cap, settled it more firmly on his head, and headed for the Rooster Bar & Grill. Letting himself inside, he paused to give his eyes a few moments to adjust to the dim light.

The smell of stale beer and old grease, ground into the floorboards over so much time that the wood now looked like walnut not oak, assailed him. The scent was once a heady perfume, but now he wrinkled his nose. The sunlight valiantly attempted to push through the film of smoke on the windows but gave up before it reached the center of the space, littered with tables scarred by more than a few brawls (some that he remembered, others he didn't; although he'd have a shiner the next day to prove he'd been in them). Most were empty at this hour. On the wall, a Budweiser sign fizzed in neon, a country ditty moaned on the jukebox, and the sizzle of a grill sounded in the back.

A bar backed by an ornate mirror ran down the right side. Behind it, a lean, tall fellow rubbed down the surface. With his black hair showing only a few white threads and matching equally black attire, he would have faded into the shadows if it weren't for a gleaming silver bolo and a pair of green eyes that targeted Andy.

"Hey, Seamus." Andy lifted a hand in greeting.

"Usual?" The proprietor asked. "Burger too?" Andy nodded, and Seamus motioned to a table in a rear corner. "They're over there."

Andy threaded his way through the tables, pleased he didn't feel even a smidge of interest in joining a group of hard-hatted guys knocking back beers over their noon hour. He still visited the Rooster on a regular basis when he was in Cordelia, but not for the beer. When he reached the table in the corner, the Mercedes's occupants looked up at him. Jon and Lil Van Castle.

"Hi, Andy. I wanted to apologize. . . ." Lil smiled up at him, but her eyes, the same laser blue she shared with Mari and their mother, were sober; her tone, apologetic. Of course it would be. She'd know about his past and present. Nothing much was secret in Cordelia. "I didn't consider that you might be uncomfortable in a bar. We just thought it would be more private than Peg's, and when you said you'd be at Beadler's this morning, we thought it would be less of an inconvenience for you to meet us here."

Noting the rather disgruntled glance Van Castle gave his wife, Andy amended her words to *she* thought it would be more convenient. Gran had told him that at one time Seamus and Jon had been contenders for

Lil after her first husband, Seamus's brother, had passed on. Van Castle obviously would have preferred to meet somewhere else. Typical that when there was a troubled child in the house, both parents started forgetting each other's sensitivities as they focused on the kid.

"No problem. I'm here pretty often."

Lil's brows raised, but with characteristic courtesy, she stayed mum.

He smiled. "Because Seamus lends out the back for A.A. meetings." He turned to Van Castle and held out his hand. "Andrew Eppelwaite."

"Jon Van Castle." Van Castle's grip was damp from his beer bottle, but firm.

As Andy relinquished his grip and took a chair, he tried to get a sense of the man. He'd read their son's— or rather Van Castle's son, Lil's stepson—case history with his therapist's and parents' permission before this meeting. It included some pictures of the family. Still, he'd never encountered the former country superstar up close. Even sitting still with his hands wrapped around his beer mug, Van Castle emanated magnetic energy. The mane of hair that had always character- ized him was cropped shorter than his old publicity photos, and silver now blended with the blond. But it was still a dramatic contrast to a pair of copper tiger eyes. His songs—written but not recorded by him since he'd retired from touring after marrying Lil— still topped charts.

Opinion colored by what he'd read, Andy wasn't inclined to like him.

"Meeting tonight." His look pointed, Seamus handed Andy a Coke.

"Thanks." Andy took the glass. "I'll be there."

Seamus nodded approval, addressed Lil. "Your burgers will be up in a minute." He didn't look at Van Castle, who ignored him back.

And Lil pretended she didn't notice. "Thanks, Seamus." When the proprietor left, she looked at Andy with renewed interest. "Is Seamus your sponsor?"

Andy opened his mouth, but Van Castle spoke up. "I don't get this. Sorry, bud, but"—he nodded at Andy, but looked at Lil—"Michael's got problems, so we hand him over to people who have even bigger ones?"

"Jon, we decided—"

"No, you and Michael's psychologist *decided* and then steamrollered me into—"

Her blue eyes were accusing. "Dr. Everheart is your counselor, too. He's the *family's* counselor."

"What Michael needs is a strong hand, not—"

"One of the reasons they hire some former drunks like me, *bud*, is because we have some experience in overcoming the kinds of problems that face children like yours," Andy inserted. Van Castle's face reddened. At first Andy thought it was anger, but a closer look showed a trace of shame, and he regretted the *bud*. A little. "Look, I'm not a psychologist, so if you're still undecided about how to resolve Michael's problems, discuss it with Dr. Everheart. Lil just asked me here to answer some questions."

"We *have* decided." Lil's chin was firm, but she laid a hand on Van Castle's wrist. "Please, Jon. Let's just move ahead with this. If I'm wrong—if Dr. Everheart is wrong—*then* we can look at other possibilities."

Van Castle slumped back, but his eyes had softened at Lil's touch. "Maybe you're right. But I still think military school might be . . ." When Lil looked outraged, he gave an exasperated sigh. "Just *kidding*."

Seamus stepped up with the burgers, and the two fell silent.

While Seamus set plates in front of them, Andy watched them, unsure if Van Castle was really kidding or not. He'd heard of cases like this during this past year at Vreeley Boys' Home—parents seeking answers, but not trusting each other's judgment. Since he wasn't intimately involved with the families, though, he wouldn't offer his thoughts. That was the realm of the counselors, and a misstep could screw up whatever therapy they were getting.

Still, that didn't prevent him from forming his own personal opinions. And from what he was seeing, what he'd suspected when he'd read Michael Van Castle's case history was true. Michael's father lay at the root of Michael's problems. What had the man expected? That there wouldn't be any? The kid had been mistreated by his birth mother until he was five, when Van Castle had suddenly taken note of him after ignoring him until then. After that, Van Castle had undoubtedly thrust him largely into Lil's care. And then when the boy had grown up and gotten curious about his birth mother, trying to make one of those all-important connections, she'd upped and overdosed a year ago. Was it any wonder Michael had a lot of bottled-up anger?

When Seamus had moved away, Lil spoke again. "We know you can't advise us, but we wanted to know more about Camp Sycamore. And since you'll be working there, we thought you could give us some—some—"

"Reassurance?"

"Yes." Lil looked at him expectantly; Van Castle addressed his hamburger.

Ignoring his food for the moment, Andy sat back. "This will be my first year at the camp, but I can tell you the people who sponsor Camp Sycamore—the Vreeley organization—are dynamite at what they do to help these kids."

"What do you mean by *these kids*?" Van Castle looked up, copper eyes intense. "You mean delinquents and druggies and—" Lil laid a hand on his arm.

"They're not bad kids," Andy said, his voice growing hard despite his efforts to keep it pleasant.

"They're troubled. There's a difference. They've acted out their problems and ended up *in* trouble."

"Jon's just concerned." She threw her husband a glance that pleaded for restraint. "Michael's had problems, but he hasn't been in jail or done drugs. We know some of the residents coming from Vreeley Home have. What Jon was trying to ask was, will Michael be safe?"

Jon Van Castle grimaced. "And will people be safe from *him*?"

"Look, Mr. Van Castle—"

"Call me Jon."

"Your son poses no dangers to other kids—he's not a hardened criminal." Andy looked at Lil, knowing her fears for Michael. Heck, he'd once wondered about his own safety working among some pretty hard-core cases—until he'd gotten to know them. "And, yes, Michael's a relatively easy case compared to some of the others. But even *they* aren't criminals. The residents of Vreeley Boys' Home who are sent to Camp Sycamore have earned the right to go. That means they've worked their way up through different levels of increasing freedom by demonstrating that they can cope with more leeway without being a danger to themselves or anyone else."

At least most of the time. Sometimes a kid just . . . popped. For the most part, these boys had learned to hide their feelings—not just from other people, but from themselves—and sometimes when it all caught up to them, they blew. But he didn't tell Lil that. The staff was trained to handle it if it happened.

He continued. "There will also be others there just like your son, referred by their psychologists for the summer—adolescents who need some time away from the family temporarily, just like you need time away from them, while you all learn new ways of dealing with each other. The camp will provide that."

As they ate their meal, Andy told them more about

the camp until Lil's questions dried up. Van Castle—Jon—hardly spoke, and Andy's opinion of him dropped further. Talk finally turned to less serious topics.

"I ran into Mari this morning." Literally. Andy smiled, thinking about her. "She seems on top of her game."

"Top of her game? Not hardly. She—" Jon stopped at Lil's frown and looked guilty. Apparently Lil didn't think her sister should provide food for gossip.

Lil looked at Andy. "She's had some troubles lately, but she'll rise above them. You know Mari."

Troubles? Hell-bent Mari? "Well, she's obviously still taking the bull by the horns whenever she can."

"You could say that." Humor glinted in Lil's eyes. "But I don't think she's ever encountered a, uh, *bull* that's quite as much of a challenge as the one she's facing now.

Chapter 3

Mari had always admitted she was bullheaded and, glancing at her mother as Thursday neared noon, she knew *exactly* who she'd gotten it from. But it was another example of gene dilution—*nobody* was as stubborn as Zinnia.

While Mari pulled up the sheets on her parents' four-poster bed, Zinnia sat to one side in a chair quilted with a pale blue floral design that matched the room's wallpaper. The chair was tilted to catch the breeze and the sun tumbling through the second-story window overlooking the half acre of backyard behind her parents' home. The light bounced off Zinnia's glasses and hair, as shiny and textured as a steel-wool pad. Periodically her mother bent to try to tug up a surgical stocking over the healing incision where a vein had been harvested. Each time she'd groan from the pressure the movement caused against her chest.

"Would you leave it, Mom? I'll help you as soon as I'm done with this." She'd thought her mother would love having the stocking off for a little while— God knew she'd grumped about it nonstop for the last five days.

"Doc says I'm supposed to wear it all the time, Mari. Not just when I feel like it."

Like her leg would fall off if the sock was gone for

five minutes? Mari clamped her teeth together, refusing to respond.

Her mother gave a long-suffering sigh, but straightened back up. "Jon bought Lil a new Mercedes, did you hear? Peace offering, I'd bet. Things have been tough for them lately." She sighed again. Then before Mari could respond, she pointed. "Pull that bottom sheet tighter, honeybunch. You sure you have it on right? Lord love a duck, you'd think I'd never taught you to make a bed the way you're goin' on with it."

Mari gave the sheet a yank, and the sound of a seam splitting echoed off the high ceiling. Tensing for an onslaught, she glanced at her mother. But instead of the outrage she'd expected, Zinnia had bit her lip and looked away. Her glasses had fogged.

Summoning patience she was shocked to know she had, Mari murmured, "Sorry, Mom," and somehow managed not to tear at her hair. It was all just . . . too much. Zinnia had always been upbeat and optimistic, but now she segued between tears and anger, anger and tears. Mari was never sure how Zinnia would react. Just that she would.

Her mother had just finished taking a bath. Or rather sitting in a shower chair while Mari sponge-bathed her limbs with great care. She didn't remember her mother's skin being this, well, *loose* on her plump frame, or so transparent. At the slightest pressure, Zinnia would squawk, "Careful, honeybunch, you know how easy I bruise"—even though Mari didn't. And she'd pinched her mouth so tight when Mari got near the jagged lines on her leg and chest, Mari had decided the visiting nurse, still coming three times a week, could handle any necessary wound care this afternoon. Touch one of those puckered, angry ridges and Zinnia would lop off her head.

But her primary reason for great care wasn't her mother's fragile skin or the incisions. Mari had been scared of a major skull-crack. The shower chair wasn't made for a big claw-footed bathtub, but her mother had insisted they use the chair. As far as Mari could make out, it was because Mom didn't want to hurt Pop's feelings, since he'd bought it. Or hadn't wanted to admit she was wrong when she'd insisted he buy it. That had been her and Zinnia's first argument.

For today. There had been umpteen arguments before that one since Mari had returned home, ranging from the "Humpty Dumpty" inanity to matters of life and death—like the damn shower chair.

Mari tugged at the blankets, careful this time not to rip them out of the bed, and decided the shower chair was history. She'd break one of its legs and blame it on faulty quality control. A hammer would do it. And it would feel good wielding one. Her mother wasn't the only person alternately verging on tears or anger. Just the only one with a real reason. Which only made Mari feel more childish and useless . . . and more like running away. She should *never* have agreed to come back here.

Zinnia interrupted her reverie. "Are you gay?"

In the process of thumping a pillow, Mari stopped her arm on the downbeat. Jaw dropping, she turned. "*What?*"

"You can tell me if you are. Might take some adjusting if you were of a mind to come out of the cupboard, but I'd still love you, you know."

Mari blinked a few times. "It's *closet*. Come out of the *closet*." She perched on the bed, her knees almost brushing Zinnia's. "What in blazes makes you think I'm gay?"

"Oh, don't get your panties all in a knot. In the eight years since you moved away, you've never once mentioned a man. And you run to the phone every time it rings like your pants are on fire—why, you snatched it right out of Pop's hands the other day. You have these whispered, secret conversations with

whoever calls, don't say squeak about it later. . . ."
Zinnia's gaze moved up. "And then yesterday you
went and got that haircut."

Involuntarily, Mari's hand went to her head. What
used to be four inches of fizz tipped with green was
now just over an inch of tight curls. "You don't like
it?"

"I didn't say that."

Nor was she saying, Mari noted, that she *did* like
it. Oh, who cared? Mari stood up. "I'm not gay." She
gave the pillow a direct hit. "And the phone calls are
just from . . . a friend. I didn't want them to bother
you or Pop." Or make any explanations at all about
who Sean was. If her mother ever found out Sean was
married when they'd, well, *met*, she wouldn't just lop
off her head, she'd torture her first. Slowly.

"Well, if you're not gay, then maybe you could get
together with Andy Eppelwaite. You two used to be
closer than two peas in a pod." Zinnia's gaze was still
fixed on Mari's hair. "Although I'm not sure with the
hair . . ." Zinnia sighed. "I want to get *my* hair done."

"*No-Account* Andy?" Mari snorted. When she'd
run into him on Main, she'd felt a surge of warmth
that she'd put straight down to nostalgia. Because
from all appearances, she'd been right to put the ki-
bosh on things between them when she had. "Sure,
right. And we'll live in a shack out in North End
where I could raise chickens when I wasn't chasing
him out of some bar."

She eyed the bed, thought it looked good enough
for an army sergeant's approval, and turned to look
at Zinnia. "You know the doctor said you needed to
be protected from viruses and can't go out yet. It's
bad enough everyone in town seems to think this is
Grand Central Station. If you want me to wash your
hair later"—she wondered if she could disable the
shower chair before that—"I'll do it. And set it."

"That's right nice of you, honeybunch." Zinnia

frowned, still studying Mari's brush of curls. "But you just call Betty on up. I'm just sure she'd come on over to do it."

Mari counted to ten. "When I was at Up-in-the-Hair yesterday, Betty Bruell had a cough that could wake the dead. So, no. It's me or nobody." This was one argument she intended to win. A Zinnia with pneumonia or bronchitis—or even a cold, at this point—could be a dead Zinnia. And, dammit, Mari was still too young to be left motherless.

Her mother didn't answer. She just sighed again, turned her face toward the window, and gave up without even a trace of Lord-loving-a-duck. Mari blinked back the sudden rise of tears. Zinnia in this shape was scary.

"I miss my gardens." Zinnia picked at her robe like an old woman. But she wasn't old—she *wasn't*. She was only sixty-nine.

Mari knelt in front of her mother. "We'll go out and walk through the backyard this afternoon. The doctor said you need to walk, just not too far." She gently rolled up the surgical stocking over the incision. Zinnia didn't even seem to notice.

"But I'll see so many things I want to take care of, and looking's just not the same. I like feeling the soil between my fingers. . . ." Zinnia looked at her hands and slowly flexed them. Mari followed her gaze, wondering when the veins winding between her mother's knuckles had started standing out like blue ridges on a relief map. And when had her mother's hands become so crosshatched with wrinkles? ". . . And smelling the earth while the sun warms my head and the robins sing . . ."

Mari placed her hands on her mother's knees. Her hands were the same shape, but still smooth and white. "Mama, you'll do that again."

"Are you sure?" Her mother's gaze rose and locked with hers.

"I'm positive." *Did you hear that, God? I just prom-ised my mom she would completely recover, and You'd better back me up.*

Tears prickling her throat again, Mari gave her mother's knee a pat and rose. "And today you won't notice anything wrong with your gardens, because Andy said he'd come by to work on them." And if he didn't show up, she'd go down to the Rooster and haul him right out. Surely a drunk could still pull weeds?

"See, honeybunch? He's just downright nice to offer to do that. You used to be closer'n two peas in a pod," she repeated. She was repeating a lot of things lately. "So maybe while you're here, you could—"

Mari's eyes went heavenward again. "I don't even want to know why you think all I rate is an Andy Eppelwaite."

"He's not the same—"

"Mom." Mari's voice was a warning. She threw open the closet door and winced when a rainbow of colors smacked her right in the eyeballs. "What robe would you like to wear?" A bra was still painful, so Pop had bought Zinnia a whole wardrobe of lounge-wear concoctions, and he was not known for an aver-sion to bright shades.

Zinnia eyed the garments the same way she'd eyed Mari's hair. "Oh, Lord love a duck, he means well, but— Bring me the pink one, I guess. The one with the purple and yellow irises. I'll look like I upchucked my garden all over myself, but I guess paying never-you-mind to the man's peccadilloes is better than a passel of hurt feelings."

Mari swallowed. It was a sentiment she should re-member.

"Those are bearded irises." Down on one knee, Andy pointed out a bunch of pale green spears rising out of the soil. Shade dappled most of her parents' backyard, but anywhere sunlight poked through, Zinnia had planted, leaving only one big oblong of grass for the family's volleyball games. After Andy had arrived, Mari had given her mother strict napping instructions. And Pop was at the grocery store. With nothing better to do—except the dishes, the parlor dusting her mother was carping about, and about six years' worth of laundry—she'd followed Andy out to the garden.

Now she nodded like she cared about irises. When what she really cared about was that Andy had arrived without any Rooster-raiding. And sober.

At least she thought he was sober.

Pretending to study the plants, she leaned over his shoulder and gave him an experimental sniff. No. No whiff of alcohol. In fact, he smelled nice—kind of earthy. And he looked pretty damn good, too, in faded jeans and a denim shirt rolled up over his elbows. The hair on his tanned forearms glinted in the sun, almost as bright as the curls on his head.

She was suddenly glad she'd given in to the impulse—surprising, since it was only *Andy* after all—to trade the old capri denims she'd scrounged around in this morning for the apple green outfit that complemented her hair. Or would, if she had any—damn her mother for putting the thought in her head that it was too short. But she guessed Andy was still as nice as her mother had said. At least he hadn't made a single comment on the hair. Unless you'd count a grunt when he'd seen it.

She blinked, realizing he'd jerked his head around and was staring at her. "What is *up* with you? You've been sniffing me like a hound ever since I got here."

She straightened, her chandelier earrings swinging against her cheeks. She felt her face heat. "I, uh, I like your cologne."

He rolled his eyes so far up, she was afraid they were stuck. "Right," he said drily. "I'll write a letter to Proctor and Gamble telling them you like their soap. Now, pay attention. If you're going to do more work out here—"

"You mean you won't come back after today?" Alarm replaced embarrassment. "I didn't mean to sniff, but, Andy, you know how you are—"

"Were," he interjected.

"—and I know my folks won't pay you if they think you've been drinking, so, you see, I was just thinking of you."

"I'll bet," he said. "And, no, I won't be back. I *do* have other work, Mari."

"I'll bet." When he glared at her mimicry, she amended that to "What work?"

But he'd gotten that jaw-jutting look she remembered that meant he wasn't going to tell her anything else. He just motioned to the irises and said in tones of strained patience, "These are the same as those over there, only those are Japanese. There's lots of different kinds of irises. Some bloom early—like the Japanese—and some later. Don't cut off the stalks when the flowers fade—the roots still need nutrients from the leaves. Where did you say you put the plants you pulled out by mistake?"

Mari decided not to mention that he looked like a bulldog when he poked out his chin that way. He might leave. "Follow me."

She led the way along a sunny side of the house's detached garage to a pile of compost. Andy leaned over and poked through eggshells and coffee grounds coated with grass clippings, setting aside some irises she'd yanked out while her mother had gone berserk on the screened-in back porch. "I think I can salvage these tubers. They won't bloom this year, but irises are pretty hardy."

Mari folded her arms and watched him. "You've picked up a lot of knowledge about this kind of stuff, haven't you?" She might as well give credit where it was due. He'd never match Sean in aspirations, but at least he'd learned *something* over the years.

He looked up, amusement lurking behind his blue eyes. He was the only person she'd ever known whose eyes could really twinkle. He didn't look so much like a bulldog anymore. He looked kind of . . . cute. "Yep, just picked it right up. That's me—a sponge."

Feeling irked that she'd thought good-old Andy, *No-Account* Andy, was *cute*, for God's sake, she let a comment rise to her lips about what usually soaked the sponge. But she bit it back. She didn't want him to bail on her now.

He stood up, wiped his hands on his backside, then bent to pick up the iris. "I'll be working over at Lake Kesibwi this summer. Maybe we can get together again."

Her eyes stayed on his buns. Mighty nice-looking buns . . . Geez. *Get a grip*. She'd obviously been way too long without . . . anyone. "Yeah, maybe."

If she was staring at his buns and remembering what they'd looked in his tightie-whities years ago, getting together might not be such a good idea. She followed him back to the garden, casting around for a topic that didn't include anything that he did now. Or that they'd done then.

He knelt, reached for a trowel, and started digging furrows. "So, Gran tells me you have your own business."

"Mmm." Another topic she'd rather avoid.

Biding her time, she looked around for something to protect her cotton gauze from grass stains, saw nothing, decided that on apple green they wouldn't show, and flopped down beside him. This *was* only Andy; nobody she needed to impress. She leaned back on her hands and considered what to tell him about her business. If his grandmother hadn't told him of her failure, it meant Tansy hadn't heard a whisper about it within Peg O' My Heart. Ergo, there wasn't a hint to be found in Cordelia.

Closing her eyes, she tipped her face to the sun and adopted a cosmopolitan air. "Designs by Mari. Very challenging work. Lots of clients. In fact, I won a huge major account and, boy, did that knock the wind out of my competition's sails, I can tell you. I added a bunch of new people just to keep up." She peeked at him to see if he was buying all this.

He just kept digging. "Hit the big time, huh? I lived in KC for a while. Where were your offices?"

"Offices? I, um, worked out of my loft. *Big* loft apartment. Wish you could see it. Lots of light, lots of space, great midtown location . . ." Andy looked up, eyes sharp. She shut hers again. "Just seemed a shame to waste rent on somewhere else, too."

"So, everyone fit in there?"

"Everyone? Oh—my employees?" She nodded vigorously, feeling her earrings bounce against her cheeks, feeling his gaze. "Everyone fit just fine."

"Mari."

"I'm not lying!" There was silence. She sighed and opened her eyes.

He'd rocked back on his heels and his brows were raised. "What's with the tall tales? This is me, remember?"

She shied away from the look of censure mixed with hurt. She'd never lied to him before. "Okay, okay. But I was *exaggerating*, not lying."

"Unh-huh."

"I *did* have my own business." Straining against nature, she chose her words carefully. Maybe Andy could still catch her out, but that didn't mean she had to tell him *everything*. "I started it up soon after I moved to Kansas City." *Because*, she didn't add, *I was afraid everyone would guess I was carrying on an affair with my boss*. Her married boss. God, she was *such* a *cliché.* "It would have been eight years in September. And it *was* called Designs by Mari."

Andy's brows were still raised.

"What do you want? To see my income tax returns?"

"Don't fly into a temper. I wasn't the one stretching the truth. What else?"

"There were no employees, just me," she admitted, grinding her teeth that she had to admit anything. Damn Andy. "But everything went *great* for the first five years or so, it really did. And I *did* win a huge major account. Which *did* kick the bucket out from under my bigger competitors." It had been a golden moment. Fool's gold.

"So what happened?"

She leaned forward, hunching her shoulders. "The account was a website design firm. It was going great guns at first, then went the way of a lot of the dot-com companies."

"Which was?"

God, did he know *nothing*? "Which, like almost all of them, was belly-up. Last month." She picked at a blade of grass. "And don't tell me it was stupid to put all my eggs into that basket. I already know that." But she hadn't had much choice after she'd refused to accept any more of Carmichael Cards' contracts from Sean.

His eyes were soft on her. "Since when did I ever think you were stupid? What you did was amazing."

She was silent. What she'd done was god-awful.

He set the iris tubers in the furrows and covered them with soil. "How many people have the guts to go out on a limb like that? You tried, Mari. Don't sell yourself short."

She wasn't. He just didn't know. She couldn't have succeeded as long as she had without Sean's contracts. She'd proved it, barely treading water for the two years after she'd dispensed with them. God, what had she done with her life?

"I guess you're right." She watched Andy's hands as they pressed the ground. They were strong and sure. "Well, once I'm done here, I'll go at it again. I don't know where, though. Maybe Chicago or New York." She'd taken one trip to New York. The Big Apple had dazzled her, in more ways than one. Even though she'd gotten lost—also in more ways than one. She thought of Sean. "Maybe Kansas City again." The thought should have cheered her, but the whole idea of starting over made her want to lie down and sleep. Maybe she was just heartily sick of anything to do with design.

His mouth had twisted in distaste at the mention of Chicago and New York, but all he said was, "So there's no special someone to clip your wings?"

She frowned. The question was careless, yet she sensed more than casual interest. "Oh, geez. You know how that goes. . . . You go out with this person or that person, but when you're building a career, you just don't have real time for a relationship." She turned the tables before he called her on that. She was not going to discuss Sean—not even with Andy. "You said you lived in Kansas City?"

"Just for a few months. With Anna. You remember her."

"Sure, I remember."

The sullen-faced brat. After their parents had died when Andy was five and Anna eight, Tansy had raised Andy while their maternal grandparents had raised his sister, Anna, in Kansas City. But every summer and winter break holiday, Anna would visit Cordelia. Andy would hang all over his sister. Mari would get jealous. Anna would get jealous when Mari interfered, and inevitably threw some kind of tantrum. She'd been a moody little brat, as far as Mari was concerned, and she'd ruined a whole boatload of good vacation days. Mari still held it against her, although she'd learned long ago not to utter one word against Anna. Andy had a tendency to get a tad defensive where she was concerned.

"She married pretty well and had an apartment she wasn't using over a garage, so when I got done with serving my community service sentence—"

"Oh, that's right, you went to—" She broke off.

"Jail." He inserted matter-of-factly, like jail was a weekend in Vegas. She'd never been to Vegas, although she'd always wanted to. Along with L.A. and Miami and . . . damn, what *had* she done with her life? "I was lucky."

"Jail is *lucky*?"

"They put me away before I followed my father's example." Gaze turned inward, he shook his head. Andy had loved his dad, but a drunk No-Account Senior had driven his car into a bridge killing himself and Andy's mother. She remembered how she and Andy had talked about it through their adolescence; it had taken him *years* to forgive his father. "It was my third offense—this time I slammed into another car. Nobody got hurt, thank God, but it still meant six months in the clink and another six of community service. Penance paid, I moved in near Anna."

"You mean, you don't drink anymore?" She couldn't stifle her incredulity.

"Nope. I'll be sober four years come June."

"Not *anything*?" Four years. It was a minor miracle. Maybe not so minor, considering how he'd practically pickled himself before he was even twenty-one. "That must be so hard for"—she bit back *you*—"uh, anyone."

A grin tickled his mouth. His hands still worked the soil. "Not really."

"Not really?" Her small trove of diplomacy dried up. "You've *got* to be kidding."

"I'm not." He sat back and looked directly at her. "Us drunks hit bottom in different ways, and some aren't lucky enough to ever get there. The car wreck did it for me. I landed in a program and I was ready and willing. I was, as they say, sick and tired of being sick and tired."

She'd always been able to spot him lying, and he wasn't now. "Aren't you ever tempted? Even a little?"

His mouth hitched up again. My God, that *grin*. Once she'd hit adolescence, that grin had always made her stomach do a hop-skip. And now it was accompanied by the sweetest little crinkles around his blue eyes. *Oh, for God's sake!*

He shook his head. "No. I'm lucky—for some it's a struggle, but for me, it hasn't been so bad. Oh, it's taken work—and help. Lots of meetings, lots of chewing things over, lots of reading—and some sponsors that have probably wanted to pitch me out on my ear for bending theirs so much. But every morning I'm grateful to wake up with a clear head and no regrets."

"One day at a time, eh?"

"That's the idea."

She'd bet it had been quite a journey. She felt a niggle of admiration. She really shouldn't have sniffed him. "So what have you been doing since Anna's?"

He bent back to his task, the skip before he replied noticeable, and she wished she hadn't asked. Obviously, he'd come back here and now worked the same odd jobs. That he'd sobered up was terrific and he should be proud, but all he had now was—she looked at his hands—dirt. Poor Andy. Maybe she hadn't taken her life to great heights—yet—but it must scratch his pride to know she'd done more with her life than he had.

He finally replied. "While I was at Anna's, I worked for my grandparents. They own a lawn and landscaping business. But I headed off after that summer, went to—"

The door to the screened porch banged open. "Mari!" Pop stood on the stoop, shading his eyes. She felt like mimicking his pose. His tall, still stalwart frame was clothed in a purple and orange plaid shirt paired with· navy pants and red suspenders. Blinding. "Could you come on in a minute?" There was a shrill note in his voice.

Mari scrambled to her feet. Easygoing Pop didn't *do* desperate. But these days, Zinnia's convalescence had them all clinging by their nails to sanity.

"Probably just a frigging chipped nail," Mari huffed as she jogged toward the door. Andy was at her elbow, taking his steps in long strides that by contrast made hers look like bunny hops. "You don't need to come." She paused. "You don't *want* to come."

"Hey, I like your folks. If I can help out, I'd be glad to do it."

She didn't try to dissuade him again. If he was into masochism, so be it. But as they reached the door, a fleeting thought crossed her mind. If Sean were here, he'd likely move at a fast clip too . . . right through the hedge that led to the street.

Chapter 4

When they entered the kitchen from the porch, the room was empty. Andy didn't even wince at the decor of Zinnia O'Malley's favorite spot in her house. Cabbage roses climbed up purple lattices on the wallpaper. Light fought for entry through a froth of foliage that hung in front of the casement windows. Every corner was packed with baskets of sewing, magazines, and catalogs, and a squat refrigerator staggered under a weight of magnets and church bulletins half a decade old. As a kid, he'd shared enough meals sitting at the scarred oak table with the O'Malleys that the sight of the kitchen only brought a feeling of warmth, not shock.

He did pause, though, at a painting centerpieced on the wall and counterbalanced by columns of plaster handprints, one for each O'Malley. The landscape, done using only a bandwidth of golds, just about took his breath away; the artist had captured the serenity of dawn in the Ozark mountains. He didn't know art, but he thought it was good. A glance at the signature told him it was Mari's. The date underneath said she'd done it in college.

Standing in the dining room doorway, as tall, solid, and unbent as Andy remembered, although his thatch of hair had gone white, Pop beckoned them with an unlit pipe. The lines around his mouth had deepened over the years and were now stretched with concern. From the parlor beyond came a murmur of voices— and one long, hacking cough.

"Goddamm—dangit." Mari straightened her shoulders and brushed past Pop.

"Exactly my sentiments, Pumpkin," Pop murmured, his anxiety visibly lessening with Mari's reaction. He raised brows as thick as bottlebrushes as he watched his daughter march through the dining room and pause just short of the parlor. He turned to Andy. "Been a while, hasn't it, son? I've been meaning to tell you how glad Zinnia and I were to hear you'd straightened yourself out, but you haven't been around much."

"No, the last few years have been a blur." Andy shook the hand Mari's father held out. His knuckles had enlarged from arthritis, but his grip was strong. He'd guess Pop O'Malley must be about seventy now. He nodded toward the parlor. "I take it Mrs. O'Malley isn't in any serious straits?"

"No, but that clucking crowd that gathers around her every afternoon is about to be."

Pop stuck the unlit pipe in his mouth—a holdover from quitting smoking many years ago—and both men turned to look toward the parlor. Mari still stood at its edge, hands on her hips, surveying the scene like a general planning her attack. Beyond her, Andy could count about a half dozen women ranged around the room, two perched on the edges of doily-clad brocade chairs, another two sharing a bench pulled away from an upright piano. Pinched between Betty Bruell with her mile-high lacquered hairdo on one side and Betty's motormouth head stylist, Rosemary Butz, on the sofa, Zinnia looked smaller than everyone else, although her personality usually filled a room.

"They're wearing her out, and since she won't listen to me, I thought I'd leave things to Mari. She'll get the point across." Pop talked out of the side of his mouth, then winked. "And I'll be out of the cross-hairs."

"And you, sir. How are you holding up?" Andy followed Mari's father through the dining room. The same lace curtains, edges yellowed now, fluttered in the open windows.

"Now that Zinnia's home, fine. She's a bit tetchy, but the doc says that'll pass with time. There's a silver lining, though. We get to take a rest from that bed and breakfast business she insisted we start up some years back. I'd rather be fishing at the lake than dishing up hash browns for some stranger's breakfast. It was fun for a while, but—" He shrugged, and came to a halt next to Mari, who hardly gave them a glance.

Sitting on the sofa, Betty Bruell let out a cough that sounded like she was about to hack up Minnesota. Andy raised his eyebrows and looked at Mari, whose face went ketchup-bottle red. Pop simply folded his arms and waited.

Not two minutes later, the door banged shut behind the last of Zinnia's guests.

"Good riddance," Mari said.

Two spots of color staining her cheeks, Zinnia choked out her words. "I have *never* been so mortified in my entire life, Miss Marigold McKenzie O'Malley. I won't be able to face them ever again. I just can't believe you called them all a bunch of cackling old *crows*."

Pop sat down next to his wife and gingerly patted her hand. Mouth tight, Mari whipped around the room, collecting coffee cups and napkins. The dishes rattled.

"And you just watch what you're about with my good china, you hear?"

"I called them *crones*," Mari muttered, but didn't break stride.

About to retreat to the sanctuary of Zinnia's garden, Andy stopped when Mari cast a wild look his way. He knew that look. It was the one that implored him to stay in the hopes her mother wouldn't paddle her behind while he was there. He gave an inward groan. Last time he remembered championing her like that was after they'd snuck down to Paley's Rock Quarry in North End for a forbidden swim. Mari had insisted it was all her idea, Zinnia had guessed it wasn't, and he'd earned a few swats of his own. Still, he shoved his hands in his pockets and stayed.

Getting no other response from Mari—who, to his surprise, must have learned something through the years about keeping her mouth shut—Zinnia snatched her hand out of Pop's and turned her glare on her husband. "This is all your fault, you—you *tattletale.*"

"Now, dear, you know the doctors said—"

Mari halted. "Do you have a death wish or something?" Pop's eyes widened. "Not *you. Her.* It's not his fault, Mom. It's *theirs.*" She gestured with the china, nearly toppling the pile.

Bearing a casserole dish, Lil pushed through the front door. "What in the world is going on? I just passed Betty and Rosemary. They looked scared witless."

"They *are* witless," Mari said.

"Don't you—" Zinnia started.

Mari overrode her mother, grip whitening on the china until Andy feared for its life. "Good God, Mom! You've only been out of the *frigging* hospital for six days and people keep swooping in here like you're all set to entertain the queen or something. Jes—I mean, jeepers—Betty sounded like she'd croak any minute, and she has the nerve to come over here and expose you to God-knows-what. You're supposed to be resting, and we're supposed to protect you from germs, and—" A cup finally gave up. It landed on the rug at Mari's feet, bounced, and cracked in two. Mari stared at it, nose pinking. "—And I don't want you to *die!*"

Expressions shifted in the sudden silence. Biting hard on his pipe, Pop blinked down at his hands. Lil's face went soft. And Zinnia stared at her youngest, high color fading.

Andy covered the ground to Mari and knelt at her feet to pick up the pieces. "I think we can fix it." He glanced up. Mari's lips trembled. He straightened and gently took the rest of the china out of her hands.

"Oh, honeybunch, I'm not going to die on you, not for a long time." Zinnia struggled to rise. Pop stood to help her, a hand under each arm. She gave him a pat, then crossed to her daughter and held out her arms. "Why, they fixed me up right as rain, dontcha know." When Mari hesitated, Zinnia added, "And a hug won't kill me, I promise."

Mari collapsed in her mother's arms, hunching to bury her face in the crook of Zinnia's neck. "Oh, Mama."

Andy tiptoed to the kitchen with the china, and dawdled a few moments. When he came back, Zinnia was back on the sofa, her hand on Pop's knee. Lil and Mari had each taken a chair. Feeling like a fifth wheel, but loyalty—and feelings he barely admitted he had—holding him there, Andy leaned against the door jamb.

"I understand your concerns, honeybunch." Zinnia frowned at Mari. "But you can't go around calling my friends names."

"But I'm right," Mari insisted. "Just look at you. You've got bags under your eyes, you're as gray as old socks—"

"Thanks," Zinnia murmured.

"—and they can't keep hounding you or you'll never get well."

"But—" Zinnia began.

"She's right, dear." Pop put his hand over hers.

Lil shifted and looked around for a place to set her casserole. Glad to be useful, Andy sprang forward to take it out of her hands.

"Thank you." Lil faced her family. "Maybe there's a solution we haven't considered. What about going to the cabin at Kesibwi? Mother loves it there. Pop wouldn't mind doing some fishing. And you"—she looked at Mari—"when you're not busy with Mother, you could paint."

There was a moment of silence, then three voices erupted.

"But what about—"

"Paint? I'll be bored out of my—"

"Very good idea, Lil—"

Holding the casserole, Andy backed from the room. An ear half-tuned to the conversation in the parlor, he busied himself with the dishes, even though the garden still waited in all its weedswept grandeur. He shrugged and put a plate on the dish rack. There were still hours of daylight left. And he was more than a little curious to find out if his old chum Mari O'Malley would spend the summer at Lake Kesibwi—only minutes away from his job at Camp Sycamore. There *was* hope for him yet.

Chapter 5

"Why don't you come with us to Camp Sycamore tomorrow so you can see we're not sending Michael to purgatory?" Eleven days later, on Memorial Day, Lil slid the door to the O'Malleys' Lake Kesibwi cabin closed behind her and joined Mari on the deck that jutted out over the Ozark hillside.

Mari didn't bother to acknowledge her. She was dog-tired. The days since they'd decided to retreat to Lake Kesibwi had rung with Zinnia's continual bleat. Mari had forwarded the mail, boxed up supplies, packed the bags, closed up the house, and strapped the damn shower chair to the top of their van. (She hadn't found a hammer in the jumble on Pop's workbench.) Lil had helped. As had Pop. And Zinnia had ordered them around like Mussolini dressed in a bright yellow robe patterned with lavender ducks.

Mari took a sip of her lemonade and looked around, thinking purgatory might be a good description, except surely purgatory wasn't this peaceful. Through a screen of trees, the cove shimmered, reflecting the mottled olive and viridian of the woods and the wash of the deepening periwinkle sky.

"Scoot over." Lil nudged her.

Mari obliged, sliding her glass down the picnic table so Lil could sit next to her on the bench that faced the lake. Despite the chill in the air, her mother had insisted on lemonade. *Fresh-squeezed lemonade*, she'd bellowed when she saw Mari getting out a can of frozen.

"I never said it was purgatory."

"You haven't had to. The way you roll your eyes whenever the subject comes up says it for you."

With an effort, Mari stopped mid–eye roll. She bunched her shoulders, shoving her bright red cardigan up toward her ears. "It's really not any of my business."

"Since when has that mattered?" Lil leaned her forearms on the table and looked across the water. Since they'd arrived Friday afternoon, rainfall had been a constant companion, but this afternoon the heavens had finally lightened. A breeze pushed left-over clouds through the sky. Sunlight flickered through the retreating gloom. It would be a stunner of a sunset—gold light mixed with blue haze. The kind of light difficult to capture on canvas.

Mari thought of her paints tucked away in the sleeping porch beneath the deck. She hadn't packed them with much enthusiasm, more as a sop to the yawnfest she expected stuck in the backwoods of the Ozarks for the entire summer. But suddenly she was glad she had. And—she stirred with some surprise—she realized she was actually happy they'd come. Falling asleep without a hip-hop lullaby last night—or her parents' snores echoing down the hallway—had been wonderful.

Lil glanced at her. "Besides, it seems to me Michael has made it your business."

Or she *would* be happy as soon as Lil, Jon, and Michael made their exit tomorrow. Too bad her mother wasn't a candidate for Camp Sycamore, too.

Mari shrugged. "He's only *talking* to me, Lil. It's no big deal, and he'd talk to you, too, if you'd really listen."

"I *have* listened. Listening isn't enough."

Mari shrugged again. To each his own. She wouldn't argue. From what she'd seen this weekend, the whole family was beyond reason. Except possibly Michael.

She looked up through the canopy of trees overhead and changed the subject. "Do you remember when Pop built the deck and Mom threatened him within an inch of his life if he harmed one twig of her dogwoods?"

A shadow flitted across Lil's face. Oh, great change of subject, *dope.* She'd forgotten both their brother, Henry, and Lil's first husband, Robbie, had helped Pop. Both men were gone, one at an early age from heart disease, the other in a car accident. When Jon and his children had come along several years later, they'd filled Lil's heart, but *of course* Lil would still feel some sadness.

But Lil didn't mention them. "If I remember right, it wasn't Pop's life in danger. It was any hope of future slices from Mother's apple pies." Lil looked around. "It's comforting, though, isn't it? To know this place is always waiting for us. To have our memories stored here?"

Mari nodded, glad for something they could agree on, although until now she hadn't thought much about it.

Rising behind her, woods pushing against it on all sides except for the clearing where they parked and the slope that led to the lake, the native stone cabin had stood for four generations. Although *cabin* was a misnomer now. Over the years, various O'Malleys had expanded the three-story structure that housed several bedrooms on the top floor and a sleeping porch and storage cellar on the bottom. A vast kitchen, opening in front to the gravel drive and in back to the deck over the sleeping porch, was sandwiched between the two stories, and arms had been added to either side: one outstretched to hold a rambling low-timbered room decorated in Traditional O'Malley—garage sale finds, family castoffs, and a mishmash of homemade knickknacks from pillows to embroidered table doilies—and where they'd played spades and Scrabble on the last two evenings while a fat-bellied stove warded off a late May chill. The other arm embraced more bedrooms and a bath Jon and Lil had remodeled last year.

No O'Malley had done more for the cabin than Lil. After she'd married Jon, they'd assumed management of the property—Mari was no longer sure who actually owned it, her parents or them—and the bathroom was the least of their renovations. While careful to preserve the cabin's original charm (most notably the dogwoods, as nobody would take a chance on a lifetime without Mom's apple pie), central air had replaced fans, and rotting wood windows had been swapped for roll-open casements that let in the view. Her sister and brother-in-law had even added a three-bedroom guesthouse near the top of the tree-walled gravel drive from the road, and had plopped a three-hole dock with a swimming platform in the place of Pop's gap-toothed one.

Mari squinted through the gathering dusk down the path that led through trees and a border of wildflowers to the dock. The sweet william was in bloom—one of the few flowers she could name, because as a little girl she'd always wondered who William was, and why he was sweet. (She'd asked so many questions back then, it was amazing Zinnia hadn't rolled her right down the hill and into the drink.)

From this angle, she could see just the bows of their three boats and two pairs of men's feet, Pop's clad in boots, Jon's in sandals, as they passed back and forth alongside Pop's bass boat. The other two boats—a Cobalt they used for water-skiing and a pontoon for cruising—rocked with the men's footsteps. A rope hit the dock as they prepared to cast off.

"Think they'll catch anything?"

Lil smiled. "Hope so, or Jon will pout all night. As soon as the rain stopped this afternoon, he whipped up fish batter, made hush puppies, and bragged how we'd all eat the best-tasting catfish this side of the Mississippi for supper."

Mari matched her smile, thinking about her brother-in-law's big talk, which had grown more fulsome with Lil's gentle ribbing. Their joshing as they'd worked side by side was reassuring, given the tension she'd felt between them all weekend. *Maybe* the tension had lifted with the rain clouds. *Probably* it had lifted because Michael had stopped storming their ramparts and closeted himself in his room all afternoon.

Lil's fingers drummed along the side of her glass, then fell still. "What exactly has Michael said to you?"

God. For a brief moment she'd forgotten that while butter would hardly even soften in her big sister's mouth, when Lil got hold of a subject she was a real rat terrier.

"He hasn't said much." Just that his stepmother *smothered* him; his dad didn't *understand* him. That he regretted what he'd done, he wouldn't do it again, and he didn't need a *frigging* (not the word he'd used) camp to straighten him out.

In short, he seemed normal. Or as normal as teens ever got. Both Jon and Lil were overreacting, but she wasn't about to open *that* can of snakes. She'd be arguing till sunrise tomorrow.

"I've watched him seek you out at every opportunity. All he's said is *not much*?"

Mari picked the least of Michael's objections. "You're sending him to a camp on the lake. And Michael is scared of the water." Michael had almost drowned once when he was young.

"But not as scared as he used to be," Lil pointed out. "Pop's helped a lot, taking him out in the bass boat and teaching him how to drive it. Although Michael's still leery of the rougher water around the cliffs out in the main channel."

"And now he likes to drive a boat. Big deal. Boys like to drive *anything*. It's not quite the same as swimming and water-skiing in deep water, which are both things that he said were on the camp's schedule." Mari kept her tone equally reasonable just to show that she could.

"Yes, but—"

"Can we talk about something else, for God's sake? All I've heard this weekend is Camp Sycamore *this* and Camp Sycamore *that*." Mari wished Lil would evaporate and leave her to the peace of her first time out of Zinnia's vocal range all week.

There was a sputter, then a roar. The men had fired up the bass boat. Both women watched as the boat puttered out of the dock then turned toward the mouth of the cove.

"I'm sorry." Lil's gaze followed the froth of the boat's wake until it disappeared around a bend. "I don't mean to drag you into our mess, but it's just I'm so hoping Camp Sycamore helps. And maybe with Michael out of the house . . ." Lil's voice held a trace of tears.

Inwardly, Mari sighed. Outwardly, she patted her sister's shoulder. "Maybe it *will* help." She paused, then barged ahead, wondering how tight her bolts were fastened. But she felt she needed to say *something*. Underneath Michael's predictable objections, she'd heard a tone of real distress. He was angry, sure, but he was also afraid. "But are you positive this is the best way to handle things? I mean, even Jon doesn't seem to think the camp will help."

Lil brushed at her eyes. "If Jon had his way, Michael would be the youngest recruit in the army."

"Oh." Mari frowned. "I wouldn't have thought—I

mean, Jon's never been harsh with Michael. If anything, he's spoiled him rotten."

"That's what Jon thinks, too. So he blames himself. And me. And thinks that Michael needs more, oh, shaking up than understanding."

"That doesn't sound like Jon."

"It's just that he's afraid Michael could repeat his own history, and Camp Sycamore might not be rigid enough to put him back on the right track. You know Jon was a screwup in high school, in and out of trouble before he ran off."

"And like *he* turned out so bad?" With an effort, Mari kept a snort out of her nostrils. "I just don't see why you're both making such a big deal about Michael. Sh—I mean, shoot—do you remember how much trouble Andy and I got into in high school. I didn't need counselors and hand-holding and *camps* and—"

"But Andy did." Lil's voice was quiet. "His grandmother was too busy making a living to notice that he did, and too poor to afford counseling even if she had. But we weren't, and we're not."

That shut Mari up. During their childhood, she'd always been aware Andy didn't live the same kind of life she did. He'd had no parents, only minimal supervision, and she'd envied the hell out of him. It wasn't until she was sixteen—shortly after that trip to the pickup where she'd had her curiosity more than satisfied—that she'd realized Andy's high jinks had gone beyond the realms of adventurous. And she'd had the sense to steer clear. Still . . .

"But Andy's doing okay now, and he's been sober for almost four years, and—"

"What Andy has done for himself is great." Lil's voice turned dry. "But I'd rather Michael not have to learn his lessons in jail."

"Sounds to me like what you're sending him to is basically the same thing."

Exasperation breaking through, Lil stood up. "Jon thinks I'm too soft. You think I'm too hard. And you know what? I'm fed up with both of you. This is Michael's best opportunity to handle his problems. Even Andy agrees. He said—"

"Andy? What does he know? His situation was way different than Michael's. Maybe Michael didn't have a bed of roses when he was little, but you took him away from his mother when he was *five*." Jon's ex-wife, Belinda, had mistreated his children until Jon had gained custody with Lil's help. Then Belinda had continued her downward spiral right into the grave a year ago. "And you've been a great mother since then. Jes—I mean, geez—you even bought Michael Christmas presents and signed the gift cards from Belinda. That's going way above and beyond. Plus Jon's been a good dad, and Michael has always had everything he's wanted. So what problems *exactly* does he have? He's just a teenager. You know that at that age every little thing becomes one big fat drama.

"Or maybe you don't." Lil had always been Miss Goody Two-Shoes. "But most kids do act up, Lil. That's normal. It's your reaction that isn't. Criminy, Michael steps out of line and Jon thinks he's bound for Lansing, and you think he's going to hell in a handbasket." Mari took a sip from her lemonade, rolled her eyes . . .

And earned a cuff on the shoulder. Lemonade spewed.

"What'd you do that for?" Mari sputtered.

"To knock some sense into you. The last time Michael 'stepped out of line' he almost got himself and Rose killed. He took Jon's Bronco—and his cousin—and almost drove them over a guardrail. If it hadn't been for that tree . . ."

Oh, *that*. "Okay, but it was still just a prank. I'll grant you a prank that almost led to disaster, but think about it. When Andy and I carted Paddy's Indian up the steeple at St. Andrew's, one of us could have broken our necks. Andy stole Tansy's old truck and we went joyriding when we were younger than Michael. I did it with Pop's Buick. The same thing could have happened to us."

"Except for one big difference. You cared whether you lived or died."

"And Michael doesn't? Oh c'mon."

The ring of the telephone wafted out through an upstairs window.

Lil's face grew hard. "You don't know everything, Mari O'Malley, even if you think you do. Michael isn't thinking of consequences. Not to himself or anyone else. Rose said that she screamed at him to slow down, but he just laughed and called her a chicken. And I know why you won't come with us tomorrow—because you're afraid I'll prove you wrong."

Brushing at the lemonade spilled on her cardigan, Mari stared after Lil as her sister stomped into the cabin and slammed the sliding door so hard it bounced back on its tracks. Lil never got that mad—well, at least not *hitting* mad. Michael had sounded so sincere about wanting to straighten out, but Michael and his cousin Rose were so close, she couldn't imagine he'd put her in danger unless *something* was wrong. Maybe things *were* worse than she thought.

Upstairs the window squeaked wide on its rollers. "Lord love a duck, what's going on down there?"

Great. Lil had awakened the sleeping giant.

"The phone's blaring," Zinnia continued. "And there's all this commotion . . ."

"Who called?"

"I don't know. It's for you."

"Why didn't you say so?" Mari scrambled to her feet and headed inside. It had to be Sean. And she didn't know what to do about him—hell, she didn't even know what she felt about him. He'd called each week since she'd left Kansas City, exhibiting that same single-minded purpose he'd always had. When Sean wanted something, he went after it—patiently, persistently, and as long as the effort wouldn't rock his world too much. And now he wanted her. The sound of his voice always left her with a disturbing sense of longing. Rapidly followed by self-loathing that she could feel any longing at all.

He was pushing to see her. She was running out of excuses. And she was surprised that she felt she needed any. Maybe the last decade had taught her that rushing into things half-cocked often caused her world to explode in her face.

She'd thought a summer sojourn might allow her to see things more clearly. Instead, she was just more confused. No *maybe* about it. Things *were* worse.

Chapter 6

Much worse. The next morning dawned under a skein of blue linen sky and earth-scented breezes. But bumping along a tangle of lake roads in the backseat of the Bronco, she felt like she was about to choke. Lil and Jon sat silent in the front seats, as silent as the boy beside her. Despite the beat of country rock on the CD player, the tension was *smothering*.

What on earth had possessed her to think *this* would be better than the litany of demands her mother had thrown at her while she'd helped her dress this morning for one of Zinnia's mandated exercise sessions? Tossing out the excuse that she'd promised to accompany Lil to Camp Sycamore, Mari had left it to Pop to ferry Zinnia to the cardiac rehab center at the hospital in Osage Beach. At that moment, anything had sounded better than getting trapped in the car with her mother.

But *this* sure wasn't any joyride.

Mimicking Michael's pose, she slumped farther down in her seat and looked out the window. It didn't help that she hadn't slept much after Sean's phone call last night. He'd persisted, she'd resisted, and things hadn't changed a jot. Why she encouraged him at all, she couldn't fathom.

Gloomily, she stared at the arrows of sunlight that darted through the leafy overhang and strobed against the glass. Maybe because she'd really loved him once. Maybe because she wanted to recapture those feelings and see if—without Jo—they had a chance. Or maybe—she squirmed—she was just playing the odds. Keeping all her options open, so to speak. Which didn't speak much to the strength of her ethics.

She rolled her head to look at Michael. His face was in quarter profile, giving only a glimpse of a high-boned cheek and an aquiline nose. Thick and straight like his father's but dark like his birth mother's, his hair swooped over his brows in front and brushed the collar of his brown I'M WITH STUPID T-shirt in back. She smiled for the first time that day. Teenagers were oh-so-subtle.

He turned his head and their eyes met. He frowned at her smile, the corners of his big dark eyes dipping down. She wiped off her grin and patted his knee, a hard knob in the folds of his sagging jeans. He grunted and turned back to the window.

She felt a pinprick of hurt, then shrugged. What had he expected from her? That she'd square off against his stepmother and actually win?

Jon slowed the Bronco and turned under an iron sign, tires skidding on the gravel strewn over red clay. CAMP SYCAMORE was spelled out overhead. Nothing else. No keep out, no WARNING: DELINQUENTS AHEAD, not even a watch house. Mari peered into the woods. From Michael's descriptions, she'd expected at least barbed wire, attack dogs, maybe an armed guard or two. But she saw nothing. She glanced over at her nephew. His expression was bored, but the hand in his lap had clenched. They passed a smaller sign on the right that indicated a turn toward a boat ramp, then the Bronco hit a steep downward grade. Before the road dipped back into the woods, she glimpsed the lake and a scattering of rooftops.

Within a minute, the road leveled, following the curve of a promontory that sloped toward the lake.

Thickly timbered hillside rose sharply on her left. Shaded by hickory trees on her right were two small buildings. Below them, through the trees, she glimpsed a cove ringed with docks.

"You know, this doesn't look so bad." She glanced at Michael.

But Michael stayed still as a post.

She switched her gaze back to the roadside. The first building was encased in glass. A greenhouse? The next building, a glorified screened-in porch, was marked with a sign that read ART CABIN. Gravel paths led up to the doorways. In a clearing dappled with sunlight between the two stood a man wielding a shovel and dressed in an orange T-shirt and a very familiar red baseball cap. She frowned. He straightened, took off his cap, revealing tousled blond hair, and swiped an arm across his forehead.

"Hey, that's Andy!" She craned to see him better, but he'd disappeared from view.

"He works here," Lil said.

"Andy works *here*?"

"Just great," Michael grumbled. "Like it's not bad enough everyone in my family knows where I'm going. Now everyone in *Cordelia* will know."

"Andy doesn't tell tales," Mari reassured him, knowing *that* for a fact. "If he did, I'd have spent most of my school years in detention and most of my time at home grounded."

She chuckled, but nobody joined in. In fact, Lil shot her a jaundiced look. She fell silent. *Spoilsport*. Still, she felt happier knowing Andy would be nearby. She'd try to find him later and ask him to keep an eye on Michael while he went about his groundskeeping chores. Or maybe he was the general handyman or janitor. She patted Michael's arm, and he jerked it away. She sighed. This was a tough crowd.

The driveway widened in front of a long rough-timbered building that stretched across the main thrust of the promontory. Another sign was nailed to a post helping support a roof that extended over a porch running the length of the building: MAIN HALL. Across from the building and down the drive, as far as Mari could see before the road was swallowed by trees, ran a row of small cabins. Sleeping quarters, she assumed. The closer they drew to the main hall, the more the inside of the Bronco felt like a graveyard.

"You know"—she poked Michael, thinking nobody could accuse *her* of not trying to paint a silver lining on the cloud—"this looks like any old camp."

He shot her a look that said, *moron.*

This time her sigh was audible.

Jon slowed to a crawl. Okay, maybe it *wasn't* like any old camp. There weren't any children running around. No boisterous shouts. Instead small clumps of people lingered silently on either side of the roadway. While the numbers in each group varied, they all held one teenaged boy bearing the same slouched shoulders, and I-don't-care expression that Michael wore. Their families looked around in various guises of confusion, anxiety, and unease. Much the same as Jon's expression in the rearview mirror.

He braked suddenly as a guy dashed across the driveway in front of the Bronco. His sand-colored hair blew back from an apologetic smile. A few years younger than she was, he sported raw-boned limbs, khaki shorts, and another orange shirt. One side of the shirt said CAMP SYCAMORE. He joined one of the groups and shook a hand with more energy than anyone had a right to at this hour of the morning. The back of his shirt said STEVE. God, was everything labeled here? She looked around and spotted more men in orange shirts. DALE, HAL, and TONY. Guess so. Each of them bore a clipboard. To prove her point, she watched Tony—stocky, muscular, and with a swatch of blond hair—scribble something down, rip it off, and pat it on one of the teenagers' chests. KYLE. Michael sank farther down in his seat.

Jon took a turn into a parking lot, a square of gravel squeezed between the main hall and two more cabins that sat side by side. More labels: THERAPISTS on one cabin, COUNSELORS on the other. And what, she wondered, was the difference?

The Bronco nudged its way along, avoiding a group of teenage boys congregated in the lot. All were orange-shirted and prelabeled. They joshed with one another and with a man in his mid-forties who sported a blond crew cut, square shoulders, a clipboard, and a key hanging from a cord around his neck: KIRK. In contrast to the boys who'd lingered silently by the roadside, these teens looked happy to be here. Odd.

Jon found space for the Bronco between a school bus that had seen better days and the wall of the therapists' cabin. On the slope to the lake in front of them, a man with VOLUNTEER stamped on his back tooled a riding lawn mower along the shore. Mari wondered if that was something Andy normally did. When Jon turned off the key, the only sound was the drone from the mower.

Lil stirred. "We're here!" she said brightly, in case someone hadn't noticed. She turned around. "What do you think, Michael? Mari's right. It looks like it could be fun."

Michael's jaw was so hard, Mari thought she could probably use *it* to break up the shower chair. She felt the beginnings of a headache.

"Yeah, right," Michael muttered.

Lil's smile faltered. "We'll give it a chance, okay?"

"What do you mean, *we*? I'm the only one who has to stay in this dump."

"Well, yes, but we'll all be participating in counseling sessions through the summer. We won't be together at the same time except for once a week, but everyone—me, your dad, your sister—will be working as hard as you."

Michael raised an eyebrow. "Who says I'll work?"

"That's enough." Jon twisted around, eyes cold as brass. "Show your mother some respect—"

"She's *not* my mother."

"—because if this doesn't work out, buddy, you *really* won't like the next place."

"Fuck that," Michael mumbled. Mari hoped to high heaven Jon had suddenly gone deaf.

"*What* did you say?"

"Jon . . ." Lil put a hand on his arm.

Michael cringed back, although Mari knew Jon had never laid a harsh hand on his son in his life. Jon's dad had beat him, and he was particularly vocal on the subject of child abuse. But since it looked like he might have forgotten all that, she interjected, "He said, *Duck* that."

Jon turned his eyes on her in disbelief.

"I mean, see . . ." She pointed. "There's a low-hanging branch, and if you get out of the car without noticing it, you could really get a clunk on the old noggin."

Jon gave her the ghost of a grin. "Liar."

"I'm *not* lying. There really *is* a low-hanging branch."

"Can we just get this over with?" Michael muttered. The ingrate.

He threw open the door and got out, looking away from the boys in the parking lot. They'd started toward the main building, following the man labeled KIRK. Hands stuffed deep in his pockets, head down so his hair shielded his eyes, Michael headed the same direction, careful to keep his distance.

The rest of them scrambled out, Lil and Jon hurrying, Mari lagging behind and still questioning her mental stability over putting herself here. Red clay, damp from the weekend rains, collected on her Icon wedge sandals. *Dang* it.

Jon nodded toward Michael. "Does he know where he's going?"

"Yes. There's an orientation session in the cafeteria, then a tour of the grounds," Lil said. "Oh, and we also need to pay some incidental fees."

Jon stopped and frowned at his wife. "On top of what we've already paid?"

Uh-oh. Mari stopped, too. A good six feet away. Michael ignored them and kept walking.

Trying hard not to listen—she'd had her fill of the Van Castle family problems—Mari looked around. A breeze blew in off the lake, and tall oaks bowed gently. A squirrel leaped between branches, chattering so madly at something below she could hear him over the whirr of the mower. Her gaze followed the animal as it leaped onto the roof of the therapists' cabin. Out of the corner of her eye, she caught a glimpse of an orange T-shirt disappearing into the brush around the back. That must be why the squirrel had his panties in a twist.

"Be grateful we can afford it." Lil's voice had risen above the mower. "A lot of these boys, like that group"—Lil motioned toward the boys ahead of Michael—"don't have families who can. They're residents at Vreeley Home in Kansas City, referred to it by social services."

"So we're subsidizing a bunch of other kids?"

"No!" Mari expected to see Lil stomp her foot. "The state pays. Donations pay. I've told you all this. You just haven't *listened*."

"I have, too."

"You have not."

Mari rolled her gaze heavenward and caught sight of a hawk. It really was beautiful out here. You never saw hawks in Kansas City. And she'd only seen a mess of pigeons in New York. For a moment she wished for her charcoal pencils to capture the hawk's flight in a few brisk strokes.

"Then why do *we* pay?" Good grief, Jon was *whining.* "A ton, I'll remind you."

"*We* pay because *our* child hasn't been in and out of foster homes. *We* pay because *our* child hasn't reached a point where the next stop is a mental institution or jail. Dr. Everheart told us this would be the best opportunity for Michael to get away from our house and address his problems without us badgering him all the time."

Jon scuffed a toe in the dirt. "What he needs is a good *badgering,*" he muttered.

"And with Michael out of the house, maybe we can address *our* problems. We're not helping him with constant arguments like this. We've got to put an end to it. Melanie will be home in the next week, and I don't want her subjected to this. It was bad enough at Christmas. We *all* need counseling, and you know it."

Jon stopped scuffing. He closed his eyes a moment, then quietly said, "The holidays were pretty bad. You're right."

They finally moved forward again. Ahead of them, the group had disappeared into the building. Michael was stepping up onto the porch. This time Lil took Jon's arm, walking close up against him. Their matching strides reminded Mari of a sack race, and she felt the sudden lack of a partner for herself. Not Sean, but *Andy* flitted across her mind, and she stumbled. Where had *that* come from?

"So what are these incidentals we need to pay for?" Jon asked.

"For one, the camp has a store. The boys earn behavior points in order to purchase things like candy. But for the families that can afford it, they ask for a donation to cover toothpaste, shampoo, items like that." She paused, pulling him up short. "Do you have your wallet?"

Jon patted his back pocket. "I left it in the console."

"I'll go get it," Mari announced, glad for an excuse to get away. While Lil murmured her thanks, Jon dug in his pocket and tossed her the keys.

With Jon and Lil continuing to the main building, Mari took a leisurely stroll back to the Bronco. Forget a partner. If her experience with Sean hadn't been enough, Lil and Jon were making her wonder if any man was worth it. Her mind skipped ahead to what she could do post-Cordelia. A bigger city this time. A bigger career. A nice fat splash. She'd leave her memories in Kansas City and just move on. She wished she could be dead certain she had the guts to leave Sean behind, too.

She reached the Bronco, unlocked the door, stretched in with one foot up on the side, and grabbed Jon's wallet. Behind her, there was a sudden movement. Someone flew by, banging briefly against the door. She hadn't heard anything coming over the sounds from the mower. Startled, she scrambled out so fast she conked her head on that damned low-hanging branch.

Pain flared, and her temper spurted. "Hey!" Rubbing her scalp, she glared after the running figure.

Tall with dark hair, a boy—a man?—had reached the main hall, his strides eating up the ground. Before he disappeared around the corner, she got an impression of dark legs under white shorts and pale arms, which didn't make sense, unless he was wearing warm-ups under the shorts. Orange shirt, of course. With her watering eyes, she couldn't make out more than a D at the beginning of the name on the back.

"Hey!" she called again, planning to force an apology.

But he didn't stop. He didn't even look around. He bounded up the side steps to the porch, tossing something into the hedge of forsythia that ran a ring around the main hall.

Idiot. She shook her head. Maybe you lost points or something if you were late for a meeting. Either that, or he was in dire need of a bathroom. But neither was any excuse for making her head pound more than it already did.

Rubbing the knot on her skull, Mari mounted the steps to the main hall, and passed under several more signs: small ones telling her the building housed the cafeteria, gym, office, and camp store. She let herself in through two big double doors. Inside, in a shallow rectangular room that ran the length of the building and was bookended with offices was a mass of barely contained confusion. About a dozen orange-shirted boys were still joking with one another, posing, she supposed, for the equal number of boys still in street clothes who lounged with their backs against a half dozen rough-hewn pillars. The latter seemed determined to ignore the former. Gazes stared up at the timbers striping the ceiling or down at the clay tracked on the linoleum around their feet. Gripping their clipboards, STEVE, DALE, TONY, HAL, and a couple of other young men who she assumed acted as camp counselors darted among them, calling out names and herding them into groups. The boys still in street clothes responded slowly.

Still massively annoyed, Mari looked around, trying to spot the miscreant who that had made her clunk her head. On her way up the steps, she'd peered into the forsythia and spotted what looked like a crowbar, one end wrapped with blue duct tape. Whoever it was couldn't have been up to much good. So much for close supervision.

Most of the teens were tall, and there were various shades of complexions—white, black, and everything between. Plus any number of DS . . . DAVID, DANIEL, DAMON, DEVON . . . and maybe it hadn't even been a D she'd seen. Maybe it had been a B. BRANDON, BRYCE, BRENT. She couldn't swear to race, hadn't gotten a look at his face . . . Criminy, it could have been anyone.

She gave up and looked for Michael instead, finally catching a glimpse. His back was flattened against the wall, as though he could camouflage himself. Squeezing between bodies, she headed in his direction.

"Where are Lil and your dad?" There were no adults to be seen.

Michael's expression was lifeless. "In there." He jerked a thumb toward another set of double doors on the back wall below a cafeteria sign. "Some stupid meeting."

"Aren't you supposed to go, too?"

"No."

Mari didn't want to abandon him, but he wasn't giving her much to work with here. "What are you doing?"

Michael heaved a sigh, like responding was taking all he was worth. "They're dividing us up into sixes— six guys to a cabin. Six guys to a *youth care provider*." He snorted. "Shit, more like *babysitters*."

Mari studied STEVE, standing nearby. With his sprinkle of freckles and a gap-toothed smile, he was kind of cute. "Is that your baby—I mean—youth care provider?"

"I guess." Michael shoved his hands into pockets that looked like they could each hold a truckful of coal.

"He looks nice."

Michael gave her another *moron* look.

"Look, Michael. You're here, and maybe it's lame, but you might as well suck it up. It won't last forever."

He stiffened, and the sullen look turned into a

blaze. "Easy for you to say. You're not the one they're throwing in here just so they don't have to deal with you anymore."

"They're not—"

"It's Michael, right?" Steve's hand fell on Michael's shoulder. "I'm your youth care provider." To her he added a pleasant smile. "The parents are gathering in the cafeteria."

"I'm not a—"

"You'll be able to see your son later."

"My what?" He thought she was old enough to have a fifteen-year-old? She should never have cut her hair. Nor was Steve as cute as she'd thought.

"She's my aunt," Michael muttered.

Steve didn't skip a beat. "Nice to meet you. You'll be able to see your nephew later."

It was a dismissal. She glowered, but his smile stayed put. It even looked genuine. Finally realizing her glower was completely glancing off Steve's white teeth, she gave Michael's arm a squeeze, turned on her heel, and headed through the cafeteria doors.

She stepped into a high-ceilinged space flooded with light from a wall of windows that looked across the lake. Outside, sunshine glimmered across the water. Inside, two basketball hoops were tipped up at either end, accounting for the wire screens protecting the glass. Fold-up cafeteria tables with benches held an assortment of parents, some singles, some couples, all seated facing the same direction, with space for an army between them. The boys apparently weren't the only ones afraid to mix. Some expressions were weary, others dazed. All were turned toward KIRK, who was holding forth in front of rolled-down aluminum shutters above a stainless-steel counter. This room doubled as gym and dining room.

"We use a technique called milieu therapy—" His voice, booming without help from any microphone, broke off when she appeared. "C'mon in. I'm Kirk, the director." He smiled, showing a row of teeth as white and even as Chiclets.

Feeling like a schoolkid caught sneaking into class late (a feeling she wasn't totally unfamiliar with), she ducked her head and scrambled into a seat without looking around for Lil and Jon. From a row of chairs facing the audience near Kirk, she heard a chuckle. *Andy*. Her cheeks fired up. Dang it, she'd kill him for laughing at her.

After she was settled, Kirk continued, gesturing, stalking back and forth at the front of the room, the key around his neck swaying with his footsteps. The man was all barely contained energy. "Those of you who have kids at Vreeley Home know about milieu therapy, but please bear with me while I explain to those whose kids are coming into this for the first time. Basically, we try to provide a structure where expectations and consequences are clear. Very clear. We want to start the boys with a stable, safe environment where they'll feel comfortable addressing their problems without the battles that have developed at home."

Stable, safe. What fun. Mari looked around. Some people stirred uncomfortably.

Kirk grinned. "Don't feel embarrassed. We know what it's like dealing with a teen who has suddenly turned on you. It can create World War III. You aren't alone."

A few parents gave each other sheepish glances. Mari's gaze, though, was on Andy. He wore an orange T-shirt like the rest of the employees. She hoped he had one with his name on it, and not just JANITOR. That'd be demeaning. She examined her fingernails. She needed a manicure.

"The kids hate the rules, especially at first. You'll hear a lot of complaining, but believe me, we do have fun here, too, once they get used to it." *I'll bet.* "And we make progress, *real* progress on their difficulties.

The staff include the youth care providers—one for every half dozen boys. The YCPs will live with your kids. The counselors, like Dr. Everheart here"—he nodded at an Ichabod Crane of a man with longish black hair and glasses so thick they hid his eyes—"are here overnight on different schedules, as their cabin only accommodates a couple of people. They conduct individual therapy sessions just like your kids have been doing from home or at Vreeley Home. If more sessions are advisable, the counselors will let you know and make themselves available."

Mari yawned, realized Andy was watching her, and covered her mouth with her hand. His blue eyes did that crinkle thing. She lowered her hand and stuck out her tongue.

"And finally we have the therapists."

Looking away, Andy sat up straighter. Diversion over, Mari went back to her nails.

"These folks specialize in various disciplines. While they have a cabin on the grounds, they largely work with your boys during scheduled hours during the day. Whatever they observe will be reported to that boy's counselor. Let me make some introductions. Rita Wagner is our recreational therapist."

Mari looked up. A large, raw-boned woman of middle age had taken over the floor from Kirk. "We'll have swimming, fishing, water sports . . ." Rita's voice boomed. Mari winced—*Sieg heil!*—and started working at a hangnail. Definitely a manicure. Maybe on Thursday when she took her mother to rehab. She doubted she could con Pop into doing the deed twice in a row.

"Thank you, Rita. And Finney Sturgeon, our art therapist . . ."

There was some light clapping. Mari glanced up again. A trim woman around her age rose from beside Andy. What kind of a name was Sturgeon? Poor girl. Fins, fish. She must have really gotten ribbed in grade school. Flipping long dark hair behind her shoulder, Finney Sturgeon launched in on the joys of self-portraits, group murals, and collages centered on pre-determined themes. Strange name or not, the woman was pretty, with a nice glow to her face. Mari pinched her own cheeks, thinking maybe tomorrow she could catch some sun while her mother napped. Maybe if she had a tan, nobody would notice her hair. Her gaze dropped to her feet. And on Thursday, she'd get a pedicure, too.

"And last but not least, our horticulture therapist—"

Mari frowned. What in the heck was a horticulture therapist?

"—Andrew Eppelwaite."

Her jaw dropped.

To a smattering of applause—nobody applauding more enthusiastically than Finney Sturgeon—Andy rose, took over the floor, and explained his work with the boys at Camp Sycamore. Apparently a horticulture therapist was much the same as an art therapist, only instead of paints and paper and colors, he used shovels and dirt and plants to increase self-confidence, foster responsibility, aid social skills—sheesh, and maybe even effect a cure for cancer?

The second that last thought entered her brain, she shrank in her seat, ashamed. Andy's expression radiated commitment and dedication—the same kind of glow she'd seen on the art therapist's face, like working with a bunch of vegetation or crayons and unruly boys was some kind of nirvana. But she'd never seen Andy look like that. Ever. Motivated, dedicated, and just like . . .

She looked at his colleagues. At Kirk. And Rita. And Finney. All of them sported a similar shine in their eyes. The same kind of gleam she'd seen in the gazes of STEVE, DALE, HAL, and TONY.

Then she looked at her hands, only this time she

didn't see the remnants of her last nail job. Manicures and pedicures. Icon wedges and Manolo Blahnik stilettos. Bikini waxes and just the right dye job. Self-contempt crawled over her. She'd treated this whole thing—she'd treated Andy—with nothing but disdain. But Andy had obviously found a purpose in life.

More purpose than she had.

Chapter 7

After the orientation was over, Mari wandered out to the main hall's front porch. The three therapists had filed out before the session had ended, Andy breaking stride to give her a chunk on the arm, looking puzzled when she'd returned only a wan smile. Most of the parents, including Lil and Jon, remained in the cafeteria, where Kirk was answering individual questions. The reception room was empty; the boys had been herded elsewhere.

She looked around for signs of activity, wondering what she would do with herself while Lil and Jon toured the premises with the other parents and had a last meeting with Michael. They, along with Michael's sister, Melanie, would gather once a week for family counseling, but other than letters, they'd have no contact with their son.

She moved to the porch railing. Nobody was in sight. Off toward the lake, she heard catcalls and an occasional shout of laughter. The boys must be taking their own tour and were somewhere near the cove. She considered her options. Off to her left, the drive stretched up toward the road and disappeared into a tunnel of trees. Off to her right, it straggled to a turn-around after the last of the residents' cabins.

That's what Kirk called the boys. *Residents*. Not campers. He hadn't put frills on what everyone would work to accomplish here. Camp Sycamore wasn't a holding area for miscreants; it was a place where real work got done on their problems. And Andy was a part of it.

Still in a state of disbelief, she shook her head.

"Hey, Mar."

She started and turned. Flipping the tab off a can of soda, Andy stepped through the door. Now that she knew about him, he looked different. The jeans and T-shirt seemed normal, as was the ball cap stuffed into his back pocket, its brim sticking out. But she noted that along with the usual easygoing amusement in the depths of his blue eyes, there was wisdom. Along with the smile lines around his mouth, there was firmness to his chin. How had she missed these things?

"Want some?" He held out the can.

She wasn't thirsty, but she was at an unusual loss for words. To cover her silence, she took it and swigged.

He leaned against the opposite post. "So what do you think?"

She swiped the back of her hand across her mouth and handed back the can. "About Camp Sycamore?" *Or about you?*

He nodded.

"It . . . seems nice."

Inane response, but she didn't really know what to think. Between Michael's opinion that the place would be nothing less than Leavenworth Federal Prison on a lake and to her own flippant idea and that it would be some woo-woo center with a lot of hand-holding, typical of what Lil would dig up, she hadn't found room yet to process the information she'd gleaned in orientation. After the therapists had been introduced— after *Andy* had been introduced—she'd finally paid attention.

He smiled, pushed off the post, and offered his hand. "C'mon. I'll give you a tour."

"Don't you have to be somewhere, do something?"

"I'm pretty much done for the day. I've already given my nickel speech to the boys, and there's nothing else until a welcome lunch after the parents leave. My real work won't start until tomorrow." He jiggled his hand. "C'mon."

Like she often had when they'd set out on some caper, she took his hand. Like he often had, he sensed her mood and gave her hand a reassuring squeeze. Only this time her discomfort wasn't because they were headed out for a forbidden dip into Paley's quarry pond or a lark in Pop's Buick. This time uneasiness rose because she didn't know where they were headed. Her disquiet felt odd. She'd always known where they were going before.

Turning left, he swung their hands between them as they headed up the drive. "I'll show you the therapists' domain."

"Okay." She stumbled over a rut, and his grip tightened.

He glanced down. "Great choice of shoes." His eyes traveled up. "Although I'm sure the boys appreciate the miniskirt. I do."

Despite the flattery, suddenly the French Connection retro-print seemed foolish rather than stylish. She blushed, then grew angry at herself. It seemed like every time they saw each other now, she fired up like a bottle rocket. She'd never blushed like this before around Andy. Okay, maybe once or twice when they were in the back of his pickup, but . . . "I'm sure they've seen better—younger—legs than my sticks."

"Mmm. I wouldn't call them sticks." He winked. "Straws, maybe. Not sticks."

"Hmph." She cast around for a new topic. "Were you surprised to see Michael?"

"Michael? No. I'd met with Lil and Jon before to answer some questions. That was the appointment I had the day I ran into you out on Main."

That was the day she'd thought he was itching to get to the Rooster to belt back a beer as soon as it opened. He must have thought she was pretty damn amusing. She halted and shook her hand loose. "Why didn't you frigging tell me?"

He looped his thumbs in his pockets and grinned. "I figured you'd find out sooner or later. Cordelia may have grown, but in a lot of ways it's still small. And once I knew you were coming to Kesibwi . . ." He shrugged.

"But we never kept secrets from each other. We always—" She stopped. Not for the last fourteen years. For the first time, she realized just how long ago that was. Plus, it wasn't like she planned to lay out her entire history now, either. There were parts she didn't want anyone to know. Least of all Andy. That last thought really tangled her tongue. What did it matter what *Andy* knew?

"Ah, Mar. I just couldn't resist. You've always been so cocksure about everything, it was too much to ask me to destroy your illusions."

"But you let me think you were—You were—"

"Still No-Account?"

She hung her head. Maybe she'd deserved his evasion. "I'm sorry."

"Me too." He grasped her hand again. "Now that we're both duly apologetic, I'll lay my life bare. Let's go."

They continued up the drive.

"So how did you get involved in all this?"

"It was a natural, really. Those six months of community service? I fulfilled the time at Girls and Boys Town in Omaha. You heard of it?"

She nodded.

"I liked working with the kids." His smile went dry. "I was rather familiar with a lot of their situations, you know. After that, I was at loose ends. I didn't want to go back to Cordelia until I'd figured out what

I was doing with my life. Gran had picked up the pieces often enough in the past. When Anna invited me to stay with her, she also finagled a job for me out of our grandparents. They own a lawn and landscaping business."

"I always forget you have other family besides Tansy and Anna."

"I didn't, not really. My grandparents were relieved that I'd dropped out of sight once Anna was in college, and you should have seen their faces when I suddenly materialized again. Even when I was working for them, they didn't like to acknowledge we were related. They'd always considered me a bad influence on Anna. That's why I never was invited there, and why Anna didn't visit us except for Christmas and a week or so during the summer."

Much to Mari's relief back then. Politely, she asked, "And how is Anna?"

He gave her a sideways look that she couldn't read. Part surprise, and part something else. "You never did like her much, did you?" he asked. "That's always puzzled me—the two of you were a lot alike."

Ouch. How to respond to *that* diplomatically? She settled for a noncommittal, "Oh, really?"

"Yeah, really. Both of you top-notch artists. Both of you with the, uh, artistic temperament to match." He apparently caught the expression on her face. "I mean, you both were spontaneous, both emotional. Both . . ." He trailed off. "I think I'm digging a deeper hole here."

"One you might not get out of." Replaying his words in her head, she frowned. "You said *were*. That we *were* a lot alike. Has Anna changed since I knew her?"

"Anna died a couple of years ago."

She halted. "Oh, God, Andy. I'm so sorry." And now, along with guilt over her assumptions about Andy, she could pile on more for her snarky thoughts about Anna. "For the last decade or so, I haven't exactly stayed on top of Everything Cordelia. Family stuff, yes, but nobody mentioned Anna."

Andy shrugged. "Not surprising. Very few people probably remember her."

"What happened?"

"She—" He broke off, started again. "It was a bad reaction to a prescription drug." Andy tugged on her hand and they resumed walking. "Anyway, I loved working in landscaping. Liked the feel of the soil in my hands, enjoyed being outside."

He sounded like her mother. And he sounded like he didn't want to discuss Anna. His sister's death must still be painful. She'd practice maturity and wouldn't pursue it. "So you combined the two things, working with kids and gardening. I didn't even know there was such a thing as a horticulture therapist until today. Did you need a degree?"

He nodded. "Almost three years ago, I took myself off to K-State. I actually passed some classes in JuCo after high school—barely, since I was drunk every night—so I finished college in a couple of years plus summer school." He noted her grimace. "Hey, I'm sober *now*."

"Not that." She waved a hand. "K-State."

He laughed. "Only the big time for you, huh? Well, I like backwaters and small towns and wide-open spaces, so Kansas filled the bill. And now I'm up to my eyeballs in school loans."

As they neared the greenhouse, they passed a half dozen boys led by Steve coming down the hill. All the boys wore orange shirts now. She spotted Michael, but he didn't see her; he was too busy looking at the ground. The set of his shoulders looked forlorn. She sighed and turned her attention back to Andy.

He was watching her. "He'll be fine, Mari, I promise."

"Andy, he's . . ." She felt tears swell in her throat

at the sympathy in his expression. Michael was *what*?
Alone, lonely, scared? "He's afraid of the water," she
finished lamely.

"I know that from his file. Nobody will make him
do anything he's not comfortable with."

He squeezed her hand again, and she fought a few
goose bumps at the warmth in his eyes. Flustered, and
amazed that *Andy* had the ability to make her
flustered—she switched subjects. "So Vreeley Home
is the last stop on your road?"

"Mmm, I've got a few other ideas, but nothing firm
yet. I'll let you know when I figure it all out." He
grinned. He hadn't changed altogether, still taking life
as it came instead of grabbing it with both hands. "I'm
actually hoping, though, I'll get stuck in one of those
backwaters."

"You wouldn't want to live anywhere bigger?" She
couldn't fathom how people like Lil and Andy were
content with places like Cordelia. Cordelia was as exciting as watching paint dry.

"Omaha and Kansas City are big enough. It'd
take"—once again his glance at her was inscrutable—
"oh, something very special to get me anywhere
bigger."

They turned onto a narrow path that led through
trees to the greenhouse, and he loosed his grasp so
they could move single file. Her hand felt surprisingly
empty. Pausing when they reached the stoop, he surveyed the clearing between the greenhouse and the
art cabin. It was little more than a rectangle of clay.
Here and there, a few scraggly saplings poked through
the earth, along with more than a few rocks and
weeds. The bags of black soil and sand she'd watched
him load in his pickup were piled against the
greenhouse.

"It doesn't look like much now, but I'll set the boys
to turning that ground into flower heaven." He
pointed. "Back there, we'll put in tomatoes."

"Free labor, huh? Break a rule, and you get sentenced to work in the rock pile?"

He tossed her another glance, and she squirmed at a glint of disappointment in his eyes. "Not exactly. It's a way to help them experience what teamwork can do. Some projects are designed to help individual growth, others to help them with socialization."

Mari shut her mouth, deciding she wouldn't say another word.

Stepping over a coiled hose next to several large watering cans, he opened the door to the greenhouse and motioned her in.

The enclosure wasn't much bigger than Zinnia's kitchen. But, believe it or not, it was much more colorful. Flats foaming with flowers and seedlings lined counter-tall tables. Around the perimeter, gardening tools dangled from pegs, and empty pots begged to be filled. Light poured through the glass roof on one side; the other was shadowed where the woods crowded close. Every window that could open was opened, and the smell of fresh air and sun-warmed earth wafted through.

Andy moved forward, motioning at the flats. "It's too late in the season to grow from seeds . . ." He leaned down to shift a crate.

Moist warmth hugged her. In July, the greenhouse would be beyond hot, but since early June mornings still held a hint of coolness, it felt lovely. Like being held close in someone's arms . . .

". . . but we'll do some planting from seeds, grow them in pots. It's a good thing for a kid to have to rear something tender. They learn a bit about taking care of themselves."

She hardly heard him. Watching his lean muscles bunch as he moved the crate, she was still rolling along with this hugging fantasy thing. A flash of sensation swept her, settling low in her abdomen, as she remembered when he'd held her at sixteen, the first time

she'd let a guy touch her. And, except for some fumbling around in college that had led to not much of
anything, it hadn't been until Sean that she'd allowed
it again.

He'd poked his fingers between fronds of flowers.
"Still damp."

Shocked out of her whimsies, she raised her eyes.
Even between close friends, was her physical state
something that needed discussing?

"What?" He frowned at her expression. "What'd
I say?"

You dope, he'd been talking about the soil. "Uh,
nothing. I, uh . . ." Willing her face to fade back to
normal, she moved beside him. "Marigolds," she said,
focusing on the flowers, grasping at a change of topic.

He still looked perplexed, but he smiled. "Wouldn't
want to be without them."

She warmed again, wondering if he'd really meant
the double entendre.

He shifted to reach for another pack of plants in
front of her. Their arms brushed and she went warmer
still. "And hollyhocks. And, believe it or not, there's
a lilac bush behind the greenhouse."

"The O'Malley sisters are all represented then." She
concentrated hard on the flowers.

"Did you know the Victorians christened flowers
with meanings?"

Concentrating hadn't helped. She shook her head,
wondering why she was finding this conversation
erotic.

"Lilacs represented love, or the first emotions of
love."

"That suits Lil."

"And hollyhocks stood for ambition."

"*Perfect* for Alcea." She touched the many-fingered
leaf of a marigold. "And what do these mean?"

His grin turned evil. "Grief and despair."

She dropped her hand. "You're kidding!"

"Nope."

"They get the nice stuff, and I get *grief?*" She cuffed his shoulder. "You made that up."

"I didn't." He ruffled her hair, his hand lingering a tad longer than necessary. Or maybe that was just her imagination. "When you were born, your mother must have had a premonition."

Laughing and forgetting they were both thirty, she lunged at him, grabbing hold of his arms. It had once been the prelude to wrestling him to the ground. Of course, that was when she had towered above him. Now he barely even staggered. They scuffled a moment until he caught her against his chest. She looked up—realizing she rarely looked up at anyone—and his eyes laughed down into hers, something flashing hot in their depths. Another something shifted deep in her gut, and she suddenly realized she'd risen up on her tiptoes.

"Mar—" He whispered her name.

"Oh, sorry—I thought you were alone."

A sweet voice sounded behind them. Andy dropped his hands, and Mari twisted around, embarrassed to be caught . . . roughhousing. *Roughhousing*, nothing else. She ignored the note of promise she'd heard in Andy's voice. Along with a whole host of other feelings that weren't going away near fast enough.

A petite figure with long hair was silhouetted in the doorway. It was—oh, what was her name? Fin Fish, the art therapist gal.

"No problem, Finney." Andy didn't look at all flustered. But he did look—a tiny thrill shot up her spine—disappointed. He swiped his forehead.

"Kirk called and wants us all back at the main hall. The parents are getting ready to leave." She gave Mari an uncertain look, and Mari's flush deepened. That look wondered if roughhousing had been all that she and Andy had been up to. "Rita's already on her way."

"Okay. Finney, this is an old buddy of mine, Mari O'Malley. Mari, our art therapist, Finney Sturgeon."

They exchanged hellos, then Andy and Mari followed Finney from the greenhouse. On the way down the drive toward the main hall, the camaraderie she'd shared with Andy evaporated. The two therapists had lapsed into professional talk, commenting on the boys they'd met today and the plans they had for the summer. Mari felt like a fifth wheel.

And she also felt something else.

While Finney's face had brightened at Andy's description of her as an *old buddy*, Mari had felt unexpectedly disgruntled. And now she just felt confused.

Chapter 8

Early the next morning, thrumming through a chorus of birdsong, a woodpecker knocked incessantly on the sycamore tree outside the sleeping porch. Mari buried her head in her pillow, then gave up, flopping onto her back and opening her eyes to a wash of ivory light that flowed through three sides of the screened-in room. The fourth wall was solid stone, interrupted only by the door that led into the storage cellar. She'd left the vinyl shades that covered the screens rolled up when she'd gone to bed. Since Lil and Jon had headed back to Cordelia last night, only Pop and Mom were left at the cabin, and there had been no need for privacy.

She pulled the blanket up to her neck. The air was cool, but damp. Everything in the lake region was always damp. To foil the mildew, she'd tucked her belongings into an old chest of drawers and hung her clothes on a rod inside the cellar. Out here on the porch, the only adornment was her bed and a trunk of art supplies that she was using for a nightstand.

She studied the white beadboard ceiling, counting the slats out of habit, although she already knew how many there were. Up until Jon and Lil had built the guesthouse, the room had held two pairs of bunk beds and was the favorite nesting place for the youngest O'Malleys. When she was little, she'd always put dibs on a top bunk, because she'd liked looking down at the rest of the world. Although the bunk beds had long ago taken the last bounce they could stand, she still preferred sleeping out here, leaving the multiple bedrooms to the rest of the family.

Bunching her pillow under her head, she looked through the trees down the slope to the cove and considered how much time she had before Zinnia pounded a stout walking stick on the deck overhead, signaling another day as a scullery maid. With the uneven ground around the cabin, and the doctor's insistence that Zinnia walk daily, Mari had thought the walking stick a find when she'd spotted it at Paddy O'Neill's Emporium back in Cordelia. Now, with summer barely started, she already wanted to burn it.

Thinking of the day ahead, she blew out a breath. She'd cater to her mom, mop the floors, grocery shop, wash the sheets—and the supper dishes still on the counter. She'd fix lunch, fold towels, then steel herself for another tussle over the damn shower chair. What a riot.

Her mind wandered to Camp Sycamore and settled on Andy. What would he be doing? Nothing involving shower chairs, she'd bet.

Yesterday, as they'd driven back from camp, she'd glanced through the schedule Lil had handed her. Reveille was at six-thirty, breakfast at seven, lights out at nine-thirty. In the morning, the residents would participate in sessions for art, gardening, or recreation. Afternoons were set aside for a full-group activity— they'd hike, swim, ski, fish, canoe. Quiet time was late afternoon. For an hour before bedtime, they journaled, and those journals were collected and read by their counselors.

Ugh. She'd tossed the schedule aside. "Milieu therapy" indeed. Not one moment of time unaccounted for, few minutes unsupervised, privacy nonexistent. She wouldn't last a day. Her sympathy for Michael had surged anew as she'd listened to Lil and Jon discuss his summer, their enthusiasm sounding forced. Still, their hands had linked tight together on the console, and they'd no longer argued.

She rearranged her pillow, her thoughts drifting away from her sister's family until they finally settled on what she *really* needed to think about. Andy. More to the point, how she'd felt when they'd stood in the greenhouse clasped together. She couldn't believe it, but truth was, she'd almost forced a kiss on him. And he'd looked like he wouldn't have minded if she had. Yikes. The inclination should give her hives, but it hadn't seemed like a half-bad idea at the time. In fact . . . it still didn't.

Frowning, she stirred. Maybe the whim simply sprang from happiness that her childhood chum had found a niche that didn't involve kegs of beer or busting somebody's head. Maybe it was just the shine of dedication in his eyes that moved her. Except . . .

She forced herself to examine her feelings. They went beyond simple pleasure in his achievements and commitment. Even while his new calling made her own life seem trivial, the direction he'd found made him attractive. *Danged* attractive. She couldn't believe it, but there it was.

Oh, well, what did it matter? She probably wouldn't see him again this summer, and her feelings would fade. The thought made her sad.

Hoping to lose her mixed-up emotions in a few more minutes of shut-eye, she rolled over. But above her head, the walking stick pounded. She groaned and swung her legs over the side of the bed. Duty—in the form of a small woman carrying a big to-do list—called.

A few hours later—breakfast made with only a minor skirmish over her selection of the dietitian-recommended low-salt margarine on whole wheat

bread instead of the butter smeared on biscuits that
her mother preferred—the washer churned away in
the cellar, the clothesline fluttered with clean sheets
(Zinnia insisted on breeze-dried), and dishes stood
like soldiers in the draining rack.

Listening to Patsy Kline croon "I Fall to Pieces"
(*Tell me about it, Patsy*) on a radio tuned low, Mari
alternately mopped the floor and peered out the windows over the kitchen sink. Doused by sunshine, her
parents walked a slow circle around the clearing in
front of the cabin. Zinnia held the walking stick in
one hand, Pop's arm in the other. He'd pulled on his
old fishing hat, and a hookless feathered lure dipped
in front of his eyes while he watched their feet. Now,
almost five weeks since her bypass, Zinnia had recovered some of her previous vigor, but her movements
were still hesitant.

Watching her, Mari leaned on the mop handle and
sighed. Despite her bluster and bravado, her mother
was afraid. Afraid she'd break, afraid to be left alone,
afraid of her own body. The formerly fearless Zinnia
now relied on crutches, from the walking stick to the
shower chair to the people around her. Mari recognized the problem, but didn't know what could be
done. The visiting nurse—now down to once a week
and soon to stop—had counseled patience. Her
mother needed time.

Well, *she* had plenty to give her. Straightening, Mari
shoved the mop in the bucket. There was certainly no
reason to rush. Even if she could escape Lake Kesibwi
today, she wouldn't get far without a job. The mop
agitated across the floor. This afternoon, she'd forgo
working on her tan and set up the Mac. Tonight, she'd
look at want ads on monster.com. Then tomorrow,
she'd . . .

The phone rang. Setting the mop aside, she picked
up and heard Sean's voice, and her pulse rate doubled
even as she dropped into the usual seesaw of emotions

he caused. They'd last talked only two days ago, and this was far too soon for the once-a-week contact she'd insisted was enough when he'd started calling daily. She wanted space to think things through. And she didn't want to answer her mother's raised eyebrows every time the phone rang.

"Are you busy?"

She looked at the half-wet floor, heard the washer chug to a halt, thought of the lunch her parents expected in half an hour. "No. But I told you—"

"Then can you get away tomorrow? Meet me in Sedalia for lunch?" This wasn't the first time he'd suggested a meeting, but it was the first time he'd sounded so urgent.

But she'd stick to her guns. "Sean, I didn't mean I'm not busy *at all*. I can't just—"

"Just this once, Mari, and then I'll leave you alone till the end of summer if that's really what you want. But I have something to tell you."

"You can tell me now."

He hesitated. "In person. Please."

An odd buzz of excitement in his voice whirred through the wire and piqued her curiosity. Her guns unstuck. "Oh, all right. But it will have to be afternoon. And can we meet in Cordelia instead?" Sedalia was closer for Sean, but further away than Cordelia for her.

There was a long pause, and Mari frowned. Was chivalry dead?

"I've been out of town. I have a lot to catch up on here, and—"

Chivalry *was* dead. "—and you're the one who works, so your time is more valuable than mine." *Everyone*'s time was more valuable than hers.

"That's not what I meant."

"It's okay, Sean. I *understand*." And she did, but she didn't like feeling less significant than dog doo.

After agreeing to meet at El Tapatio, a popular Mexican restaurant, they hung up.

Thinking thoughts like *Curiosity killed the cat dead, dead, dead* and *You're an idiot* and *You've got as much backbone as a Twizzler,* Mari set the mop back in motion. The phone bleated anew.

She grabbed the receiver. "What!"

"Good morning to you, too." It was Lil. Sounding breathless, she rode right over Mari's mumbled apology. "Something's happened. Is Mother there?"

"Is Michael all right? Did—"

"Everyone's fine. I just need to talk to Mother."

"But—"

"For Pete's sake, hand her the phone, Mari. Jon and I are leaving to pick up Melanie from college, and I'm in a rush. Mother can explain everything."

Grumbling, Mari carried the cordless outside to Zinnia. Then loitered nearby. Pop dragged over two lawn chairs, helped Zinnia lower herself onto one, then settled himself in the other with a grunt. After some "mmm's" and "I see's," Zinnia glanced up at Mari. "Well, we got the space, that's the Lord's truth, and I don't see why she wouldn't be up to it."

Mari frowned. "Up to what?"

Zinnia waved a hand to shush her. "Okay." She nodded. "All right. We'll see them then." She clicked off and stared up at Mari. "Got some things for you to do this afternoon, honeybunch."

"You wanted me to go to the grocery store. See *who*?"

"We can put that off until later."

What was with this *we* stuff? "See *who*?" Mari repeated. "And what am I supposed to be *up to* doing?"

"Seems we'll be having some summer company, and the guesthouse needs readying." She patted Pop's knee. "Pop will help."

Not showing a whit of curiosity, Pop nodded, complacently chewing on his pipe stem.

Her plans for an afternoon job search suddenly fell apart. *"Who?"*

Zinnia glared at her. "Don't get yourself in such a tizzy. From what Lil says, this morning when she called that camp you all took Michael to yesterday— I guess Jon left his wallet there someplace—she found out they were in a bit of a pickle. Some cabins were vandalized or something, and they found out this morning they can't be repaired in short shakes. So a few of the folks there need a nearby place to stay. Lil volunteered the guesthouse." She paused. "Oh, and they found Jon's wallet."

"Great. Just *great.*"

"Lord love a duck, it sure is." Zinnia nodded. "What a mess that is, canceling credit cards, replacing your driver's license—"

"That's not what I meant! Now I have to take care of you, this place, *and* clean up after a bunch of boys."

Zinnia frowned. "You should know your sister better than that—she wouldn't even think of sticking us with a bunch of boys that have been in and out of trouble."

Mari closed her eyes a moment and begged the universe for patience. "Mother. *Exactly* who is coming?"

"Why, just that nice Andy Eppelwaite and some gal he works with."

Chapter 9

After that announcement, Zinnia shooed Pop off to do the shopping—"Get plenty of extra, as we'll ask them to join us for supper"—admonished Mari to get the guesthouse readied, and then looked surprised at Mari's lack of argument.

But not more surprised than Mari. Instead of annoyance, she felt excited. And her excitement confused her. Not the least because it seemed that the spirit of Martha Stewart had invaded her psyche. She forgot the Mac, monster.com, Sean, and her aversion to things housewifely. She flew up the drive to the guesthouse and scrubbed it top to bottom until it shined. She even picked some wildflowers and deposited them in a vase on the kitchen table, along with a note from her mother inviting Andy and their other guest—she assumed either Rita Wagner or Finney Fish-whatever—to supper. Then, leaving the guesthouse unlocked, she headed back to the cabin to fix a huge pot of spaghetti. While she suspected the idea of having Andy nearby drove her, she didn't pause to examine her feelings too closely. All she knew was that summer suddenly looked brighter.

But as day advanced into evening, and the supper hour came and went with no sign of their guests, the glow dimmed.

And by the next day it had completely gone out,

despite June-blue skies and an afternoon of freedom in front of her.

Behind the wheel of her several-year-old Volkswagen Cabrio, Mari emerged from the Ozark hills, Lake Kesibwi an hour behind her, and decided to pin her continuing dark mood on the oppressive bank of clouds to the north. But she knew better. She just didn't want to look too closely at *what* she knew better.

What did she care about Andy, anyway? She turned her car onto a four-lane highway, a seam through a carpet of pastureland. Her thoughts moved with the highway ahead to Sedalia. For that matter, what did she care about *Sean*?

With the top lowered on the Cabrio, the wind furrowed its fingers along her scalp and set her beaded earrings dancing. At least the wind felt good. And being out of Zinnia's vocal range felt even better. Guilt rose with the thought.

This morning, she'd sniped at her mother and grumped at Pop. But instead of giving her the backlash she'd deserved, Zinnia had waved her off to see *a friend* with a wan smile that was so pathetic, and so frigging understanding, it had cut deeper than anything her mother could have said. Well, at least she'd left her parents enough stew in the Crock-Pot (as well as spaghetti sauce in the refrigerator) to feed a battalion. They wouldn't go hungry if she wasn't home until late. Not that she *planned* to get home late. But she'd be damned if she'd spend another evening with her tongue hanging out like some lonesome puppy waiting for Andy.

On the CD player, Mary Chapin-Carpenter belted out "I Feel Lucky." Mari snorted. *Lucky* was obviously about as far out of her reach as *fame* and *fortune* and *getting her hair to grow faster*. Let alone figuring out what in the hell was going on in her head.

Last night, after Mom had retired and Pop had settled in for his usual before-bedtime reading, she'd wandered down to the cove. Clasping her knees, she'd sat on the dock listening to the rising *ree-ree* of the cicadas, the stirring of an occasional raccoon, and the soft lap of the water against the shore. Luxuriating in the lack of traffic noise that had throbbed beneath her windows in Kansas City day and night, she'd tilted her head back to watch a bat swoop over the lake, had admired the stars pin pricking the sky, and—dammit—had glanced over her shoulder at least fourteen hundred times to see if lights from the guesthouse glimmered through the woods.

And when they finally had, she'd glanced at the neon numbers on her watch, realized it was nearing eleven, and had suddenly felt too shy to take herself up the hill.

She'd awakened this morning, cursing herself for her sudden attack of bashfulness—it was only *Andy*—then found an excuse to walk up the drive. But while tire tracks were fresh in the still-soft clay, he was already gone.

When she'd returned to the cabin, Zinnia rattled off another litany of instructions which—to Mari's amazement—included shouldering their company's *laundry*. "They're helping your nephew after all." Incensed, Mari had made it abundantly clear she'd be damned if she'd wash Andy's socks. It had taken sharp words, tears, and some groveling on Mari's part before they'd finally made up. And the sock matter still wasn't resolved. So much for her hopes that things would change for the better with Andy around. So far, he'd made everything worse.

Socks. She pressed on the accelerator, knowing Sean was already waiting. She'd timed her departure to a T, but Zinnia had blown her schedule, insisting Mari drive her to rehab that morning, not Pop: "I spent my whole trip Tuesday clutching the armrest. The man never did know how to handle traffic." Considering the sock argument, Mari hadn't dared to refuse her. Next week, her mother would be able to drive by herself. Next week couldn't come soon enough. She sighed. But probably Zinnia would still be too scared to head off on her own.

And, as if all *that* wasn't enough, on the way to the rehab center, Zinnia had sprung more news. News that stank *worse* than Andy's socks. The party her mother usually held in the spring to celebrate the family's spring and summer birthdays had, of course, been canceled because of her heart problems. So she'd (*she'd?*) hold a big O'Malley gathering in a little over two weeks. Her mother ticked off her plans. Beds to prepare. Menus to plan. Food to buy. Dishes to prepare. *Won't that be fun?* Stifling a groan, Mari had only smiled and nodded like a dashboard dummy.

Shaking her head and muttering, "Tourists," Mari darted the Cabrio around a lumbering Cadillac. The road was full of people coming and going to the lakes. As she neared Sedalia, countryside gave way to motels (Bell Tower Motel always confused her—no bell, no tower), Texaco StarMarts, and farm implement showrooms. She passed John Deere on the right, then the state fairgrounds on the left, and was in the thick of the small city. She tensed at the bumper-to-bumper traffic. It didn't begin to compare with Kansas City's jams—let alone the honking and hollering she'd experienced that one time in New York—but she actually found herself wishing for the uneven streets of Cordelia and the potholed roads at the lake. Sheesh, she couldn't have gone that soft in only three weeks. Stomping on the accelerator, she buzzed in and out like a Manhattan cabdriver just to prove she could. Reaching the junction with Highway 50, she turned right, then pulled into the parking lot of El Tapatio and waited for her hands to stop trembling. See? Nerves of putty.

Easing out of the car, she glanced at her watch. Twenty minutes late. But she knew Sean had waited. Sean always waited, largely hoping things would fall into place without any conflict. She'd once thought that a virtue—one she'd never had—but she wasn't so sure anymore.

Finger-combing her hair, then tugging to straighten the silk blouse she'd donned over a pair of tight floral-print cropped pants, she walked across the lot. The straps of her slingback sandals dug uncomfortably into her heels. The spandex in her pants felt like a girdle. Criminy. After the outing to Camp Sycamore Tuesday, she'd decided designer wear was best left to the city—and *already* the ancient flip-flops, T-shirts, and khaki shorts she'd dug out of her (and Lil's) old dressers at the cabin felt as comfortable as second skin. Just as she'd feared—it didn't take much time to drop back into old ruts.

Hmph. Old *traps*.

She let herself into the restaurant, spotted Sean in a booth against the far wall, and started toward him. When he glanced up and saw her, a smile split his face. She almost melted right on the spot. She did have her doubts, but they didn't include the chemistry between them.

Old traps, she reminded herself, and slid into the booth. "Hey, there."

"Hey, back." He reached across the table and took her hands. "It's good to see you. Really good. I like the hair."

"You do?" She gave him a look of disbelief, slid her hands out from his, and grabbed a menu. "I'm starving. And I have to hurry."

Beyond sitting back in his seat, he didn't react to her rebuff. "I've ordered you a margarita. What's the rush?"

"Birthday shopping to do. The O'Malleys are hav-

ing a party in a couple of weeks." She frowned as a
waiter stopped at their table, salt-rimmed glass in
hand. "And I don't want a margarita."

Holding the drink just short of setting it down, the
waiter hesitated and looked between them.

She'd once been a party-hearty kind of gal, but
she'd learned the hard way that her impulsiveness and
alcohol didn't mix. Sean knew how she felt. Hell, he'd
taught her the lesson. Their affair had been a start-
and-stop ride on a fast track to nowhere. They'd race
along, she'd bump over her guilt and put on the
brakes. He'd renew pleas and promises, invite her for
drinks, and wait for a loss of resolve. Which always
happened. God, she'd been such an *easy* lay, it was
pathetic. She tried to ignore the fact that she'd also
loved him. She looked at him now. And maybe still
did.

"One won't hurt." The smile he gave her was cajol-
ing. And familiar.

"Still, I don't—"

The waiter gave a long-suffering sigh.

"Oh, criminy." Glaring at the waiter, she snatched
the drink from his hand, pleased to see him flinch. His
sigh hadn't held a candle to the disdainful stares of
the waitstaff she'd encountered in New York. With
them, she'd had to restrain herself from scrambling up
to offer her chair. And the cabdrivers? Don't get her
started on *them*. She couldn't understand most of
them, and those that she could, she hadn't wanted to
hear. Rude wasn't the word for it.

After the waiter (with a new measure of respect)
had taken their order of *chimi del mar* for her, and
pollo borracho for him, Sean asked, "So how's life in
pastoral Missouri?"

"Wonderful, if you're into masochism. I'm a char-
woman under the control of a little dictator." She ran
a finger along the rim of her glass, removing part of

the salt. "But I shouldn't complain. Things could be worse."

Sean raised an eyebrow. "How so?"

She frowned at him. "Geez, Sean, think. At least Mom is recovering. There could have been complications, or we could even have lost her."

"Oh, right."

She sighed and forgave him. Sean's parents had retired to Florida, and from what he'd told her, they'd never been close. Not that she was all that fond of being *this* close to her mother herself, but still.

She changed topics. "What's going on in the big city?"

"The usual. Frieda over in production is still being a pain in the ass, but I think I've found a way to cook her goose."

He rambled on about Carmichael's, filling a good hour while she sipped her drink, the waiter brought their food, and she emptied half her plate.

"Anyway, I'll be glad to leave it all behind." The words were airy, but his expression had shifted into barely contained excitement.

"What?" She paused with a forkful of shrimp halfway to her mouth, chagrined to discover she'd let her mind wander. Worrying that Pop would forget to wake Zinnia in time to watch *Oprah*. Worrying her mother might forget to take her evening meds. Even, for God's sake, worrying if there was enough stew should Andy make it for supper tonight.

"That's what I wanted to talk to you about." Pushing his plate out of the way, Sean sat forward and leaned his elbows on the table. He smiled. "I've accepted a new job."

"You have? I didn't know you were looking." She dipped her fork back into the shrimp.

"I wasn't. Not really. I'd left my résumé in a couple of headhunters' hands just in case something came along. And something did. A big something: senior art director."

"An upward move for you." Like there had ever been any doubt that that was the direction he'd go. "Where?"

"An advertising agency."

"Great," she mumbled around a mouthful of food. Sean had always wanted to move into a larger arena.

"A *big* advertising agency." Sean waited like he heard an internal drumroll, and his smile broadened. "In New York City."

She swallowed in one gulp. *"New York?"*

"That's where I've been the last few days. The offer came yesterday. And they said I could hire an assistant." He winked. "And I know just who I want."

Oz! Mari was transported into the middle of Manhattan. The bustle of the city crowded against her, exotic smells drifted through the air, voices chattered in a hundred different tongues. Color. Sound. *Excitement.* Even remembering hair-raising taxi rides, the occasional garbage strike, all those supercilious waiters, and the throngs of people crowding the sidewalks and staring straight through her, in her mind's eye, she stared up at mile-high skyscrapers and felt she could fly.

Then reality returned and she sat back with a thump. "There's Mother. I can't desert her." Plus *assistant* wasn't exactly floating her boat.

He grasped her hands, and this time she let him. "That won't be an issue. They don't want me until September, so the timing couldn't be more perfect."

Still, for reasons she didn't quite understand, she hesitated. "Sean, I can't just—"

"Don't say no. Remember how much fun we had there? It could be like that all the time."

"I *did* have a good time, but . . ."

They'd done the tourist thing—walks through Greenwich Village and SoHo, ferry to Staten Island, trip to the top of the Empire State Building, hours spent at MoMA. It *had* been fun. Too much fun. Like a Disney ride that thrilled her while at the same time making her want to get off. Then, after a carriage ride through Central Park and too much champagne (*cliché, cliché, cliché*), she'd fallen right into bed with a married man. It hadn't been her finest moment.

Oh, criminy. What was *up* with her? It was exactly what she wanted. Wasn't it? This time she'd have Sean all to herself. No muss, no fuss . . . No Jo.

And no nearby family if things didn't work out.

She almost toppled off her seat. Where had *that* thought come from?

Sean had been watching her face. "You aren't sure of me, are you? I guess I can't blame you, but . . . Look, I love you, Mari. I won't deny there have been other women since Jo died—"

Probably even before then, Mari thought cynically.

"—but I could never commit. And when I heard you were leaving town, I knew that was because I'd never *stopped* loving you." He paused. "Say you'll go."

"I want to go. Or at least I *want* to want to go. I'm just . . . In answer to your question, no, I'm *not* sure." *I'm not sure how I feel about you.* Another thought surfaced and this time she nearly choked. *And I'm not sure how I feel about Andy.*

Hurt descended over his face. He let go of her hands.

She was stung by the rejection. "Hey, no fair to give me that kicked-dog look. Our whole affair wasn't exactly easy to take, you know. You stayed with your job while I turned one down so people wouldn't find out. You stayed with your wife, while I waited around and used your contracts to keep my business afloat. I finally had the courage to end our relationship. And then had the courage to try to get by without Carmichael's business. I was—I *am*—all used up. It was *wrong*. *We* were wrong. When Jo—"

Sean made an exasperated noise. "I keep telling you that wasn't your fault."

"It doesn't matter if it is or isn't my fault. It *feels* like it is!" People at the next table looked over, and she lowered her voice. "I'd be a complete moron not to have doubts." She sat back and ran both hands through her hair. She felt as confused as she had the one time she'd wandered out on her own in Manhattan and gotten lost in a maze of streets. "You can't just waltz in here, make an announcement, and expect me to make a commitment this huge. Not after all that's happened. Not after all this time. It's just not *fair*."

He was quiet. "You're right. I shouldn't have hoped mention of New York would push you into my arms." He gave a slight smile. "But I did anyway."

"I need time, Sean. The summer. Without your influence." Andy flickered through her mind. "And without commitments on either side." Talk about not fair. She was trying to have her cake and eat it, too. Her instincts were whispering, *Say sayonara and be done with it,* but she couldn't. She couldn't just let everything she'd ever thought she wanted slip through her hands.

Could she?

Mari pulled her Cabrio into a spot near the cabin and yanked to a stop. She'd noted Andy's pickup outside the guesthouse but hadn't paused. Now that he *was* here, she wasn't sure she wanted to see him. She was thinking of him too much. *Way* too much.

She clenched her hands on the steering wheel and dropped her forehead on top of them. What was *wrong* with her? Sean had offered her everything—the Golden Apple and the Golden Boy all rolled into one. He'd even agreed to give her this summer to make up her mind. Without his influence. Without a commitment. Exactly as she'd asked for. But it was a two-edged sword she'd put into play—no commitment meant he might just find someone else.

Wondering if she'd just executed commitment hara-kiri, she groaned. Once upon a time, she would have jumped on his offer. Jumped him, actually. Why hesitate now? Because she couldn't make up her mind if she still loved him? Because he hadn't fought harder to change her mind? Or was she just a big fat scaredy-cat? All talk, no action. Or was it something else? Even . . .

Some*one* else?

She turned her head and stared across the clearing in front of the cabin. It was nearing seven-thirty. Bathing the atmosphere in gold light, the sun poked fingers through tumbling clouds that had moved overhead in the last half hour. Pop's red geraniums, stuffed in pots around the front door, glowed as if lit from within. Everything looked surreal.

Everything *was* surreal. To emphasize the point, thunder cracked and the skies opened up. Scrambling, she raised the convertible top, grabbed her bags, and made a dash for the cabin. She flung through the door, slammed it behind her. Muttering a curse, she shook herself off. Water from her hair showered the floor. From across the room, at the table in front of the sliding glass doors, someone chuckled.

She halted mid-shake, looked up, and met Andy's amused eyes doing their crinkle thing. Her gaze moved sideways to Finney's brown ones. Which were doing a laughing thing. Wonderful. Mari muttered a hello, aimed for a smile, but hit only a grimace.

Mom and Pop had twisted around in their seats.

"Glad to see you got back, honeybunch, before the storm got itself all worked up. What you got there?"

"Not much. Birthday presents." She looked at her bags. "I shopped in Cordelia on the way back."

"Well, get yourself something to eat and join us."

"Um, let me just put this stuff away."

Taking time to compose herself, delaying the inevitable moment when she'd have to pretend everything was a-okay, and hoping she could come up with some feasible excuse to refuse supper instead, she slogged downstairs and made slow work of putting her bags away, pulling each gift out and examining it. She'd bought an antique beaded necklace for her niece Melanie (birthday this past April), and a used-but-in-great-condition book bag for those business classes her sister-in-law Patsy Lee (birthday in a couple of days) took at night. As usual, O'Neill's Emporium with its bevy of good, cheap junk had coughed up some prizes for everyone except Lil (birthday midmonth). But what had Mari expected? Her sister had everything.

She sighed and put everything back in the bag. There was no polite way to decline supper; hell, she couldn't even drum up a rude one. Her brain just didn't want to work. She wandered back up to the kitchen, catching a whiff of the stew as she passed the Crock-Pot. Surprisingly, given her state of mind—although, come to think of it, maybe not so surprisingly, since she'd abandoned her *chimi del mar* when Sean had started discussing New York—her stomach growled. She reached for a bowl and cast a sideways look at the table where conversation had resumed.

Looking like a sleek spaniel, Finney had exchanged the uniform orange T-shirt for a crisp white blouse that contrasted with her dark hair and tanned skin. She looked great. Mari plopped a wad of stew in her bowl. She knew *she* looked like a wet poodle. Andy leaned toward Finney and said something Mari missed, and was rewarded by a lilt of laughter. Mari yanked out a drawer to grab some silverware. Great again. Along with that glow the art therapist had mastered, she *also* did melodic laughter. Sometimes *she* could manage a throaty chuckle that sounded rather sexy, but usually it was more like a bark from a seal.

She settled herself in a chair at the end of the table, Zinnia to her right, Andy on her left. Outside the sliding glass doors, rain lashed at the deck. Inside, she addressed her stew.

"Did you have fun with your friend?" Her mother's voice held an arch note.

"Mmmph," Mari said, mouth full.

"Who was it?" Andy asked. "Anyone I know?"

Mari swallowed. "No."

One of Andy's brows lifted at her less-than-candid reply, but before he could say anything, Zinnia spoke up. "That *friend* that keeps calling here from Kansas City, I'll bet." Her mother winked at the table at large. "Some man with a sexy voice. Lessen you all think she's gay."

"Mother!"

Andy choked, Pop's eyebrows went up, and Finney raised a napkin over her mouth.

"And why would I think that?" Andy's voice was strangled.

Mari glared at him. He knew darned well not to encourage her mother.

"That haircut of hers." Zinnia patted her hand. "Don't you worry none, honeybunch. It will grow back."

"I am *not* worried. I wanted it this way."

Finney cast a dubious glance at Mari's skull.

Andy lowered his head and raised *his* napkin. "Think I got something in my eye."

That *something* was about to be her finger.

Mari knew her face was flaming, but she straightened her shoulders and changed the subject. "I hope you found your accommodations suitable." Cool as a cucumber.

Andy and Finney chorused their thanks, then Finney looked at Zinnia. "May I bring our laundry down here every once in a while? There are washing machines at camp, but it's easier for me to get to it in the evenings."

"Well, Mari here will—"

"—show you where everything is." Mari cast a triumphant look at her mother, who clamped her lips together, then looked at Finney. What was with this *our laundry* bit? "I'd make him do his own."

Andy smiled. "Then it's a good thing it's not you I'm bunking with."

Mari's eyes narrowed. What did *bunking with* mean, exactly?

"Oh, he doesn't get off scot-free." Finney bumped her shoulder against Andy's, and Mari's eyes went to slits. "He's in charge of grocery shopping and we'll both do the cleaning. We've divided up all the chores."

God. The picture of domestic bliss. "Why do you have to live here anyway?" She cleared her throat. "I mean, what happened at your camp?"

They both sobered.

"Somebody—or somebod*ies*—took a strong exception to the therapists' and counselors' cabins," Andy said.

"Those two next to the parking lot?" Mari asked, remembering the running figure that had made her thunk her head.

Finney nodded. "They wrecked the plumbing, ripped mattresses, destroyed furniture, even tore some holes in the walls. The cabins are completely unusable. Andy shared Kirk's quarters in the main hall that first night, and Rita and I bunked on the floor in an office." She rotated a shoulder. "I'm still sore."

"We were hoping everything could get fixed p.d.q., but the plumbing is history." Andy put a hand on Finney's shoulder and massaged it briefly. Despite her attempts to keep them down, Mari's eyebrows crept up. "And you know how hard it is to find reliable help around here, plus—"

"—there's a lack of funds," Finney inserted, smiling thanks at Andy. "There's always a lack of funds."

"So Kirk decided the boys should have a go at it— another project for them. One of the volunteers knows plumbing, so he'll supervise that part of the work. And Finney—"

"—gets to add fashioning end tables from crates to my list of art projects," Finney concluded.

Mari figured her eyebrows had by now hit her hairline. Did they always complete each other's sentences?

"And all of that will take most of the summer." Andy spooned another mouthful of stew.

"But since your sister volunteered your guesthouse," Finney said, "our problems are solved. The counselors rotate, so they'll bunk in Kirk's quarters when they're at camp."

"What about that other therapist—the recreation one?" Mari asked.

"Rita has an aunt with a trailer at Macks Creek; she said she'd be happy to settle in over there." But nobody looked happier than Finney. Pretty neat the way Rita had gotten shuffled off somewhere else.

Pop was listening with interest. "I thought you all had to be on the grounds all the time. At least that was the impression Lil gave me."

"The YCPs—youth care providers—do. And Kirk, of course. But not us." The way Finney said *us* set Mari's teeth on edge. "We're day help. And even if Kirk wanted us there 24/7, there wouldn't be the—"

"—funds. We know." Mari could complete sentences, too.

Zinnia frowned at the note in her voice. Finney seemed taken aback, and Andy glanced over, a question in his eyes.

"I'm sorry," Mari murmured. "It's been a long day, and I'm not feeling very good."

She pushed back from the table. She should mention she might have seen the vandal, but decided it could wait. She didn't have much to offer beyond *orange shirt* and *dark hair*, anyway. And that covered more than half the boys who had arrived at camp from Vreeley Home. Right now she wanted nothing more than solitude. It *had* been a long day. And her stomach *was* upset. Whether it was from the *chimi del mar*, the margarita, or the mix of emotions roiling around in her innards, was a toss-up.

She looked at her mother. "Do you need help getting ready for bed?" She tried to sound pleasant and patient and all the things she wasn't feeling right now, but her tone implied *still*.

Andy frowned.

"Why, no, honeybunch. Pop can help with whatever I need if you're tired, but—" Zinnia's hands fluttered to encompass the mess on the table.

"We'll handle k.p." Andy stood up and nudged Finney. "Won't we?"

"And I'll help." Pop rose, too. Concern deepened the creases around his mouth. "You just get some good shut-eye, pumpkin."

Pop's sympathy in the face of her, well, *boorish* behavior made her feel worse. And watching Andy and Finney jostle each other and laugh while they cleared the table didn't make her feel any better.

She walked to the cellar door and paused. "Well, um, thanks, everyone."

With all the bustle—even Zinnia was reaching across the table to hand off plates—her words went unacknowledged. Shoulders drooping, she opened the door, then glanced back at Andy standing elbow-to-elbow at the sink next to Finney. She had a sudden urge to hurl herself between them.

Andy looked over his shoulder and their eyes met. That inscrutable light was back in his. "G'night, Mar."

His voice was soft, and she felt a pinprick of tears.

Ducking her head, wondering why she was PMS-ing when she was only mid-cycle, she pulled the door shut behind her. Downstairs, a sullen light clouded the sleeping porch, and the wind whisked through the screens. But she didn't bother to lower the shades. Instead, she fell on her bed fully dressed and indulged in a silent fit of tears.

Chapter 10

A few days later, on Sunday, the storms were long gone, leaving behind a big bowl of blue sky and a cove shimmering with reflected color. For once, the humidity was low.

On the swimming dock, clothed in an old one-piece navy swimsuit she'd dug out of a trunk in the attic (in Kansas City, she hadn't needed swimwear), Mari resolutely snapped her easel into place in the shade of the boat dock's overhang.

As Mother Nature had eased up a little, so had her emotions. Even though she wasn't any further along to making a decision. And even though she refused to look closely at the feelings that rose when she watched Andy and Finney across the supper table— as she had for the last three nights. She couldn't quite get a handle on what the relationship was between them. While she'd caught Finney casting what could only be called adoring (and cute and sweet and everything Mari was not) looks at Andy, Andy seemed oblivious to Finney's obvious interest.

She pushed thoughts of the duo aside and squinted upward. The sky would be easy to duplicate—heavy on the ultramarine—although midday didn't provide a very exciting light, not like twilight or dawn. Almost from this very same spot, she'd captured daybreak for the painting that now hung in her mother's kitchen.

It might be interesting to do a similar view, only at twilight. But not yet. She needed to exercise her artist's eye again before she took on *interesting*. It had been a long time since she'd seen her acrylics. Actually, it had been a long time since she'd seen a swath of sky like this, uninterrupted by rooftops. The sight caused an itch in her fingers—and also stirred something deeper inside.

Behind her, on a canvas-back chair on a corner of the boat dock, her feet up on a plastic crate topped with a flotation cushion, Zinnia gave a satisfied sigh, expressing Mari's feelings exactly. "Now, you just never mind me, honeybunch. I'm just pleased as punch to be down here enjoying the sunshine." She opened a book in her lap.

Mari flashed her mother a smile, pleased *beyond* punch. This was the first time Zinnia had felt she could negotiate the climb back up the hill to the cabin. She was making progress. Maybe the nurse had been right: All her mother needed was time. And maybe that was all *she* needed, too. Well, God knew, she had plenty of it.

Mari hunkered down and rummaged in her trunk of materials, piling a palette knife, brushes, and a jar of water onto a rusting TV tray set up near the easel. She'd carted a radio down, too, but opted to leave it off, preferring the faint slap of the water against the dock and the tune of the swallows that nested under its eaves. Even though she was pretty certain she'd botch her first efforts at painting in nearly a decade, at least this was a break in the routine. Which had seemed even more unbearably dull in contrast to the Camp Sycamore stories she was hearing around the supper table. Andy and Finney were so *involved* with their lives, while she felt as stagnant as the rainwater that had collected in Pop's watering barrel.

Straightening, she arranged her paint tubes in some semblance of color progression. She *had* set up her Mac—a step in the right direction, not that it had done her much good. With Andy and Finney's voices echoing in her ears, she'd spent two nights combing the Internet for jobs, finding nothing of interest in Kansas City and even less in New York. New York . . . Unless something popped onto the screen in the next couple months, if she wanted to go there, it would be under Sean's wing. As his *assistant*. She wrinkled her nose. She wanted to fly on her own; it was wiser to fly on her own, but . . .

Argh, if only there was some way to be *sure*.

Pushing worries aside—plenty of time left in the summer to figure everything out—she squeezed out blobs of paint. The sharp scent of the resin set her nose quivering. Like the fragrance of new school supplies or the first whiffs of spring, paint held for her the smell of limitless possibility. Picking up a soft-bristled brush, she studied the scene before her. It was about as far away from Manhattan as you could get. Instead of jagged strips of blue between gray buildings, the sky filled a world framed by green hills. Instead of skyscrapers shooting up from the sidewalks, limestone cliffs far out on the main channel rose from deep water. It was a mosaic of blues and greens.

She dabbed at the ultramarine, then, taking a deep breath of clear Ozark air, washed a blue base across her canvas. She'd love a broader spectrum, except . . .

She thought again about the painting hanging in her mother's kitchen, created almost entirely of various intensities and values of one hue. It was the best thing she'd ever turned out. Maybe because narrowing the color range forced her eye to see things she might otherwise have missed.

As they said, sometimes less was more.

An hour later, Zinnia had dozed off, looking (deceivingly) cherubic with her chin resting on her ample breast, her book facedown in her lap. Mari was still at it, applying a darker wash for shadows, when a creak sounded behind her. She glanced over her shoulder. Finney had stepped onto the dock. She was dressed in a red bikini, revealing everything her orange T-shirt usually hid. She had a towel in her hand, a carryall over her shoulder.

"May I?" Finney motioned toward the easel.

Thinking there was nothing dowdier on the planet than an old navy swimsuit, Mari put a finger to her lips, indicated her mother, and stepped back. "Not much to see yet," she whispered. "Plus, I haven't done this in quite a long time."

Finney stopped in front of the canvas and studied it with a critical eye. "Maybe not, but you've got a sure hand." She kept her voice low. "Will you do the whole canvas in blue? Nice way to add interest."

Mari felt a smidgeon of pride and thought, despite the red bikini, maybe she liked Finney after all. "I need to let this dry before I go on." She motioned toward the end of the dock. "Let's move over there so we don't wake Mom."

After spreading their towels on either side of the swimming ladder, they sat and dipped their feet in the water. Mari leaned back on her hands, tilted her face to the sun, and closed her eyes, listening to Finney rummaging in her bag. She felt more peaceful than she'd felt in . . . well, forever.

"Want some?"

She opened her eyes. Finney held out a container of suntan lotion.

"I suppose I should. I don't tan, I crisp." She eyed Finney's golden arms. "Bet you don't, though."

"No, lucky me."

While Mari slathered on lotion, Finney rummaged again, emerging with a couple of sodas. She handed one off to Mari, who popped the tab and took a swig. "Thanks."

"Andy told me you owned your own design company."

"Yes, I—" About to launch in on the rendition that painted the whole endeavor in a rosy glow, Mari stopped. If Andy had told Finney that much, he'd undoubtedly also mentioned that her business had tanked. "But I had to close up shop last month when I lost my biggest account."

Finney nodded sympathetically. "I tried to start my own business when I first got out of college. It's tough. But we can pat ourselves on the backs—it takes courage to try."

Case closed. She did like Finney. "So how did you get involved with art therapy?"

"Process of elimination, I guess." Finney laughed. "I couldn't make enough to feed a sparrow on freelance work. I wasn't interested in big firms, and I was too snobby to lower myself to doing ads or the like. Teaching sounded like it could be fun, but who wants to deal with a school administration? So I hit on this."

"Do you like it?"

"I do. I like working with people, and I have a lot of autonomy. And I like the idea I might be doing some good." Finney set her can down and leaned back on her elbows. "But, oh man, the work is intense. And I wouldn't mind earning more money. Art therapy requires a master's, so I went back to school. Now I have the piper to pay."

"Where did you go?"

"Emporia State University."

"Why there?" About a hundred miles from Kansas City, Emporia sat on the edge of the Kansas Flint Hills. She'd driven through them once on a college road trip to Texas. Interstate 35 was a long white ribbon unwinding between pillows of pastureland that stretched from horizon to horizon—an undulating blanket of green as far as the eye could see.

"There aren't many programs available. It was there

or Chicago in this region. Emporia was cheaper. And I love the Flint Hills."

They *were* lovely—but to truly appreciate them, you needed an affinity for cattle. "So you think you'll change jobs soon?"

"If something came along that wasn't supported by donations and state funding, it'd be great—maybe working at a senior residence or something where my job isn't so dependent on some government lobby and the success of the last charity ball. Don't get me wrong. I adore the boys, but I'm not married to them. Not like Andy. This is a calling for him."

Mari wiggled her feet and watched the water eddy. "You know Andy well, don't you?"

"Probably not as well as you."

Mari wished. Then wondered why she wished.

"I wish he—" Finney broke off, and Mari glanced over her shoulder. Finney's pretty face had gone rosy. "I mean, I wish *I* knew him better. But he's . . . busy. Like today—he went to Cordelia this morning to pick up supplies he ordered from Beadler's, and then planned to go to an A.A. meeting."

There was sure a lot of wishing happening here. "Well, yeah, he works and all, but so do you."

"Except, you know, he's also writing those articles."

"Oh, that." *What* articles? "Um, how are those going? We haven't had much chance to catch up." Much chance? *Any* chance. As soon as they finished supper each night, Andy disappeared. Maybe the articles, whatever they were, explained the vanishing act.

"He just submitted to *Child & Family Behavior,* but I'm sure he told you that. And now he's started one he'd love to see in *Psychology Today,* but he said he needs more credentials before he gets published there. Well, those will come after he's back in school." Finney pushed herself up. "I'm hot. Do you want to get in?"

"No, but you go ahead." School? Was that among the *few ideas* he'd mentioned back at Camp Sycamore? "With work, it will probably take him a long time to get his"—she stabbed in the dark—"master's."

"Master's?" Poised to jump off the edge of the dock, Finney stopped and gave her a puzzled look. "He's going for his doctoral degree in clinical child psych." She winked. "And knowing Andy's drive, it probably won't take him long at all."

Finney leaped, the water splashed, and Mari blinked. Andy's *drive*? Still blinking, she watched Finney splash around, wondering how else he'd changed.

The boards beneath her jounced, and she glanced back. Speak of the devil. Andy had stepped onto the dock. He paused to study her canvas, then flashed her a smile that about blew her into the water. A pair of khaki swim trunks rode below his waist, and a short-sleeved cotton shirt hung from his square shoulders, unbuttoned to reveal a tanned chest. A nicely muscled tanned chest. And an equally impressive set of abs. Throwing around bags of potting soil had its payoff. Realizing she was staring, Mari averted her eyes and looked at her mother. Zinnia slept on, her lips puffing in and out with each breath.

Andy moved to the edge of the dock and waved Finney over. An expectant glow lit up her features. Mari grimaced. Liking Finney or not, she was growing tired of this glow thing.

"Kirk just phoned. He wants you to call him back about a scheduling problem."

Finney's expression dimmed a few watts at the prosaic message. What had she expected? A declaration of love?

"Thanks. I'll go do it now." Finney clambered up the ladder and grabbed her towel.

In Mari's jaundiced view, the pose Finney struck while she toweled off was worthy of *Sports Illustrated*'s swimsuit issue. Taking a gander at Andy's expression, it looked like he thought so, too. Her lip curled.

When Finney had gone, Andy ignored the towel Finney had left spread out on the dock and settled himself on the edge of Mari's, much to her glee. Then she blushed at the childishness of her mental reaction, which had been something along the lines of sticking out her tongue at Finney and singing "nyah-na-na-na-boo-boo."

He leaned back on his elbows, closing one eye against the sun and squinting at her with the other. "It's good to see you painting. That piece hanging in your parents' kitchen is great, not that I'm any critic."

She shrugged and picked up her soda. "Just something to do while you and Finney are off saving the world."

His brows dipped. "What's up with you?"

"Nothing at all." She swigged from the can, then scowled. The soda had grown warm. "But the real question is, what's up with you, *Dr.* Eppelwaite?"

"Doctor . . . ? Oh, I guess Finney mentioned the doctoral thing."

"She did. Which begs the question, why didn't you?" She set the can down with a snap.

"Because nothing's firm yet. I haven't completed the application process—I'm still building up some credentials."

"Even if you start in the fall—"

"Won't be this year. The process takes time. If I get in, I'll start next fall."

"Then won't it take you another four years to get that degree, even if you go full-time?"

"I'd *have* to go full-time; it's required. And it would take me five. What of it?"

"If you start a year from now, you'll be thirty-six when you finish."

"Wow, you can add." He sat up. "What is it with

you? You're overwhelming me with all this encouragement."

"Well, it just seems a little late to start blooming."

"Maybe you're right." His brow knit. "Hmm. Let's see. If I go back to school, then in another six years, I'll"—he slapped his forehead—". . . well, whaddaya know! I'll be six years older. Same as I'll be if I *don't* go back to school. And still not doing what I want with my life."

Mari chucked his shoulder. "I get your point."

"But I don't get yours. You don't think it's a good idea?"

"It's not that, it's . . ." She blew out a breath. Confession time. "It's just, I think I know you, and then I keep finding out I don't really know much about you at all." Tit for tat, she supposed, since he didn't know everything about her, either.

He stilled. Then he shifted, moving closer until their thighs brushed. His was cool against the beginnings of what she knew would be a sunburn despite the loan of Finney's lotion. Ripe, red, and nothing like the other woman's golden *glow*.

Andy dipped his head to study her face. "And that's important to you?" he asked softly. "That you know me?"

Under the steadiness of his deep blue gaze, thoughts of Finney faded away. Mari swallowed a sudden lump, not knowing if it had jumped into her throat because of fear or anticipation. But she knew she'd just reached a crossroads. And that her answer could fling her in a direction she hadn't expected. And maybe didn't even want. She didn't reply right away, but when she finally did, she told the truth.

"Yes," she said, equally softly. "It *is* important."

Deftly, he brought his head up and caught her lips with his. The kiss took her by surprise, even though she'd done no less than invite it. It was gentle, not too long, the kind of kiss you might give a friend.

Except that it wasn't. She knew it from the way her toes curled under the water. Knew it, as well, from the way Andy suddenly squirmed. His reaction thrilled her no end.

And also set off alarm bells. This was not the way to get her head straight about Sean. Or about New York. She was muddying the waters, further muddling her mind.

And on that thought, she kissed him back. His lips were soft; they tasted sweet. They made her *feel* sweet, and she hadn't felt that way in such a long time. Oh, what the hell—she'd un-muddle later. She twisted to loop her arms around his neck, and Zinnia made a noise.

They broke apart and glanced back. Mari could swear she saw her mother's eyes snap shut, and when she looked up at Andy for confirmation, he grinned. But except for a tug at the corner of Zinnia's mouth—which could have been gas—she appeared to sleep on.

Mari didn't want to tempt fate in the form of her mother. Instead of turning back to Andy, she once again faced the cove, staring out across its mirrored finish, gently stirring her feet in its waters. Andy held her hand loosely entwined with his. His grasp was warmer than the sun on her shoulders. She didn't know exactly what she'd set in motion, but she didn't feel prone to stop it. Nor did she plan to think about it. Before they could start grinding away again, Mari switched off the gears in her head.

It was summer. She'd give it the summer. She'd give *everything* the summer. By fall, surely her way would seem clear.

Andy spoke up. "I have an idea."

"But this isn't what I'd planned," Zinnia complained. No, Zinnia *whined*.

The next morning, in the sunlight that winged through the trees and between the simple blue curtains at the kitchen windows before landing with a splash on the floor, Mari folded laundry at the table while her mother sat across from her and indulged in a fit of hand-wringing. Pop had escaped to the peaceful task of watering his flowerpots.

"Mom, I'm taking Andy up on his idea, and there's no good reason why I shouldn't. And a lot of reasons why I should—he said the camp *needs* volunteers. I've *said* I'll stay here until the end of summer, and I will. But you've been out of the hospital now for over three weeks, and it's five since your surgery. By next week, you'll be able to drive, the nurse won't need to come anymore, and you can give up that damn stupid shower chair."

"But I need that chair!"

"No, you don't."

Zinnia folded her arms across her chest.

"And I'll still be here full-time for another week. Maybe longer. They have to do a background check before I can work with the boys."

Andy had suggested Mari volunteer at Camp Sycamore for the rest of the summer, assisting Finney. When Finney had returned to the dock yesterday, she'd looked appalled by his idea. And even less thrilled at the sight of Mari's hand in his. But she'd agreed. Of course it would be hard for her to object, since she'd apparently told Andy she could use some help. And Mari was determined to give it. It would get her out from under her mother's thumb, maybe help Michael feel more secure. And she'd be closer to Andy. She didn't know which she wanted more, because she hadn't paused to inspect her reasons. Impulsiveness had always been her strength, if you ignored the fact that it was also her downfall.

"You've gotten much better. You don't need me like you did at first, and I—"

"That's not what I'm fretting about. Or at least not *all* that I'm fretting about!"

"Then what *are* you worrying for?"

"It's just—just *everything.*" Behind her glasses, Zinnia's eyes were wet. "My oldest daughter has a husband who cavorts all over the place—"

Mari wanted to laugh but didn't because Zinnia looked so serious. "Dak doesn't *cavort*; he's a writer. And since he writes travelogue-type books, it'd be pretty damn—I mean, danged—weird if he *didn't* travel."

"But Alcea says sometimes Dak goes off just because he wants to be alone. I don't understand their marriage at all."

Mari's eyes rolled. "Yes, you do. You know Alcea and Dak love each other very much. More to the point, they understand each other. He needs some solitude every once in a while, and she gives it to him, so I don't see any reason to call in—what's the name of that guy you watch on *Oprah?*"

"Dr. Phil," Zinnia supplied grudgingly.

"Yeah, him." Mari had always envied Alcea her marriage the most, even though Mari had once had kind of a *thing* for Jon (just like a million other country music groupies). "I think it's great that they're able to give each other the space they each need without getting all bent out of shape over it."

Zinnia abandoned Alcea and Dak. It must have been because Mari had evoked the name of Dr. Phil. "And Lil . . . I always thought that of you all, Lil would be fine, but she and Jon are arguing all the time because of Michael, and—"

"They're just going through a rough patch, Mom. Marriage does have some." At least, that's what she'd heard. "And you *know* they adore each other. They even held hands all the way home from Camp Sycamore. Things will be fine soon—Lil has always made sure of that."

"And then there's you—" Zinnia cast wild eyes at Mari's head.

"Chri—criminy, *not* the hair again." Mari ran a hand through her hair. Actually it didn't look too bad now. She'd grown an apricot nimbus around her head—or maybe it looked more like long peach fuzz. Whatever. She was much less Howdy-Doody than she had been. "The only thing wrong with me is that I'm going frigging stir-crazy here. You are getting—*have gotten*—better. And the more you are able to do, the less I need to. I won't be spending full days at the camp, just part-time hours. I'll still be around to do whatever you and Pop can't."

Zinnia folded her lips in a tight line.

And Mari folded the last of Pop's bright-colored shirts, put it on the top of the laundry basket, and pulled up a chair next to her mother. "I don't think this uproar is about any of us. I think it's about you."

"No, it's not."

"C'mon," Mari coaxed. "Tell me what's really wrong."

"You made a danged mess of that shirt. You need to fold it again."

"Forget the shirt." She put her hand on her mother's.

Zinnia looked at their hands, and the tightness left her mouth. She drew in a long breath. "I wish I knew. Sometimes I think I'm going plumb crazy, I've got so many mixed-up thoughts in my head."

"You and me both," Mari said, then bit her tongue. Her mother would pounce on that remark like a cat on cream.

But it hadn't seemed to register. "It's just—this whole thing wasn't on my schedule, you see."

"I doubt a heart attack is on anyone's schedule."

"But I always thought I'd be fit as a fiddle up till the day I died. Now Pop . . . With that smoking he used to do, I figured I might end up taking care of him, but never in my wildest dreams did I ever think

I'd be the one needing tending. And it doesn't feel right."

"No, it doesn't." Mari gave Zinnia's hand a squeeze. "You weren't the only one thinking you were immortal. We all did. What you've gone through . . . It's been scary."

Zinnia looked indignant. "I didn't think I was *immortal*. I—" She broke off and looked at Mari, who had raised her brows. Zinnia's smile flickered. "Why, Lord love a duck, I think I *did* believe I'd never pass on. Leastways not before I saw Pop into his grave at some late date down the road, and then made sure each of you was settled. And that each of my grandchildren was taken care of. I just never felt old." Her smile faltered. "But I do now. And it *is* scary."

"But you've come out okay. And you're *not* old."

Zinnia stared out the window. "I was always a glass-half-full kind of person, but lately I've been letting the doldrums take me over. Maybe if I didn't have so much time on my hands . . ." She puffed out a laugh. "You know, I never did cotton much to daytime television—soap operas and *Oprah* and Court TV. Pish. No wonder I'm feeling blue." She looked at Mari again. "When did that pamphlet stuff from the hospital say I'd be able to use a shovel again? I think it's time to plant me a new garden. Kind of late in the season, but if Andy'll pick me up some plants next time he's at Beadler's, I'll keep 'em watered and see what happens."

Mari felt immeasurable relief. Some of the old Zinnia was surfacing. "No shovel for a while yet, but all of us can help do whatever you need. Pretty soon you'll be back to doing all your own gardening again, and taking care of us in the bargain." *God help us all.*

"You're right. I do believe you're right." Zinnia gave an emphatic nod. "And none too soon, because I think you *need* taking care of."

Mari pulled her hand back and eyed her mother warily. "What do you mean by that?"

"You know how much I like Andy Eppelwaite. Apparently from what I saw down on the dock yesterday, so do you."

"So you *were* awake."

" 'Course I was." Zinnia looked smug. "I just didn't want to embarrass you any."

That was a first.

"So," Zinnia continued, "when are you going to tell him you've got another young man calling you up on the phone? And is that why *your* thoughts are all mixed up?"

Mari sighed. Her mother was back. "Sean won't be calling me—"

"Sean? That's his name?"

She sighed again. "Yes."

"But you've broken up with him."

"Kind of."

"*Kind of?* Marigold McKenzie O'Malley, don't you go waltzing that nice Eppelwaite boy down the wrong path. You own up to him, you hear?"

Guilt, that familiar companion, gnawed at her, but she leaned in toward her mother. "Mother, I am thirty years old. I don't need your help to figure out my life. What I decide to do about Sean—and Andy—is up to me. And—"

"Well, I'm just saying—"

"*And,*" Mari butted in, knowing she was risking her life, "if you breathe one word of any of this to anyone else, I-I'll *leave*. Discussion over and out." She rose from the table, grabbed the laundry basket, and headed for her parents' room to unload the clothes.

"Hmph," Zinnia retorted at her retreating back. "When you find yourself swimming in hot water, don't you come crying to me."

Ha. She was *already* lost at sea. And since her feelings were buffeting her in conflicting directions, she'd decided for now that she'd make no decisions, make no commitments.

Until the end of summer, she'd just. . . . float.

Chapter 11

It wasn't until Saturday evening, almost a full week after that kiss he'd snatched the previous Sunday, that Andy managed to snag some real time alone with Mari again. Days were sapped by his work at camp; nights by the article he was trying to complete—more to help his chances for admission into the child psych doctoral program than anything else. Competition for the available slots was stiff. Still, he might have played hooky some evenings if he'd thought he could grab more than some chitchat from Mari over the supper table, but the O'Malley homestead didn't provide much privacy. The two of them always seemed within arm's reach of Finney—she'd developed a nasty habit of popping up when he didn't want her—or within call of Zinnia's voice. And Mari's mother had a very loud voice.

But tonight he'd foiled them. He'd picked up tickets for the drive-in movie theater that was tucked into a valley not too many miles from the cabin. Over the supper table, he'd handed them off.

Mari had stared at the ticket in her hand. "You thought I'd like a Screech Theater Extravaganza?"

"You used to like horror movies." They'd sat through quite a few together, and she'd crawled into his lap every time. Which was the point.

"Let me see." Finney took the ticket from Mari.

"Teen Rebel Rampage, Midnight Massacre on Locust Street . . ." Finney giggled. "These are *classics*. If she doesn't want to go, I will."

"Let's live a little." Addressing Mari, Andy ignored Finney's comment and also the flicker of hurt he saw cross her face. Her interest was flattering, but he liked her only as a friend. Nothing more.

Mari took the ticket back from Finney, and he could almost see her mind wheeling to find a reason to turn him down. What was with her? Three back-to-back movies beginning at nine. They'd have hours alone, and it wasn't like they had to *watch* the damn things.

"But I'd planned to work on my painting."

"In the dark?"

"Well, up until then, yes." Mari was still working on the twilight twin to the morning landscape hanging in her mother's kitchen.

"We could still—"

"I didn't even know that old drive-in was still up and running," Zinnia interrupted, casting a look of concern at him that turned to disapproval when her gaze moved to her daughter. He'd seen that look frequently this week, and it left him puzzled. "Remember how we loaded everyone in the car on Saturday nights when you were little, Mari? It'll be a trip back in time. I think you should go."

"But—"

"Pop and I can take care of the dishes. You can work on your painting any ol' time." Zinnia had said, with a note of finality in her voice. "Now, you just have your evening out."

Mari had looked around the table and finally at him. He'd tried to keep his face blank, but she must have sensed his confusion, because she'd ceased her objections. "Then Screech Theater Extravaganza it is."

And now they were rolling over the lake roads in his pickup, stars pricking through a blanket of violet overhead, windows open to the caress of the wind and the scent of lingering honeysuckle. He inhaled in appreciation, then glanced at Mari. If she squeezed any closer to the passenger door, she'd fall out.

"Careful, that door latch isn't too reliable. What is *with* you?"

"Huh?"

She eased a few inches away from the door, tugging to adjust her turquoise terry cloth shorts and top. They weren't new; in fact, he thought he'd once seen them on Lil. But Mari looked nice—very Mari-like. The clothes were more like what she'd once worn—and suited her far more than that hoity stuff she'd adopted after college.

"Don't give me *huh*." He knew she'd heard him. "And what is with your mother and all those weird looks she's throwing my direction?"

"Who knows what Mom ever thinks?" She toyed with one of her earrings, a bead concoction with turquoise feathers that emphasized her eyes. "Not me, that's for sure."

But he thought she did know. "Forget your mother, then. What are *you* thinking? Why didn't you want to go out tonight?"

He slowed to take the turn into the drive-in. The yellow light at the ticket booth glowed up ahead.

The truck rocked over the potholed lane, and Mari grabbed hold of the door frame. "You'd think they could level this off."

He made an exasperated sound and decided not to force the issue until they'd parked. Woods surrounded the drive-in. There was no place for her to run.

He handed off their tickets, wound around to the rear, and pulled into the last row next to one of the old speaker posts that stuck up at haphazard angles throughout the lot. Only about two dozen cars and trucks populated the spaces, leaving plenty of room between them all. Their windshields flickered with reflected light from the screen. The trailers had started.

A concession stand—a pale white shack—crouched in the middle of the clearing.

He threw the truck into park, turned off the engine, and twisted to look at her. "Mar—"

"I want some popcorn."

"Oh, for God's sake—" He yanked open his door, got out, and slammed it harder than necessary.

She leaned toward the window. "Andy, I—"

About to stalk off, he paused. "What?"

"Could you get me a Coke, too?" Her voice was small.

He didn't bother to reply, just turned on his heel.

When he returned, juggling two large drinks and a vat of popcorn, she leaned over to open the door. In the glow from the overhead light, her face looked contrite. "I'm sorry."

He waited to reply until he'd handed off her drink, put his own in a cup holder, and settled the popcorn between them. Reaching out the window, he turned down the volume on the static from the speaker, then twisted so he could see her profile, flashing blue and white in the light from the screen. "Tell me what's going on. I was under the impression—and maybe I was just whistling Dixie—that what happened on the dock last Sunday meant something."

"It did. It does. But maybe I shouldn't have kissed you before you knew"—she looked down at her hands, then sucked in a breath—"there's somebody else."

He thunked back against his seat. "Great."

Hitching up her knee, she turned to face him. "He's a guy I went out with in Kansas City. We were serious, but we broke up almost four years ago because, well, because he thought, um—because he thought he might love someone else." Her words tumbled over one another, like she couldn't get the weight off her chest fast enough. "I haven't even seen him at all for the last two years, but then he showed up right before I

came here. And then I saw him not too long ago—
that day when I was in Sedalia—and when I did, he
told me he had a new job. In New York." She swallowed hard. "And he wants me to go with him."

His stomach sank. "And you said yes."

"No!"

He looked at her. "You said no?"

She looked away. "Not exactly. I said I'd think
about it. We agreed to give it the summer, and then
I'll give him an answer. We won't even have any contact until then." Her voice turned wistful. "I've always
wanted to live in New York, but I'm not sure I want
to go with him. And then when you kissed me—" She
met his gaze again. Her face was wreathed in misery.
"I don't *know* what I want." It was practically a wail.

He drummed the steering wheel with his fingers,
then turned to her, stretching his arm along the back
of the seat. They'd played enough games. It was time
for straight talk. "When we were growing up together,
you had your big family, but I just had Gran, occasionally Anna—and you. When you decided not to have
anything more to do with me after *that*"—he jerked a
thumb at the pickup bed—"it left a big fat hole in my
life. Until I saw you again, I didn't realize just how
big. And I realized I'd . . . missed . . . you for a
long time."

"I never meant to hurt you back then, Andy. I
really didn't. That whole first time was confusing, even
though I tried to pretend it was just one more prank
we'd shared. But it wasn't. It was a Big Deal, even if
we didn't love each other that way."

She could speak for herself.

"And I—*we* were young—and I didn't know how
to tell you how I felt."

"How *did* you feel?" he asked.

She scrunched her nose in thought. "I was glad my
first time was with you because it made it, oh, I dunno,
more comfortable I guess."

Comfortable. What every man ached to hear.

"But afterward, everything felt awkward between us, and I didn't know how I was supposed to act around you. And that made me mad because I'd never had to act like *anything* around you. Then there were the things you'd started to do—the fighting and drinking and speeding and hill-hopping. It all scared me. They weren't just mischief. It wasn't fun anymore. But I really didn't mean to hurt you."

He touched her cheek. "I don't blame you. I was one messed-up kid—you grew up, but I didn't. Not for a long time." He paused. "But I'm grown-up now. And I'd like to see where things go, but I'm not going to tangle with some kind of love triangle." Anna flitted through his mind. "People get hurt. Nobody wins."

"I—I don't have a commitment. I haven't made any promises. We even decided we'd see other people if we wanted. I wanted you to know about him, but this—*us*—isn't a betrayal or anything."

He frowned. She sounded like she was trying to convince herself. He studied her familiar face in the half-light: the sprinkle of freckles, upturned nose, stubborn chin, and eminently kissable mouth. She was so . . . dear. He picked up the popcorn and wedged the bucket on his other side. "Come here."

She slid closer, until her head nestled under his chin.

He settled his arm around her shoulders. "It took me this long to find you again, this long to realize you've always been important to me. This long, even, for you to figure out I'm worth something to you." His pulled her closer. "I'm probably pushing too hard, but I pissed away a lot of years and want to make up for lost time. I just need to be sure of one thing."

"Which is?" she murmured.

"That you're telling the truth. That there's no commitment."

"There isn't." Her hand crept up his chest and settled there. "I promise, there isn't."

Relief swept him, turned his voice light. "So I just need to convince you that you prefer backwaters to city life, is that it? And me over him."

"I don't think you over him will be all that difficult." A smile in her eyes, she looked up at him. "But persuading me to stay in someplace like this? *That's* a pretty tall order." He dipped his head, but she put her fingers against his lips. "Actually, I'm not joking, Andy. When summer is over, I don't plan to stay. That's one thing I'm sure of."

"I can be pretty persuasive." With her breath soft on his face, his body was taking over whatever sanity was left in his mind. He pulled her hand from his mouth, ran his tongue briefly along her palm. "Let me show you."

No little kisses this time. Nothing she could remotely define as *comfortable.* Sliding one hand up into the warm hollow of her neck, the other wrapping itself in her hair, he took possession of her lips, deepening the kiss, pulling her tight against him until her breasts were crushed against his side. And her feathered earring was in his mouth. He spit it out.

She twisted, wiggling until she faced him, her back wedged against the steering wheel, her long legs stretching the length of the seat. When her thick-soled sandals clunked against the door, she kicked them off, then locked lips with him again. Her fingers curled through his hair, ran along his face, traced lines of fire along his neck. He groaned and angled for better position, sending the popcorn shooting from his side. Puffs of white showered around them.

Mouth still fastened on hers, he slid a hand under her top, his breath hitching when he found her braless. Cupping a breast, his finger and thumb found a hard nub to squeeze and worry. She gasped, her breath growing fast, her fingers fumbling wildly at his shirt. A thread snapped. Opening his eyes, he saw a button fly past.

Withdrawing his hand from under her blouse, he swept it down the length of her side, then slowly moved back up along the smoothness of her calf, around to the back of her knee, softly up the inside of her thigh. Her tongue ran over his chest, found his nipple, pinched it gently between her teeth. Trembling now, his fingers bumped up against the hem of her shorts, then worked their way further, creeping under the elastic of her panties. Writhing, groaning, she sought his mouth again, and he plundered hers. She broke off to pant against the side of his face, her body tensing, her breath a rasp. Bare feet pressing against the far door, she pushed against his hand.

Then came with a yelp louder than a coyote. Her legs jerked. The door flew open. The horn blared.

He laughed despite the pain in his ear—and the greater one in his groin. "You never do anything by half, do you? Let's get the hell out of here."

Three hours later, on top of a hillside at the end of a narrow back road that had petered out into barely enough room to turn the truck around, they lay on their backs on an air mattress. When they'd arrived, Andy had hardly set the brake before they'd flung open the doors and sought the bed of his pickup.

Mari had stopped dead when he'd lowered the tailgate, revealing the air mattress he'd strapped at the bottom. Her eyes narrowed. "You had this planned!"

"No, I'd hoped. There's a difference."

"Not much of one."

"And I remembered the last time. I was a youngster then. If I repeated that performance without that mattress, I wouldn't be able to walk in the morning. You should be thanking me for the consideration I'm showing your buns." The night air was balmy, but chill. "Hurry up, get in." If she didn't, he'd ravish her right there on the ground.

Tilting up her nose like a queen, she allowed herself

to be helped up. She nodded at him graciously. "My buns thank you."

He caressed said buns on their passage by, his pulse beating so hard he thought he'd choke. "And take this." He tugged a quilt out of a storage bin and tossed it at her, rummaged again and came up with some condoms.

She shook her head. "You must think I'm pretty easy."

"No, I think I'm pretty hard."

She grinned, then stuck out her tongue. He clambered up, had her clothes off in mere minutes, and was all over her.

Twice.

They hadn't needed the quilt. And Andy was pretty damn sure Mari wouldn't term his lovemaking *comfortable* ever again.

In a state of contented exhaustion, arms linked under their heads, they gazed at the sky. It was black crepe, dusted by a zillion stars. He felt like he'd zoomed straight into the heavens. Holding Mari, caressing Mari, *making love* to Mari hadn't been anything like that first time when they were inept adolescents, high on Boone's Farm and bravado. This was his fantasy come to life, the way he'd known it could be between them. He'd poured his need for her through his hands as he'd explored her flesh, his body as he'd covered hers, and in the words he'd murmured in her ear.

But he'd bitten back *I love you.* Even though he knew he did. And probably always had.

He glanced over. In the meager light from a crescent moon, her profile was only a pale shadow against the side of the pickup, her chin—that resolute chin—tilted up at the sky. He grinned to himself. Mari was a contrary cuss. Pressing her would send her running in the opposite direction. So he wouldn't push anymore. He'd woo. He'd rediscovered his best friend, and he didn't want to lose her. Unlike in the past, he wouldn't be careless.

He turned his gaze back to the sky and pointed. "Shooting star. You don't see that much in the city."

"No, you don't," she murmured. She swatted at her leg, showed him the mosquito she'd flattened. "Nor do you see as many of these." She sat up to grab the edge of the quilt.

"And the smells." He breathed in deep. "No traffic fumes. Just honeysuckle and fresh air."

She sniffed at the air. Then sneezed.

He ran a hand up her spine. "A score of two for each side," he murmured.

She tugged at the quilt, then settled back, propped up on an elbow, her cheek resting on her hand. "Will this be an ongoing competition between city and country all summer?"

"Only if you want it that way." He smiled at the moon. "Or you could just cave now and save me a passel of trouble."

"Be serious. This could become a big problem."

"Or not." Now wasn't the time to discuss potential problems. She would come up with so many objections that she'd talk herself right out of a relationship with him before it had barely taken off. "Let's just take things as they come."

"One day at a time, just like A.A."

"I don't think they had *this* in mind, but yeah." He turned his head to look at her. "Look, Mar, I don't mean I'm just messing around with you. If I only wanted a summer fling, I could have picked Finney. God knows, she would have been an easier choice."

"Are you saying I'm difficult?"

He tucked a curl behind her ear. "Are you trying to tell me you're not?"

"Nope. But I'm worth it." She grinned. "I'd wondered if you'd noticed Finney's interest."

"She's a nice gal and a good friend, but I've never

felt anything for her beyond that, so nothing was ever going to come of it, even if you hadn't come along when you did."

"Hmm. That's not the Andy I remember."

"That's because I'm not the same Andy I was, goofball. Since my conviction, I've hung up, uh, *flinging*. I had a relationship while I was at K-State, but that's about it. And it didn't go anywhere."

"Why not?"

He paused. *Probably because I had you stuck somewhere in my head and didn't even realize it.* "Because she had a wandering eye, to tell you the truth. She didn't have the guts to tell me her feelings had changed until I found out she'd done a little *flinging* herself. With a so-called friend of mine, no less." He'd never decided which one of them he blamed more, or how much his sister Anna's experience had figured into his feelings.

He rolled over and raised up on his elbow. In the dim light, Mari's eyes were wide, her jocularity gone. He didn't pause to puzzle it out; he needed to set something straight. "I know you need time, and I'm not going to push. But I'm in this for the long run."

"Andy, I—"

He placed a gentle hand on her mouth. "Let me finish. I'm okay with this guy that's waiting in the wings, because none of this would have happened if he had a snowball's chance in hell with you."

"You can't know that." Mari sat up, her movements agitated. "*I* don't even know that."

"No, you don't." He ran a hand down her back. "But I know you. You're honest and forthright. But sometimes it takes your head a lot longer to figure out what your heart has already told you."

"Andy, I'm afraid you'll be hurt. I'm not sure—"

Dammit. He'd just told himself not to push, and he'd given her a shove. "Let *me* worry about *me*, okay? I know what I'm doing. There's just one condition." With Mari, he didn't think he needed conditions, but he didn't intend to be careless with himself, either. That last time *had* hurt.

She looked over her shoulder. "What's that?" Her voice was wary.

He gathered his courage. She wouldn't like this. "I'm willing to give you time to make up your mind. But I'm not him, and I'm *not* okay with your seeing other people. Not even him. While we're together, we're *together*. If you decide to move on, I expect you to tell me. I won't like it, but I'll recover. No dishonesty. Okay?" He braced himself for her response.

But instead of attacking, she caught her lip between her teeth and studied him a moment. Then she breathed out a sigh. "Okay."

Just what he'd wanted to hear, but not what he'd expected. He frowned. It wasn't a big deal and he should be grateful, but her lack of reaction disturbed him. He'd thought she'd launch into a how-dare-you speech at his insinuation she'd ever be less than straightforward. Because the Mari he knew . . .

His thoughts stumbled. Out in her mother's garden, she'd told him some tall tales about her business before coming clean. Was Mari being upfront with him now? The young Mari always was, but . . .

But maybe he didn't know the older Mari as well as he thought.

Chapter 12

It was just past mid-June—twelve days after they'd kissed on the O'Malleys' dock, six days since they'd made love, and three since she'd joined him at Camp Sycamore. Kirk had rammed her background check through in record time.

As summer had advanced, the temperatures had, too. Afternoons now topped out around ninety; the humidity—while not as grasping as it would eventually get—had climbed. Although morning still granted some comfort in the shade, out here in the garden next to the greenhouse, under a searing Friday morning sun, it was already hotter than hell. Andy lifted his ball cap and gave his forehead a swipe. Mother Nature was a bitch—she no longer held anything back on summer.

And Andy was still trying to persuade himself that Mari hadn't held back on anything at all.

While he would have liked a repeat of last Saturday night, it was impossible to catch Mari alone for long at the cabin. Not that he hadn't tried. On Wednesday night he'd snuck inside the sleeping porch, lowered himself to Mari's bed while she slept, and murmured sweet nothings to rouse her. He'd roused her all right—into a kicking and yelling whirling dervish. And when her foot had connected with his chin, he'd added to the mayhem by yelping. Between the two of them, they'd made enough noise to wake the dead. Or at least Zinnia. Above their heads, the sliding door had banged open, Zinnia had assaulted the deck with her walking stick, and Pop had leaned so far out over the railing trying to see into the porch beneath it, he'd nearly toppled off. Mari had collapsed on her back, laughing like a hyena, while Andy had cowered against the stone wall away from the probe of Pop's flashlight. Grabbing a shoe, he'd lobbed it at her, and she'd recovered enough composure to finally get out a strangled, "Sorry, bad dream!" Reassured after some more fast talking on her part, her parents had toddled back off to bed. But the event had successfully cooled—if not slaked—his ardor. He'd tried, but Mari's renewed giggling hadn't offered much in the way of an aphrodisiac.

Then, as if a sore chin and bent pride weren't enough, he'd also gotten a dose of guilt. When he'd returned to the guesthouse, he'd found Finney poking around in the refrigerator. She'd said she couldn't sleep, but he'd known from the hurt in her eyes that she'd guessed where he'd been. Crawling between his own covers a few minutes later, he'd sighed, resigning himself to seeing Mari over innocent swims, long walks, and the supper table. While he didn't want to hide his relationship with Mari, he didn't need to rub Finney's nose in it, either. And he *really* didn't need to risk Zinnia's ire.

So they now spent most of their time talking. About his work. ("You really love it, don't you?" "Helluva a thing, isn't it? I do.") And about hers. ("I wish I could drum up more enthusiasm.") About his schooling. ("Why KU? What is it with you and *Kansas*?" "Easy answer. I've got residency established on that side of the state line. Plus, it's one of the best programs around.") About their childhoods. ("Do you

remember . . ." started most of their conversations.)
And the painting she still worked on at dusk. ("It's
driving me nuts! I can't get the light right.")

But Mari said nothing about her years in Kansas
City. Oh, trivia, like things she'd done and reasons
she'd liked it, nothing of any importance. She evaded
his questions—especially concerning the waiting-in-
the-wings guy—and changed the subject. He wanted
to believe she wouldn't discuss her banked old flame
because she thought it might hurt his feelings. But he
suspected there was more to it than that.

But he wouldn't find out anything this weekend.
Her whole family was hitting Kesibwi for some O'Malley birthday party that had been postponed in the
spring. The pickup truck would have to wait.

He gave a mournful sigh, knowing he sounded
childish, and glanced at the art cabin tucked under a
bower of hickory and mimosa trees on the other side
of the garden. Behind the screens that made up the
upper half of the art cabin's walls, shadows moved,
but he couldn't identify Mari's. Giving up, he switched
his attention back to the six boys toiling in the garden.

Squatting in the narrow shade next to the greenhouse, two boys were busting up small clay pots then
dumping the pieces into a half dozen bigger ones.
Once topped with soil, the shards would provide a
layer for drainage. That pair had seemed overcharged
when they'd arrived at the greenhouse after breakfast,
so he'd set them that particular task to let them work
off some steam. The other four, including Mari's
nephew and a beefy, carrot-topped boy named Malloy,
worked in easy silence, yanking weeds from between
the cannas and hollyhocks they'd set in place during
the first week of camp. Between pulls, they kneaded
fish emulsion into the soil. They'd need a swim or
showers before lunch—the stuff enriched the earth,
but it stank. Pleased at their progress, pleased by the
healthy new blossoms on the hollyhocks—the cannas

would bloom later—Andy folded his arms, soaking up sunlight, soaking up the feeling of well-being this job gave him. And forgetting for a moment how Mari could rattle that peace.

The screen door on the art cabin banged open. Finney trotted down the step and moved toward him, stopping for a moment to turn around and study the rectangles of foam core board she'd tacked in a row to the side of the cabin underneath the screens before the boys had arrived this morning. Dappled light reflected off her hair, but the shine was no match for the usual one in her dark eyes when she turned back to him. She was a looker, no doubt about it. But, for him, the chemistry just wasn't there. It sure would be easier on him if he could concoct some. His sense of well-being faded. Finney wasn't complicated . . . unlike another person he could name.

When she reached him, he nodded at the boards. "What's up with that?"

"There's more room out here to work on group murals. Mari's inside, gathering supplies and pairing up the boys. I just came out to make sure the boards hadn't fallen down." She studied them again. "What do you think?"

"Good idea."

While each of the boys attended individual counseling sessions as well as the usual once-a-week family ones—if he had a family—all these boys were at a level where they could learn the benefits of "playing well with others." Like Finney, Andy had designed most of the summer projects—like the garden—to teach lessons in unity, cooperation, and the pride of achievement in reaching a common goal. At the same time, the boys had individual projects too—important for self-expression and self-esteem.

"How's Mari working out?" He kept his voice casual and professional.

"Fine." Finney responded in kind. "The boys already like her. Sometimes she steps out of line, but I have to admit, I'm glad to have the extra pair of hands."

Mari would always step out of line. "Spouting off sometimes, is she?"

Finney nodded. "But so far she hasn't said anything that will set anyone's progress back more than, oh, a decade."

Andy couldn't help it; he unleashed a grin. "She never did have much mouth control."

This time Finney's nod was emphatic, but not unkind. "And Damon's already got her wrapped around his little finger." Damon was a handsome mocha-skinned boy with a stunning smile that they both knew from his years at Vreeley Home. "I don't think she's fully aware of what she's dealing with here." Finney paused. "Do you think Damon's our vandal?"

Mari had told them what she'd seen on the first day of camp, and they'd reported what little she knew to Kirk. But a rummage through the forsythia for the blue-taped crowbar hadn't unearthed anything, and *dark hair, orange shirt* wasn't much of a clue. Especially since Mari had stressed she wasn't even sure of anything anymore except the orange shirt.

"It could be anyone. Like Kirk said, the only way we're likely to find out is if the scoundrel brags and someone else decides to squeal." He shook his head. "No sense in speculating. It could be Damon—or anyone. Damon thinks he's got everyone snowed. What worries me is that, in the boys' cases, he's mostly right. They fear him, they admire him, they want his approval." He nodded toward Mari's nephew. He cared about all the kids, but he was trying for the O'Malleys' sake to keep a special eye on Michael—difficult, since he rarely saw him except when Michael worked in the greenhouse. "Take Michael for example."

Like the other boys working in the garden, Michael had shed his shirt. The muscles in his back bunched and relaxed, keeping time with his movements. As they watched, he said something to Malloy and the two exchanged a brief laugh. When he bent over again, his jeans slid below his boxers, revealing a couple of inches of yellow cotton and a few small scars along the waistband, white against his tan skin.

Andy called out, "Hey, Michael, pull up your britches."

Michael tossed him a grin and hitched up his pants.

"Michael is coming along pretty well, though," Finney said. "Rita says she got him to swim with the other boys yesterday. And he's lost some of that surly edge." They liked to see the boys reach a level of calm where they could deal with their deeper issues.

"But he'd do better if he stuck with kids like Malloy rather than buddying up to Damon. All the boys would."

"Granted," Finney said. "But since Michael and Damon are bunking in the same cabin, it's hard to keep them apart." Michael and Malloy moved to the side of the garden and each picked up one end of a bag of mulch. "And it seems there's a friendship blossoming between him and Malloy, so that's good. Plus, Michael and Damon chose different programs this summer."

After the first week of camp, each boy had picked a program—horticulture, art, or recreation—as an area of concentration. Finney's group numbered eight to Andy's six. As usual, the rest had chosen Rita's more popular recreation program. All the kids took part in afternoon recreation with the recreation therapist and Kirk, but mornings were devoted to their preferences. They also alternated in helping with repairs on the vandalized cabins.

Finney continued. "Besides, like Kirk says, sometimes the boys learn more from their bad choices than they do from their good ones. Steve says he's keeping a close eye on Damon."

"Not close enough. Do you see those scratches on Michael's legs? Looks like he was out in the woods last evening—maybe during quiet time. They weren't there yesterday afternoon."

Finney frowned. "So you think Damon has him running to the Pit Stop for cigarettes?"

The Pit Stop was an open-all-night convenience store not a half mile down the lake road. Cigarettes were, of course, forbidden, which made them all the more attractive to kids who wanted to show their disdain for The Man—and for Vreeley Home and Camp Sycamore's rules in particular. And despite the bright smile and his continuous show of courtesy, Damon harbored a lot of disdain. With good reason, considering his history. But compassion for his past didn't mean the staff wasn't mindful of his present problems, or the ones he could pose for the others. A natural leader, Damon was both feared and respected. And one way the boys proved themselves to him was to be his runner.

"I wouldn't doubt it. Just like he used Malloy back at Vreeley, until Malloy got caught."

Malloy had never said who had sent him on cigarette runs at Vreeley. But Damon ruled Vreeley, sitting at the pinnacle of the boys' pecking order. When Malloy had shown up black-and-blue two days after Steve had nailed him sneaking back into the dorm with a couple of packs of cigarettes, the staff figured Damon and a couple of his sidekicks were the culprits, punishing Malloy because he'd gotten caught and was now refusing to do Damon's bidding. But they couldn't prove it, especially since Malloy had insisted that his bruises were the result of a tumble down the steps and that he'd swiped the cigarettes for himself. While every effort was made to keep the boys supervised and safe—both from one another and from themselves—the residents figured out ways around their watchdogs.

Andy had never known a teen who couldn't. "And you know that every dollar counts in this neck of the woods; nobody at the Pit Stop would card him."

"Maybe Kirk can talk to the store manager. And I'll mention it to Steve. Poor Steve. He'll have to sleep with one eye open."

Mari waved from the stoop of the art cabin. The boys in Finney's group were crowded around her. "We're ready!"

As usual, his chest hitched at the sight of her.

Glancing at Andy's expression, Finney sighed. "Well, I'll see you later. The garden's looking good, by the way." Walking off, she tossed the remark behind her.

Embarrassed that Finney had caught him mooning over Mari, he tore his thoughts away from her to look at the garden. It *was* thriving. Which was good. The kids could see what a little nurturing would do. They'd fight battles later on—against aphids and mites, fungus and rust—also good, since it taught them something about frustration.

Maybe he could use the lesson, too.

He watched as Mari and Finney herded the boys toward the mounted boards. They positioned four boys on stools with markers in hand. Another four stood behind them. The boys would take turns, one of each pair drawing, the other directing. As with all Finney's projects, she'd guide a discussion of their work when they were done. The conversation would center on autonomy and dependence issues, albeit cloaked by their activity.

Mari knelt near Damon, getting his attention with a tug on the long-sleeved shirt he always kept on, wearing it under his orange T-shirt, wearing it even when swimming. Andy shook his head. He knew from Damon's counselor that the shirt hid the boy's disfigured arms. Understandable that Damon would be self-conscious, but if he didn't get beyond his embarrassment, he'd roast this summer. Gesturing at the board, Mari spoke rapidly. Even from this distance, Andy could tell by Damon's smiling nod that he was pouring on the charm. Smiling back, Mari kept yakking. Until Finney drew her away. Out of earshot of the boys, the two women exchanged words, Mari looking belligerent, Finney resolved. Ending the talk with a sharp shake of her head, Finney moved back to the kids, missing the disgruntled look Mari sent heavenward.

Andy grinned. Mari was always so sure of herself. Her cocky streak could be exasperating, but he admired it. Except that lately . . . The grin faded. Lately, she hadn't seemed sure of much of anything at all.

Mari stretched and looked around. Spotting him, her face lit up with a hundred-watt smile and she headed over.

He pushed aside his concerns and smiled. "Are we havin' any fun yet?"

"I *was*, but Finney spoiled it, the party-poop. All I did was make a few suggestions, but you'd think I'd swiped the marker out of Damon's hands to draw it myself, the way she jumped all over me."

"The ideas for the murals—"

"Have to come from the boys. I know, I know. That's what she said."

"Everything here has a purpose, Mari. It's not fun and games."

She snorted. "That's obvious. In fact, in that volunteer handbook Kirk gave me, I think that among the five gazillion rules there's one that specifically *prohibits* fun." Crossing her arms, she turned to watch the boys.

He felt a stab of impatience that quickly faded. Like Finney had said, Mari didn't understand what they were up against, and it was his fault for not filling her in. While details about the boys' histories had to be omitted, she needed more grounding.

"I mean, look at them, Andy." She gestured to the teens. "They're just all so darned *cute*. Especially that Damon kid and Malloy. Damon's one of the nicest teenagers I've ever met. And with all those freckles, Malloy reminds me of a redheaded Dennis the Menace, only bigger."

Nice. Cute. Andy sighed. He really did need to take her aside and explain a few things before she'd volunteered another day. Damon was as trustworthy as Eddie Haskell. Less so. And at one time in his life, Malloy really had been a menace. Nothing cute about it.

Mari grabbed a tray and joined the line at the lunch counter. At noontime, everyone congregated in the cafeteria. The youth care providers took charge of the boys, joining their residents at designated tables. The therapists, Kirk, whatever counselor was here, and various volunteers dined where they wanted.

Technically, she'd finished her workday—she was scheduled only for mornings—but for the last two days she'd hung around through lunch, snatching a few words with Michael, then joining Andy and Finney to eat. So far, she enjoyed the work. No, more than enjoyed it. She lapped it up. She liked the boys, liked their high energy and creativity, and she thought—no matter Finney's complaints—she had a real knack as a teacher. It felt normal, natural, like she'd done it for years. Plus, after so much drawing on a lifeless computer monitor, it was fun to get her hands back on real art projects.

Dragging her easel down to the dock on the evenings when Andy worked on his article hadn't provided quite the same thrill (especially since she still hadn't nailed that smoldering light as the sun went down). Sure, it beat doing the supper dishes—mentally she gave a grudging thanks to Finney for getting her out of *that* chore—but she'd realized last night that

her joy in painting paled next to the rewards of working with the boys. She knew they all had problems,
but, *God*, from the broad smiles at the merest hint of
praise and the boisterous high-fives at even the small-
est of accomplishments, you'd think most of them had
never had a lick of attention.

But everything wasn't *all* rosy. Although she knew
she wasn't qualified to do more than act as Finney's
assistant, she chafed in the role. She also felt a tad
put out that Finney (and Andy, for that matter) both
frowned on what they called her *overinvolvement*.
Take this morning, for example. She'd only been *talking* to Damon, for Pete's sake, when Finney had practically wrenched her arm off, given her a scold like
she was six years old, and then left her with nothing
to do except fool around with a sketchbook. Stewing
and steaming—especially after Andy had backed Finney up—she'd whipped out a few studies of Michael
working in the garden. (Actually, a couple of them
weren't bad—they would be her birthday present for
Lil.)

Waiting impatiently in line, she bounced on the balls
of her feet. She wanted to beat Michael's youth care
provider to his cabin's table. She'd already learned
that Steve, with that ever-pleasant smile of his, would
butt in to shoo her off if she tried to do more than
just say howdy to her nephew. Criminy. Before she'd
started work on Wednesday, Kirk had explained they
wanted Michael free of family concerns except during
his counseling sessions, but this was ridiculous. Her
mouth twisted. As *she* saw it, she wasn't part of Michael's *family concerns*, nor were a few friendly words
and a pat on the back going to damage him for life.

Everything around here was such a big deal. Okay,
these kids might have some problems. But none of
them seemed all that far off the benchmark for most
teens. Besides, Finney had explained that this morning's project had been designed to aid socialization.

Well, geez, what better way to *socialize* than to have a conversation? She thought the whole "milieu therapy" thing was worshipped to extremes. These boys were regulated and scheduled out the wazoo.

Off to the side of the cafeteria, Andy was sliding his tray into his usual place at a table with Finney and Rita. Just spotting him made her pulse jump. She hadn't a clue where this whole thing with Andy would go, since it seemed their goals could never mesh. A definite country mouse, city mouse kind of thing.

But, even so, even if she was stupid to get tangled up with him, it felt right.

Very right.

She handed off her plate to a cafeteria worker and watched while he loaded a bun with sloppy joe mix. Sean flickered through her mind.

The fact Sean was waiting for an answer didn't feel right at all.

She should dash Sean's hopes now. Even if things didn't work out with Andy—and who knew, maybe she could convince him there were plenty of great schools outside *Kansas*—she had no business stringing Sean along. Taking back her plate, she grabbed a bag of chips and glanced behind her. Steve was still well back, chatting with Hal, another of the youth care providers. She faced forward again. And she owed it to Sean to tell him in person, but that would mean taking a day off just as she'd gotten started. Besides, it wasn't like Sean *expected* to hear from her before Labor Day.

Finally reaching the end of the line, she grabbed a bottle of water, paid the nominal fee they charged volunteers, and headed off to her nephew's table, looking around to make sure nobody was charging forward to stop her. Steve hadn't reached the end of the line, Kirk was engrossed in conversation with Dr. Everheart, and Andy had his back turned.

She breezed down the farthest side of the cafeteria,

her passage fluttering a row of papers tacked to the wall. Each sheet was headed by a boy's name, each one decorated with stars, and each one indicating how many points the boy had earned since camp began. Just getting to reveille on time counted for something, as did every other achievement, small or large. When the points totted up to a certain number, the boy would "move up a level," which largely meant more freedoms—like staying up late to watch a movie in the cafeteria or joining an excursion to ride go-karts on the other side of the lake. Of course, they could also lose points for rule infractions and be busted a level (or more, if things were serious), too. Andy had explained that displaying these papers gave each boy a feeling of personal success and control over his life. To her, it smacked of something more akin to Pavlov's dogs, but she guessed she could see the point.

She paused briefly to examine Michael's sheet, tacked up next to Damon's. From the stars and exclamation points, it was obvious Damon had more points than anyone else, but—she smiled with satisfaction—Michael had earned five stars from Rita Wagner for taking a dip in the lake yesterday and wasn't too far behind him.

Reaching Michael's table, she looked around for Steve. The YCP had made it through the line, but had stopped to chat with one of his cohorts. Still, she'd have to make this fast.

She dropped into a chair beside Michael. "How's it going?"

Engaged in an animated conversation with red-headed Malloy on his other side, Michael suddenly stopped and dipped his head. "Okay, I guess." He gave a big sigh. "I hate it here."

She frowned. When she'd seen him earlier working in the garden, he hadn't looked hangdog. In fact, he'd seemed engrossed with what he was doing. "There isn't anything you like?"

"No. I wish you'd tell my parents to get me the hell out of here."

"Oh, c'mon. It's not that bad."

"What do you know? You don't know *everything* that goes on. They don't understand me. Dr. Everheart is a jerk, and Mr. Kirk is even worse. Even Steve—" He glanced up through his bangs, and as quickly as he'd sunk into the doldrums, he now lit up. "Wazzup?"

Damn. Couldn't they get through one conversation uninterrupted? Mari twisted around. Damon stood at her elbow. "Hey, dawg." He and Michael lightly punched their fists together. With a puppy dog look— half hopeful, half fearful—Malloy held out his fist, too. When Damon ignored it, Malloy's face fell. Mari's frown deepened. What was with that?

Damon turned that great smile on her. "And how are you, Miz Mari?"

At the inane question, her irritation increased. How lame. He knew how she was; he'd just seen her in the art cabin ten minutes ago. But when he just continued to smile, his brows politely raised as he waited for a response, she scolded herself. Finney's morning reprimand had made her a shrew. She was an adult, not a child. And she could act accordingly. She returned his smile and scrambled up. "Here, take my place. I was just leaving."

Besides, in three short mornings, she'd already noticed Michael admired the year-older boy, and she was glad to see his friendship returned. Damon could help Michael bear the weeks ahead, and with all those points on his chart, he'd also provide a good example. She high-fived Michael good-bye, turned around . . . and nearly upset her tray all over Andy.

He was standing behind her with folded arms. "What are you up to?"

He looked so sanctimonious, her dander went up.

"Planning a massive breakout. Bring your spoon to their cabin at midnight. We're digging our way out."

Unnoticed by Andy, Damon gave her a thumbs-up. Feeling like a co-conspirator, she grinned back, then started to push past Andy, but he grabbed her elbow.

She jerked, but he held on. "For God's sake, Andy, I was only *talking* to Michael."

"Come with me."

He steered her toward the cafeteria door. She gave another jerk, and he finally lost his grip but just kept going. Unless she felt like making a big scene—and she didn't, at least not on her third day here—she had little choice except to follow. Flushed, she trotted behind him, tray still in her hands, feeling like a serving wench following her master. And she didn't like it. Not one little bit. Without stopping, she slid her tray onto the nearest table, but it didn't make her feel any less servile.

He stalked through the lobby and out the double doors. When they hit the front porch, she grabbed his arm, effectively halting him in his tracks.

"What in the hell was that all about? You don't have any right to treat me like that. I was simply talking with my nephew, not that it's any of your business."

"It *is* my business, Mari. This is what I'm trained for. What we've all trained for—except you. And what you're doing isn't in Michael's best interests."

"And what exactly am I doing that will have such dire consequences?"

"You're letting him get to you, that's what you're doing."

"Chri—criminy!" She stomped a foot. "He's my nephew. Of *course* he's going to get to me. He's *supposed* to get to me. That's what families are for. We watch out for each other."

Andy took a deep breath and blew it out. He motioned to a bench. "Sit down."

"I won't sit down just because you say so. I'm not—"

"Sit down!"

Mari sat.

Andy lowered himself beside her. "And quit sticking out your chin like that. You look like a mule."

"Then give me one good reason why I shouldn't talk to Michael."

"Because he'll manipulate you."

"Michael wouldn't—" She stopped, remembering how quickly her nephew had adopted that pathetic look. And how fast it had disappeared once Damon had shown up.

"I'll bet that he was telling you how much this place sucks, wasn't he?"

She didn't give him the satisfaction of an answer.

"They're all like that, Mari. Some worse than others." He paused. "And I wouldn't encourage Michael's relationship with Damon."

"Oh, for Pete's . . . What's wrong with Damon?"

"Damon's spent a lot of time at Vreeley Home, but he hasn't really worked the program, he's just learned to beat the system. Some of the smart kids do that— they learn what they have to do to move up levels, figuring the faster they do it, the sooner they're outta there. Despite all those points he racks up, Damon is a long way from solving his problems."

"What exactly *are* his problems? He seems like a good kid to me."

Andy sighed. "You know I can't talk about the kids' files with you. Even if Vreeley and Camp Sycamore didn't have policies on confidentiality, there's the Privacy Act. So you'll just have to take my word for it— Damon can't be trusted."

She didn't entirely believe him, but she let it go. She was more interested in Michael anyway. "Can you talk about Michael?"

"Up to a point."

Fine. He could keep his secrets. "Why would he manipulate me?"

"A lot of it's habit. Many of these kids are pros at taking advantage because they've had to be in order to survive. It's the only way they know to get what they want, or need."

"But Michael was never in a desperate situation."

She frowned when Andy hesitated. What didn't she know about Michael?

"He was before he went to live with your sister and Van Castle. Those first five years of his life, he couldn't trust his mother, the person he should have been able to trust the most." She narrowed her eyes. Andy was picking his words carefully. More carefully than usual. "He spent a lot of those young years hiding under a bed with his sister to keep out of his mother's reach. You don't think that marked him?"

"But Melanie grew up fine. Why wouldn't his sister have a bunch of emotional problems, too? She lived with that situation longer than he did."

"I didn't say it was logical. Different personalities come into play. One kid can ignore things, another one can't. It happens even in what you'd term a good home. That's why these boys are here—we take them out of whatever environment isn't working for them and hope everyone in the family—if they have a family—will be able to make some changes so that when they get back together, it *does* work."

"But that doesn't make sense with Michael," Mari insisted. "With Lil and Jon, he got everything he needed and lots of love from both of them."

"From what I understand, Michael tried to make a connection with his real mother in the last few years."

So what? Mari wrinkled her nose. "I never could understand why, though. Belinda really *was* manipulative. A grade A, number one bitch."

"But she *was* his mother—that's why he wanted to know her. And he'd feel something for her, no matter how she'd treated him. When she died of an overdose, I'm sure in Michael's mind it was like he was being abandoned all over again. He's carrying around a lot of anger."

"Abandoned?" Mari raised her brows. "Michael was never abandoned."

"The famous Jon Van Castle didn't deign to make his son a part of his life until he met Lil." There was a harsh note in Andy's voice she'd never heard before. "As far as Michael's concerned, his father abandoned him first. And he'd see Lil as his rescuer, not Van Castle."

"You think Michael's problems are all *Jon's* fault?" Mari bristled. Good God, when had Andy decided he was judge and jury? "You forget that Belinda's mother lived with them, too. Jon trusted *her*. And he really thought the kids were better off with their grandmother and mom than living a musician's life; he toured all the time. But you don't know Jon. He *never* would have left them if he'd known Belinda was mistreating them. As soon as he did, he went for sole custody." She could see from Andy's expression that he didn't believe Jon was much of a saint. Exasperated, she shook her head. "Besides, from what Lil told me, the abuse was pretty mild, comparatively speaking. Some slaps, yelling, a few skipped meals, and she locked them out of the house in the dark a couple of times when their grandmother wasn't home."

"She also—" Andy stopped.

"She also what?"

"Never mind."

Damn those confidentiality rules.

Andy stood up. "I have to eat and get back to work. Let's call a truce and talk about this over the weekend."

She didn't move. "You shouldn't blame Michael's problems all on Jon."

He sighed. "I'm not. I know Michael's mother is

largely at fault. Look, I'm sorry if I've made your brother-in-law out to be a monster, but in my view, when you have a kid, you've made a commitment that should be as honored as marriage vows. More so, because that kid depends completely on you. And just like a husband and wife, trust has to be the foundation or the whole house comes tumbling down. When trust is gone . . ." Andy's gaze drifted over the clearing in front of the building. The shadow crossing his face made her wince. "It results in tragedy."

Somehow she knew he wasn't thinking about Michael anymore.

He held out his hand. "C'mon. I'll walk you to your car."

Still thinking about that dark expression on his face, she didn't raise any more objections. She slipped her hand into his and let him pull her up.

"That's better." His grin erased the shadow. "I sure wish your family wasn't coming this weekend. Guess the drive-in is out."

"Guess so. I don't suppose you'd like to visit the sleeping porch again, would you?" The question was idle. Her mind clanked away, processing his remarks.

"And risk having your mother string me up by my . . . thumbs? No thanks."

"'Fraidy-cat. We could be quiet. And no jawbreakers—I'd keep my feet to myself, pinky-swear it."

Exchanging silliness, swinging hands, they walked to the parking lot. The sun was hot on her back. But inwardly she shivered, wondering what Andy would think—what he would do—if he knew she'd once encouraged a husband to break the vows Andy held sacrosanct.

Chapter 13

By midmorning Saturday, the official launch date of the O'Malley Spring and Summer Weekend Birthday Celebration, Andy still hadn't fulfilled his promise to discuss the whole Camp Sycamore thing with her again. Actually, Mari couldn't blame him. He hadn't had a snowball's chance in Zinnia hell, which was just as well, since she still felt shaken by their conversation yesterday.

Between work and supper last night, Andy had helped Finney load her car for a weekend trip home to St. Louis to visit her family. (Finney was smart to escape the onslaught.) Five minutes after supper had ended, Zinnia had shoved fishing poles at him and Pop and charged them not to return until they'd caught enough to feed the entire family. When they'd returned—late; they'd been afraid to come back without a good haul—Lil, Jon, and Jon's daughter, Melanie, had arrived. Good thing, too. Because even with the extra hands, they'd been up till midnight cleaning the catch for this evening's fish fry. Then, early this morning, as soon as her mother had opened her eyes, she'd started barking orders and thunking that walking stick, and the whole whirlwind of preparations had started anew.

Fortunately, the day was fresh-scrubbed, with only a few whipped-cream clouds in the sky. Even though their clan had crowded into the cabin before on bad-weather days, it was a stretch of space—and nerves—to have them all under the same roof at once. With good weather, they'd spread out—floating on rafts in the cove, water-skiing behind the Cobalt, fishing from Pop's bass boat, or just lazing in one of the several hammocks tied between trees. Meals would be served outside on the deck, beginning with hot dogs for lunch today and ending with a late-afternoon cookout before everyone went home tomorrow.

After covering the picnic table with a red-and-white-checked oilcloth, Mari walked to the edge of the deck and leaned over the railing, nudging the tendrils of what Andy had identified as Virginia creeper out of the way. (He'd stopped her just before she'd lopped it all off, thinking it was poison ivy.) Until Melanie returned with a couple of card tables to extend the ends of the picnic table—or unless Zinnia spotted her idling—she had a few loose minutes.

In a clearing downslope, near the water where the ground leveled out as much as it ever did around here, Andy was poking one pole of a volleyball net into the ground. Pop stood nearby, holding stakes and a hammer.

Andy stood up and spotted her. "Look about right?"

She gave him a thumbs-up. "Looks fine to me!"

His smile came complete with eye crinkles, then he tugged on the brim of his cap and returned to his task. Hugging his grin to herself, heart warming, she lingered at the railing and watched him. Over the past week, she'd realized there had been a definite gap in her life since she'd stepped out of Andy's, and now he'd returned to fill it. Fill her. It didn't take much to recognize that the warmth that enveloped her was love.

"Has my baby sister finally fallen in love?"

Mari started and turned to find Lil had materialized

at her elbow. "Don't scare me like that!" *Don't read my mind like that.*

Lil just smiled. "Well?"

Mari started to tell her to mind her own beeswax, but then she glanced back at Andy and her heart melted into a gooey, sentimental mess. "Yes," she sighed, dropping her elbows to the railing. "It just feels like, I dunno, natural. I guess I've always loved him in some form or other."

"Like the harvest of something planted in childhood."

Mari would have given that piece of poetic nonsense an eye roll, except she thought Lil had hit the mark dead-on.

Lil leaned on the railing, too, still smiling. "So I assume he feels the same way."

"I think so."

Andy looked up and blew them both a kiss. They both blew one back.

Lil raised an eyebrow. "But you don't know?"

"Okay, I do know. He does." She knew it just like she knew almost everything he thought. *Almost* was the key word. "But we haven't exactly said the words yet."

"Why not?"

"Shouldn't you get back to making potato salad?" Jon and Lil had spent the morning peeling potatoes without a murmur of dissension between them. With Melanie home from college, Michael off at camp, and the family therapy going well from what Mari could tell, all now seemed quiet on the Van Castle home front.

"It's done. Jon headed off to get bait for fishing later on." Lil nudged her. "So what gives?"

"All right, all right." Mari watched Andy take the hammer and a stake from Pop. "I've held back because right now I just want to wallow in a little newfound— and well-deserved, by the way—contentment. I think he's doing the same thing. Once we say the words, well, then we're going to have to look at the big fat messy future."

"And what's so messy about that?"

"I want glitz and glam. He wants . . . *Kansas*." Now she did roll her eyes. Beyond, Andy pounded in the stake with sure strokes. She sighed, thinking of how supremely righteous he'd looked yesterday when he'd lectured her on Michael. "And he's not the aimless goof-off he used to be."

Lil looked puzzled. "And that's a bad thing?"

"No, but it means convincing him he can reach his goals in somewhere other than cow-and-wheat country isn't going to be easy."

"Mari . . ." Lil took a deep breath, and Mari braced herself. Lil could never resist giving advice. "Maybe you should—"

"Aunt Mari, do you think these will work? Do we need both?"

Mari turned around to see Melanie struggling through the door with two card tables. Bless the nineteen-year-old's timing. "Probably." Mari and Lil hurried forward to help her. Melanie was slender and slight. The card tables almost outweighed her.

"Thanks." Mel swept back a fall of straight dark hair, revealing her high cheekbones. "When will Aunt Patsy Lee be here? I haven't seen Daisy since I've been home."

"And, gee, it's been such a long time since you and Daisy were together at college," Lil said. "What is it now? Two weeks?"

"Plus a couple of days," Mel added, a smile lighting her brown eyes. "Don't forget those."

"Patsy Lee was minding Merry-Go-Read this morning, but I told her to close the shop early. She and Daisy—along with the other three kids—will be here soon." Patsy Lee had started managing the Cordelia store for Lil after their oldest brother Henry's death almost a decade ago. Never remarried, Patsy Lee was as much a part of the family as any of them. Lil looked around. "Why don't you set these up over there and make two tables," she suggested. "I'll go see if I can find some more oilcloth." Handing off her table to Mel, she headed inside.

"So how was spring semester? Any decisions?" Mari asked as they straightened the table legs. She knew from Lil that Melanie was trying to choose a major.

Mel juggled a table into place next to Mari's. "I'm still torn. I wish I was as sure as Kathleen." Alcea's daughter, Kathleen, had wanted to become a writer since she was young. This summer, Alcea's author husband, Dak, had arranged for Kathleen to intern at a publishing company, thinking it might pay off for her to make the contacts. Mel shrugged. "But I guess I still have time to decide. . . ."

Chatting about Melanie's upcoming sophomore year, the two women unfolded some canvas chairs, then Mari handed Melanie one of her two damp rags to help wipe them down. When the topic finally lagged, Mari thought of the conversation she'd had with Andy yesterday.

"Mel, can I ask you something about Michael?"

"Sure. But Mom said you were working out at Camp Sycamore now, so you probably know more than me. I just saw him for the first time since spring break at family counseling Wednesday night."

"How's that going?"

"Okay. At least Mom and Dad aren't yelling at each other anymore. And Michael—I don't know. I can't tell what he's thinking, but he's at least talking more to them now. What did you want to ask?"

"I just wondered . . . why do you think you turned out so different from him?"

"We've discussed that in therapy." Mel rubbed down the arms of a chair. "When I met Mom—Lil—

I was older and we really bonded, as they say, right from the beginning. I always knew I could trust her. And I think—well, I think I have a more forgiving nature than Michael."

"You mean you forgave your dad for not being around when you were little, but Michael didn't?"

Mel paused in her cleaning. "I don't know that I ever felt I had anything to forgive Dad *for*. Maybe because I was older, I understood he didn't really have a home for us to go to when he was still on the road. But as soon as I told him how things were with Belinda"—Mel never called her birth mother *Mother*—"he never took us back there." Melanie's voice went dry. "And I also understood that Belinda would never turn into Mother Teresa. Michael, though . . . I think Michael always held out hope that she'd somehow become a loving mom, even though he had it worse from her than I did. I never wanted to see her again after Lil adopted us, but Michael did. Dr. Everheart says I just process things differently.

Mel set one chair aside and grabbed another. "Like, when she died last year, I felt sad. But not sad for *me*, sad for *her*. Because her life was just such a waste. And then to die from an overdose . . ." Mel's hair swung as she shook her head. "But Michael was really upset." She paused. "You know, Belinda lied all the time."

"I remember," Mari said. Who could forget? Belinda had almost gotten away with lying to the court and ruining Jon's chances for custody.

"Whenever Michael saw Belinda, she filled him up with all these sob stories where she was forever the victim. He started slipping her whatever money he could scrounge up before he went to see her. I told him not to; I told him Dad paid her mortgage and her household and credit card bills, and she'd probably just use the money he gave her on dope. But he felt sorry for her—she'd convinced him that the way she'd turned out was all Dad's fault. But Aunt Mari, it *wasn't* Dad's fault. He tried to help her, but that was just the way she was. Selfish and bitter and—"

"Am I interrupting?" Andy stood at the top of the deck stairs, his gaze resting on Melanie. Mari hoped he'd overheard their conversation. It might put paid to his idea that Jon was some kind of ogre. At the same time, she wished he hadn't spoken up so soon. She wanted to know why Melanie felt Michael had suffered more at Belinda's hands than she had. *He had it worse from her than I did.* Maybe she'd just meant because Michael was younger during those years when they'd been alone with Belinda and their grandmother.

"Nope, you're not interrupting." Melanie turned to Andy with a smile that dazzled in the same way her father Jon's did. "In fact, you can finish this up while I go cut up all those carrots Grandma put out for me."

Andy laughed. "This family is full of bossy women."

"Here, use this." Mari tossed him a rag.

"Aye-aye, Captain." He snatched it up. He winked at Mel. "But I think Mari's the bossiest one of all."

Thinking about her conversation with Lil about talking Andy around to the beckoning lights of a big city, Mari smiled sweetly. *You ain't seen nuthin' yet.*

Four hours later, everything that could be prepared in advance of the evening cookout was done. Patsy Lee and her brood (Mari rattled their names off in descending order for Andy's benefit—Daisy, Hank, Rose, and Lily—then told him "Hey, you" would work, too) had arrived an hour ago. Moving with gentle calm among them, Patsy Lee looked not too unlike the Virgin Mary with her fall of dark hair and her comfortably plump frame. Which made sense; it took a saint to put up with the four children Henry had left Patsy Lee to raise alone after he'd died. After a flurry of greetings, renewed activity, and a quick snack, everyone had scattered: Lil and Jon to take a nap (yeah, like *that* excuse fooled anyone), Patsy Lee to study for the business classes she took at night. Sixteen-year-old Hank had headed out in Pop's bass boat, and college roommates Daisy and Mel had slipped to the room they were sharing for a gabfest. Near the water, Pop was snoozing in a hammock strung up between two bur oaks while Zinnia relaxed with a game of solitaire inside.

Andy and Mari sat on a low stone wall outside the kitchen door, charged with waiting for the last remnants of the O'Malley clan to arrive so they could help with luggage. Andy had tucked Mari's hand in his. Overhead a few cloud puffs drifted through the sky.

Off to one side of the drive, Patsy Lee's two youngest daughters picked wildflowers to decorate the tables, their voices wafting across the clearing, their matching blond heads gleaming in the sun. Shy eight-year-old Lily held up every flower for her fourteen-year-old sister's inspection. Rose seriously considered each one, then nodded approval when Lily added it to her bouquet. Mari smiled. Everyone was gentle with Lily. The youngest O'Malley was like a deer, easily spooked. But normally Rose was far from serious, up to raising almost as much hell as her best friend Michael, the same as Mari had done with Andy at that age.

She nestled a little closer to Andy and sighed with contentment. Her oldest sister and her husband should be here soon, but Alcea and Dak could take as long as they wanted as far as Mari was concerned. She felt like she could sit here forever. Maybe it was just Andy, but a deep peace had settled over her. Just like in Cordelia, time here moved at a slower beat than the tempo she'd set in the city. And, believe it or not, she was actually looking forward to seeing everyone.

"Want to tell me why two people coming for just

one night need help with their luggage?" Andy asked. He spread her hand out on his knee and played with her fingers.

"It's not just Alcea and Dak," Mari answered. Andy groaned, and she smiled. Sorting out her family with all its extensions was a big headache. "They're bringing Florida and Florida's daughter, Missouri. And you can't travel anywhere with a three-year-old—Missouri's three, almost four— without a mountain of stuff."

Andy frowned. Mari didn't blame him. She tried to help. "Do you remember Florida Jones? She was a knockout blonde a few years ahead of us in high school—God, I always wanted to look like her. She's Alcea's partner at the diner. Hey, that makes her your grandmother's boss, I guess. And she's Alcea's sister-in-law—Dak's sister."

Andy's hand had stilled. She glanced at him; his expression was still odd. "What?"

"Nothing." Dak's Jeep Liberty crunched over the gravel at the top of the drive. Andy stood up and muttered, "This'll sure be fun."

Mari frowned. What bug had crawled into his britches? But before she could comment, he'd already started toward the Jeep. Brushing off the seat of her denim shorts, she hurried after him, nearly getting knocked down by her nieces, who ran past her. Lily stopped just short of the vehicle to twine a piece of hair around her fingers, and the more exuberant Rose yanked open Alcea's door so she could climb out. On the other side of the vehicle, Dak eased his long frame from the Jeep, flashed Mari a smile, lightning-bright against his tanned skin, then moved straight to the rear to start unloading. Her writer brother-in-law had slid easily into the O'Malley family, but Mari knew Dak would prefer solitude to this throng of people. After a short flurry of greetings, Alcea followed to help him.

When Andy would have joined them, Mari held him back. "I want you to meet Florida." When his mouth thinned, her puzzlement jumped another notch.

In the backseat, Florida was stuffing an assortment of toys scattered over the upholstery into a canvas bag, helped reluctantly by her daughter. Gathering the bag's handles in one hand, Florida finger-combed a riot of long hair with the other. "What a trip! Dak can't go anywhere without turning this darned ol' Jeep into a wind tunnel. I thought maybe when he traded the Wrangler for a Liberty, we'd finally travel with some dignity. But, no, now he has to leave all the windows down." Rose held out her arms for Missouri, and Florida helped her daughter clamber out, narrowly avoiding a tennis shoe in the face. "Y'all mind your cousin now, Missouri. Don't go down to the docks without an adult. And a life jacket. No mischief."

The youngster shook a head full of dark curls. "No misjef, Mommy." But the dance in her eyes belied the dutiful words. She squirmed down from Rose's grasp, caught Lily by the hand, and the three took off, flowers scattered and forgotten.

"Do watch her close, Rose!" Florida called. Unfolding her long legs, she climbed out. "That girl will be the death of me." She and Mari exchanged a hug, then Florida held out her hand to Andy. "I'm Florida Jones, Alcea's sister-in-law. I remember y'all from high school."

Andy hesitated a moment, then took Florida's hand. "Andrew Eppelwaite. You graduated at the end of my freshman year." The words were frosty, his gaze cold, and the shake lasted the barest nanosecond. Florida's blue eyes turned puzzled.

Mari stared at Andy. Well, *that* wild enthusiasm should make Florida feel welcome. She gave him a what's-with-you look, but, face bland, he only quirked an eyebrow. Covering up the chill in the air, she tugged at his hand. "Let me introduce you to Dak." *And see if you want to eat him for lunch, too.*

She dragged him to the back of the Jeep, performed the niceties, and Andy shook Dak's hand. "I've read some of your *Road* series books. Really enjoyed them."

She frowned. So it was only Florida who somehow merited boorish behavior.

Behind Dak, Alcea was rummaging through the mounds of stuff piled in the Jeep. Stacking a few items on top of each other, she turned and dumped them into Mari's arms. "Be careful with that container; it's the birthday cake."

"Made fresh this morning with her own hands. Along with another half dozen she sold in the bakery." Staring at the mountain of suitcases, bags, and toys still left, Dak ran a hand through an overly long crop of dark hair shot through with a few strands of silver. "And I thought taking Kathleen to college was bad. Missouri is spoiled rotten. Well," he sighed, "let's do it."

For the next twenty minutes, they unloaded the piles into the cabin, helped along by the chatter that flew between all of them. Or, at least, between all of them *except* Andy and Florida. While he was his usual charming self with Alcea and Dak, Andy talked to Florida only when he had to. And when he had to, his gaze stopped just short of freezing her to death. The puzzlement in Florida's eyes changed to hurt, and Mari saw her whisper a few words to Alcea. When both women glanced in Andy's direction, Alcea's mouth was tight. *Uh-oh.* Mari had been scrambling to make sure Florida and Andy had few opportunities alone. Now she redoubled her efforts to keep him and Alcea apart, too. Geez, this weekend was really shaping up to be a good ol' time.

But after her last trip inside, where she'd gotten delayed by Zinnia, who was fussing over who went in what room (who cared?), she returned to the clearing to find Alcea and Andy facing each other at the back of the Liberty. With nobody else around. Groaning, she hurried forward. Not that hurrying would help. She could tell from her sister's poked-up chin and Andy's stubborn one that she was too late to curb Alcea's tongue.

"I don't know what your problem is, but Florida is my best friend—"

Mari interrupted her. "Hey, sister dear, why don't you let me take that?" She inserted herself between the two of them and reached for the last suitcase.

"—and I won't have you acting like she's carrying the plague. What happened to your manners, Andy Eppelwaite? You might have been a screwup before, but you were never rude."

Andy flushed, but his expression wasn't conciliatory. "I just—"

Alcea waved a hand. "Spare me further commentary on your notion of morality." She grabbed the suitcase out of Mari's hand and jerked her head for Mari to follow. Giving Andy a helpless shrug, Mari did. When they were out of earshot, Alcea muttered. "Does he know about your past?"

Confused, Mari frowned. About Sean? Four years ago, when Alcea was sorting out the destruction of her first marriage, Mari had confided in her—Hock was the only person in the family who knew about her affair with Sean—and it had been Alcea's advice to dump him that had helped Mari decide to . . . well, dump him. Now, with Alcea's sharp but not unconcerned gaze on her, she suddenly wanted to confess and explain everything all over again. But with Andy glowering at them just yards away, now certainly wasn't the time. Besides, what did her past have to do with Andy's behavior now?

Not knowing what to say, she answered with a rise and drop of her shoulders.

"I didn't think so. Not the way he's acting toward Florida." Alcea shook her head and stalked off. "Gawd. *I'm* the only one here with reason to hate her. . . ."

Still confused over what Sean had to do with Florida, Mari watched her go.

Dak met his wife at the door and held it open. "Anything else?"

"We're *plenty* done." Alcea stepped into the cabin and slammed the door.

Mari returned to Andy. "You want to tell me why you've ignited World War III?"

He raked his hair back. "I'm sorry."

"I'm not the one you should apologize to."

"I know. And I will. But it's just . . ." That haunted look she'd seen a few times before spread over his face.

"Just what?" Something was very wrong.

"Everyone treats Florida like a member of the clan—"

"Technically, she *is* family. She's Dak's sister. But even if she wasn't, she and Alcea are really close and they're practically raising Missouri together. So what?"

"Maybe I've got things twisted up, but Gran told me Florida was responsible for breaking up Alcea's marriage to her first husband—Sam, Steve . . ."

"Stan."

"Yeah, Stan. And that Missouri is Florida and Stan's kid. I mean how can you or anyone, let alone Alcea, act like what Florida did doesn't matter a hoot in hell?"

Mari felt a tremor of fear. He was skating close to her own history, and his face was so *hard*. "They're *friends*, Andy."

"How could they possibly be friends?"

"Well, Alcea fell in love with Florida's brother. And then Florida inherited the diner Alcea worked at, but she didn't know how to run it like Alcea did, and that was Alcea's opportunity to become a partner in the business she loved, so they ended up depending on each other. . . ." She looked at Andy's face, which hadn't softened a bit. "Uh, I guess it's complicated," she wound up lamely.

"It would have to be." The words were clipped.

Feeling hopeless, Mari tried again. "Alcea and Stan's marriage was a big fat farce. Florida wasn't Stan's first affair, you know; she was just the last one before Stan and Alcea's marriage fell apart. It would have all blown up anyway. Besides, Florida didn't get pregnant with Stan's child until well after he and Alcea divorced." She swallowed. "And don't you think maybe *Stan* shares some blame?"

If possible, Andy's features grew more rigid. "Maybe most of it."

Mari felt a little bit better. But only a little bit. "And don't you think it's possible that maybe Stan made promises to Florida. Maybe he said things like he and Alcea were separating, or he planned to divorce her, or something? And maybe Florida was in love, and she wanted to believe him, and so she just *did*?"

Andy considered a moment, then shook his head. "It's just not right, Mari. It's not right for anyone to screw around with someone who's married."

Mari's heart was stuck in her throat. "Why do you feel so strongly about this? Is it because of that woman at K-State and your friend?"

He hesitated. "That's part of it. Before that, though, I watched Anna's marriage go up in smoke because her husband catted around." His gaze grew distant. "And then she—"

"She what?" Mari was almost whispering, but Andy didn't seem to notice. When—more important, *why*—had Andy become so judgmental?

"Nothing." He shrugged as if shaking himself back

to the present. He looked at her, then smoothed the hair back from her face and smiled crookedly. "You look like a basset hound, all sad eyes and droopy mouth."

"Thanks tons. It's a look I've aspired to." She couldn't manage to put any lilt into her voice. And it made her feel worse when Andy's expression grew concerned.

A blond head poked out the door, eyes ringed in violet that clashed with a hot-pink-and-green-striped bikini. "Hey, Aunt Mari! You seen my sisters and Missouri?"

"Which one is she, again?" Andy said sotto voce. "She's scary."

Mari mustered a smile. "Daisy. Melanie's college roommate and Patsy Lee's oldest. You can always tell her by the gobs of eye shadow and the wild clothes. We think she shops wherever Pop does." She pointed up the drive and raised her voice. "They went thataway."

"I didn't mean to make *you* feel bad." Andy touched the corner of her mouth. "You can do better than that."

She bared some teeth, and he recoiled in mock terror. "Geez, Mar. That's pathetic."

"Lily! Rose! Missour-eee!" Daisy hollered from the door. When the threesome appeared from around the bend in the drive, she yelled, "Mel and me are going swimming. Who wants to go?"

"Me, me, me . . ." Missouri ran pell-mell down the drive as fast as her thin legs could carry her, with Rose not too far behind. Lily followed at a more leisurely pace, stopping to sniff a flower, then watch a butterfly, until her exasperated older sister ran back to tug her along.

Andy stood up and took her hand. "C'mon. I *am* sorry. I'll throw apologies all over the place and act like Florida's my best buddy, okay?"

Feeling wiped out, realizing the future held not just a few bumps but a majorly huge roadblock, Mari let Andy pull her along. They walked toward the cabin, meeting Rose at the door. The fourteen-year-old's earlier enthusiasm was gone, her expression sad.

"What's the matter, hon?" Mari asked.

"Every once in a while, it hits me."

"What does?"

"That Michael's not here." Rose's eyes filled. "It doesn't seem right. He can be a skunk, b-but he's my best friend."

Mari could relate. She hugged her niece, and glanced up at Andy. She'd feel exactly the same way if she lost him. And she had little doubt now that if he ever learned the truth about her affair with Sean, that's exactly what would happen.

Chapter 14

True to his word, within the hour Andy had apologized to both Alcea and Florida, and then had proceeded to pour on the charm. Mari didn't know what excuse he used for his earlier behavior, but—even if he sat so far away from Florida at the fish fry that he practically had a foot in the next county—his act was so good it could have won an Academy Award.

Mari busied herself with some Oscar-worthy acting of her own. Still burdened by her awareness that the man she loved would toss her right out on her ear if he learned of the part she'd played in Sean's tumultuous marriage, she stuck a smile on her face and managed to carry off the evening without garnering more than a few puzzled looks from Andy at her performance. Which was saying something, since he knew her so well. Or thought he did.

When night fell, she lay in bed staring at the ceiling with Missouri snoring little-girl snores at her side (the inn was running out of room) and wondered exactly how well *she* knew *him*. The old Andy would never have shown such a self-righteous streak—judging Florida, judging Jon. And where did he get off judging anyone at all? He'd done his share of screwing up. You'd think the years he'd spent at A.A. meetings would have made him *more* understanding, not less. He'd obviously worked through the anger he'd once felt at his father, and he'd told her about his struggles with his own self-forgiveness, but it was plain he still had *issues. Big* issues.

But he wasn't the only one. Careful not to wake Missouri, who had chattered a blue streak for an hour before finally dropping off to sleep in a tangle of sheets and dark hair, Mari rolled onto her side and stared into the dark. She could rant inwardly at him all she wanted for his sanctimonious behavior—the hypocrite—but it didn't get rid of all the guilt she still felt at her role as the Other Woman in her own love triangle. She sighed. How could she learn to forgive herself—attend Tarts Anonymous, ha-ha? And even if she did know how to forgive herself, how could that help her and Andy? Not that she wanted to tell Andy *anything,* but she knew she couldn't live a lie forever. If they even had a *forever* ahead of them.

When morning broke after a restless night, Mari awakened to the usual pounding of the walking stick on the floorboards above her. But instead of her mother's voice, she heard giggles.

Noting the empty spot next to her in the bed, she yelled at the ceiling. "Cut that out, Missouri, or I'll have to use you for fish bait."

The giggling increased. "Grammy Zinnia says, *Get. Up. Right. Now.*"

The kid had an uncanny talent for mimicry. Grumbling, Mari swung her feet to the floor. As she threw on her swimsuit and belted a short kimono over it, she decided she wouldn't say a word to Andy. Yet. What was the point of bringing up her past now when she wasn't even sure of their future?

Upstairs, Pop was preparing a marinade for the steaks and hamburgers they'd have late afternoon before everyone went home, and everyone else was preparing a pancake breakfast. The kitchen was bedlam. And a mess. But when the meal was over, to Mari's surprise, Zinnia refused help either cleaning up or getting ready for the next big feed. "You kids just go have your fun. I can take care of what little there's left to do, and Lord knows, it's about time I started being useful again."

While the others hunted down coolers, towels, snacks, and suntan lotion for a day of swimming, skiing, and fishing, Mari hung back. When she was finally alone with her mother, she asked, "Are you sure you don't need any help getting ready for the cookout?"

"Of *course* I'm sure. I'm ready to take the world by storm again."

Oh, boy. Look out, world.

When Mari still hesitated, Zinnia smiled a small, secretive smile and headed toward the door that led to the clearing. "Let me just show you a little something."

Puzzled but curious, Mari followed. Zinnia stepped out on the stoop, bent, and rummaged in a rusting trash can behind a fat lilac bush just outside the door, and then, looking triumphant, lifted out a mangled piece of something . . .

Mari peered closer, then laughed. Zinnia had found Pop's hammer. And then had used it on the shower chair.

"Silly thing." Looking satisfied, Zinnia dropped the chair back in the can, then patted Mari's shoulder. "Now you just run along, y'hear?"

Mari didn't offer any more arguments.

Still smiling, she wandered downhill toward the dock, which was almost submerged under a blanket of beach towels. Just off the path, Lil was seated on a glider. Mari started to pass her by with a wave, but a sadness in Lil's eyes made her sigh and change her mind. She detoured and settled next to her sister. A colorful flotilla of water rafts, all topped with children, littered the cove.

"What's wrong?"

Lil gave her a small smile. "It's the first time in

years that we've done something like this and Michael hasn't been with us."

"He's fine, Lil. Really. I saw him three days last week, and I'd let you know if he wasn't." She'd chosen to believe Andy—that Michael's complaints were more manipulation than not.

"I know. And I do think his time at camp is helping. At least we're all talking again without yelling. But I still worry about him. I wonder if he's lonely, or scared, or—"

"He's made some friends, so he's not lonely. And what would he have to be scared of? He's in Andy's horticulture group, did you know that?" Mari culled her mind for other reassurance. "And Steve—his YCP—is really nice." Even if he could be a pain.

"I know he's safe with the staff. It's the other boys I worry about." Lil sighed. "Dr. Everheart says he's not so sure one of Michael's new friends is a good influence."

"Who?"

"Damon something. One of the boys from Vreeley."

"Oh, don't worry about Damon." Leaning back, Mari stretched her arms out along the back of the glider. She'd given Damon some thought. Maybe his unfailing courtesies were bogus, but she could remember putting on the same act when she was a teen for the benefit of the parental units. That hadn't made her a bad person. "I swear, sometimes I think all those psych types look for problems where there aren't any. I've met this kid—talked with him, even—and I wouldn't worry. Besides, you know Michael wouldn't take up with anyone who wasn't nice."

"Oh, yes, he would." Lil gave her a level look. "At school, Michael sought out the wrong crowd. And he would have dragged Rose with him if she'd let him. Fortunately she's made of stronger stuff, so she held back and didn't get into all the messes he did. It's an old pattern with him, Mari. He's a follower. And he doesn't always pick the best people to follow. He doesn't want to take responsibility for his own actions, so it's easier for him if he has someone like this Damon telling him what to do."

Mari was momentarily stymied. "Okay, let's say you're right." Which Lil might very well be. Michael and Rose sounded an awful lot like she and Andy once had been. "But Damon couldn't get Michael into much trouble around *there*, believe me. The boys can't jump without asking how high."

Lil gave her a jaundiced look.

"It's true. Besides, Michael has also made friends with this boy, Malloy—and Malloy's a great kid. I haven't a clue why they think he belongs in Vreeley, or in Sycamore, for that matter. Why, he's no more troubled than Mi—" She broke off. She didn't want to argue Sycamore's merits with Lil again.

Lil was still looking at her. "It's obvious you don't have children."

Well, neither do you. Mari bit her tongue before the words escaped her mouth, appalled at the impulse to hurt her sister more than Lil had just wounded her. Her turmoil over Andy had her totally addled. She hadn't even decided if she ever wanted kids—she'd only been aware that the window of opportunity was narrowing. Lil, though . . . Lil loved Jon's children as if they were her own. And she would have moved mountains to actually bear her own. But Lil had suffered a miscarriage during the trauma of her first husband's young death. One that had taken her child and her ability to have any more.

Turning her gaze back to the lake, Lil apparently didn't notice Mari's face had heated with shame. "They can be sneaky. You think you know them, but sometimes . . ." Lil's voice turned mournful. "Well, sneaky or not, I miss Michael. Especially today."

Still feeling contrite, Mari swallowed the rest of her

opinions. She sat with Lil a few more minutes, unable to think of anything she could offer to make her sister feel better (or to make up for her earlier thought). Then Andy hailed her from the dock. As she rose to join him, she wondered again what their future would hold—and, for the first time, wondered if it included the pitter-patter of little feet. Maybe it shouldn't. Considering the genes any product of their loins would inherit, their kids would be *way* beyond sneaky.

She mentally smacked her head. Children were the least of her worries.

By four that afternoon, all that was left of the mid-afternoon cookout was crumbs from the garlic bread. The family had demolished the vats of potato salad and coleslaw, eaten every last one of Zinnia's deviled eggs, and stuffed themselves on the steaks Pop had cooked to perfection on the grill.

Supervised by Patsy Lee's teenage children Rose and Hank, young Lily and little Missouri had headed back to the cove for a swim. ("Make sure Missouri gets all that egg filling washed off her," Florida had yelled after them.) The men had loaded themselves into the pontoon boat and taken off for a last round of fishing. ("We'll have nothing but fish fries for the next week," Mari had complained.) And, as was usual—and completely unfair, in her opinion—the womenfolk had been left to take care of the detritus. (She decided to overlook the fact that the guys had taken their turn swabbing the decks last night.)

Prepared to utter a scathing comment, she looked around the kitchen, and the comment died on her lips. The feeling of companionship among all the women was palpable. Zinnia and Patsy Lee had commandeered the sink to do the dishes, her mother rubbing shoulders with the woman she still considered her daughter-in-law. Patsy Lee used a soapy hand to brush a strand of dark hair back over her shoulder and

smiled at something Zinnia had said. Wrapping leftovers, Lil stood near Florida, whose blond shade
matched Lil's so closely that Alcea's partner and
sister-in-law looked like just another O'Malley. And
at the table, still chattering madly with each other,
coeds Daisy and Melanie helped Alcea dish out the
cake they'd consume before everyone left. The scene
might not be one Gloria Steinem would applaud, but
seeing all these O'Malley women gathered in the
kitchen, Mari could imagine how generations of their
ancestors had done the same before them.

Nice sentiment. But she could still be glad all bases
were covered and they didn't need her help.

She moved toward the cellar steps. She'd slip downstairs, grab a short nap, and—

"Take this."

She turned, and Alcea dumped a cardboard box in
her hands.

"You can put the presents out on the picnic table."
Her oldest sister didn't wait for a response, but headed
off to elbow between Zinnia and Patsy Lee at the sink.

Mari looked down at the gaily covered packages
and swore under her breath. While the presents she'd
bought in Sedalia for Patsy Lee and Melanie were
wrapped and waiting in the cellar, she'd forgotten to
bring home the sketches of Michael that she'd planned
to give Lil. They were still at camp. For a moment
she toyed with the idea of mailing them off to her
sister later, but then she remembered the sorrow in
Lil's eyes earlier today.

Dang. She'd have to go get them. She hurried to
the deck, deposited the box on the table, trotted back
inside, and grabbed her purse. "I'll be back in a sec.
Something I forgot."

Her sisters exchanged a look, sure they'd guessed
her predicament.

"Not much gift selection at the Pit Stop, Mari,"
Alcea called after her on a laugh.

Mari didn't pause to retort. If she stepped on it, she could make it to Sycamore and back within forty minutes.

Twenty-five minutes later, she rocketed down the drive from Camp Sycamore, Kenny Chesney belting it out on the radio. She put up a hand to shield her eyes. Damn, she wished she'd remembered her sunglasses. The sun flicked through the trees like a strobe light hitting a disco ball. Proving a simple matter to retrieve, the sketchbook lay on the seat beside her. She'd yanked to a halt in front of the art cabin and, after a quick rummage around inside, had found it among the drawings from a self-portrait exercise Finney had led the kids on last week. Since the art cabin was only halfway down the drive and not near the main hall, she hadn't seen a soul.

The Cabrio rattled its objections to her speed as she serpentined between potholes. Hit one of those babies and they might have to send in a search party. Glancing at her watch, she turned without a pause onto the lake road. If she was back at the cabin in fifteen minutes, she'd have another hour to frame at least one sketch with matte board before everyone congregated for ice cream and cake. She'd mount the other sketches later.

She rounded a curve, and the sketchbook slid across the seat. Cursing, she reached over to catch it before it dropped to the floor. Then she looked up. In front of the car, a figure nearly camouflaged by the light glancing off her windshield threw up its arms and dove for a ditch. She slammed on the brakes. "Omigod!"

Gravel scrunched as the Cabrio's wheels fought for purchase and finally found it. She threw the car into park, leaped out, and dashed to the side of the road. Someone crouched in a ditch amid sprays of wild orange daylilies and tall grasses. Oh, *God.* Michael.

"Are you okay?" She scrambled down to join him, her voice several octaves higher than usual. She knew she hadn't—*thank God, thank God*—hit him, but as still as he was, maybe he'd sprained an ankle or something when he'd jumped.

But after glancing around and registering that it was her, Michael rose easily, slid the wallet he must have lost on his tumble into a saddlebag-sized pocket, then swooped to pick up something small that winked brightly before he pocketed it, too. Maybe some coins; maybe a lighter. She hoped he hadn't taken up smoking, but now wasn't the time to address it.

"I'm fine. I just— *Shit*, Aunt Mari." He brushed himself off with choppy movements.

"Yep, that's almost what I just did, too." The feeble joke didn't sound very funny—not surprising considering how badly her voice was shaking. "I'm *so* sorry." She felt him all over. "Does everything still work? I was in a hurry and I wasn't paying attention and . . . What are you doing out here anyway?"

Michael shrugged off her hands. "I was just taking a walk. It's quiet time and we get to do what we want." He tugged down his T-shirt.

She reached out to straighten it, too, just for good measure. "Off the grounds and out of Steve's eyeshot? That's allowed?" She doubted it.

He hesitated only the barest moment, then shrugged again. "The grounds are boring. I've seen everything. So I walked up to the road. So what? I'll get some points knocked off for disappearing, but I'll just say I fell asleep someplace." His eyes narrowed at her. "Unless you tell."

"I don't care what you were doing as long as you're all right." Ignoring his stiffness, she hugged him and aimed for jocularity. "Because if I'd flattened *you*, Lil would flatten *me*, and then—" Abruptly she let him go and started clambering out of the ditch. "Shi— shoot—*Lil*. I've got to get back to the cabin."

Michael didn't move. "Lil's at the cabin? Dad and Melanie, too?"

"Yeah, the whole O'Malley clan has—" At the top of the ditch, she halted, wondering if she'd *ever* learn to keep her mouth shut. Slowly she turned around. Michael's expression was bleak. She held out her hand. "Come on, I'll take you back to camp."

He shook his head. "The next activity isn't for an hour."

"But I can't just leave you out here wandering the road. Come on, be a sport and come with me. I'll tell them I found you sleeping in the art cabin."

"I want to walk back."

She could tell by the obstinate look in his eyes that he planned to do whatever he felt like the moment she left. And with that expression in his eyes, she wondered if that included returning to camp at all.

She frowned, then threw caution to the winds. "Ah, hell. Want to go see your family? Or at least Lil and Melanie. Your dad's out fishing." And Andy, thank God. There would be hell to pay if he found out. She'd have to swear everyone to secrecy.

"Sweet." His face lit up, but there was a sly cast, and she wondered what had excited him more—the idea of seeing his family or screwing the camp establishment.

Oh, who cared? It wouldn't hurt anyone. Every boy deserved a little mischief, and as far as pranks went this one was lame. She'd have him back here before anyone knew.

She walked over to the Cabrio and opened the door. "Your chariot awaits."

When they arrived at the cabin, she parked at the top of the drive where they were still hidden by trees and told Michael to wait. On the drive over, she'd deduced the fewer O'Malleys who knew of Michael's quick visit, the better. No way would the youngest ones keep quiet, nor—she thought of Zinnia—would the oldest. Especially not the oldest. She hated leaving

Rose out, since she was Michael's best friend, but had decided it would be wiser if she clued in only Lil and Melanie, hustled them up to the car, and swore them to secrecy before unveiling her prize. Lil would be overjoyed.

And at first Lil did seem thrilled. While Mari, feeling magnanimous, stood a polite distance away, Lil hugged Michael to her so hard Mari was afraid he'd burst at the seams. Continually touching his face, Lil talked with him for a few minutes. Watching them, Mari felt smug. She'd always known Sycamore should give the kids more freedom. This little meeting hadn't hurt a thing. But then Lil announced she'd fetch Michael some cake while Melanie took a turn hugging her brother, and Mari knew by the way her sister stalked toward her that Lil probably didn't share the same opinion. Before she could sidestep out of Lil's reach, her sister had grabbed her arm and dragged her toward the cabin.

"What in the world were you thinking?" Lil hissed when they stopped out of Michael's earshot. "You've broken every rule in the book. Worst of all, you've encouraged Michael to do the same thing. If he gets caught, he'll—"

"He won't get caught." Mari wrenched her arm away. "I'll have him back before—"

"Plus you've put me in a position of having to keep something from Jon and the rest of the family. And I—" Lil's voice was actually shaking.

"Jes—geez, Lil." Mari rubbed her arm. "Get a grip. It's not like I broke him out of prison."

"—and I won't do it."

Mari stilled. "What? You'd get Michael in trouble because he came to see you? I thought you'd *want* to see him."

"I *did* want to see him. I *do*. All the time. But not like this. I'm not suggesting we tell Kirk or Dr. Everheart, although that's what *should* happen. But the last thing I need is another barrier between Michael and me. If Michael got punished, he'd blame *me,* even though it would be your fault—*and* his for going along with you. But I can't and won't keep this a secret from Jon. I won't ask Mel to keep it a secret, either. From anyone."

"But if Andy finds out, they might not let me volunteer at Sycamore! And I want to go back." By God, she really and truly did. For those three mornings last week, her work with the boys had absorbed her. So much so that she'd forgotten her own problems. And, wow, that was saying a lot.

"Maybe you should have thought of that sooner. And maybe you *shouldn't* go back to Sycamore. This isn't a game. Michael needs to learn his actions have consequences." Lil's eyes shot blue fire. "And it sure doesn't look like he'll learn that from you."

Lil turned on her heel and headed into the cabin. Mari watched her, mouth gaping. Lil *couldn't* tell. But knowing her straitlaced, play-by-the-rules sister, Mari knew Lil could. And would. She'd been an idiot to think otherwise.

She sank onto a boulder and dropped her chin in her fists, her mind churning with how she'd ever explain this to Andy.

Chapter 15

Monday morning, before dawn was more than a few minutes old, before Zinnia could pound her walking stick, and before anyone could tell her she couldn't wear it anymore, Mari had shrugged into her Camp Sycamore T-shirt. She'd realized yesterday during her, uh, *talk* with Lil that the most unfashionable thing in her wardrobe had become more important to her than her Shelli Segal embroidered jacket. And she was determined to keep it on.

She glanced at her watch. There was still over an hour before it was time to leave for camp, and she didn't want to run the risk of encountering her parents before then. No telling what her mother had in mind—maybe roping her to a chair to prevent her return. Zinnia had been appalled at Mari's "butting into other people's business." Mari hmphed. Like butting in wasn't an inherited trait?

Mentally running through the excuses she'd give Andy about her escapade yesterday, she tiptoed upstairs to grab a glass of juice, started the coffeepot, and set out her mother's favorite mug. Back in the cellar, she dumped a load of sheets in the washer. Then wondered why she was being so nice. Maybe she thought a few brownie points would deflect her mother's disappointment in her. Like that had ever worked?

She set the detergent box down with a thump. She was in hot water up to her eyeballs, and she knew it. But she still didn't understand why all the big whoop-de-doo over a minor infraction of the rules. Gads, she hated rules. While the washer chugged, she slipped outside through the sleeping porch and pulled up a lawn chair to watch the sun rise. The sky was old-fashioned lavender overlaid with a doily of pink-edged clouds.

When she'd arrived back at the cabin after dropping off Michael (just for the record: in plenty of time for him to make it back to his quarters before anyone knew he'd left), everyone was bustling to depart, loading up their cars while little Missouri chased Lily around the clearing. But despite all the activity, Mari could tell they all knew what she'd done. She could see it in the stern look Jon gave her, hear it in the snap of her mother's voice and in the doleful note that underwrote Pop's. Alcea had shaken her head in a gesture that said Mari was hopeless, and Patsy Lee's doe eyes had held such disappointment, Mari had wanted to poke them out. As for Lil, she hadn't even said good-bye.

In fact, except for Zinnia, who could be counted on to never stifle an opinion, nobody had said anything. Nobody had uttered one word of censure.

Maybe because Andy had been casting such black looks in her direction, they'd figured she was done for anyway.

She took a sip of her coffee. Somewhere over the shoulder of the cabin, the sun topped the hills and the lavender paled to blue.

Knowing she couldn't escape Andy forever, but also knowing it wasn't a bad idea to give him time to cool down, in the flurry of her family's departures near twilight, she'd slipped away. The grounds were vast, wooded, and she knew any number of places to wander unseen. So she'd grabbed a tote, loaded it with a sketchbook, a box of pastels, a can of soda and another of bug repellent, and had done just that: wandered. From a seat in the Cobalt boat to a log on a promontory; for a walk on the road, a ribbon of gray in the fading light, to a concrete perch on a boat ramp. She'd stayed there—not having any more luck capturing the evening blush with her pastels than she had lately with her acrylics—until a fat moon hung in the night sky almost straight overhead. Oh, Andy had tried to find her. She'd heard him call, sounding angry enough to rip her head off. No fool she, she'd waited a long while after his voice quit bouncing off the hills across the cove before she'd tiptoed back to her sleeping porch, somewhere around midnight, reconnoitering the place first to make sure he wasn't lying in wait.

She took another sip of coffee. Call her a coward, but she was a coward still in one piece.

The washer quit chugging. She set her mug on an upended bucket and ducked back into the cellar to fill the laundry basket. Lil's words actually *had* penetrated her thick skull yesterday. And there was even a small—very small—chance that Lil was right. But, really—she dumped the sheets into the basket—she just didn't see that what she'd done was such a big deal. Nobody in her family would have done anything different if they'd seen that bereft look that had crossed Michael's face as he'd stood in the ditch. Dammit, even *Andy* would have done the same thing.

After tossing a handful of clothespins after the sheets, she carted the basket down to a line strung along the water's edge. Sticking a clothespin between her teeth, she shook out a sheet and stuck one corner over the line, careful to avoid the clematis (she was becoming quite the botanist hanging around Andy) that wound around netting hung from the cross-poles at either end. The large violet flowers had a neon glow in the early light.

"Are we done playing hide-and-seek?"

Nearly swallowing the clothespin, she whirled around.

Leaning his back against a tree, arms crossed, Andy eyed her with a level gaze that definitely lacked humor. "Pretty mature behavior, Mar."

She turned her back so he couldn't see her flush and clipped up the fabric. Suddenly all the excuses she'd drummed up for what she'd done seemed beyond lame. "I didn't think you were in any condition last night to listen to reason," she finally said in a prim voice.

"You want to tell me what was so *reasonable* about your actions?"

She poked up another corner. "Quit talking to me like I'm a three-year-old."

"Then quit acting like one."

How original. She'd seen that response coming from a mile away.

Andy pushed off the tree, stalked forward, and grabbed her arm. "Don't roll your eyes at me, Mari O'Malley. We aren't in high school anymore. What you did with Michael wasn't a funny little prank. It could have—and still might have—some serious consequences."

"Let go of me, and let me explain." Mari yanked away. "It wasn't like I planned what happened. I went to get some sketches I'd done of Michael for Lil. On my way back, I almost ran him down on the lake road and—"

"What was he doing on the lake road?"

Shit. "Taking a walk. It was quiet time. He wasn't doing anything wrong."

"Right. He was probably running cigarettes for Damon."

"Running—what are you talking about?" She remembered seeing Michael slip something into his back pocket. She'd thought it was his wallet. Cigarettes?

"Never mind." Andy folded his arms again. He looked so pompous, she wanted to slap him. "Go on."

"I came so close to hitting him, he actually dove into a ditch to—"

"Hide."

"No! To keep the car from plowing into him." She remembered how still Michael had been as he crouched in the ditch. "He was scared stiff—"

"That someone would see him."

"Would you *stop* that?" Mari dragged in a breath, trying to keep her anger under control. "And when I said the family was all at the cabin—"

"Why in the hell did you tell him that?"

"It just . . . slipped out. I wasn't thinking."

"Are you *ever* thinking?"

She blinked against the tears that suddenly spouted. She *really* didn't like having Andy mad at her. "Of course I *think*. But I, well, I just said something, and he looked so crushed, I couldn't just leave him there. I told him to go back, but I could tell he wouldn't. So what else was I supposed to do? I mean, hell—heck, what would *you* have done?"

"I would have taken myself down to Sycamore, rounded up a youth care provider or Kirk, and told them to go get him."

Her tears dried up. She stared at him. "You wouldn't do that. You wouldn't snitch on a friend and get him in trouble. When did Andy Eppelwaite turn into such a prig?"

"It's not a matter of snitching." His teeth clenched. "These kids are *not* my pals. I love them, maybe too much, but I'm there to take care of them. Not be their best friend. *You* are there to take care of them, too. And egging them on in the wrong direction is not doing them a favor."

"Would you get off it? Like what I did will damage Michael forever?" If she was the spitting type, she would have spit. "Shi—shoot—it's not going to damage him at all." She bent to pick up another sheet.

"Except now he has the idea that if he plays the

right hand, you'll fold. It's manipulation, just like I told you before."

"And so what if it is?" In three sharp movements, she pinned up the next sheet. "I took him to see his stepmom and sister, not on a heist. It probably did him good." She turned to face him, hands on her hips. "Camp Sycamore has all those boys so shackled, they can't pee unless the rules say pee. Kids need some freedom, you know. Maybe all this manipulation you talk about is because *they* know that, even if *you* don't. What's going on at Sycamore just isn't"—she looked for a term he'd relate to—"healthy."

"Healthy?" He stared at her, face incredulous.

Good, maybe she'd given him some food for thought. "So, you see, I do have their best interests in mind. And even though I don't agree with all the rules, I promise not to break them again." She took a deep breath. "So will you let me go back? Or are you going to snitch on me to Kirk like you would on Michael?" She'd thrown down a gauntlet. They'd *never* told on each other before.

Emotions battled for control of his face. Incredulity, a flash of anger, exasperation . . . and it finally all slid into resignation. "No, I won't tell on you," he muttered. "But I *would* like to turn you over my knee."

She felt a surge of triumph. "Interesting idea."

That tore a reluctant grin from him. "Come on." He gestured. "Get your sheets up, and let's take off. Finney and I need to be in early for a meeting."

"But how will I get back if I don't take my car? I finish a good five hours before you do."

"Finney can drive your car." He started up the hill toward the guesthouse, then turned back to look at her, all traces of smile gone. "Because you and I need to have a little talk."

Her self-satisfaction wavered.

*   *   *

Less than a half hour later, ears still ringing from the lecture Andy had poured into them during the entire drive to Camp Sycamore, Mari found herself unceremoniously dumped in front of the greenhouse. Along with a forty-pound bag of potting soil and instructions to haul it inside. Following Finncy in Mari's Cabrio—and without looking back—Andy had steered his truck down the hill to the main hall for the meeting.

Trying not to grumble—after all, this was pretty paltry punishment and she was still here, wasn't she?—Mari half-dragged, half-carried the bag toward the door. Snippets of their conversation as they'd rolled down the lake road replayed in her head, despite her efforts to shut them off. Andy was so damn certain about *everything*, it was driving her nuts.

On the rules: "The rules aren't there because someone likes rules. They're there because these boys grew up—whether for one year, five, six, or more—without being able to count on a thing. At places like Vreeley Home and Sycamore, they know, without a doubt, that each of their actions has a result—good or bad. When they follow a rule, they earn points. And with every point, a little more self-worth. When you help Michael break a rule, it only confuses the hell out of . . ."

Yadda-yadda-yadda. She *got* it, okay?

On manipulation, Andy had waxed eloquent, telling her again that it was a learned art: "Take Damon for instance. He's one bright kid, smart as all get-out, works his points, and is leaps ahead of the rest in levels. But don't let him fool you. He's never had that breakthrough we look for—that point where he hunkers down and really works on his problems." Andy had paused. "And he has some real doozies to work through."

"Like what?" she'd asked.

But, of course, he'd refused to say, pleading the

need for confidentiality and all that other rot she'd heard before. Who did he think she'd tell, for God's sake?

And then more on the rules, always the rules: "The rules are also there to protect you and everyone else. Nobody at Sycamore is a real danger to anyone— mostly. But, Mari, you can't forget that quite a few of these boys once landed in some pretty hot water."

Okay, maybe some had been involved in . . . oh, gang activity or thievery or vandalism or something. But most were probably guilty of no more than a Michael-style joyride. Otherwise they'd be in jail, not committed to the great outdoors. Brother.

He'd continued in that pedantic tone he'd adopted, reminding her of their old high school science teacher. "But you don't need to worry about safety—"

She wasn't.

"—the boys that came to Sycamore from Vreeley Home are tough cases, but all of them had to earn the right to come here, to prove they could socialize with boys with lesser emotional problems, like Michael, without losing their cool. Most will make the transition back to the real world within the next two years, maybe less. Camp is another step in their progress, which has so far been successful." Andy had paused again. "Damon might be an exception to that. But he made the grade, so we had to let him come. And Damon—well, he's more a danger to himself than anyone else."

She'd wondered about that last comment, but of course, Andy had once more grown tight-lipped when she'd pressed him for details.

Reaching the greenhouse entrance, Mari dropped the bag and paused to catch her breath. She'd also wondered about his comment that Michael had *lesser emotional problems*. She assumed that meant that the abuse Michael had suffered hadn't been as bad as what some of the other boys had experienced. Or maybe it was just that Michael's hadn't lasted as long as some of the rest. Well, she was no Mary Sunshine, so she could have figured that out if she'd thought about it. And now that she had, it bothered her. A lot. But . . .

She was also curious. Damn, she wished Andy weren't such a stickler for all that privacy stuff.

Holding the door open with her hip, she picked up the bag by two corners and swung it inside. Stepping in after it, she stopped at the sight of Malloy standing near a table filled with flats of flowers and one big clay pot. Dirt dusted his hands. The greenhouse should be empty—the boys weren't scheduled to arrive until after breakfast, in another hour.

The husky sixteen-year-old flushed, blue eyes wide. "Hullo, Miss Mari. I wasn't hungry so I thought I'd come up here and get started, but I really wouldn't have if I'd known Mr. Andy wouldn't be here yet, because I know the rules say I'm supposed to stay with someone if—"

"Bugger the rules," Mari muttered.

"Huh?" Malloy's freckles stood out like tiny pale pockmarks on his round red face.

"I mean, just go on with what you were doing. Mr. Andy will be here in a few minutes." She waved him back to his flowers.

The tension easing out of his shoulders, he gave her a grin and shoved his hands back into the soil.

She moved closer to see. Big hands working inside the pot, he was mixing some—she tilted her head to read the label on a bag of white stuff—vermiculite into the dirt. Despite the large hands, his movements were delicate, and enthusiasm flattered his homely face.

"What's next when you're through with that?" she asked.

He motioned at the array of color and greenery lined up in the flats. "Mr. Andy said we could each choose about six of those plants and make our own arrangements. Mine's going in front of Cabin Three," he said proudly.

Mari nodded. Everyone in the horticulture group would undoubtedly have a flowerpot displayed in a public location, just like the murals the art group had started on Friday would end up gracing the cafeteria walls. Every accomplishment was exhibited and admired.

Malloy continued puttering. Mari leaned against another table and watched him. Andy had explained that gardening often reduced anxiety because of the absorption it required, which, therapeutically, made a person with their hands in the dirt more approachable.

She wet her lips. "Do you like it here, Malloy?" She kept the question casual. She didn't know if she should even ask, but she didn't see why not. When Malloy's shoulders stayed relaxed, she decided she hadn't blundered.

"Yes, ma'am, I do. The bus ride here was fun—I ain't never, I mean, haven't ever been on a bus. But I like it back at Vreeley Home, too."

Never been on a bus? "How long have you been at Vreeley?"

He scrunched his nose, considering. "About four years now. It was my first home."

Malloy considered a residence hall at a boys' facility a *home*? "You mean the first place you felt at home?"

"Well, that." He reached for a salmon-colored geranium. "But it was my first *real* home. Oh, I had another one, when I was really little, but I don't remember it. It was before my ma died. She died when I was about four."

"Oh, I'm so sorry."

Malloy just shrugged. "I don't remember much about her either."

Poor child. "Where did you live after that?"

He tipped the geranium upside down, carefully supporting the base of the flower with a couple of fingers. "In the streets." His reply was matter-of-fact, but it was like a lightbulb had dimmed behind his eyes.

"At four?" She couldn't help the shock in her voice. "All by yourself?"

He shook his head. "Not all the time. I had some people who took me to stay with them. Off and on."

The shadow had deepened on his face, and she decided she'd asked enough questions. "Oh. That's good." *Off and on?* Where had he been between times?

"No, it wasn't good." He shook his head again, slowly. "They wasn't—I mean, weren't—good people." The tug he gave to release the plant wasn't as gentle as his earlier movements. "They . . . hurt me."

Part of her wondered how he'd been hurt; another part really didn't want to know. She was glad when his face brightened.

"But I'll never forget that first night at Vreeley." He pushed the plant roots into the soil, his movements again careful. "It was the first night I had my own bed. And the first time that I wasn't a-scared to fall asleep."

He'd been twelve. Twelve before he'd fallen asleep without fear. Mari felt the prick of tears. She just wanted to take this big kid into her arms and hold him. And she might have, if Andy's voice hadn't stopped her.

"Nice job, Malloy."

She started. She hadn't heard him enter, didn't know how long he'd been listening. Grinning at the praise, Malloy looked over at Andy, who crossed the room and laid a hand on the boy's shoulder. "What else you planning to add to that pot?"

Malloy nodded his head at a cluster of small plants with tiny ultramarine blue flowers so iridescent they looked like they'd glow in the dark. "That lobelia and an asparagus fern." He looked proud of his use of the proper names.

"Good combination of color and foliage." Andy squeezed Malloy's shoulder. "But you know you aren't supposed to be up here before breakfast is over."

The boy's face fell. "I know."

"And I know you were just excited about getting started and didn't mean any harm. But you know the rules—I'll have to dock you some points. You'll maybe have to sit out that movie tonight."

Malloy frowned, then shrugged. "That's okay. But can I still finish my flowerpot?"

Andy smiled. "Of course. And maybe—just maybe—if I like it enough, you'll get those points back. But if I'm feeling stingy, you just volunteer for more time working on the cabin repairs. I hear you wield one mean belt-sander."

"I like working with stuff like that."

"It shows." Andy glanced over at Mari, then back at Malloy. "Do you mind finishing up outside, though? I need to talk to Miss Mari."

Beaming, Malloy gathered up his pot and headed outside. Without looking at her, Andy picked up an empty flat, filled it with the plants Malloy had selected, and followed. Mari hoisted her rear up on a table. Legs dangling, she tried not to think about Malloy. Alone, afraid, no home . . .

Then Andy returned. The gentleness she'd seen on his face while he'd talked to Malloy was gone. He looked grim.

Mari let out a long-suffering sigh. "What have I done now?"

"You don't know?" Andy looked like he was about to pull his hair out. "What did I tell you all the way up here this morning? When you discover a kid breaking the rules, you need to report it."

"You mean Malloy? For Pete's sake! He was just here a few minutes early. No need to get out the rubber hoses."

"The rules aren't in place just for them. They're also in place to protect *you*."

The rules again. *God.* "From *Malloy*? That sweet, gentle boy?"

"Granted, Malloy's come a long way, but he still has further to go or he'd already be out of Vreeley. Dammit, Mari, you're not trained to handle certain situations. Anything can happen."

She scoffed. "Like what?"

"When he was *ten*, that *sweet, gentle boy* tried to kill another kid."

Chapter 16

For the rest of the morning, while she mixed paints, handed out supplies, and cleaned up messes, Mari stewed over what she'd learned—and *not* learned—from Andy about Malloy. Kids had filtered into the greenhouse and art cabin immediately on the heels of his pronouncement, so she'd had to swallow her questions.

Oh, well. She couldn't have dug another scrap of dirt out of Andy anyway. From the way he'd clamped his lips together, she knew he already regretted telling her that one tidbit. Good *God*. Malloy had tried to *kill* someone? When he was *ten*? It must have been self-defense. Or an accident. There must have been some kind of—what did they call them?—*extenuating circumstances*.

She was dying to know what they were.

When she'd tried to wheedle more out of Andy, he'd pulled "Policy" out of his hat again. And apparently "Policy" read, *Volunteers shalt not be privy to squat*. The therapists did have access to the boys' case histories; Andy read them, Finney didn't. Apparently she wanted to avoid preconceptions. Like the YCPs, whose access to the files was limited, Finney preferred to rely on the boys' counselors, like Dr. Everheart, to tell her whatever was essential for her to know about each boy.

So Finney probably didn't know the details surrounding Malloy's past. Not that Mari would ask her,
anyway. The way the woman eyed her, she knew
Andy had dropped a word of warning about her into
the art therapist's ear. Nope, she'd find out nothing
there.

By noon, her curiosity had reached fever pitch,
joined by a niggle of alarm for Michael. If that's what
Malloy had done, what about the other kids who had
come here from Vreeley Home? Specifically, what
about *Damon*? Andy suspected Michael did Damon's
bidding. What if Damon was coercing him? Was Michael in danger?

Get real, she chided herself. If Michael really felt
threatened, he'd report it . . . wouldn't he? Remembering her nephew's dark comment, she felt her concerns balloon: *You don't know* everything *that goes on.*

In the main hall before lunch, she and Finney
ducked into the ladies' restroom to scrub off remnants
of a free-form painting exercise. Finney was chatty,
pumped that one of the boys, thin, quiet David, had
finally unburdened some concerns during the group
discussion.

Mari spotted opportunity. "So will you write a report for David's psychologist?"

Finney grabbed a paper towel and nodded. "Nothing formal, though. We—the therapists—don't take
clinical notes at every session; we just report our observations to the boys' counselors if we think they're
important." Frowning, she paused. "I'll also need to
write up something on Damon. In fact, once it's dry,
I'll put Damon's painting into his file for Dr. Everheart to see. Maybe he can get something out of him
about it. I sure couldn't."

Using a minimum of red and black slashes, Damon
had depicted a bunch of people, with one figure isolated from the others. The stark bleakness of his painting had done nothing to reassure Mari. "I don't think

it takes a psychology degree to see he's feeling lonely or separate or something."

"No," Finney agreed. "But all his other artwork has been bland to the point of boring. Usually he hides his feelings. So why this particular picture at this particular time? It could mean he's reaching a crossroads. Or headed for a crisis."

Mari shrugged. The whole process—how art was used for everything from rapport-building to understanding the boys' self-perceptions—intrigued her, but that wasn't what she was interested in now.

"Those files must be inches thick," she said casually, yanking a towel from the roll. "Or are they all computerized?"

Finney smiled. "Figuratively speaking, they *are* inches thick. Especially if the child went through intensive therapy."

"So the files *are* all on a com—" Finney's last words registered. "Wait. I thought *all* the kids were in therapy."

"They are, but we have a special dorm at Vreeley for the kids who are victims of things like sexual abuse. They go through intensive therapy during their first months with us."

God. She supposed on some level she'd known some of them must have experienced that horror, but it hadn't really hit home. She swallowed hard. Those particular kids must have a ton of anger to deal with— and what did that mean for Michael?

Finding out more about the boys he'd befriended took on increased urgency. "It must be difficult to maintain all that secrecy Andy says the Privacy Act requires. Hackers, you know." How could she get someone's password? She was no Mata Hari.

"Hackers?" Finney snorted. "Most of the paperwork is still that—paper. Not only does lack of funds keep us from upgrading our software, but where would we find time to enter it all? Kirk just keeps the files in his office and makes sure the door stays locked." She held the door open. "Coming?"

"Uh, sure." Mari shoved her towel in the trash can and followed Finney. Before she entered the cafeteria, she took a gander at Kirk's office door. It was closed. Probably locked. And she'd bet the only thing that opened it was the key Kirk always wore around his neck. *Dang*.

But fortune decided to smile on her. Or so she thought before she caught a look at those files.

In the cafeteria, she grabbed an apple and sandwich before joining Andy. Seated by himself, he was examining the day's schedule. When she pulled up a chair, he smiled and tweaked her nose. "Do you want to stick around this afternoon for the group recreation activity?"

"And that would be . . . ?"

"A canoe trip."

"Sounds fun. Sunburn. Sore muscles." She picked up the apple and bit off a chunk. "You'll have to do some pretty fast talking to convince me," she mumbled around a full mouth.

"Hmm. Everyone's going. We won't be gone that long. About two hours." He smiled his crinkled-eyes smile. "And you won't notice the heat or the pain because you're so besotted with me."

"Besotted? Hmph." Although spending the rest of the day with him, even under those conditions, was tempting. Maybe she would—

A thought struck her.

The camp would be deserted. Her heart sped up as she wondered what kind of lock-picking skills she could develop within a couple hours. She darted a look at Andy. If he knew what she was thinking, he'd not only kick her out of Sycamore, but all the way to the moon. "Well . . . Oh, *shoot*. I don't have a swimsuit with me." Thank God. Andy's face fell, and she added, "But I'll stick around and wait for you. I can . . . keep an eye on things. Do some sketching." She gave him a bright smile.

He frowned and opened his mouth, but Finney picked that moment to waltz up, bless her. "Rita wants our help porting the canoes to the shore. I'm changing into my suit in the ladies'. Steve said you could use Cabin One, Andy, since the boys are already done."

Still frowning at Mari, Andy hesitated.

Mari put on her most innocent face and waved a hand. "You go on. I'll just finish my lunch and grab my sketchbook." She took another bite of apple.

After another pause, Andy finally left. As he walked off, Mari thought she heard him mumbling to himself.

As soon as he was gone, she stuffed the rest of her lunch in the trash, headed for the art cabin, picked up her drawing materials, and returned to the main hall, where she loitered on a bench out front, sketchbook open on her lap. Gears meshed in her head. It might be easy. There was a chance that Kirk would leave and forget to lock his office door. Or, if that didn't happen, there was also a chance she could pick the lock. She sighed. Yeah, a *fat* chance. What a brilliant plan.

Finney let herself out of the main hall. No red bikini today, just a modest black tank suit. Kirk emerged almost immediately after her, also dressed in swim gear. The director cast Mari a puzzled look, probably wondering what she was still doing there, but shrugged his square shoulders when she bent over her sketchbook and scribbled wildly. Out of the corner of her eye, she saw him lock the door to the main hall. Then drop the key on its chain back under his shirt. So much for Plan A. She slumped back on the bench. And now Plan B was even more complicated. There were *two* locks to pick.

Wait a minute. Mari straightened and stared straight

ahead. Finney hadn't said she'd ask *Kirk* to put Damon's painting in his file. She'd said *she'd* do it. She'd
bet Finney had a key. And Andy. Probably the counselors, too. They'd need access to the files, wouldn't
they? Of course they would.

"That's interesting."

She jumped as Finney's voice sounded right beside
her, then looked down at the sketchbook in her lap.
Her drawing was a mess of nothing. She slammed the
book shut. "I was just warming up," she said. Her
gaze moved to the bag Finney had hooked over her
shoulder. "I'm sticking around while you're out there.
Do you want me to watch your purse?"

"Thanks, Mari, but no. I'll put it in Rita's locker
down by the docks."

Her shoulders slumped. Nice try; no cigar.

Finney angled to get a glimpse of Mari's watch, then
looked across the drive. "And they say *women* take
forever to get dressed."

Mari's eyes followed Finney's to Cabin One, where,
inside, Andy was changing. Her brain started churning
again. She'd bet he'd leave the contents of his pockets
behind. After all, he wouldn't chance something ending up on the bottom of the lake. Something like, say,
his ring of keys. But he wouldn't leave them in Cabin
One—too much temptation if one of the kids returned
before he did. And he wouldn't have time to climb
the drive to secrete them in a supply cabinet in the
greenhouse with everyone waiting. And Kirk had already locked up the main hall and disappeared down
the path to the lake. . . .

She smiled. Gee, good thing she was here.

At that moment, Andy stepped out the door and
their eyes met. His brows snapped together, and she
wiped the smile off her face. Still frowning, he turned
up the drive.

"Andy," Finney called. "You don't have time—
everyone else is already at the cove."

"It'll just be a minute. I need to stick this stuff in my truck." He held up his wallet. A ring of keys dangled from a finger.

It was Mari's cue. Feeling very Mata Hari–like, she rose, glided down the steps, over to Andy, and batted her eyes. "I'll take care of them for you."

His eyes narrowed.

Hers widened. "Don't you trust me?"

"Andy . . ." Finney nodded toward the path Kirk had taken.

Andy hesitated another moment, then sighed and dropped his wallet—and a big fat set of keys—into Mari's hands. He leaned down to whisper in her ear. "I don't know what you're up to, but I know it's something."

Mari only smiled demurely.

His frown deepened until you could almost get lost in the crevices, but Finney beckoned again—really, God *bless* her—and he had no choice.

After they'd headed off, Mari tucked his wallet in her pocket, then moved around to the back of the building where she had a view of the lake. She took a seat on a stone wall and twirled the key ring around a finger. Soon, one by one, the canoes appeared. She took a head count and waited another four beats until they'd all glided out of sight. Reassured that she was now alone, she hopped down and trotted back to the front. Even though Andy had said the trip would be two hours, they were late starting off, so she'd limit herself to thirty minutes tops with the files. *If* she was right about the keys.

She was. After fumbling around with a half dozen on Andy's ring, a brass key slid right into place and she slipped through the main entrance, closing the door behind her.

The main hall felt weird—too quiet, too dim. She shivered. Too cool. The only light filtered through the frosted window of the office door, forming a milk

white square on the floor. She approached and tried
the key. As she'd thought it would, it turned easily.
She stepped inside, leaving the door cracked so she
could hear if anyone came in the main entrance, and
looked around. A lump of a chair crouched behind an
old wooden desk, a couple of others stood straight-
backed for guests, and photos of past summers at Sycamore papered the walls, most shots of the backs of
kids' heads or taken at such a distance that nobody
was recognizable. (The Privacy Act had dictated that
nothing identifying the residents could be displayed.)
Her gaze moved to a computer table topped by an
ancient PC. And then on to two four-drawer filing
cabinets.

She glanced at her watch. Five minutes had already
passed. She hurried to the first filing cabinet, yanked
at the top drawer, and nearly pulled her arm out of
its socket. Damn. It was locked. Rubbing her shoulder,
she thought. Kirk carried only *one* key. She tried the
brass one to no avail, then looked around. There must
be another, it must be in here, and spartan as the
office was, there weren't that many places to hide it.
Hastily, she hunted—nothing in the desk, nothing
taped beneath the chairs. She felt along the top of the
windowsill. *Voilà!* Nancy Drew had nothing on her.
She unlocked the cabinet and pulled open the drawer.

Manila files, some two inches thick, fit tightly inside
hanging folders, all of them alphabetized—by last
names she didn't know. Groaning at the waste of time,
she ran through the tabs but didn't spot the first names
she wanted. She slammed that drawer shut, opened
the next one, and repeated the process. Eureka. There
were Damon (Underwood) and Malloy (Young). She
yanked them out and grabbed Michael's file for
good measure.

Without examining the names, she set two files on
the corner of the desk, perched on the guest chair,
and studied the one in her lap. It was Malloy's and

looked innocuous enough—too innocuous to warrant the shiver that ran up her back.

Slowly she opened it up, blinking in surprise at the photograph stapled inside the cover. It must have been taken when Malloy had arrived at Vreeley when he was around twelve. There was no gentle smile. No eager eyes. No round face. His hair was greasy and tousled, his eyes dead, his cheeks thin.

She rifled through the papers, finally pulling out a sheaf that said ADMITTING REPORT. She skimmed it, skipping over the psychological terms describing emotional problems she didn't understand. Her eyes slowed over a section labeled HISTORY. Like Malloy had already told her, he'd existed under society's radar, basically homeless from age four to ten, no formal schooling, unable to read. He'd been shuffled around— Her grip tightened on the pages. Oh, geez. He'd been shuffled around by *gang members*. They'd adopted him like some pet dog, and once he was old enough—good God, *six*!—they'd had him run drugs. She looked up, considering. Her education on this matter was supplied by *NYPD Blue,* but she'd heard of that practice. A six-year-old caught with drugs got off lightly compared to older cohorts. She returned to reading. Midway through the section was the incident Andy had mentioned.

At age ten, in mid-January, Malloy had taken a knife and slashed a boy walking to school. Her eyes bugged. Not in self-defense. Not by accident. Malloy had explained to the police he'd done it only because the boy was about his size, his feet were cold, and he'd simply wanted the boy's shoes. Shaken, Mari sat back. To the young Malloy, his act wasn't immoral; it was survival. Fortunately, the boy had lived. Malloy had been placed in juvenile detention then sent to Vreeley Home two years later.

Mari slid the Admitting Report back, then glanced through a doctor's notes. Malloy had entered detention malnourished, with no vaccinations, no education, and a body scarred by beatings. The page blurred as she remembered Malloy's words. *They . . . hurt me.* She slapped the cover down on the file. They'd treated Malloy *worse* than a dog. And it had started when he was not much older than Florida's daughter, Missouri.

Stomach now in knots, she touched the other files and finally picked up Damon's. She pulled out the same reports and read. The seventeen-year-old had once lived with his mother and uncle in Camdenton, not many miles distant from Cordelia. At age eleven, he'd started a journey that began with a short stint in a state mental health facility, then led him through a series of foster homes. Deemed unmanageable by the foster parents who had tried to help him, Damon was referred to Vreeley four years ago.

Mari flipped the page, searching for the reason the state had taken him from his family in the first place. Her eyes stopped on a stark paragraph in the middle of the text. Family Services had removed him from the home after he'd started hemorrhaging in class and a school nurse had reported . . .

Omigod. Bile rose in her throat. Mind reeling, she shoved the papers back, grabbed the other files, and crammed them all in the drawer. Only sheer willpower preventing her from heaving, she rushed from the office and out the front door. She gulped in mouthfuls of air as she ran for the back of the building. In the forsythia bushes, she upchucked her lunch.

From the time Damon was six, he'd been regularly beaten and sodomized by his uncle. And his mother had *known.* She'd looked the other way in return for the crack her brother had supplied. And when Damon was ten, they'd turned him into a prostitute. Sitting in class—in his *elementary* school class—the rectal hemorrhaging that had led to his visit to the school nurse had probably ultimately saved his life.

Staring sightlessly across the lake where the sunlight

glanced off serrated waters, Mari inhaled one ragged breath after another. A breeze kicked a clump of wild-flowers near the water's edge and flung pollen around like gold dust. In a dim corner of her brain, she realized the canoes were returning. But she couldn't move.

She'd known all kinds of horror lurked in the world—everyone *knew*. But now the victims had faces. Damon's bright, false smile; Malloy's sincere, shy grin. Her mind ran through all the other young faces that were growing familiar, her mind skittering away from what terrors might have visited them before they'd arrived here. *Abuse. Abandonment.* Clinical terms, lacking in passion. Horrors cleaned up into something sounding palatable and impersonal. But the actuality *was* personal. It lurked nearby, reaching its insidious hands everywhere—including into the rural towns that she knew, touching hapless children in the guises of mothers and fathers and uncles. And falling on Damon and Malloy when they were just *babies*. Children who should have been enjoying a mother's kiss planted on their foreheads, a hug from their dads, children who should have spent their time climbing a tree and tossing a ball and bobbing for apples and finding presents under a Christmas tree. *Dammit.* They were *still* children. Denied all the things she'd experienced . . . and that she'd taken for granted.

She didn't know how long she stood frozen before she realized her face was wet. Hearing footfalls, she swiped her cheeks but didn't turn around. Warm hands fell on her shoulders, ran down her arms, extracted the key ring from her pocket. She didn't have to look to know who it was. Andy wrapped his arms around her, and she leaned back against him.

"How did you know?" Her voice was hoarse.

She felt his shrug. When he spoke, his voice was gentle, free of remonstrance, and it helped heat the chill in her heart. There was no mention of rules or

policy. She supposed he knew that he'd likely never
need to mention them again. "Finney told me you
were curious about the files. It didn't take a giant leap
to get from that to why you'd hung around after lunch
and volunteered to lock up my things. I also found
the office door unlocked and the files a jumble—I
straightened it all up. And . . ." He paused. "I knew,
just because I know you."

"I got sick."

"Understandable."

Staring at the water, they fell quiet.

Finally she stirred. "Have you read all of Damon's
history?"

"Yes."

"Why does he wear long sleeves all the time?"

There was a beat of silence. "He doesn't want anyone to see his scars." Rough emotion underwrote
Andy's voice.

"Scars?" she whispered. "From his uncle?"

"No . . . from himself. He's what we call a self-
harmer. He started carving up his arms when he was
eight."

Her niece Lily's age. Tears welled again. "Even with
what they did to him . . . How could anyone that
young try to kill himself?"

"People who self-mutilate usually aren't trying to
get rid of themselves—it's a form of psychological release. He hasn't done it in quite a while." Andy
smoothed back her hair from her forehead. "He's safe
now. They're all safe now. Except maybe from
themselves."

"And from bumblers like me."

Andy pulled her tight against his chest. She could
feel his heart beating between her shoulder blades. It
felt odd, but right. "Your intentions were never bad.
I can't remember a time when you couldn't drum up
some reason for whatever you did." There was a smile
in his voice.

She thought of Sean's wife, Jo. She'd tried to justify all that, until she just couldn't make excuses for herself anymore. "I don't belong here. I can't—"

"Take it? Ah, Mari. Each of these boys can break your heart. They break mine all the time. But I'm still here."

"You have a big heart; you can handle it," she murmured.

"And so can you. You have a bigger heart than you know."

She didn't think Jo would agree. Mari knew *she* didn't.

Claiming she wasn't feeling well—which was totally *not* a lie—Mari readily acquiesced to Finney's offer to do the dishes and excused herself early from supper that evening.

Concern in her eyes, Zinnia watched her, but when she opened her mouth, Andy stepped in. "Why don't you go to bed early, Mar? I'll help Finney."

Darting a glance between Andy and Mari, her mother subsided. Mari descended to the sleeping porch, flipped on a fan to stir the muggy evening air, and stretched out on her bed, feeling too stripped of emotions to even undress. Instead she watched the beadboard change from white to pale blue to violet, and then finally grow gray. Outside, a chorus of cicada song filled the night.

Her thoughts tumbled with what she'd learned today about Damon and Malloy, and what she might have learned about the others had she been able to stomach further reading. She might argue with her mother and squabble with her sisters and wish she had more money for more stuff. But these kids . . . they'd never had any of that. All the things she'd taken for granted through her life, they hadn't been able to count on at all. Their images mixed with thoughts of her own nieces and nephews, memories of her girlhood self and her sisters. In her family, every child was surrounded by a dozen people who stood between her and disaster. Her eyes blinked against a sudden film of tears. And her family still protected her that way.

She was still wide awake when her night table clock glowed midnight and Andy slipped in through the screen door. She held out a hand. She'd known he'd come.

Without speaking, as easy as if they'd done this every night of their lives, he quietly shed his clothes, then eased down beside her and removed hers. Pulling her close, his mouth and hands offered her the comfort words couldn't. He smoothed away the chill the night air pressed against her uncovered skin, filled the hollow that had grown in her heart, and finally awakened her deadened emotions. She clung to him, feeling like she was holding solid rock while currents pulled and eddied around her. And when they were done, they lay quiet and still entwined, her head on his chest listening to his heart beat in rhythm with her own.

She finally broke the silence, speaking softly. "I didn't look at Michael's file."

His arms tightened around her. "Nothing happened to Michael that's as bad as anything you read about Malloy and Damon, I promise."

"But there are things I don't know, aren't there?"

Andy's silence was answer enough.

"Please. Not knowing is worse than whatever it is."

Andy pulled her even closer and spoke quietly. "Michael suffered some things at his mother's hands that Melanie didn't. Melanie didn't even know—nobody knew until Michael started leveling with Dr. Everheart recently. Which is good—he needs to get it all out and examine it, no matter how painful remembering is."

"What happened to him?" Even while her dread grew, she felt calm. She wanted to understand.

Andy squeezed her tighter. "Michael has some

chicken pox scars. At least that's what his birth mother had claimed they were."

Yesterday when she'd tugged down Michael's T-shirt, she'd seen some of the scars, a small patch of puckered white dots trailing down to disappear beneath the band of his boxers. "What are they really?" she whispered, already afraid she knew.

"For punishment with Michael, Belinda sometimes used her cigarettes."

Mari closed her eyes against the tears that welled. Andy stroked her hair, not offering platitudes, just comfort. Oh, *God*. Oh, *Michael*. She remembered when she'd first met him. Five years old. Big brown eyes full of mischief and excitement. A grin that hid the monstrous things Belinda had done to him, because he didn't know any better. Because he didn't know his mother shouldn't have treated him that way. And nobody had been there to save him.

She swallowed, and when she could speak, said, "So that's why you blame Jon." She could understand it; it was hard not to. But Jon hadn't known.

"The guy should have been there. But . . ." Andy stirred. "I heard his daughter talking to you Saturday. Maybe . . . I don't know. I just see so much tragedy that could have been avoided if someone had just taken notice. Jon could—should—have taken notice."

Mari remembered what Lil had said about Andy. She splayed her fingers over his chest. "Like your grandmother should have taken more notice of what was happening with you?"

"That was different," Andy said, too quickly. "Gran tried. She was working hard to make a home for me. I ran wild; it wasn't her fault."

"I agree. Tansy did the best she could." She caressed the taut skin under her hand until it relaxed again. "But you think Jon didn't?"

Andy was silent, and she thought she'd goofed, but when she twisted to look at him, that mule-set to his chin wasn't there, just that same thoughtful expression she'd seen when he'd overheard Melanie. She relaxed back against him.

"I want to help. At Sycamore. Not just fill my time, but really help. You need to teach me how," she said slowly. Maybe her contribution for the summer was just a drop in a bucket, but she *did* want to help. "I won't screw up anymore. I won't break rules and make things more confusing for them."

"Good. Because you're confusing enough as it is." She could hear the smile in his voice.

She gave his chest a half-hearted punch. He caught her hand and held it there. He turned his head to murmur into her hair. "But I love you anyway, you screwup."

She hadn't realized how much she'd wanted to hear him say it. A glow lit her from within and spread clear out to the tips of her fingertips and her littlest toes. "You do? That's good. Because I love you, too."

She tilted her head up to study his face again. Bathed in the half-light from the moon, it was a good face, strong and committed and dear. She closed her eyes to accept his kiss, remembering how his expression could also turn hard and unforgiving. And as his lips found hers, she fervently hoped he'd never find out how big of a screwup she could be.

Chapter 17

By the time the Fourth of July weekend rolled around, summer had blazed onto the scene like a woman scorned, leaving a trail of searing heat in her wake. The temperatures hovered near one hundred, the humidity not much lower. In Camp Sycamore's cabins, ceiling fans stirred the air but didn't do much to cool anyone off.

As the heat had soared ever upward over the last twelve days, the boys were restless, their tempers more likely to flare. Mari sometimes wanted to sound off in kind but instead took her cues from Finney, copying the art therapist's soothing touch and her soft, level voice. Mari would never manage melodic, but at least she was now thinking before she ran off at the mouth, and pretty soon her calm demeanor had become habit. Who'da thought?

And the boys responded. Just like some of the boys who maneuvered for Finney's attention, Malloy now jostled for a place next to Mari at the table whenever he was in the art cabin. Quiet David gave her a drawing he'd painstakingly done of the marigolds flourishing in the camp's garden. And sometimes Damon slipped when he was around her, allowing glimpses of the serious, thoughtful kid he'd be had he not learned to cover up his pain with a facade. She wished he was open all the time—she was never sure what his smile hid. A bruised heart or a black one? Maybe both.

The times she made a real connection became moments to treasure. And the times when Finney or Andy treated her observations with the same respect they'd give each other's, she felt a flush of real accomplishment. If she didn't watch it, pretty soon she'd glow just like Finney. The days she'd once spent isolated in her loft, churning out brochures and advertisements and logos, seemed in the far distant past. As did Sean, who remained uncontacted and unresolved in the back corner of her mind, where she'd shoved him.

Her curiosity about the boys' backgrounds had been sated for the most part. She was no longer as eager to learn why they'd come to this place in their lives, but occasionally she *did* wonder. A few days ago, after David had given her his drawing and the boys had left for lunch, she'd asked Finney about him. "But don't give me too many details." She didn't need another close encounter with the forsythia bushes.

Mari had told Finney of her foray into the boys' files. While Finney hadn't exactly approved, something in Mari's face had stilled Finney's lecture before it had scarcely begun. Finney had relaxed more around her, no longer strictly adhering to the Sycamore Code of Silence.

Sweeping magazine clippings from the collage they'd just done into a wastebasket, Finney smiled. "That's easy. I don't *have* many details. All I know is that David came to Sycamore on advice from his counselor. Apparently his sister died a couple of years back. Since then, he's had trouble in school, at home. . . . Sounds rather like Michael's situation."

Stacking a batch of magazines, Mari frowned. "Oh, yeah. Andy said you didn't read their case histories like he does."

Finney nodded. "That's right. Some of these kids have made some pretty serious mistakes. I don't want what I might read in their files to prejudice me against them, so I let their counselors tell me whatever I *have* to know. For example, to help keep Damon safe, Dr. Everheart told me about his history of self-mutilation, and that's why I ask you to count things like the scissors at the end of a session. And that's why there aren't mirrors in the cabins—possible shards that the kids could use against other people or themselves." She straightened, and examined the room for any scraps that had gotten away. "I think I'm more effective if I meet them without any biases. It's also self-protection. Sometimes their problems are so wrenching, they'd consume my entire soul if I let them. Avoiding their files keeps that from happening." She didn't sound certain, though.

"Still, this work must tear you up."

"It does. No matter how hard everyone tries, sometimes we just can't reach a kid, and we find out after he's left that he's ended up in prison—or worse." Finney sighed. "I try to keep some emotional distance. If I get too involved, I become too much a part of their lives. And then I can't help them."

Mari set the magazines on the top shelf of a metal cabinet where they kept the supplies. "But Andy doesn't feel the same way you do?"

"I'd think you'd know that." Her voice was dry.

Glad her back was turned, Mari blushed. Finney had to be aware that almost every night for the last twelve, Andy had joined her on the sleeping porch. Sometimes they made love, but with the humidity so high, sometimes they just wandered out to the docks, stretched out on their backs on the still-sun-warmed wood, and talked. Staring at the stars, weaving dreams, just like when they were kids.

Finney continued. "For Andy, his job is a crusade.

He thinks that if he can figure a kid out, he can save him. But for me, that's not what it's all about."

"What is it about for you?" Mari turned around, picked up a sponge from the edge of a utility sink, and started wiping down the tables.

"I don't think in terms of success and failure. Some of the boys—like Damon and Malloy—spend years at Vreeley. But at camp, and even at Vreeley, some are with us for only a short time. We're often just a stop on a child's journey. I give them what I can while I'm with them, and I hold on to the hope that whatever that is, they'll take it into their next experience and have a better chance at succeeding through whatever that might be." Finney bundled the trash bag to put out in the Dumpster. "In fact, that's a philosophy of both Vreeley Home and Camp Sycamore. Kirk would agree with me. But Andy . . ."

Mari thought about the conversations she'd had with Andy. "Andy wants to fix people."

"Exactly. But you can't. People have to fix themselves. We can help them see how, but you can't take these kids and *make* them understand that while they may have been handed some hard knocks, their lives are now up to them. They have to grow into the knowledge that what happens from now on will be the result of their own choices. And that those choices aren't—or shouldn't be—the result of what anyone did to them in the past. They have to let go of blame."

Mari stilled. "Andy has a problem letting go of blame."

"Andy hasn't had much time on the job yet. Nor does the horticulture therapy program require that many psych classes. But if he continues with his schooling, he'll learn." Finney had thrown the bag of trash over her shoulder like a knapsack. "Ready for lunch?"

Mari had picked up David's drawing and they'd

headed for the cafeteria. When she'd come through the door, a slow smile had spread across Andy's face like it always did—like she was heaven on earth or some damn thing. And she wasn't. Oh, she loved the way his expression made her feel, loved the way *he* made her feel, because every day she loved *him* more. But her mind was a jumble. Finney was right—Andy would grow less judgmental as he gained more education and experience. But right now he still wanted to find fault. . . .

God, she needed to talk to *somebody*.

After thinking it over, she'd decided that the somebody should be Alcea. Alcea knew at least some of her history with Sean. Also, and more important, Alcea was in Cordelia while Mari was miles away at Lake Kesibwi. Since Mari didn't want to hold the discussion by phone, distance provided a perfect reason to procrastinate.

Until her mother, dang her, presented her with an opportunity the day before the Fourth of July.

Never without a host of chores to thrust on somebody, Zinnia had ordered her and Andy to pick up fireworks for a holiday picnic at the O'Malley cabin. Since Andy also had some supplies waiting at Beadler's, they'd decided to combine the errands with a run to Cordelia followed by supper with Andy's grandmother (how romantic). Even though the distance wasn't that great, they'd also stay overnight at her parents' house; she had to check on things anyway. For one blessed night, they'd be free of that knowing look Zinnia gave Mari when she headed for bed. The look that said her mother was pretty certain what went on under her feet.

This holiday weekend wouldn't be a big shindig. Lil had arrived last night with Jon and Melanie, but they were the only branch of the family putting in an appearance. The Fourth was *the* big summer weekend for all the merchants in Cordelia. Since Patsy Lee was spending evenings studying for end-of-session tests in her summer classes, she'd volunteered to stay behind and keep Merry-Go-Read open. Alcea and Florida were also staying put in Cordelia, raking in the tourist dollars at their diner.

Mari had been thrilled to get a day away with Andy all to herself. But just before they'd left, Zinnia had thrust a big vase of red and white roses into Mari's hands. "Mind you take these directly to Alcea. I told her I'd perk up the tables at Peg's for the holiday weekend." And, just like that, the thrill was gone. She'd just been handed the chance to confide in her oldest sister . . . dammit. And she needed to take it, even though she'd almost managed to convince herself that maybe there wasn't any reason to let Andy know of the infamy in her past. Even though she'd bet money Alcea would say different . . . And even though she knew Alcea would undoubtedly sound *reasonable* when she did.

Because her secret from Andy was eating her up.

Now, tooling along the highway to Cordelia in the pickup, Mari's stomach gurgled to prove the point. She pressed a hand to her diaphragm. She'd brave Alcea's reaction because if she didn't unload soon, she'd have an ulcer big enough to drive a truck through.

Which made it difficult to concentrate on the subject Andy had just brought up: The Question of Their Future. *God*. Why today?

She picked up the conversational gauntlet from where he'd just slapped it down. "I *do* love you." She glanced at him. Wind ruffled his curls, and if she squinted, she could pretend they were both still sixteen. Her eyes traced his profile. She really did love him. "And I *do* want to be with you." And she really wanted that, too.

"Then what's the problem?" Wrist casually hooked over the steering wheel, Andy frowned.

She frowned back. He knew what the problem was. They'd only recently started struggling over their plans—leaving out the M word for now, although it hovered between them—but defining the problem wasn't the problem. It was finding a solution—and all they did was talk in circles.

"I know we need to talk about what happens after camp ends, but can't we just enjoy the rest of the summer and forget the real world for a little while longer?" She pointed at one of the many fireworks stands that had blossomed along the roadside in the past week. "Let's stop there on the way back. It's the biggest one we've seen."

"I've made plans, you haven't. You don't even have a job." He picked up the ball where he always picked it up: his plans, her lack of them.

She wrinkled her nose. Between what she expected to hear from Alcea and what she was hearing from Andy, she was getting more sound logic than anyone should be asked to swallow in one day. And it was particularly annoying when the other person was right.

"But why do your plans have to involve Kansas?"

She was whining; she already knew the answer: Because he'd established residency there and school would be cheaper, and if he lived near Kansas City, he might be able to commute to a part-time job at Vreeley and blah-blah-blah. But, *criminy*. She'd already given up the idea of New York. (Actually, she'd relinquished that dream with alacrity because there was a chance—however remote—that they would run into Sean. And another chance—not so remote—that the place would stir up bad memories. And, well, also because—but this was only a teensy-weensy little bit of her reasoning, mind you—the traffic, the congested sidewalks, and especially the *waiters* got on her nerves.)

But that didn't mean she planned to cave altogether. "Why can't you go to school in Chicago? They offer child psych . . . psych—whatever that degree is—too. God knows, there's probably more need there than here. You'd find a job in a snap." She didn't know if that was true, but it sounded good.

"You know that's not what I want."

No, dammit, it wasn't. He wanted help out kids in rural, back-of-beyond areas around here . . . the poverty-stricken wounds in certain parts of the Ozarks where domestic violence was a way of life, welfare was a career aspiration, and beer was considered a major food group. She sighed. It was laudable, and she knew his help was needed and that he'd understand the people in a way others couldn't because he was a native . . . but what in the hell would *she* do? "What about what *I* want?"

"And what *exactly* would that be?" He kept his voice pleasant.

Fuming, she slumped back. Except for her yen to try another city, who knew? In the last week, she'd updated her résumé, but her Internet search hadn't coughed up any place she wanted to send it. There *were* a few jobs she was qualified for, but they'd sounded about as exciting as watching water evaporate. Unfortunately, she'd told him that.

When she didn't answer, Andy looked smug. She hated it when he looked smug. Lip curling, she closed her eyes.

"C'mon, Mar. Quit acting like Kansas is some vast prairie wasteland. It's a beautiful state, full of big skies, rolling hills, friendly people."

And cattle and wheat and guys with gun racks mounted in the rear windows of their pickup trucks. She yawned. Loudly and rudely.

It didn't deter him. "You'd like Lawrence. It's not exactly a city, but it's not a small town either."

"I know," she said irritably. "I've been there." And she *had* liked it . . . but *live* there?

"It's only an hour from K.C., and it's on the cosmopolitan side—not backward. And hilly, not flat. Old Victorian homes, tree-lined streets, K.U. sitting up on Mount Oread. Parks. Low crime . . ." He went on and on about the university town, sprawling riverside among the rolling hills of eastern Kansas. She yawned again, but this time because his voice had lulled her. She had to admit he painted a nice picture. "With the college, there's all that culture you yammer on about, and the place is full of liberal minds." She could sense he'd smiled. "And just think. Green-tipped hair, earrings hanging down to your knees, and shoes with heels three stories high wouldn't stick out like a sore thumb at all."

Her mouth quirked, but, half asleep, she didn't have the energy to punch his arm. Even though Lawrence was a busy little metropolis, they'd have a quiet, slow-paced life, free of stone-faced pedestrians crowding the sidewalks and traffic clogging the freeways. She'd exchange friendly hellos with the clerk she'd grow to know at the post office, the bag boy at the grocery store, a smiling waiter at some pub that would become one of her and Andy's favorite haunts. And she'd never have to take a cab anywhere.

Eventually Lawrence would probably be as familiar to her as Cordelia.

Her eyes flew open. What was she thinking? *Cordelia?* She pushed herself up straight. "Competition for real jobs in a college town is fierce, and the pay usually lousy."

His sigh held a world of patience, and she wanted to pinch him. "You can *commute*. You worked in Kansas City before. Why not again?"

Her mouth twisted. There was just no beating common sense. And it wasn't like what he was asking was selfish—he hadn't said they'd live in Lawrence forever, just until he finished school. But she'd already tried Kansas City on for size. It hadn't fit. At least not the way she'd thought it would. The way she thought Chicago—or somewhere else—might.

Mari let her hand creep over to Andy's thigh. "Let's not discuss it today, okay? We've still got weeks to figure things out." And there might be *nothing* to figure out if she told him about Sean.

"Only five before camp's out." Sycamore closed after the first week in August to give the kids time to prepare for school's start midmonth. "That's not all that long."

"Quit being logical. It's too *pretty* outside for logical." It was. The humidity was low, the sky a jigsaw puzzle of blue and white.

Andy laughed. "All right. No more discussion until next week."

Relieved, she ran her hand up his thigh. He batted it off before she reached the finish line. "And none of that either." He gave her a slow, lopsided smile. "At least, not until later."

Satisfied that she'd diverted his thoughts, she looked back out the window. They were traveling through new housing tracts on the outskirts of Cordelia, then the highway narrowed and turned to tree-shaded streets lined with gracefully aging homes before they entered the heart of the old town. The familiar rose-brick buildings with their white-trimmed windows and flower boxes rose around the square, watched benignly by St. Andrew's Church, sitting stalwart as always smack in the middle. Funnily enough, her heart warmed. Well, that wasn't really such a big surprise. It stood to reason she'd be fond of the old joint; it didn't mean she wanted to live here. It didn't mean, like, she'd gone soft or something.

Andy pulled into a slot in front of Peg O' My Heart Cafe and Bakery. The tale she wanted to spill into Alcea's ears pushed into her brain again, and her earlier relief evaporated.

He leaned across her to push her door open. "I'll meet you at the Rooster around noon."

Halfway out the door, she stalled. "No messages for Tansy?"

"I'll see Gran tonight." When she still loitered, his brows rose. "Something wrong?"

Oh, I'm about to tell my sister that I'm the next best thing to a murderer. She lowered her eyes. "No." She gathered up the roses, backed onto the sidewalk, and mustered a parting smile.

Andy glanced at his watch and apparently decided he didn't have time to question her further. Still frowning his I-don't-believe-you frown, he pulled away. She hesitated for a moment, hoping the heady perfume of her mother's roses and the aroma drifting across the sidewalk—Alcea must have Blueberry Bright Scones in the oven—would boost her spirits. They didn't. She drew a deep breath and turned toward Peg's.

No time like the present, and all that rot.

Trying to swallow a blueberry scone down a dry throat, Mari sat in a booth backed to the wall and watched her oldest sister bustle around the diner, snatching up dishes left from breakfast and cleaning off tables for the upcoming lunch crowd. Andy's grandmother, Tansy, and Florida had retired to the kitchen in back where they were undoubtedly elbow-deep in dishwater. Through an adjoining doorway, Alcea's bakery was doing brisk tourist business.

Peg O' My Heart Cafe had been a Cordelia institution through two generations, and the familiarity of the place where Pop had once jounced her on his knee and where the family had squeezed in for noisy brunches on special occasions wrapped Mari in warmth and settled her nerves. Kind of.

Abandoning the scone, she plopped her chin in her hand and stared out the window. Cordelia snoozed in the bucolic haze of summer. On the square directly across Main, the dappled shade under a host of maples and sycamores invited lingering, even in the midday heat. Seated on a bench, old Paddy O'Neill swapped gossip with Up-in-the-Hair's owner, Betty Bruell, who shoved at her towering do every few seconds. Nearby, one of Betty's hairdressers, Rosemary Butz, stooped to talk to one of the Tidwell grandchildren—the Tidwells lived next door to her parents. And along one of the paths crisscrossing the green, Julius, the town's oldest mechanic and a close friend of Alcea and Dak's, pushed Florida's daughter, Missouri, along on a red bike with training wheels. The child's curly hair floated around her face like a dark cloud.

Nobody looked at a watch. Nobody raced to make an appointment. If a horn honked, it would be the one on the handlebar of Missouri's bicycle. Cordelia moved with the speed of a glacier. The scene hardly ever changed; it just came in different versions.

Damn. Instead of disdain, unfamiliar affection had enveloped her heart. Maybe she *was* getting soft. Or scared. Or whatever it was that kept people trapped in this town. This—this *sappy sentiment* was *exactly* what she'd been afraid of before she'd come back. Sitting up straight, she shoved another piece of scone in her mouth and chewed fast. It was probably just nerves.

As Alcea worked, she barked orders to the Bartlesby twins, Lisa and Liza. Mari couldn't tell one from the other. In matching orange uniforms, both girls had gobs of blond hair, gobs of black eyeliner, and more curves than sense. But despite the curves, the makeup, and their youth, neither held a candle to Alcea.

Mari studied the sister more than a decade her senior. When Mari was small, the physical paragon that she'd lived with had awed her, and she'd been more than a little intimidated by Alcea's sharp tongue. But, because of Alcea, she'd learned to give as good as she got. Lil had always played peacemaker, and it wasn't surprising that Mari had gravitated to her middle sister's gentler nature. But Lil was also easily shocked, so when Mari had needed to talk about Sean four years ago, Alcea had been the lucky listener. And, gosh, it looked like Lady Fortune was about to smile on Alcea again. Just wait until she got a load of what Mari had to tell her this time.

Her scone suddenly had all the flavor of dirt.

Finished with her chores, Alcea had gathered the roses, a dozen or so bud vases, and a pitcher of water. Now, with the waitresses' help, she carted it all over to Mari's table and, after waving the twins back to work, withdrew two pairs of shears from her apron pocket.

She handed one off to Mari. "Here, get to work." Alicia slid in on the opposite side of the booth, filled a bud vase with water, cut off the stem of a rose at a slant, and plopped it into the vase. "Like that."

Blueberries bouncing in her stomach now that the moment of truth was near, Mari pushed her plate to one side and reached for a rose.

"So," Alcea said before Mari could open her mouth, "I'd guess from the number of roses, Mother's back in business."

"Um, yeah." Mari nodded, not sure if she was relieved or disappointed at the delay. When she didn't say more, Alcea gave her a sharp glance. Mari hurried to fill the lull. "Full of vim and vigor, as she puts it. She can drive now. And since her cardiac rehab stint is done, she's joined a gym in Osage Beach. Can you believe it? Says she loves the rowing machine, and she's getting strong as an ox. Which adds some symmetry, since she's just as hardheaded."

Alcea smiled. "I can just picture it. The spandex crowd is probably cowed."

"She also got it in her head to put in a new garden, then decided—*after* Andy and Finney and I had spent three evenings clearing the ground, of course—that it was too late in the season. So she turned her attention to babying her roses."

"I'm glad."

"Not more than I am. I knew next thing she'd have us doing is spreading sh—I mean, manure." Mari went with the flow, looking for and dreading an opening to bring up her past affair. She clipped and stuck a rose in a vase. "She even junked that old shower chair— pounded it to pieces, actually. I had a burial at sea the other day; I pulled it out of the trash, weighted it with rocks, and sank it."

Alcea's arching eyebrows arched even more.

"I didn't want to take a chance she'd get her hands on it again." Suddenly distracted from her mission, Mari touched a rosebud. "Criminy, Hock, it was tough to watch her acting so *old*."

"She's not young anymore, Mari." Alcea's gaze was steady. "We all have to get used to the idea that Pop and Mother won't be with us forever."

"I know, but . . . well, at least things are okay now."

"Yes, for now."

Mari didn't like the temporary sound of that, but let it go, mind once again fumbling with how to broach what she needed to discuss. Blurt it out, she guessed, just like she did most things. Squirming, she took a deep breath.

But Alcea was already talking. "And how's Michael doing?"

"Um, Hock—" Planning to ignore Alcea's question now that her courage had peaked, she started in.

Alcea looked up, a line of concern between her brows. "He's doing okay, isn't he?"

Courage sputtering out, Mari sighed. "Pretty well. Lil said last night that he's opening up more in their counseling sessions, and he and Jon are getting along better. At least Jon no longer wants to stick him in boot camp. Andy says he's made progress—I'm not sure if he means Jon or Michael—but Michael still hasn't made what they call a big breakthrough. Andy says just give it more time. And Michael's also made some friends at camp." Sidetracked again, this time by thoughts of her nephew, she frowned.

Alcea's forehead wrinkled. "You don't like the friends?"

"No, it's not that. I like all the kids so far. But there's this one . . . he's had it really, really hard. He's smart, and he knows the ropes, and he can be really nice."

"But . . . ?"

"He's . . . well, he's not sincere, you know what I mean? Andy calls him Eddie Haskell. He's also a leader, though, and the boys—well, they want to be his friend, but he also scares them."

"Have you told Lil?" Alcea's glance was sharp.

"She knows. And I don't think Michael is all *that* afraid of him." She thought of the cigarettes. Maybe he didn't need to be scared—as long as he did Damon's bidding. But what would happen if Michael stopped playing the suck-up? "But Andy and Finney, and Kirk, too—he's the director, has Lil told you that?—think the boys need to experience the natural consequences of their choices, so they won't interfere unless they think Michael is in some kind of real danger."

"Well, they must know what they're doing." The bells on the entrance sang, and Alcea glanced over her shoulder. Satisfied that one of the twins was helping two early lunch customers, she returned to her task. "Now, what did you want to talk to me about?"

"Huh?"

Vases filled, Alcea placed them all back in the box. She motioned to Lisa-or-Liza. "Put a rose on each table." When the waitress had collected the box, Alcea looked at Mari. "You've been fidgeting around

ever since you got here. It's not Mother and it's not
Michael, so what's got you in knots?"

"It's—it's Andy. Well, not Andy, exactly, but something that he doesn't know, and I—"

"About your married . . . friend, right?"

"Sean . . . yes."

"No surprise you haven't told him, considering how
Andy treated Florida."

"That's the problem." Lowering her voice, Mari
leaned toward Alcea. "He's got some chip on his
shoulder about . . . Well, I guess he *should* have a
chip on his shoulder about women who have affairs
with married men, but his seems more like this great
big boulder. I don't like not telling him everything,
but I'm afraid to tell him about Sean." She looked
down at her hands. "I really love Andy, Alcea. I don't
want to lose him."

Alcea stared out the window, then looked back at
Mari. "What you did was wrong, but people make
mistakes. Surely Andy understands that, especially
given his line of work. And I'm here to tell you that
affairs don't happen if the marriage is sound." Alcea
would know—her first husband had been a serial
cheater. "Not that *unsound* is any excuse for screwing
around." Her look at Mari was pointed.

That was Alcea, subtle as a sledgehammer.

"But if I'm recalling right, you did regain your sanity and broke it all off." Alcea paused. "You did break
it off, didn't you?"

"Right after you and I talked four years ago, although I did have a business relationship with him for
a while longer. But then I cut that off, too,
because . . ." The words stuck in her throat.

"Good." Alcea nodded. "You know, my wonderful
first husband gave me some practice with deception,
and I've never seen a lie—"

"I haven't lied! I just haven't told Andy."

Alcea's mouth pursed. "You're quibbling. As I was saying, I haven't seen a deception that hasn't hurt people when the truth finally came out. And you know it will eventually. You aren't exactly the kind of person who keeps a secret very long. Tell Andy. If he can't live with it, it's better—and will hurt both of you less—if you find out now instead of later."

She knew Alcea was right, except— "There's more to it than you know."

"What more could there be?"

"Sean's wife, Jo . . ." Mari sucked in a breath. "Sean told me his wife had problems."

Alcea's voice went dry. "Gee, what a surprise that he'd tell you *that*."

"No, I mean *real* problems. She was emotionally unbalanced. It was why he couldn't bring himself to leave her, but he also couldn't cope with her. That's just the way he is. He doesn't confront things as much as he just aims for the best and hopes."

"Sounds like a winner."

Mari probably should have been offended at Alcea's implied opinion of her taste in men, but she could see Sean more clearly now, and Alcea was right. Sean wasn't a bad person, not really, but he, well, he had about as much spine as a flounder.

When Mari didn't say anything, Alcea reached for her hand. "What is it? Just tell me."

Mari looked at the table. "Two years after Sean and I broke up . . ." She swallowed past the lump of guilt and misery that always threatened to choke her whenever she thought of Sean's wife. "Jo . . . Jo killed herself."

There was silence. She didn't look at her sister, and Alcea didn't utter a word, but Mari could feel her shock vibrate through her hand. To her surprise, though, Alcea didn't let go.

"And you blame yourself."

Wanting to throw her arms around Alcea for the

matter-of-fact note in her voice, Mari sat back. "Oh, I know that I'm not the only reason she did it, but—"

"Of course you're not. You're not a reason at all. I'm not saying you didn't add to her misery for a time—if she even knew about you at all—but it wasn't your fault. Not yours. Not even Sean's, much as I'd love to pin it on him. We all go through hardships and tragedies, and a good chunk of us go through bad marriages, but very few of us decide to kill ourselves over them. Blame his wife's emotional problems if you have to blame something—but she made the decision to die for herself. You didn't make it for her."

The bells on the door jangled again, this time admitting two couples. Some other customers crowded behind them. Alcea looked over her shoulder. "Damn. I've got to get back to work." She reached up to brush a curl back from Mari's forehead. "If you need to talk more, call me." Alcea rose, then stooped to give her a fierce hug. "Everything will be okay."

Mari watched Alcea greet her customers, thinking over her words. While she wasn't sure she really believed what her sister had said, she already felt like Alcea had lifted a hundred-pound weight off her shoulders. Whoever had said that confession was good for the soul was *absolutely* on target.

Feeling a new resolve, she stood up and straightened her shoulders. Now all that remained for her to do was tell Andy. She hoped she felt this good after *that*.

Chapter 18

"What's up?" Inside the Rooster Bar & Grill, Andy slid onto a stool and hailed Seamus. He still had a half hour before Mari arrived, which gave him time to catch up with the man he'd asked to be his A.A. sponsor for the summer.

Busy dunking mugs into soapy water, Seamus gave him a sharp glance from dark eyes. Everything about Seamus was sharp—his features, the cut of his boots, the crease in his sleeves. "Better question is, what's up with you?"

Andy shrugged. "I know I haven't made it to meetings regularly."

"For nearly a month, you haven't made them at all." Seamus dried his hands on a towel, quietly appraising him from under black brows. "You doing okay?"

Andy couldn't help it. A grin split his face. "More than okay."

The brows went up. "The look of a man in love. Dangerous to let a woman—or anything, for that matter—come between you and continued recovery, even after four years of sobriety. You've done good. Don't let anything trip you up." Flipping the towel over a shoulder, Seamus picked up a glass, filled it with ice and Coke, and slid it in front of Andy. He poured a mug of coffee for himself.

"Don't worry. I haven't even been tempted." Andy took a drink, set down the glass. "After those first few months, I kinda got to like waking up to sunshine and blue skies instead of a big wad of pain and regret from the previous night's binge."

"Meetings help keep things that way." Seamus settled his forearms on the bar, mug between his hands. "But I can see I'm talking to a hardhead. Who is she, anyway?"

"Mari O'Malley."

A rare grin flashed across Seamus's face. "That's a handful."

Seamus should know. When Lil had been married to Seamus's brother, Seamus had formed tight connections with the entire O'Malley family.

"You can say that." Andy's mood dipped. "We've already had a difference of opinion on where we should live after the summer."

"Things gone that far, eh?"

Andy nodded. "But I'll work her around to my way of thinking."

"Ah, for the certainty of youth." Seamus stared off, gaze distant. "Be careful there, Andy. We reformed drunks have this habit of thinking we know what's best for everyone. We get our lives cleaned up and think it's given us some kind of step up on the righteousness ladder." He paused. "But people will do what people will do. Best to accept that and not fight it."

For Seamus, it was a mouthful. Andy frowned, thinking of the gossip that had swept Cordelia some eight years back. After Seamus's brother had died, Seamus had held out hope that he'd eventually win the widowed Lil. But then Jon Van Castle had swept onto the scene in his country star glory. Seamus's maneuverings had just served to push Lil further into Van Castle's arms.

"She should have chosen you," Andy blurted, then

flushed. Despite the closeness that had developed between them, they'd never discussed Seamus's personal life.

Seamus didn't ask who Andy was talking about. Nor did his expression change. "Wish she had, but she didn't. And she's been happy with her choice—that's what counts." Seamus shifted his gaze back to Andy's face. "What have you got against Van Castle?"

Andy lifted a shoulder, let it drop. "His son is at Camp Sycamore."

"And you've pinned the boy's problems on his father."

"With reason."

Seamus was quiet a moment. "Pains me to say it, but Van Castle is a good man. He made mistakes." He paused, eyeing Andy. "But then, haven't we all?"

Andy tightened his lips. "But some mistakes are bigger than others. Some hurt people more than most."

"Yep. Like the mistakes that can happen when you drive drunk, right?"

Andy looked down at his glass. "Maybe."

Seamus's gaze was level. "Hook up with Mari O'Malley, and you'll be dealing with every member of her family for the rest of your life. Hold a grudge against Van Castle, and you've set yourself up for trouble. Those sisters have their differences, but they're 'all for one,' and you know it." He paused. "Besides, from what you've told me, it's not Van Castle that put that judgmental chip on your shoulder."

Maybe Seamus was right. Maybe he should cut Van Castle some slack. And not only Van Castle, but Alcea's partner, Florida. She'd be part and parcel of family gatherings, too. He could do that. For Mari's sake, if not for theirs. And if he pretended friendliness long enough, he might even feel it. His heart hardened. But there was one person he'd never absolve. . . .

The Rooster's door opened, sending a slash of sunshine across the dark wood floor. A party of tourists trooped in, looking for lunch. Behind them, he glimpsed Mari's apricot curls.

Seamus straightened. "Back to work." He reached under the counter for a few vinyl-wrapped menus. "Make the next meeting. And in the meantime, take another look at Step Ten." Seamus abandoned him to tend to his customers.

Trying to remember the tenth step, Andy frowned. He'd worked all twelve steps during his first year in A.A., but it had been a while since he'd looked them over. Something about continuing to take personal inventory. His frown deepened. What in the hell did that have to do with anything? He'd had nothing to do with what had happened to his sister.

After grabbing a burger at the Rooster that wasn't settling too well on his stomach after his conversation with Seamus, he and Mari headed up Main. Cordelia's town square was ready for the holiday: The buildings were dressed in red, white, and blue bunting for the parade scheduled after St. Andrew's bell tolled an end to services tomorrow; on the church green, families had spread out picnics in the shade; signs in shop windows heralded Independence Day sales; and tourists moseyed along the sidewalks. He and Mari joined them, browsing through O'Neill's Emporium, stopping in at Merry-Go-Read to see Mari's sister-in-law, Patsy Lee, grabbing an ice cream soda at Sin-Sational Ice Cream and drinking it two straws to one glass, just like when they were kids. From Mari's distracted air, he wondered if she, too, had indigestion.

Now, as the sun slanted from the west, Andy pulled the pickup to a stop in front of his grandmother's house. Tansy lived in North End, an area of hit-or-miss poverty. Some of the small ranch bungalows were tidy like hers, with clipped lawns, pots stuffed with petunias, and the occasional windmilling yard ornament. Others were little more than shacks with faded plastic toys strewn across straggling grass, sofas abandoned on porches and left to the weather, paint peeling down to the wood, and cars oxidizing in the sun. Smoke curled from rusting barbeques in front of most houses. Few had air-conditioning, and, even just past the brink of July, he knew that it was cooler outside than in. He hoped Gran had all her window fans buzzing.

When he switched off the engine, the squeals of children, the slap of a screen door, and the sound of someone flipping the tab on a can of beer drifted in through the truck window. Inside the cab there was silence. Not only distracted, Mari had been uncharacteristically quiet all day. From what she'd said, nothing was amiss with Alcea, and he wondered if she was still stewing over the conversation they'd had on the way up from Lake Kesibwi.

If she was, she wasn't the only one. Convincing Mari the grass wasn't necessarily greener in Central Park or along the shores of Lake Michigan was something that had consumed a lot of his time lately. Then Seamus had put him in mind that he needed to come clean with her about his sister. And he would, because he didn't want any secrets between them. Whatever future they had together, Tansy would be part of it, even if from afar. And it would be easier on Gran if she didn't have to keep up the subterfuge in front of Mari that she'd carried off in front of the rest of Cordelia. He knew he could trust Mari to keep his confidences to herself, but he'd avoided the conversation because talking about Anna was still painful.

Mari reached for the door handle, but he stalled her with a touch on her arm. "Before we go in, I need to tell you something about Gran."

A frown creased her forehead. "Tansy's not sick or something, is she?"

"No. Actually, it's more about Anna."

Mari turned toward him, hooking a knee up on the seat. "What about Anna? Is Tansy still deep in mourning or something? Should I not mention her name?"

"That's not it. It's about how Anna died."

"You said she had a bad reaction to a prescription."

"That's the story Gran gave out because she didn't want people gossiping about Anna. And I agreed to go along for her sake. But it's not the truth." He took a breath past the tightness in his chest. "Anna committed suicide."

Shock apparently knocked her silent, then she reached for his hand. "Oh, no. Oh, Andy, I'm so, *so* sorry. How hard for you . . . for Tansy."

"At first I was just angry with her. But now the hardest part is wondering why. She didn't leave much of a note, nothing more than an *I'm sorry*. I have a few ideas, but . . ." Jaw tightening, he leaned his head back and stared up, not really seeing the split vinyl that crisscrossed the ceiling.

"Her problems probably started a long time ago— when your parents died. That would be rough for anyone."

"Yeah. Being orphaned hit us both hard, but her harder—she was really close to our mom. Then, from what Gran says, there was wrangling between Gran and my mom's folks about who would take us in. Gran wanted both of us; they only wanted Anna." He gave a rueful smile. "I guess even then they knew I was like my dad, and they didn't want any reminders. They'd never wanted Mom to marry him in the first place. And, of course, they blamed him for her death."

"I guess that's not too unreasonable," she said softly. "He *was* driving the car."

"Yeah. And drunk as usual."

Forgiving his dad for that was still tough, although the fury he'd once felt had abruptly ended when he'd realized how easily he could have killed someone himself in the exact same way. As Seamus had once pointed out, Andy wouldn't have dragged himself out of his own gutter had it not been for the example set by his father. To Andy's mind, seeing that bit of silver lining in his parents' deaths was a reach, but in A.A. there was the constant reminder to give up *stinkin' thinkin'*, as they called it.

"So is that why Anna always came here instead of you visiting her in Kansas City?"

He nodded. "Gran was the one who insisted we stay in touch and wouldn't take no for an answer, even though my mom's parents seemed to think that if they kept her out of Cordelia, she'd forget all about her life here. From what Anna told me, it was like they wanted to turn her into a miniature of Mom, somehow replace the daughter they'd lost. Gran says my other grandmother was a little strange. They even called Anna by my mom's nickname."

"That's kind of sick."

"Their intentions were good, but they wanted to erase her past—not just my parents' deaths, but the poverty, the teasing. Remember the names that the kids called Anna and me? I could shrug it off, but it really got under Anna's skin. Of course, she'd been putting up with it for several years by the time you and I started kindergarten."

A ghost of a smile crossed Mari's face. "You *shrugged* it off? You *beat* it off, you mean. By first grade, nobody bothered you anymore."

He echoed her grin. "Or you. You weren't so bad in the fistfight department yourself."

Raggedy Andy, Raggedy Anna, Raggedy Andy . . . started by one kid, then picked up by others until the schoolyard rang with the chant. And when five-year-old Mari had stuck up for him, she'd gotten a taste of it, too. He smiled briefly, remembering Buster Bradwell sticking his fat tongue out at Mari and hollering, *Marigold, Fairy Mold.* Mari had decked ol' Buster be-

fore Andy could jump him first. It had been one of
their first—but not last—trips together to the
principal.

"No, I wasn't." Mari's look had turned distant.
"Poor Anna. The way she was raised after she left
here must have confused her a lot. No wonder she
spent some of her visits crying practically all the time."

"But other times she was a lot of fun." He realized
he sounded defensive. He knew there had never been
any love lost between Mari and Anna, but he felt
compelled to shield his sister, even though she was
now beyond his help. "She'd be so full of energy we
could hardly keep up with her."

"Yeah, she was . . . fun." Mari sounded doubtful.

"She was always a person with intense emotions. A
lot like you," he pointed out. "But by the time I lived
near her in Kansas City, she'd become distant. No,
worse than that. She seemed numb. Oh, she put a
good face on things, but I could tell something had
changed her. It was like all the life had gotten sucked
right out of her." His thoughts darkened. "Probably
by that scumbag of a husband she had."

"Her husband? Was he . . . was he abusive?"

"No. At least not in the way you're thinking. He
screwed around." He heard Mari suck in a breath.
"Yep, he was a real piece of work. One day she broke
down and told me all about it. About how it had been
going on throughout their entire marriage. And about
how afraid she was of losing him. Losing him? I told
her she *should* lose him. But she got hysterical, said
she needed him too much, said I didn't understand. I
didn't. Especially since, after that, she wouldn't hear
a word against him. In fact, for the rest of that week,
she wouldn't talk to me at all. I talked to him, of
course. All he'd say was that an outsider couldn't
know what went on in a marriage.

"And with both of them keeping me at arm's
length, what could I do?" Andy shrugged, although

guilt welled up inside of him. Since Anna had died, he'd tried hard to dispel that mountain of regret, but he supposed he'd always carry it around. And he wasn't sure that he shouldn't. "I've always thought, though, that she could have coped with her history. That is, if she'd had a man who deserved that kind of loyalty instead of someone who betrayed her every chance he got. She must have finally lost all hope. She just gave up."

"I-it sounds like her marriage was hard on her." Mari's hand slipped from his.

And when he glanced at her, he saw she'd gone pale. "You okay?"

"Yes." She bit her lip. "I just—I knew someone who committed suicide—a, uh, friend, nobody you'd know. This just brings up bad memories."

"Do you want me to stop?"

"N-no."

He was glad. It felt good to get this all off his chest. He'd talked to Seamus about it before, but not in this much detail. He returned his gaze to the truck's roof. "I should have done more. But I was so damn consumed with *my* plans, *my* feelings, *my* recovery that I told myself it was useless. And after that summer, I took off for college still full of myself. Anna killed herself less than a year later. Intentionally overdosed on an antidepressant she was taking. I hadn't even known she was on anything." He closed his eyes against a familiar wave of pain, then a flare of anger swept guilt aside. "The scumbag wasn't around, of course. If he'd come home that night, he might have been able to save her, but he was out tomcatting. As usual."

Mari made a funny sound.

He opened his eyes and rolled his head to look at her. Her eyes were glassy. He wasn't too surprised. Despite a veneer of sophistication and a kick-ass attitude, Mari always had been an innocent. Look at how much of a Pollyanna she'd been over the kids at Camp Sycamore. Reaching up to play with one of her curls, he tried to lighten the mood. "Well. That's all in the past, but . . . it's quite a soap opera, isn't it?"

She blanched and looked away.

"Hey, what gives?"

"N-nothing." She opened her door. "Tansy's waiting."

He grabbed her hand. "Mar, I'm sorry if this whole thing upsets you. Anna's death probably won't even come up—and if it does, Gran sometimes seems to forget her version of events isn't the truth. I just needed you to know. I don't want secrets in our family because I hope someday we'll all *be* a family."

"I—I want that, too." There was a mournful note in her voice.

He frowned. What he'd said had come pretty close to a proposal, and while he knew they still had a lot to sort out, he'd expected a little more enthusiasm than that. "And I want you to know that I'll do my level best to learn to like Jon—and Florida, too."

"I—I know you will." Head turned away, she pulled from his grasp, and his frown deepened. By the muffled sound of her voice, he thought she'd teared up.

But Tansy came out on the porch and Mari started toward her before he'd rounded the truck. By the time he caught up with her, he saw no sign of tears. Still, although Mari greeted Tansy with a warm hug, chattered like a magpie all through dinner, and even volunteered to do the dishes, she was odd, almost manic. He put it down to nervousness—she wanted to win Tansy over, and Tansy wasn't always easily won. Still, he wasn't sure that was it, and it bothered him. He'd always read Mari—at least most of the time—so why couldn't he now?

While Mari busied herself in the kitchen, he chatted with Gran. Like usual, she slid into her memories of a time when her son and daughter-in-law were children: best friends who later turned into lovers. Much like him and Mari. After his parents had married, even after they'd had him and Anna, they'd lived squeezed underneath this very roof. His dad might have been a drunk unable to hold a job, but he had been charming, ready with a laugh or a hug, and there had been no question of his love for his wife or his children. And while his wife had despaired of what she called *his weakness*, she'd never given up on him.

He'd heard all Gran's stories a million times or more, but he encouraged them, loving the light in her face that took years off her age.

When she finally ran out of rope, he picked up the slack. "Remember that night Dad came home drunk with a box of candy, thinking that was all the apology Mom needed?"

Tansy cackled. "And then she chased him clean out the door . . ."

"Pelting him with chocolates all the way down the road."

The noise from the kitchen had ceased. He looked up. Holding a tray loaded with cups and apple pie, a smile on her lips, Mari leaned against the doorway to the tiny dining room, waiting for the story's end. He winked.

Grinning, his grandmother shook her head. "You and your sister—and soon half the neighborhood kids—went running after them, catching up them dirty chocolates and stuffing them in your mouths. Looked like some kind of parade. Ever'body had come outside to watch and were rootin' your mom on. And when she finally caught up to your dad, she squashed that last chocolate—big old cherry-filled sucker, if I'm rememberin' correc'ly—right on his nose. By then, you were all laughing to split a gut, and she couldn't even remember why she was mad." Tansy hooted and wiped her eyes. "That was our Jo."

"*Jo?*"

The word erupted from Mari's lips. Or he thought it had. The tray slipped from her hands and hit the floor. And whatever she'd uttered was lost in the smash of the crockery.

Chapter 19

The night sky erupted in a cascade of color. Watching the fiery glitter trail down and sputter out, Mari *oohed* and *aahed* along with Finney, Lil, Melanie, and her parents, all lounging in canvas chairs Jon had set up earlier on the dock for their Fourth of July display. But her enthusiasm was an act. *Everything* she'd done and said today was an act. The booms echoing through the cove mimicked the same explosions that had been bursting in her belly ever since Andy's grandmother had uttered Jo's name.

They even called Anna by my mom's nickname.

Behind her, on the slope between the dock and cabin, flashlight beams bounced around as Andy and Jon reloaded the steel pipe they were using as a launcher. True to his word, Andy had not just greeted Jon civilly, he'd been downright friendly since they'd returned from Cordelia. Mari suspected a lot of that was pretense, too.

But nothing compared to her charade. Nor was she fooling Andy. She knew by the confused gaze he leveled on her when he thought she wasn't looking.

Last night, she'd forestalled his questions with desperate lovemaking. Through the day, she'd pleaded a stomachache—and hadn't needed to pretend that at all. Tonight, she'd use the same excuse; tomorrow morning she'd call in sick. Because until she got this all sorted out, until she had her horrible suspicions laid to rest—or, *oh, God*, confirmed—she couldn't bear to even meet Andy's eyes. Ten minutes alone with him would be all it would take before she was baring her soul—and maybe losing him forever.

Snatching at any spare moments she'd had alone today—which hadn't been many—she'd tried to phone Sean, needing to know for absolute certain. But all she'd gotten was his answering machine. Not wanting him to call her, she'd mumbled messages about trying again later before she'd hung up. There were probably nine hundred tries piled up by now.

A *ker-thump* sounded from the pipe, and she turned her gaze to the heavens, barely registering the spew of red and gold that lit up the faces around her.

They even called Anna by my mom's nickname.

It just couldn't be. Sean had been Andy's brother-in-law? She'd always known God had a wicked sense of humor, but this was . . . Just. Not. Funny.

Clutching the arms of her chair, she waited out the fireworks, wanting only for everyone to head for bed so she could try Sean again . . .

And fervently praying he'd tell her he'd never laid eyes on Anna Eppelwaite.

Two hours later, fireworks over and chairs put away, everyone had headed for bed. Andy had frowned when she'd fobbed off his invitation to watch the stars from the dock, but with her family and Finney around, he hadn't argued. After one last bewildered look at her, he'd finally followed Finney up to the guesthouse.

Mari lingered in the kitchen, neatening things that didn't need neatening, washing things that didn't need to be washed, and flipping through magazines until she was sure everyone was safely asleep. Nearing one in the morning, she picked up the cordless and curled up in a far corner of the darkened family room where her voice wouldn't carry down the hall to the bedrooms. She punched in Sean's number.

On the third ring, he answered, his voice husky with sleep, but once he realized who was phoning, he sounded pleased. "Well, hey . . ." She pictured him sliding back onto his pillow, one arm looped under his head, that Harry Connick, Jr., smile spreading across his face. "That was a lot of messages. What's up? Good news, I hope."

"Where were you?" Her voice was dry as rust. She didn't care where he'd been—but now that he was on the other end, she didn't know how to ask the question. Correction. She was delaying because she was scared witless of what he would answer.

He chuckled. "That's not jealousy I'm hearing, is it? Nowhere special—just a July Fourth barbeque that went on forever."

"Oh." Stomach churning, heart hammering, she took a deep breath. "Sean, this might sound strange, but I need to know if Jo . . ." Oh, *God*. "If Jo and a woman named Anna Eppelwaite are—*were*—the same person."

There was a confused silence at the other end. Hope vied with despair, and her pulse thundered so loud in her ears, she was afraid she'd miss his answer. Then—

"Yes."

Her heart went flat as a pancake.

Jo.

Anna.

. . . *JoAnna*.

"How did you—?" Sean cleared his throat, started again. "I guess I probably should have told you she was from Cordelia. Did you know her?"

She couldn't answer. She sat frozen, the phone gripped so tight in her hand she almost broke it in two. She'd known. At some level since Tansy's, she'd known, but hearing it verified, a chill had spread from her spine until she felt like she'd turned into ice.

"Mari?"

"Why *didn't* you tell me she might be someone I knew?" Her voice was a croak.

"Well, I . . . What difference does it make?"

Tears leaked from her eyes.

"Mari?"

"It makes no difference. Not anymore. I—" She drew in a long, shuddering breath. She needed to tell him it was over, needed to tell him never to contact her again, but further conversation was beyond her tonight. "I'll call you in the morning. I have to go now."

"Wait. This isn't a big deal. Let's talk."

Isn't a big deal. God. "I have to go now," she repeated. "Please don't call back tonight; you'll wake my family."

Without waiting for an answer, she shut the phone off, sat for a long while in the dark, and then stumbled her way downstairs.

She'd have to tell Andy. She had to. Even though she knew her confession would likely mean the end of her friendship, her romance, and her dreams with her best friend, Andy Eppelwaite.

Chapter 20

Only four hours later, Mari woke from a fitful doze just as the first rays of sunshine crested the hills. She felt bruised and battered, but now that she had faced the worst—now that she *knew* the worst—she'd decided she wouldn't give up. She'd battle for her future with Andy, although she didn't have much of a plan. Or much hope. But at least she had enough to give her a reason to crawl out of bed.

After belting on her kimono and rinsing her mouth, she crept upstairs, where the household still slept. She'd said she'd call Sean back—and she would. She wanted to make it clear their relationship was ended, never to be resurrected again. Before she murmured one word about her past to Andy, she had to sweep it entirely away. When she told Andy, she wanted him to know she hadn't held a Plan B in reserve.

Phone in hand, she headed to the deck where she could talk without waking her parents. Her footsteps scattered some chipmunks breakfasting on the corn Pop had scattered across the boards. It was only six. She'd catch Sean before he joined the Monday morning rush hour.

She settled in a chair near the railing and punched in his number again. Unbelievable that less than five hours ago she'd called him and learned the truth. She felt like she'd aged a hundred years since then. When the phone started ringing, she slid down in her seat and hooked her feet onto the lowest rung on the railing. He picked up immediately.

"I worried about you all night. I don't know what dif—"

"Sean," she interrupted, then drew in a breath and willed herself to be patient. She wanted to have this done, and she felt like raging at him, but that would just make things worse. He couldn't have known—nobody could have known—what his wife's identity would end up meaning to her. How such a horrific coincidence could have happened was beyond her grasp. Despite her normally insatiable curiosity, she'd gone to such pains during their affair to learn as little as possible about Jo. She'd known that the more real the woman was to her, the more her guilt would swamp her. That she'd known Sean's wife all along—that she'd been the sister of her best friend—was a cruel, ironic, and astonishing blow.

"Don't say it, Mari. Please. Let's talk."

"We are talking. And I—"

"In person. I'm not sure what's going on, or what difference it makes who my wife was, but I want to explain—"

"There's nothing to explain, Sean. I've just decided that we can't—"

"You said your family's cabin is on the far shore, right? You'll be in the phone book down there," he added, probably suspecting (accurately) that she wouldn't give him directions. "I'll come today."

"You can't come here!" She gave a wild look around the deck as though he'd materialize right in front of her. Then, realizing she'd raised her voice, she dipped her head and spoke into her lap. "You just *can't*." Work wouldn't stop him—she knew that. He could take off from Carmichael's whenever he wanted.

"Then tell me where to meet you." He was the epitome of patience.

She hesitated. Behind her she heard a scraping on the steps. The chipmunks were busy again. If she didn't agree to meet him, he'd probably track her down. She had experience with his quiet tenacity. And maybe she owed him a personal meeting. She'd let him twist in the wind all summer—and he'd once been her whole world. "All right. In Cordelia, at Peg O' My Heart at noon." It might not hurt to have her sister nearby. And it sure wouldn't hurt to unburden this latest development onto Alcea's shoulders anyway. She'd need her sister's moral support before she told Andy.

Just thinking about *that* yanked at the knot in her stomach.

"That's the diner on the main drag, isn't it?" Sean had hesitated at her suggestion. "Isn't there a park or something in the middle of the square? Let's meet there instead."

For a second, she wondered why he was objecting to the diner, and then it hit her. Of course, he'd know something about Cordelia. Jo—Anna—must have taken him there at some point to meet her grandmother. And her brother. She swallowed hard. Good thing Sean had been thinking. She didn't want Tansy to witness their meeting any more than he did. Tansy might tell Andy she'd seen them before Mari could explain. And grovel. And beg.

"Fine. I'll be there."

After they hung up, Mari dropped the phone in her lap and stared across the cove. The lake rippled like satin. She'd play sick this morning, wave Finney and Andy off to Camp Sycamore, then drive into Cordelia. She'd be back before . . .

From behind her came a slight cough. Startled, she twisted around. Finney stood at the top of the steps in a pale pink wrapper, holding a cup. She wiggled it. "We're out of coffee. I thought I'd sneak in and steal

some. Is everything okay? You look pale as a sheet."
Eyes concerned, she glanced at the phone.

"Um, everything's fine." Mari rubbed her stomach,
wondering how long Finney had been there. She'd just
looked around the deck a moment ago, so it couldn't
have been very long. She played back her side of the
conversation since then and decided there wasn't
much to latch on to. "Go on in and help yourself."
She motioned toward the door.

Finney started toward it.

"Uh, Finney, I'm not going in to camp today. My
stomach . . ."

"I thought that might be it." Finney turned around.
"Has it gotten worse? Maybe you should see a doctor."

Mari was hit by sudden inspiration. "My thoughts
exactly. I just called my doctor—uh, Dr. *Peg*—in Cordelia." Dummy. Doctors' offices wouldn't be open yet.
"I mean, I talked to his service. They said he'll
squeeze me in. Around noon."

"Oh, good. I'm glad they're open today, but it's too
bad you have to spend your day off in the doctor's
office."

Why wouldn't the doctor's office be open? "My
day off?"

Finney nodded. "Since July Fourth fell on a Sunday,
we all have today off. Oh, not Kirk and not the YCPs,
but the rest of us do."

Mari gave herself a mental clunk on the head. Of
course. Well, she'd just have to avoid Andy until she
left for Cordelia. Starting right now. "I think I'll go
back to bed." What she really planned to do was go
downstairs, dress, and leave. "Um, could you tell
Andy what's up? And ask him not to wake me?"

"Sure. Is there anything else I can do? Do you want
me to ask Andy if he can drive you up there?"

"No! I mean, thanks, but I, uh, have to take my car
in. Brakes are slipping," she lied.

"Okay. I hope you feel better." Finney's face was full of sympathy.

Which only made Mari feel worse.

Trying to make sense of the worries about Mari that Finney had spilled in his ears over coffee this morning—and Finney's suspicions of what might be wrong—Andy sat in the back booth of Peg O' My Heart Cafe and Bakery. It was just past noon. When he'd arrived a half hour ago, the diner had already been stuffed to the brim, but he'd managed to claim this spot before the thick of the lunch crowd swarmed through the doors. In a corner, next to a wall of windows, the seat offered a full view of the restaurant and a good chunk of Main Street and the square. If Mari had indeed traveled up to Cordelia today, maybe he'd catch sight of her from here.

The phone book had turned up no Dr. Peg—maybe Finney had gotten the name wrong. Nor had casual inquiries to Lil, Alcea, and Patsy Lee unearthed Mari. Her car wasn't with Julius at Cowboy's Tow and Service, nor had she hauled it to the new garage out on the highway. He didn't know where she was. Or what she might be doing.

He picked up his fork and looked down at his cranberry-pecan cake. It was one of Alcea's concoctions and it was probably great. He wouldn't know. Everything tasted like lint.

Mari had acted strange since that evening at Gran's. He poked at the pie with his fork. No, since he'd told her about Anna. And now she was sick? Or was it something else, like Finney suspected? For the first time in their lives, he didn't have a clue what she was about.

Early this morning, Finney had come back from fetching coffee looking concerned. She'd overheard part of a phone call, she told him. While she'd spooned the grounds into the coffeepot's basket, she'd said Mari had made arrangements to visit a Dr. Peg today, which made sense, since her stomach had been hurting for the last few days. But Mari had acted funny about it, Finney had continued, which made Finney suspect something more than a tummyache was bothering Mari.

Mari, Finney had said, might very well be sick, or she might be . . .

Pregnant.

His grip tightened on the fork. It would explain everything. Mari's uncharacteristic quiet. The stomach problems. The reason talking about the future would upset her. They hadn't even found a compromise on where they could live, let alone discussed marriage . . . or children.

He dropped the fork on his plate, unable to eat. The more he'd thought about it, the more he was sure Finney was right. He was torn between elation and frustration. It would be just like Mari to carry the knowledge by herself, to put her ducks in a row, and then announce a decision. He was here because he wouldn't let her make it alone. Dammit. Whatever choices needed to be made needed to be made by *both* of them. And abortion or adoption were *out*.

After Finney's recital, he'd headed to the O'Malleys' cabin. Mari's car was already gone. He wasn't surprised—it would be like Mari to disappear so she wouldn't need to handle explanations. Not knowing what else to do, he'd gotten in his truck and had made off for Cordelia. His only clues, *Dr. Peg* and *noon*.

He looked around. This was as close as he'd gotten to a "Peg" of any stripe. And it was a good deal past noon. And he'd seen no sign of Mari.

This was stupid. He'd pay his tab and head back. Whatever Mari was up to, he'd force it from her tonight. She couldn't avoid him forever.

But before he could rise, Alcea paused next to his table and refilled his cup. "Hey, Andy. Haven't you found your partner in crime yet?"

He couldn't quite manage a smile.

Alcea frowned. "Is there something wrong? Did she tell you— Did you two quarrel?"

"No." He paused. "Did she tell me what?"

"Nothing." Alcea pushed a few tendrils of hair back, and gave him a smile. "I'm so frazzled today, my mouth's working without benefit of a brain."

He eyed her, knowing she was lying.

But Alcea's smile didn't waver. "Well, you have a good day. I need to get back to work." Glancing out the window, she started toward the counter. "By the way, there's your lady love now." She stopped to refill another cup, then continued on.

Wondering if Alcea already knew Mari was pregnant, he looked across Main to the church green. Sure enough, Mari, identifiable at this distance by her apricot curls, was settling onto a bench under a tree. Rising, he dipped into his pocket for his wallet and, throwing a couple of bills down on the table, he glanced out again.

And was startled to see a man take a seat beside her. Close beside her, too close for a casual passerby.

Something about the guy was familiar—Andy leaned over the table, nearly pressing his face to the glass. As he watched, the guy ran a hand through a shock of dark hair that tumbled over his forehead à la Hugh Grant. It was a familiar gesture, one just like Anna's husband . . .

Andy stiffened, feeling grimness settle into every line of his body. *Sean Reynolds*. What in the hell was he doing with Mari? A growl sounded deep in his throat when Mari reached for Reynolds's hand.

Mind reeling, he grabbed up his check, squashed it in his grip, and turned toward the exit. His jaw clenched. The line at the cash register was eight deep.

*   *   *

Mari squeezed Sean's hand. "And so I can't go with you. I've fallen in love with somebody else."

"And you're sure." Sean's eyes were grave.

Mari nodded. "There are some stumbling blocks"— that was an understatement—"but I couldn't go with you even if it doesn't work out with . . . him." *Oh, God, please let it work out.*

"At least you're honest."

No, she wasn't. She hadn't been honest at all. But somehow she'd make up for lost time.

Sean withdrew his hand from her grasp. "I probably should have known when I came to your apartment in May that I'd waited too long." Settling elbows on his knees, he stared out across Main. Around them, folks still enjoying their Fourth of July weekend strolled along by the shop fronts or gathered on blankets spread out on the green. "I wish that when Jo was alive, back when we were together, that I'd just—"

Mari didn't want to go there. "I know. But you *didn't* leave her, so it's kind of pointless to wonder *what if* now." She paused. "Why didn't you ever tell me that Jo had relatives here in Cordelia? That she was someone I might know. Was it just because you were afraid I'd mention it to someone here, and it would all get back to Jo?"

"I'll admit that was part of it."

Mari folded her arms. "Afraid that she'd toss you out if she had proof, that you'd have to pay a fat alimony?"

Sean smiled. It was a sad smile. "No. I told you the truth when I said she got hysterical at any mention of divorce. She . . . Mari, Jo already knew. Oh, not about you in particular, but she knew there were other women through the years. If it had gotten back to her that I was seeing someone from her home town, though, she would have been *beyond* hysterical. You have no idea." His expression grew distant. "I just didn't want to rub her nose in it."

"How . . . gentlemanly . . . of you. Did you ever think what it might mean to me?" This was old territory—Sean's balancing act between concern for Jo and love for Mari. It had always made her see red. She tamped down her anger, knowing it was just a knee-jerk reaction from long ago.

"Yes, but . . . You probably won't believe me, but the main reason I didn't tell you I had any connection with this place was because I loved you. I wanted you. And I was afraid that even if you hadn't known Jo, you'd probably known—maybe still knew—her family here, and that would just make you feel even more guilty than you already did. You'd use it as another excuse to leave. It was hard enough as it was to hang on to you as long as I did."

"Dammit, Sean." She couldn't help it—her eyes filled. "Her brother was—*is*—my best friend." At least for another few minutes.

He looked down, and she scrubbed the tears away. "How did you meet her anyway?"

"Same way I met you. She was an artist, too."

"She applied for an internship?"

"Several years before you."

Mari let that soak in. "And you offered her marriage. And me . . . You offered me an affair. Gee, thanks."

He winced. "I offered you love, Mari."

He had, but it hadn't been hers to take. "So maybe you were right. Maybe I would have stopped seeing you altogether because I would have felt I owed some kind of loyalty to her." Frowning, she thought a minute. Would she have quit seeing Sean? She doubted it. She'd been so over-the-top in *loooove*. And stupid, to boot. She wouldn't have cared what anyone thought or given two snaps how much consternation local knowledge of her affair might cause her own family. Now . . . well, now it was different. *She* was different. She narrowed her eyes. "Or was the real reason you

kept quiet because you wanted to avoid unpleasantness? Just like you waited to drop the *I'm married*
bombshell on me until the week *after* I'd gone with
you in New York?"

"I'm not proud of that." Sean sat back. "Yes, I was
trying to avoid unpleasantness. For you as well as me.
You know how small towns are, always with their fingers in everyone else's business. Hell, you're small-
town."

Mari blinked. "I am?"

"Well . . . look at you."

She looked down at the terry shorts and top she'd
snagged from Lil's dresser of old lake-wear before
heading off to the drive-in movies with Andy in June.
With repeated wear, the turquoise had faded. She'd
accessorized the outfit with flip-flops. She hadn't even
thought about what she was throwing on this morning,
but she marveled now that her getup hadn't included
makeup or a single dangling earring.

Sean's voice had lacked any censure, but still, his
words riled her. Beyond reason, really, which was tes-
tament to the state of her nerves. "What difference
does it make what I *wear*? And I prefer to think that
around here we're in 'everyone else's business' because we care about each other." This wasn't what
she really wanted to rail about—she wanted to rail at
fate. But this would do for the moment, so she barreled on. "It's not like the city, where people duck
their heads and pretend not to notice anyone else's
problems. We might quarrel and have our differences,
but we band together, too." She pointed at Peg O'
My Heart, looked back at Sean. "Did you know that
everyone here is responsible for my sister's business?
The diner burned down four years ago, and the whole
town got together to help Alcea and Florida rebuild."

Sean looked where she was pointing and turned
white. "Shit," he muttered. "Shit, shit, shit. I just knew
this would happen if I came here."

Startled, Mari glanced across the street, and her stomach flopped over. *Shit* was right, but it didn't nearly begin to cover the situation. Glowering like he was ready to kill someone, Andy was headed directly toward them.

Chapter 21

By the time Andy reached them, Sean had already put the bench between them. He stood behind it, leaving Mari, too shocked to move, first in the line of fire. With the unerring radar of small-town folks, a number of people had sensed a scene and turned to watch. Near the curb, Paddy O'Neill looked over, thumbs stuck in his suspenders.

When Andy was just a few feet away, Mari's paralysis broke. She rose and threw her hands out in a gesture of appeal. Red-faced and almost foaming at the mouth, Andy looked angrier than she'd ever seen him. "Andy, please, not here. Let's go someplace private and we can—"

Eyes pinned on Sean, Andy ignored her. He stopped just short of the bench, fists clenched at his sides. "Get the hell out of here, Reynolds."

Mari wouldn't have thought that it would take more than that for Sean to turn tail and run. But to her surprise, even though he looked as spooked as a deer in headlights, Sean stiffened. "Listen, Eppelwaite. I have as much right to visit an old friend as you have to be here. I won't—"

"Old friend?" Andy turned to Mari. "Old friend?" he repeated. Stunned, horror dawning in his eyes, Andy looked slowly from her back to Sean.

A flash of heat traveled from her toes to her head, and her skin grew clammy. "Please," she whispered.

"And I'm sorry," Sean continued. "More sorry than you know about what happened to your sister. I know you mourned Jo . . ."

Andy wheeled back to him. "Anna." He bit the name off.

"Anna, then. But I mourned her, too."

"Like hell you did. You mourned her probably as much as you loved her. Which was *not at all*."

Sean stood his ground. "I did love her. I tried to help her. You can't know what it was like."

"Tried to help her? You've got to be kidding. You killed her with your affairs." Andy turned his gaze on Mari. She cringed at the mix of hurt and contempt in his eyes. "Including the one you had with her. That's what this is, isn't it, Mar? He's the scumbag who's been waiting in the wings."

Andy and Mari stared at each other. Hope flickered at the back of his eyes. He wasn't completely sure—he wanted her to deny it. She opened her mouth, but no sound came out. Andy's face dissolved into a moment of pure pain before hardening like a rock. Knees trembling, she thought she'd pass out. His look was not only full of scorn; it was full of *hate*.

Sean looked uncertainly between them, then looked at her. "Good God. Is this *him*?"

Speechless for once in her life, Mari just nodded. This couldn't be happening.

"Look, Eppelwaite, you can't blame her. And you can't blame me. What happened—"

"Was your fault." Andy's chin jerked at Mari. "And hers."

"No, it wasn't!" Sean seemed to struggle with himself, then blurted, "Your sister was sick. Mentally ill."

Mentally ill? Jo . . . Anna .had been mentally ill? Sean had always just called it *emotional problems*. Mentally ill implied something more serious.

"You *slime*." Andy's fists clenched. "Don't you slander Anna. Don't you dare blame her for—"

"She *was*. And she'd tried suicide before." Sean didn't flinch. He leaned both hands on the back of the bench and spoke earnestly. "I thought it was my fault for a long time, too. I wasn't the best husband, I'll admit it. I should have stuck by her completely—and faithfully. Or left her all together. But she needed me. And I—" He swallowed. "It wasn't fair. It wasn't fair to any of us. Not me, not Jo, not Mari. But even if I had been as faithful as sundown, it wouldn't have made any difference; she still would have killed herself. I've learned in therapy since then that—"

"I don't give a rat's ass about your therapy!" Andy roared. Birds twittered overhead, but everyone else within shouting distance had fallen deathly still.

Mari looked around, took a tentative step toward Andy. "Andy . . ." She reached out to touch his arm, but he jerked away. Out of the corner of her eye, she saw Paddy hustle across the street toward Peg's. She let her arm drop. "Please, calm down. I can explain . . ."

"How can you explain this away, Mar? How? You can't. All this time—"

"I didn't know! Until this weekend, I didn't know!"

The door to Peg's banged open, and Alcea came flying across the street, her face determined. "Andy! Mari! Butts inside. *Right now*." They might have been six again.

Even Andy looked startled. Alcea reached them and grabbed each by an arm. "What do you think you're doing? Providing the July Fourth entertainment?" She turned them toward Peg's, saying over her shoulder to Sean, "Better for everyone if you just move on."

Good Lord. Mari hadn't realized until now how much of her mother's genes Alcea had inherited.

Sean looked bemused. "Yes, yes, that's probably

best." To Mari, he added, "I'm sorry. So sorry, Mari. Call me if you need me. I mean it."

Steering them toward Peg's, Alcea scolded them all the way there. Inside, she pushed them toward the kitchen, then into the cubby she and Florida used for an office. Windowless and small, the entire utilitarian space was practically filled up by the desk and computer.

"Rip each other's heads off in here if you want. Nobody will stop you—nor will anyone *see*." She made a sound of disgust, then looked at Andy. "And *you*— You know what? My ex-husband cheated on me fifteen ways to Sunday for *years*, and I didn't find it necessary to put a period to my existence. You might think about that."

Andy's mouth just tightened. Shaking her head, Alcea harrumphed and slammed the door behind her. Mari and Andy stood staring at each other.

For a while, neither of them said a word. Then Andy shook out a folding metal chair, plunked it in a corner—as far away from her as he could possibly get—and sprawled onto it, hands stuffed in his pockets, legs out. The look he gave her was a dare. "Well?"

Seeing the hard cast of his face, Mari's heart splintered. She might have awakened with hope, but as she looked at him now, hope faded. He'd already made up his mind. Still, she had to try. Pulling nervously on a lock of her hair, she settled into the chair behind the desk. She spoke in a monotone. "When I met Sean, I had no idea he was married until . . . until it was too late. And then I didn't want to give him up. I loved him, Andy. Or at least I thought I did. And at the time, he was separated from Jo—"

Andy shifted.

"I mean, *Anna*. And then he went back to her. And then they separated again." She tugged a hand through her hair. "Their marriage was a ping-pong game, but I hoped . . . well, each time I hoped he'd leave her for good. I knew it was wrong, me and a married man, but—"

"And look how everything ended. Are you proud of yourself?" Andy's voice was colder than the arctic tundra.

Mari looked at her hands. "No." Then she felt a flash of spirit and looked back up. "But I was young, and I was in love for the first time. And—and, I was *selfish*. But I wasn't totally without ethics. I did give him up. *Two years* before Anna—Anna . . ."

"Killed herself. Just say it, Mari."

"So are you going to hate me forever because I was *immature*? Is that such a sin? I didn't understand the full consequences of what I was doing. I didn't think. I . . . just didn't!" She groped for something, anything to excuse what had happened. "The affair was wrong, okay? I know that, and I'll always feel *horrible* about it, especially since Sean said Anna was mentally—"

"Stop!" Andy slammed a hand down on the desk and she jumped. She watched him struggle to regain control, then he looked at her with disgust. "*Mentally ill*. The guy is a self-centered asshole. He'd say anything to wiggle out of responsibility."

Feeling more desperate than she'd ever felt in her life, she reached across the desk toward him, even though he wasn't within her grasp. "*I love you*, Andy. I do. And I want—"

"Do you know why I followed you here today?" he interrupted. "Because Finney thought that you might be pregnant. And I decided she could be right. I thought that was what had made you so quiet—that you'd gone to have a test while I was at the Rooster on Saturday and had learned about it then, that you were sick to your stomach because—" He stopped, his expression losing some of its edge. "Hell." He looked away, and his Adam's apple bobbed as he swallowed.

"I was worried for whatever you were going through emotionally, but the more I thought about a baby, I—I was thrilled."

Tears blurred her vision. "We can still have a future together, Andy. We can talk it all out, get through this, figure out where to live, and—"

"I can't." Andy's voice was soft. He stood up. When he looked at her, his expression was bleak. "I know I didn't see Anna much, and I know we weren't as close as you and your sisters, but she was my only family besides Gran. Maybe you can't understand how I feel about them since you've always taken your family for granted, and you're always looking for the next way to escape them. I can forgive a lot of things, Mari, but this—" He shook his head. "I'm sorry." His voice broke. "I am so sorry."

Quietly, he opened the door and slipped out, then closed it softly behind him. Mari stared at the place where he'd stood.

Then she dropped her head on her arms and cried.

Mari thought she'd cried herself out by the time a rap sounded on the door an hour later. Without waiting for an invitation, someone opened the door. She raised her head, hoping against hope. . . .

But it was Alcea. She'd let herself in and was closing the door behind her.

When her sister turned and their eyes met, Alcea's expression tightened with concern. She hurried around the desk, dropped to her knees, and swiveled Mari's chair to face her. Without saying a word, Alcea pulled her into her arms. Mari's weeping began anew. But within the circle of her sister's embrace, and with Alcea's murmurs of comfort, she calmed down enough to spill the entire nightmare into her big sister's ears.

"How could this *possibly* happen?" she wailed. "Why *me*?"

Alcea pulled back. Slipping a tissue from her apron

pocket, she wiped Mari's cheeks. She smiled slightly.
"Is it really that far of a reach? I've heard lots of
stories about Anna from her grandmother since Tansy
and I started working together, especially around the
time she was mourning Anna's death. It sounds like
the two of you were alike in many ways. Both artistic,
both highly talented, both stubborn and determined
to get your way . . ."

Mari sniffled. "Watch it."

"It'd be a wonder if you didn't attract the same
kind of man."

"But the exact *same* man?"

"Why not?" Alcea sat back on her heels. "I know
it seems unbelievable, but coincidences happen all the
time. They're just part of life—and I think they occur
for a reason. Maybe not one that's apparent at the
time, but . . ." Alcea patted her knee. "Well, look at
me. What were the chances that I'd fall in love with
the brother of my ex-husband's mistress? And what
were the chances that she'd become my boss before
she became my partner? Why was I forced into situations where I had to get along with her, when what I
really wanted to do was twist her head off?"

"I dunno." Mari took the tissue from Alcea's hand
and blew her nose.

"I think I do. I was one big fat ball of resentment
and pain, an absolute joy to be around. To find love—
both with Dak and in my work—I had to let all that
go. Working through my feelings about Florida and
becoming her friend were big reasons why I could.
Call it providence. Call it fate. Call it karma. But when
you think about it, flukes like that aren't that
unusual."

"Sean told me he met Anna the same way I met
him—different years, but we both interviewed for intern positions," Mari allowed.

"Not surprising at all, then. Carmichael's offers internships through local colleges, both of you went to

one, both of you were artists. Considering that artists think landing a job at Carmichael's is a major coup . . ." She shrugged as if to say, *Case closed.*

Mari eyed her sister. Since linking up with Dak, who had a tendency to philosophize, Alcea could sometimes get all woo-woo. Not very often, granted, but sometimes. Mari didn't know if she bought into Alcea's theories, but she wasn't up to arguments. "Okay, so maybe twists of fate are meant to be, and this isn't that strange. But somehow that doesn't make me feel a single bit better." Tears welling again, Mari held her hands to her hot cheeks. "I love him, Alcea. I just love him so much!"

Once more, Alcea gathered her close. "I know you do, sweetheart. Hang on to hope. Something good is bound to come from all this. I just know it."

Chapter 22

Three weeks later, Mari hadn't seen a scrap of Alcea's promised good, had lost whatever lingering hope she'd still had, and had pretty much decided fate was simply cruel and her sister was simply nuts. So it was nice that the last Monday of July had ushered in a storm that perfectly suited such bright-eyed optimism. While afternoon lightning flashed against the windows, she sat at her computer in the cabin's family room and watched while her printer purred out the umpteenth job description she'd answered in the last fourteen days. At a card table in the corner, her mother and Pop played a desultory game of rummy.

She lifted the piece of paper from the printer tray. This position was in Phoenix. Phoenix was a cool city, right? Well, not exactly *cool*, but it was a good many miles from where she'd screwed up her life. Quite a distance from Andy, so she'd never need to see that self-righteous, hostile expression again. Her eyes filled. Damn. She'd already cried the proverbial river. She should be all dried up.

For the first week after her relationship with Andy had crashed and burned, she'd returned to Camp Syc-amore, determined to carry on, reminding herself that even if Andy blamed her (and Sean) for Anna's death, and even if she still tended to blame herself (and Sean), too, both Sean and Alcea had argued she shouldn't. She'd blundered big time, yes. But *Anna*, not Mari, had made the biggest blunder of all. And although she wasn't entirely sure she believed either Alcea or Sean, their words had helped her hold up her chin. She had her pride. And she cared for those kids. She wouldn't let what had happened with Andy drive her away, not this close to the end of camp.

But seeing Andy hurt like a spear through the heart. When they had to talk—and at camp, it was a necessity, although they avoided each other as much as they could—he was courteous, but distant, his eyes never quite meeting hers. And Finney wasn't much warmer. That hurt, too, but she could understand Finney's loyalty.

And she could have handled it. She really could have, except it wasn't more than two days into the week when the kids noticed the strain and started asking questions. Maybe she could have even coped with that, too. But on Thursday afternoon—when Finney had snapped at her over spilled tempera paint, and she'd snapped right back, and the boys had chosen sides, resulting in one big yell-a-thon—she'd realized her days at Sycamore had to end.

That Friday, she'd told Kirk she wouldn't return Monday. Then, disregarding the camp rule *Thou shalt not say more than* boo *to your nephew*, she'd looked for Michael, finding him near the greenhouse, working with the other boys under Andy's guidance. When she'd pulled Michael aside, Andy had opened his mouth to object. She'd given him one hard glare. He'd subsided with only a glare back. She and Michael had settled themselves on a bench under a nearby tree, where she'd explained this was her last day at camp.

"But why do you have to go?" Michael brushed his bangs back, his chocolate-drop eyes looking so much like they had when he was small, she wanted to hug him. But one didn't do that to a fifteen-year-old, especially in front of his friends.

She settled for scooting closer so their knees touched. "I think you know Andy and I are no longer . . . getting along."

"So what? You work over there, and he works over here."

"Yes, but . . . Well, Finney isn't happy with me either. The differences between all of us are causing tension, and that's not good for anyone here."

Michael's frown deepened. "I've never liked her."

"Please don't choose sides. I don't want—"

"Not because of *you*. She, like, says the right things and everything, but she doesn't let you get too close or something." He looked at Andy, who was helping Malloy stake tomato plants. "She's not like Andy."

Guess Finney had succeeded in her quest to retain some emotional distance. Mari followed Michael's gaze. Done with the tomatoes, Andy clapped Malloy on the shoulder. The youngster grinned, gazing at Andy with near reverence. Maybe Andy's way *was* better than Finney's. But Mari wasn't about to put a spoke in the art therapist's wheel. What happened here was too important. "Finney's a good person, Michael. She really does care, she just—"

"It's all her fault." Bangs tumbling back over his eyes, he dug his hands in his pockets.

"No. No, it isn't. It's mine. *I* caused the problems between Andy and me, and Finney's just being loyal to Andy. You know how it is—I'm sure you're like that with your own friends."

"Yeah, but I'd be loyal to *all* of them. And you and Finney *are* friends . . . right?"

She thought about it. "Well, we were." Or at least had been well on their way to becoming friends.

Michael withdrew his hands, pulling something out of his pocket and absentmindedly rotating it in his fingers. "Then they shouldn't make you leave."

A trickle of sunlight struck whatever Michael held and bounced off. Blinking, she recalled the object he'd swooped to pick up from the ditch on that day she'd nearly run him down. "Nobody's making me leave. I decided to do that myself."

His fingers stilled. "You mean, you *could* stay?"

She nodded. "But I'm not going to. It would cause too many problems."

"But I don't want you to leave," he burst out. "You're like—" He stopped.

"Like what?"

He dipped his head. "Well, it's just . . . It's like having my family around with you here."

Having expected not much more than a shrug and a *see ya later*, she was touched. "There's only four more weeks of camp left. You'll be home before you know it." Afraid of tears, she kept her tone brisk and changed the subject. She nodded toward his hands. "What's that you've got?"

Michael looked down. "Nothing." He closed his fist.

"What kind of nothing?"

Reluctantly, he uncurled his fingers. A small Swiss Army pocketknife rested on his palm.

She recognized it. "That's a Christmas present from Lil, isn't it?" How he'd smuggled it past everyone here was anyone's guess. Now she'd need to weasel it away from him before he got into trouble. Still, it was sweet that he'd carried something here from home, especially something from Lil.

His hand closed in a tight grip around it. "It wasn't from Lil. It was from my mom."

Mari frowned. "But Lil showed it to me before she—oh." Too late, she remembered. Mari could have cheerfully cut out her tongue. The knife had been a present, like many others through the years, that Lil had bought and wrapped for her stepchildren, signing the gift tags from Belinda. "Um, you're right, it was."

Michael stared at her through narrowed eyes. "The card said so. It's one of the only things I have from her. It's the *last thing* I have from her."

"Uh-huh. I remember now. Your mom just asked Lil to wrap it for her. That's why I got confused."

Opening his palm, Michael stared at the knife. He looked back up. "Lil *did* buy it, didn't she?" His voice was dull.

She couldn't look him in the eyes and flat-out lie. She tried to dodge instead. "Michael," she said gently. "You know you can't have a knife at—"

He stood up, stuffing the knife into his pocket, dragging his hair back. His eyes had reddened. "What do you care?" His voice rose. "You're leaving."

"I *do* care." She reached out and touched his fingers. "That's why—"

"What's going on here?" Sounding very official, Andy interrupted.

Undoubtedly he'd been waiting for an excuse to butt in, and Michael's raised voice had given him just that. Damn him. A few more minutes and she not only would have calmed Michael, but she would have had the knife for safekeeping until camp ended. She glared at Andy and glanced at her nephew. Michael dashed a hand across his eyes, then locked his gaze on her, fearful and defiant.

She sighed. She couldn't fink out her own nephew. Besides, he'd had the knife since day one, and it hadn't posed a problem. He wouldn't harm himself with it, nor anyone else. It was a memento to him, not a weapon. She shook her head. "Nothing's going on. Nothing at all."

"Michael, go help Malloy." Andy had waited until Michael obeyed, then had looked at her. "Mari, I've told you—"

"Oh, for cryin' out loud. Get off your high horse, Andy. I've had about as much of your judgments and strictures and rules as I can take." She'd risen and met him nose to nose. *Criminy*, she hated looking up at him. "Someday you'll find out you don't have a monopoly on morality."

"What's that supposed to mean?"

"It means the world isn't painted in black and white. There are a lot of shades of gray."

Feeling that was probably about as profound as she'd ever get in her life, Mari had turned on her heel and left him staring after her, pulling off his cap, scratching his head.

That was the last time she'd seen him. Since then, her days had fallen into a routine—helping her mother and Pop with chores and errands in the mornings, job-hunting in the afternoons, and evenings spent with her easel on the dock. That was an exercise in frustration, since she still couldn't whip the vision in her head out onto the canvas. But the painting wasn't as frustrating as seeing Andy's mirage everyplace she went, no matter how hard she tried to expel him from her brain. Not that it was his fault. He no longer joined them for supper, nor did he use the dock or wander the grounds like he'd once done. He didn't slip alongside her at night or flash her his lopsided, crinkle-eyed grin. Nor did he . . . Her eyes welled again. Hell! Looking at the Phoenix job description again, she shoved her memories so far back in her brain she hoped they were lost forever.

Pop slapped down a card. Out in the kitchen, Lil bustled around. From the smell of things, her sister had whipped up a batch of oatmeal cookies. The Van Castles had come for the weekend. Just to check up on Mother, Lil had said, although Mari thought she'd more likely been prompted by whatever Alcea had told her about her and Andy's showdown on Main. Jon had returned to Cordelia yesterday with Melanie, but Lil had decided to stay on for a few more days.

Pop yawned and folded his hand. "Think I'll go take a nap. Want to join me?"

Zinnia glanced at Mari. "No, go on with you. I'll just keep Mari company."

"You don't have to stay, Mom. I'm fine."

Pop wandered out of the room and Mari watched him go, wanting to call him back, just in case this was the opportunity her mother had been waiting for to let her know how she *really* felt about the mess she'd made of her life. When she'd returned from Cordelia on that awful day, she'd spilled the whole horrible story into their laps. She was sick of secrets and had figured they couldn't make her feel any worse than she already did. Since then, they'd stayed mum on anything to do with her love life, and they'd also treated her like she was made out of glass. Which had surprised her, since she'd expected to be shunned— after Zinnia had strung her up by her big toes, of course.

"You're looking tired—you sure you don't want a nap?" Mari asked. Alcea's words echoed through her mind. *Pop and Mother won't be with us forever.* "You really should rest, you know."

"I'm fine. What you got there?"

Mari glanced down at the paper in her hand. "Another job to apply for." Another yawner of a design job. She just couldn't drum up the enthusiasm she'd once had for the field.

"Good one?"

"I suppose." Mari dropped the paper on top of a pile. Some companies accepted applications electronically, but this one, like the others in this pile, wanted it mailed. She tapped a few strokes, waited for her résumé to pop up.

"You don't sound none too excited about it."

"I'm not. But I need to make a living. And this is what I do."

"Well, if it doesn't toot your horn anymore, why don't you learn to do something else?"

Mari snorted. She pulled up the print menu, inserted a number, stuck some linen paper in the printer. "On whose money? I'm broke, in case you haven't noticed."

"Ours." Lil stood in the doorway, a plate of cookies in her hand.

"And ours," her mother added.

Mari's jaw went slack. She stared at them both.

Zinnia smiled. "Listen, honeybunch, you keep yammering away—"

"Talking," Lil inserted, offering the plate to Zinnia.

Zinnia took a cookie. "Okay, *talking* about how you want to make a fresh start. What better way to do it than with a brand-new career?"

Mari recovered her powers of speech. "With your money? Mom, you paid for the degree I already have with a second mortgage on your house. I couldn't—"

"Jon, the dear heart, took care of all that after he and Lil got married. We're free and clear now. We'd like to see you spend your inheritance, such as it is. Why wait until we're gone?" Zinnia took a bite of her cookie. "Mmm." She nodded approval at Lil.

"Don't talk like that," Mari snapped.

Zinnia looked surprised. "But these cookies *are* good."

"I'm not talking about *cookies*." Forgetting her résumés, Mari stood up—and almost toppled over. Figuring she'd have to get used to heels again, she'd put on her wedge sandals this morning. Now she impatiently kicked them off. Stupid things. "You and Pop still have a lot of years left—a *lot*!—and you might need that money."

"Come sit by me a moment, honeybunch." Zinnia patted the seat Pop had abandoned, and Mari reluctantly joined her at the table, knowing she was about to be talked into something whether she wanted it or not. Her mother took her hands and stared into her eyes. "Pop and I are doing fine now, but this recent scare with my ticker . . . Well, no telling what can happen and at any time. It's something we all have to face sometime."

"But not—not now." Mari felt tears dangerously close to the surface again.

"Yes, now." Lil laid a hand on her shoulder. "We talked about it after you went to bed last night. Although we all hope Mother and Pop have a lot of years left, they've faced that they won't be around forever, and they don't want us pretending otherwise. What they do want—"

"Is to know before it's our time to go that all our children are right and tight." Zinnia squeezed her hands, then let go and settled back in her chair. "You know, Patsy Lee is older than you and she's set her sights on a different future with that business degree she's working on evenings. And we're paying for her schooling."

"You are?"

"Least we could do for Henry's widow." Zinnia's eyes misted as they always did when she talked about the eldest child who was no longer with them. "So she's set. And Lil and Alcea are happy. Or, leastaways, most of the time. Lil's got her problems now with Michael, but that'll eventually pass. But you—"

"Have screwed up as usual." Mari looked down.

Lil pulled up another chair. "You haven't screwed up; you've just taken some detours."

Lil would forgive the devil himself. But her mother . . . Mari looked up at Zinnia. "I don't know how you can stand to help me again. I thought you and Pop would hate me after I told you about Sean."

"Hate you? Lord love a duck, child, I can tell you aren't a parent. We might not always like the choices you make. Nor your sisters—I 'bout raised the roof when Alcea told me she was set on marrying that no-good first husband of hers, and Lil almost drove me into the nuthouse, what with worrying her and Jon would never find their way together after they met."

"But that's not the same," Mari said miserably.

"What I did—I knew people could—*would*—get hurt. I knew Sean had a wife."

"Their marriage was in trouble, and from what you've said he told you, it sounds like their problems stemmed mostly from her emotional state." Lil smiled grimly. "And I know how much stress that can put on a family. Mari, you were a symptom, not the cause."

"That's no excuse! I could have waited—waited until I saw whether or not Sean really meant it when he said he'd leave her. But, *nooo*, not me. I always had to have everything *right now* and *my way*. I didn't give two shakes about what Jo—Anna—felt, I only thought of myself!"

Lil opened her mouth to object, but Zinnia spoke up, her voice quiet, her eyes serious behind her glasses. "Mari's right, there isn't a good excuse, but" —she addressed Mari—"did you really *not* care? Didn't you say you gave up that good job because you felt too uncomfortable to be around him at work?"

"So what?"

"And didn't you tell me you threw the man out of your life at the same rate that he moved in and out of his home?"

"But—"

"Plus you put a stop to letting him into your bed four years ago."

Mari flushed. "Yes, but—"

"And then gave up the business contracts that kept your own company going after that." Zinnia finally stopped and eyed her.

"What in the hell difference does all that make?" Mari burst out.

"Ah, Marigold McKenzie, you gave up your job, you gave up your social life, and you brought your business down around your ears. And not for that man, but because your morals have been tussling with your hormones since the day you met him. You thought about his wife, all right. Probably didn't think of much else. But you've always been a one who— well, you couldn't learn nothing unless you experienced it firsthand. I don't cotton any to what you did, but I think you've doled out your own punishment. So, no, we don't hate you. We love you. And when you love someone you take the good with the bad." Zinnia's eyes glinted. "Pity young Andy Eppelwaite hasn't learned that yet."

Mari looked at the tabletop. "Until Andy, I thought I'd loved Sean. Really loved him."

"We know you did," Lil said gently. "Otherwise you wouldn't have done what you did."

"And now you know the difference between the real thing and a mirage," Zinnia added.

Mari frowned. "What do you mean?"

"I'm thinking maybe you didn't love that Sean fellow for himself as much as you loved that picture you carried around in your head of what kind of life he could give you. You've always thought something better lay outside your own backyard."

Mari didn't like the way that sounded, but . . . Maybe her mother was right. Sean's looks, his clothes, his lifestyle, his ambition . . . Would he have turned her head if she hadn't thought some of his sophistication would rub off on her? Would she have fallen in love so fast if she hadn't seen in him the promise of a more exciting life? Instead of getting there on her own, had she latched onto him because she'd thought he'd provide a fast track to the cosmopolitan glamour she'd always wanted?

She fingered the cards Pop had abandoned. "So what exactly have you both figured out that will make me all 'right and tight'?"

Zinnia and Lil exchanged glances, then Zinnia launched in. "You hit some kind of stride working out at that camp. It was obvious from the way you bubbled about it every time you walked in the door after you'd been there. It wasn't just Andy putting that glow on your face."

Great. The Finney Glow.

"We've heard you talking to Finney about art therapy," Lil said. "I've asked her what it took to work in that field."

"And with the degree you have, you're only two years away from the master's you'd need," Zinnia inserted. "Lil talked with Jon—we'd all chip in to pay your tuition and expenses."

Both women beamed as though an enthusiastic *whoopee* was a given. And Mari did have to admit she felt more than a stirring of interest. Camp Sycamore was a far cry from glamour, but the work she'd done there had fulfilled her like design never had. Still, she rebelled against strong-arm tactics. "What about *my* plans? I was thinking of Seattle or L.A. Or Phoenix."

Zinnia's smile dulled. "Still that eager to get out of the neighborhood, are you? You might do well to remember that no matter where you move, honeybunch, you drag your problems along with you."

Lil's chin set. "And Seattle is wet. Phoenix is hot. And L.A. is . . . is *concrete.*"

Lil *would* think like that. Mari ignored her remark while her brain raced ahead. There was nothing written that said she had to take an art therapy degree and live in the Ozark hills like Andy planned to. She could practice her new occupation in any city she wanted. Still . . . "I don't know. . . . Another two years of school? I'll be thirty-two—no, thirty-three—by the time I graduate." It would be impossible to get in anywhere for this fall's semester.

Lil motioned at the pile of job descriptions next to the computer. "And you have something better to do in the meantime?"

Her sister echoed what Andy had said as they'd sat

on the dock in June. *Let's see. If I go back to school,
then in another six years, I'll be six years older. Same
as I'll be if I don't go back to school. And still not
doing what I want with my life.*

Mari slowly sat back in her chair. "I'll be dam—I
mean . . . Oh, hell, I don't know what I mean. But I
think you're right." *Andy* was right.

"You *know* we're right." Zinnia looked smug. "And
watch your mouth."

Mari frowned, trying to remember what Finney had
told her about graduate programs in the region. "Of
course!" Perfect. It would be the best of both worlds.
She reached out and grasped her mother's fingers in
one hand, Lil's in the other. For the first time in what
seemed like forever, she felt optimistic; there really
would be life after Andy. "You both are the absolute
best. But there's one condition."

"What's that?"

"That we treat this like a school loan. I'll pay back
every penny." The more she thought about it, the
more her blood stirred. The idea was good. The idea
was *right*.

"But—" Lil began.

"No buts. Agreed?" She might need their help ini-
tially, but this time she'd get where she wanted to go
on her own, owing no debt. And without a Sean. Smiling, both women nodded, and Mari stood up. "Then
it's back to the Internet. I'll bet I can download the
applications I'll need."

"Oh, I'm so glad, honeybunch." As Mari crossed
the room, Zinnia's voice matched her rising excitement. "Finney told Lil she was real pleased with that
school in Kansas. And Emporia's not so far away.
Why, you can come on home whenever you want."

"Who said anything about Kansas?" Kicking her
sandals out of her way, Mari plopped in front of the
monitor. "Finney told me there's a great program in
Chicago."

She tapped *art therapy* and *chicago* and *graduate program* into Google's search engine. So glad to be distracted from her old problems by the new plans now crowding her head, she barely noticed the silence that fell over the card table. Or the sense of unease that shadowed her high spirits.

Maybe the unease had been a premonition.

That night, while her parents and Lil watched an old Jimmy Stewart movie, Mari sat at the kitchen table penning information onto the applications for the University of Illinois at Circle Campus in Chicago. Might as well get things rolling, even though the application deadline for the following fall semester wasn't until February (they accepted grad students into the art therapy program only once a year). But waiting another year to start school wasn't going to keep her tied here any longer. She'd jump the gun—move up there as soon as possible, take some of the undergrad psych courses she needed, find a job, meet some people . . .

After all, jumping the gun was something she'd always done well.

She wrote slowly, still trying to pinpoint the source of the anxiety that had crept over her earlier and settled into her brain. Yes, it bent her pride to have Lil and her parents funding this next great adventure, but if she wanted to be an art therapist—and the more she thought about it, the more she realized she did— she couldn't do it on her own, not with the whopping tuition at UIC. Guilt stirred. Emporia would cost less. But, really, not *that* much less. Just a couple thousand dollars difference. That wasn't *that* much, was it? Not to people with money like her sister. At least Lil hadn't flinched when Mari had told her what it was. Bless Lil. And bless Mom. And, especially, bless Jon Van Castle's very deep pockets. Warmth twined around her heart. Just like the town of Cordelia, the

O'Malley family had always hung together. There might be some scrapping, but they always came through for each other.

With a flourish, she crossed a *t*, dotted an *i*. But as the warm glow faded, she realized that the knot of discomfort still lingered. She sat back and tried again to unravel it. It wasn't the choice of career or even the specter of another few years of school. And it wasn't guilt about the tuition. She *would* pay them back. Maybe it was simply the impulsiveness with which she'd seized on the whole idea. Impulsiveness had definitely gotten her into trouble before.

She threw down the pen. More likely, her disquiet was caused by regrets over Andy. Except since her conversation with her mother and sister this afternoon, her head had been stuffed with visions of leisurely walks along the Magnificent Mile (where she probably wouldn't be able to afford a thing), the feeling of ascending to the heavens in Sears Tower (was the view as good if you were alone?), and long hours spent wandering among the masterpieces at the Art Institute (where she'd longed to get her degree until she'd gotten a load of *their* fees), leaving little room for reminders of what she'd lost. . . .

At a tap on the sliding door, Mari looked up. Finney stood on the deck, her petite figure silhouetted against the fading blush of last light that had arrived after the thunderclouds had rolled away. And that's when Mari decided the unease was premonition.

Putting a sweet smile on her face, she slid open the door. "Run out of coffee again?" She shouldn't blame Finney; she'd brought down her future with Andy all by herself. But if Finney hadn't run to Andy with tall tales, things might have turned out differently. She didn't quite believe that, but she wanted to spread the blame, and Finney's treatment lately had stung.

Finney flushed. "N-no."

"Well, come on in anyway."

She stepped out of the way, but Finney hesitated.

Mari waited a beat, then shrugged. "Or I'll come out." She stepped through the door, avoiding the puddles on the deck. "So, what do you want?"

Finney shifted from foot to foot. "Mari . . . I miss you," she finally blurted. "I feel horrible that it was because of me Andy followed you to Cordelia. Maybe he had a right to know what he found out, but I shouldn't have interfered."

Thinking of her earlier pettiness, Mari felt two feet tall. "Forget it."

"And since then, I've been rude to you. I'm sorry."

Mari lost another six inches. "I hurt your friend, so you wanted to hurt me back. I understand, and I could have told you I understand. I haven't been very nice to you either. But, well . . . I'd planned to tell him everything." Her voice turned dry. "Just not quite that way."

"I should have asked you first before I said anything to him. I made everything worse by butting in. I just thought—"

Mari thought they'd probably wailed and gnashed their teeth enough. "Oh, forget it. It doesn't matter. He would have reacted the same way no matter how he found out. Come on in. Lil baked cookies this afternoon, and I know Mom and Pop have missed you. Besides, I want to show you what I'm up to and see what you think."

Finney had started to follow Mari to the door, but now she halted.

"What's the matter? You're being a bigger person than me, coming over here to apologize. The least I can do is feed you."

"You said Lil's inside? Maybe I'd better tell you the rest of what I came to say before we go in. I just got a call from Kirk. He wants you to go to his office first thing in the morning." She glanced uneasily at the door. "And he wouldn't want you to tell Lil anything until he can get this whole thing sorted out."

"Get what sorted out? If something's wrong with Michael, Lil should—"

"Nothing's wrong with him. Not exactly. But a little while ago, Steve found a crowbar like the one you described. They think it's the one the vandal used on the cabins."

"And Kirk wants me to identify it?"

Finney nodded. "But that's not all."

Mari didn't like the grimness that settled over Finney's face. "Where did they find it?"

"Stuffed in Michael's mattress."

Chapter 23

Early Tuesday morning, waiting for Mari, Andy stood arms crossed, leaning against a filing cabinet in Kirk's office. Silent like the others in the room, he stared at the light flattening itself against the one window. Still recovering from yesterday's storms, the sky was bruised.

Steve stood in a similar stance next to Kirk's desk. The youth care provider's face was grim, his usual smile erased. Behind his desk, Kirk tilted his chair back, his gaze moving to a clock that ticked off audible seconds. In two straight-backed chairs across from the camp director, Michael and Malloy shifted. Michael kept his eyes pinned on his hands, lying palms-up and loose in his lap, but the redheaded boy sent Andy a scared glance. In a folding chair, Damon sat perfectly still, the shadow of a confident smile on his face as he watched a point over Kirk's head. On the desk, a lamp illuminated the crowbar, its handle wrapped in blue electrical tape.

Tires crunched, and Kirk swiveled to look out the window. "She's here."

Andy shifted, but otherwise didn't react. Since the day after the Fourth of July, he'd done his best to avoid Mari and had largely succeeded. After she'd left her volunteer work, he'd even achieved some ability to erase her from his thoughts. At least during the day. At night, she still stumbled into his dreams, unbidden and unwanted.

Seeking freedom from the emotions she'd stirred up in him, he'd made it a point to attend A.A. at least once a week since they'd parted. But serenity was hard to hang on to, even there. He and Seamus had come as close to an argument as they ever had, Seamus unyielding in his insistence it would do Andy no good to refuse to examine his actions and feelings; Andy equally obstinate that to do so would only result in needless pain. *Ignorance is bliss*, he'd told Seamus jokingly, trying to deflect the older man's adamancy. *You're simply ignorant*, Seamus had retorted without any answering grin.

Remembering, Andy shifted his feet again. He didn't like being on the outs with his sponsor, but the knowledge of Mari's affair with his sister's husband had smacked up against a wall within him that separated right from wrong. There was no breach. There was no chink for her to slide through, shored up as that wall was by his anger and grief over Anna. Emotions he'd thought he'd dealt with had resurfaced with tumultuous force when he'd laid eyes on that bastard Sean Reynolds.

Outside, footsteps sounded as Mari crossed the parking lot. Andy shifted his gaze away from the window and waited, willing himself into a hardened state where the sight of her couldn't affect him. Seeking distraction, he looked at the crowbar.

Michael couldn't be the vandal. Kirk knew that. But the three boys didn't—because the real vandal didn't know he'd had a witness. While Mari's memories were vague, there was one thing she'd been sure of: the culprit had worn the orange Camp Sycamore T-shirt that the Vreeley boys had donned before they'd arrived. Michael hadn't been issued his shirt until later.

His gaze moved to Michael. But since Steve had found the crowbar in Michael's mattress, Michael must

know who had done it. And for his sake, it would be
best if Mari's nephew came clean. The boy's determination to protect someone he considered a friend was
admirable, but he needed to learn his first loyalty had
to be to himself.

Pricked by the irony, Andy shook his head and
looked away. He'd felt a little bent out of shape at
Finney when he'd realized she'd offered an olive
branch to Mari. He'd expected more loyalty from her.
But here he was, expecting Michael to disregard loyalty to *his* friends. Maybe Mari was right. Maybe he
was too entrenched in black and white. His mouth
tightened. But in some cases, there were no shades
of gray.

He didn't want to be here and wouldn't be if he
hadn't decided to get a cup of coffee before heading
to the greenhouse this morning. Kirk had nabbed him
in the cafeteria and asked him to join Steve in his
office "in case things get ugly." Andy didn't know
exactly what the director had planned for this meeting,
but in any confrontation like this, it was possible one
or more of the boys might need to be physically
restrained.

A tap sounded on the door. Kirk rose to answer.

"I'm sorry I'm late. My mother needed—"

At the sound of her voice, Andy winced, Damon
and Malloy looked puzzled, and Michael's face grew
hard. Kirk stepped out with Mari and closed the door
behind him, cutting her off. Having been a party to
this sort of thing before, Andy knew Kirk was likely
warning Mari not to say anything until he asked for a
response. Andy felt a sliver of amusement. Kirk didn't
realize what a tall order that was.

The pair entered the office. Seeing her up-close-and-
personal again gave him a jolt. So familiar . . . yet
different. He'd grown accustomed to her casual
clothes, but she'd reverted back to high fashion—she'd
donned that apple green outfit she'd worn on that

long-ago day at the O'Malleys' house in Cordelia. High heels arched her feet; earrings, intricate and ornate, once more brushed her cheeks. It wasn't just the clothes, though—there was a purposeful air she hadn't carried before.

Her eyes swept the room, widened when they fell on him, then quickly slid off. As Kirk seated himself again, she unhooked her bag from her shoulder and looked around uncertainly for a place to put it, finally setting it on the floor. Then, with no other place in the office to go, she leaned back against the door and crossed her arms, keeping her gaze averted from him. Watching her from the corner of his eye, he saw her give Michael a reassuring smile. Michael glowered back and her smile wavered.

"So," Kirk began, "we need to discuss why this crowbar was in Michael's mattress."

Michael didn't hesitate. "I know I shouldn't have kept it, but I found it in the woods, and I didn't think it was any big deal but I knew you'd take it away so I put it—" He ground to a halt under Kirk's steady gaze.

Kirk continued as if Michael hadn't said anything. "We have reason to believe this crowbar was used to damage the cabins at the beginning of the season." He glanced up at Mari, who looked at the crowbar and gave a nearly imperceptible nod.

Michael stared at his hands.

"Let's start with you." Kirk motioned at Steve.

The YCP straightened. "Last night when Michael didn't show up for the movie in the cafeteria, I went to the cabin to see if he was there. He was. And I found him with an arm shoved into his mattress . . ." Steve continued, explaining that he'd recognized the crowbar from the description Kirk had given out to the staff, but while he was trying to question Michael, the movie had ended and Malloy and Damon had wandered in. "Michael had been feeding me the same story he just started to tell you, then Malloy and Damon started talking at the same time. None of them made any sense. I got suspicious that all of them knew something. So, I brought them to you."

"I don't know anything." Face flushed, Malloy glanced at the other boys. When Damon's face hardened around his smile, he added quickly, "And neither do they."

Kirk ignored him and looked directly at Michael. "Did *you* vandalize the cabins in June?"

Andy heard Mari suck in a breath. Despite the chill in his heart, he itched to give her shoulder a reassuring pat. Kirk was merely offering Michael an opportunity to explain the evidence—or one of the other boys a chance to save their friend with a confession.

Michael glanced at Damon, then tilted up his chin. The pose was defiant, but there was fear in his eyes. "Maybe."

"Maybe?" Mari spouted. "*Hardly.* He—"

Kirk frowned, and Mari shut up.

"You did, didn't you?" Kirk said gently, looking back at Michael.

"No, he *didn't!*" Mari erupted again. Kirk looked so astounded at having his orders ignored, Andy had to bite back a laugh. "He wasn't wearing—"

"*I* did it!" Malloy burst out.

Everyone stared. Michael looked stunned, Damon irritated. The redhead's face went fire-engine red.

Brushing a hand over his crew cut, Kirk leaned back. "*You* did?"

He sounded so surprised, Andy knew that, probably like Steve and himself, Kirk had suspected Damon. And, truth be told, that would be easier to take. Damn. Malloy had come so far and had done so well—up until now.

"Y-yes." Malloy chewed his lip. "You see, when we came to camp, I was mad about, well, just—just things.

Maybe it was Steve that did something. I don't remember now."

Skepticism suddenly flickered over Kirk's face, but he just nodded encouragingly at Malloy. "Go on."

"I—I found the crowbar. Um, I can't remember where."

Andy frowned.

Kirk's eyebrows had gone up. "And . . ."

"And I busted things up in those cabins, then hid it." He glanced nervously at Damon. "In—in Michael's mattress."

"Ah." Kirk nodded. "You hid it right away. You didn't put it someplace else first?"

"Uh . . ." Malloy looked at Damon, then Michael, uncertainty crowding his homely features. "Uh, no. I—I put it straightaway into the mattress."

Damon's gaze darted among them, as he tried, Andy thought, to judge if Malloy had been believed.

And maybe he would have been. Except the culprit couldn't be Malloy, and every adult here now knew it. The crowbar had been in the forsythia bushes before it had found its way into Michael's mattress. Which meant the vandal had to be Damon.

Mari was practically vibrating apart. "But he couldn't have—"

Kirk skewered her with a look, his brows falling so fast that she sucked her lip between her teeth. The director waited until he was sure she'd stay silent, then looked back at Malloy. "Good try, Malloy, but the crowbar was seen in the bushes next to the main hall right after the vandalism."

Damon's eyes went granite hard. Glancing at him, Malloy winced as it dawned on him that he'd unintentionally botched the whole "confession."

"So, who are you protecting—Michael or Damon?"

Kirk would know it was Damon, but Andy knew he wanted Michael or Malloy to name him. Probably

Kirk realized that if one stood up against him, the other would too, helping to break the hold Damon had exerted over a lot of the kids in this camp.

Still squirming under Damon's glare, Malloy tried again. "But . . . I—I *did* do it. I—it was just like I said. I . . ."

Damon turned a threatening gaze on Michael.

Michael muttered, "Malloy didn't do it. I did."

Mari was practically purple from holding her tongue. Kirk stared at Michael long and hard, but while color crept up his face, Michael said nothing more.

The director sighed and finally looked at Mari— fortunately before she popped a blood vessel. "Tell us who you saw running away from the cabins on the day they were vandalized."

In varying shades of surprise, all three boys twisted to look at her.

"It was . . ." She stumbled under their stares, then cleared her throat. "It was Damon. I know it was a Vreeley boy because he was wearing an orange T-shirt—Michael had on a brown one. The boy's hair was dark, not red like Malloy's. And—" She paused. "I couldn't tell if the boy was black or white because . . ." She motioned at Damon, who underneath his T-shirt was wearing his usual long-sleeved shirt. It was white—a contrast to his café au lait legs. "I'm so sorry, Damon. But I couldn't let Michael get blamed. . . ."

Her voice trailed off at the cold look the boy sent her.

Even to defend her nephew, she'd hate getting anyone in trouble, Andy knew. She'd always impulsively shouldered more than her share of the blame on one of their escapades, often because she usually felt more shamefaced than he did. Even lately, she hadn't rationalized her affair like Sean Reynolds had. *Mentally ill.* He should have smacked the slimeball while he'd had the opportunity. His thoughts faltered, feeling more like bluster than truth, but then his heart hardened again. Mari was at least partially responsible for Anna's death.

He turned a shoulder.

Kirk stood. "Thank you, Mari. Steve, if you'd escort these gentlemen to their cabin, I'll come see them in a moment."

Mari squeezed over to Kirk's side of the desk so the boys could get to the door. She put a hand on the director's arm. "What will happen—"

Kirk put up a finger and watched while the boys left with Steve. Malloy had his head down; the other two walked stiffly upright. When he reached the door, Michael looked back at Mari, his gaze hard. The door slammed behind him.

Andy lingered, wanting to get away from Mari, but equally interested in what Kirk planned to do.

Mari was staring at the door. "Why does Michael hate *me* all of the sudden? Damon was the one about to let him take the rap."

"It's just misplaced loyalty." Kirk sat down, leaned back, and looked at the ceiling, his expression momentarily defeated. "I'm sure Damon convinced Michael that if he took the fall, he'd get off lightly. I can hear it now: Michael's rich parents would pay the damages, Michael would be sent home. Which, by the way, is exactly what Michael has wanted. He'd do anything, admit anything, to get out of here." The director rolled his head to look up at Mari. "Don't worry, we'll work with Michael on it."

"What will happen to Damon? You won't press charges, will you? I mean, I know he has problems, but I've seen what a great kid he can be."

Kirk smiled grimly. "Yes, he can be a great kid. You always hope . . . But, no, we won't press charges. We'll handle it ourselves."

"How will you handle it?" Mari persisted.

Andy watched her with some surprise. She really did care about all these boys.

"We'll—"

Yelling erupted outside the door, followed by the sound of scuffling and the noise of fist meeting flesh. All three of them rushed through the door. In the reception area, Steve had a slim hold on Damon. Teeth bared, the boy was straining toward Malloy.

Some thirty minutes later, after the scuffling was over and the boys calmed, the men held a brief conversation, then Kirk, Steve, and another of the YCPs led the boys outside. Seeing nothing left to lose, Damon had clocked Malloy for screwing up. Holding ice up to a swelling jaw, the redhead gave Andy and Mari a watery smile as the boys filed out. But the look Michael threw them was hateful.

Mari sank down on a bench outside Kirk's office. "I still don't understand all this." Her voice held a tremor.

On the verge of following the others, Andy glanced at her white face and hesitated. "Malloy has no love lost for Damon, but is loyal to Michael. Michael is trying to be loyal to them both."

"Well, *that* certainly clears things up." Mari's voice was dry. She leaned her head back against the wall and closed her eyes.

Unable to help himself, Andy grinned briefly. "Michael and Malloy like each other—they're friends. For Damon, Michael feels a mix of admiration and fear. And Damon has given Michael a measure of respect around here." He pulled his cap from his back pocket and sat down beside her. "Damon convinced Michael he'd get off easy—that he'd probably only get sent home—if he took the blame for the vandalism. Since Michael wants to please Damon *and* he wants to go home, he did."

"So *will* Michael get sent home?"

"No. Kirk will impose some kind of consequences for both Michael and Malloy. I don't know what, but he'll be fair."

"What will happen to Damon? I don't think I can stand it if he goes to jail."

"He won't. Because of the vandalism, because of the fighting, Damon will start over at square one. As soon as they can get him there, he'll return to the intensive therapy dorm at Vreeley, where hopefully they can finally reach through all that anger. Meantime, he'll bunk with Kirk in his quarters. He'll be safer under Kirk's watch than in his cabin."

Mari's eyes popped open. "I don't care what Malloy did in the past, he wouldn't hurt Damon. Neither would Michael!"

"Relax. I didn't mean safe from them. I meant safe from himself."

She winced. "Oh." She was quiet a moment, then, "I feel so bad that I—"

"Don't. Getting caught is the best thing that could have happened to Damon. He isn't saying why he busted up the cabins—he probably doesn't even know why himself. When he starts over this time, maybe he'll actually do the work he needs to do and not just pretend."

"I hope so."

Again, she fell quiet. Andy turned his cap over in his hands, hoping she'd calmed enough that he wouldn't feel bad leaving. While she hadn't turned the conversation personal, he'd felt himself slipping into their old camaraderie. That wasn't good. There wasn't a hope here, and he didn't want her to get the impression there was.

He started to rise, but her voice stopped him. "But why did Malloy try to take the blame too?"

Stifling a sigh, he sat back down. "Malloy must have

known Damon had asked Michael to take the blame—maybe Michael told him. Malloy also knew that if Michael didn't, Damon would hurt him."

"Hurt Michael?" Mari sat up straight. "How?"

"Back at Vreeley, right after Malloy got caught being a runner and then grew enough spine to refuse to do it anymore, some guys snuck into Malloy's room, wrapped him up in blankets, and gave him a good pounding. Broke a rib."

Mari gasped.

"We always thought Damon was behind it, but we couldn't prove it, and Malloy never told. Given what happened today, I'd say we were right. Malloy was afraid the same thing would happen to Michael. But if Malloy took the blame—well, he might get busted a few levels and sent back to Vreeley, but he would have kept Michael out of trouble with Damon and earned himself back into Damon's good graces. I don't think Malloy intended to run cigarettes or anything else for Damon anymore, but at least he wouldn't be afraid of future beatings. Damon would owe him, you see. It's a kind of code of honor."

"Some code." Mari stared at him. "Some honor. I thought you said it was *safe* here."

"It is. At least as safe as it is anywhere you have a bunch of hotheaded boys packed tight together. Probably safer, with the way we try to watch them. You know, this kind of thing doesn't just happen in Vreeley Home and Camp Sycamore, Mari." He looked away to hide a small smile. Even now, she was still an innocent in many ways. "Emotions can get out of control anywhere. Occasionally people hurt each other. And sometimes they don't even mean to. It happens all over."

She was so quiet, he looked back at her. Their eyes met.

"Yes. It does." Her gaze was level, her voice a near whisper. "Too bad not everyone realizes that."

He looked back at his cap.

Mari sighed and made to rise. "I've got to talk to Michael. He's obviously more than a little upset with me for finking on his friend."

"I'd let Kirk handle things first." Still seeing that unwavering blue gaze even though she'd looked away, still hearing the words she'd whispered, his voice had roughened. He cleared his throat. "Mari, I—"

She sank back down on the bench. "What, Andy?" Hope quivered in her voice.

"I—" Emotions suddenly rose up inside him. His grief over Anna warred with his love for Mari. He didn't know what he owed the past or what he owed the present. *Mentally ill*. He didn't even know what he believed. He glanced up. Her face was naked with longing. Mari could never hide an emotion. Mari could never stifle a desire. His mouth tightened. Not even with someone else's husband.

"Nothing." He stood up and tugged down the cap over his brow. "Just—nothing."

Pretending not to notice the anguish on her face, he left her sitting there alone.

Chapter 24

That night, in a large, windowless storage room behind the Rooster Bar & Grill, Andy eased into a chair next to Seamus. Talking to the fellow on his other side, Seamus only nodded at Andy's arrival but his dark eyes held approval. When Andy had seen his sponsor last week, Seamus had suggested he stop in for tonight's A.A. meeting, a step meeting. Already quite familiar with each of the twelve steps, Andy preferred meetings geared toward general discussion instead of those that read and thoroughly discussed one of A.A.'s basic instructions. But perhaps there was a newcomer here that Seamus felt would profit by hearing from the more experienced members. Looking around at the twenty men and women ranging the rectangular Formica table already littered with foam coffee cups and brimming ashtrays, Andy frowned. All these faces were familiar.

On the opposite side of the table, two women exchanged a hug, a quick press of one overly rouged and lined cheek to the fresh-scrubbed polish of another: Betty and Tara, one nearing seventy, the other barely out of her teens. Several men stood together nearby, one in a sleek suit, another in denim and a western hat, the third wearing overalls with ted stitched over his heart under a streak of grease. The mechanic's overly long brown hair still held the day's sweat; his fingernails, the day's work. That didn't prevent the man in the suit—Jack, a lawyer who lived out in one of the new condo communities on the outskirts of Cordelia—from giving Ted's hand a heartfelt grasp. Old, young; rich, poor—none of that mattered in here.

Whatever Seamus might have up his sleeve, Andy felt calm settle over him as it always did at A.A. All afternoon, he'd been troubled—bleak from the recently resurrected memories of Anna, haunted by Mari's clear-eyed gaze that morning, and troubled that he couldn't shake Sean's comment about mental illness. He could use a dose of serenity.

Leader for the evening, Ted glanced at his watch and turned. Putting his hands on the back of a folding chair, he cleared his throat. At his signal, the other two men took empty seats, and the room fell quiet except for the sounds of revelry filtering through from the other side of the door, a reminder to all those who sat here of what they'd left behind. Hopefully for good.

Ted remained standing. "Good evening. My name is Ted, and I'm an alcoholic."

"Hi, Ted." The greeting echoed around the table.

"Let's get started." Ted picked a paper off the table and read the preamble, which explained the purpose of A.A.—a sharing of experience, strength, and hope.

Andy knew it by heart. Nudging Seamus, he whispered, "What step are they on?"

"Ten." Seamus's eyes glinted with humor.

Ten—the step Seamus had badgered him to study again when he'd seen him over that awful Fourth of July weekend. Resigned, Andy shook his head. His sponsor usually got what he wanted out of Andy. One way or another.

Ted leaned his hands on the table. "Just want to remind you all: What is said here, stays here." Ted picked up a familiar slim volume. *Twelve Steps and*

Twelve Traditions. He opened it to a bookmarked page. As was usual at these kinds of meetings, they'd read the step and its explanation out loud, passing the text around the room until they'd finished the chapter. Ted passed the book to Jack, then settled into his own seat.

"I'm Jack, and I'm an alcoholic."

Greetings bounced back.

Jack straightened in his seat. "Step Ten: *Continued to take personal inventory and when we were wrong promptly admitted it.*" He began to read.

Again, Andy wondered exactly where his assessment of his own personal strengths and failings held a bearing on his latest experiences. Like most drunks, he'd worked every step with the fervor of the newly converted when he'd found the program kept him sober, but many of the details were lost in the haze of activity over the last four years. While he relied on the discussion meetings to help keep him on the wagon, he couldn't even remember when he'd last cracked the *Twelve Steps* book.

Jack passed the book to the next person. As the words continued to roll over Andy, it all came back. No wonder Seamus had connived to get him here. He closed his eyes, trying to reject every phrase but at the same time knowing it was these words and all the other words and all the other drunks he'd run across in meetings like this that had helped him find—and keep—his sobriety. Still, his mind fought against what he heard.

In a voice roughened by drink and smoke, Betty spoke of the danger of justifiable and self-righteous anger. The book called them "emotional dry benders" that could threaten the recovering alcoholic with relapse.

Her voice light and airy, Tara admonished him to hold a willingness to forgive, to learn true tolerance, to remember that people suffer the same growing pains equally, addicts or not.

Seamus took the book, and with a stern look in Andy's direction, cautioned him of the dangers of doling out punishment in the guise of trying to teach another person a lesson.

And finally the book came to him. He read the last pages, keeping his voice steady with difficulty, torn by equal parts confusion and, yes, continued anger. He didn't want to be wrong; he wanted to hold on to his fury and hurt.

With the chapter ended, discussion commenced, each person taking a turn, a lot of folks raising the tenet to *Let go and let God*. Not written in those precise words in this book, the phrase was a solid brick in A.A.'s foundation, whether one believed in God or not.

Just before his turn to speak, he rose and excused himself, for the first time leaving before they recited the Serenity Prayer, before the admonition to "Come back—it works!" He couldn't help anyone here, not even himself. Because he didn't know if he could ever let go.

Feeling Seamus's eyes on his back, he slipped out the door. If he let go—if he forgave Sean and Mari— there would be nobody left to blame for Anna's death.

And sometimes people deserved to be punished . . . Didn't they?

Pausing just outside the door, he bowed his head. He no longer knew.

He stalked through the raucous atmosphere of the Rooster and out the entrance. Humidity enveloped him in a sweaty fist. Reaching his truck, he leaned against the door, swiped a hand across his forehead, and looked up. The stars overhead flickered like wavering candles, the haze promising storms in the week to come.

•

*　　　*　　　*

The first storm broke the next morning at camp, although the bright eye of the sun couldn't find a single cloud in the stark blue sky.

After breakfast, as Andy was collecting his usual cup of coffee, Michael halted a few feet away, glaring at him through his fringe of bangs. "What they're doing to Damon, it just isn't fair!" When Steve touched his shoulder, attempting to herd him toward their cabin, Michael jerked away.

Signaling Michael's YCP that everything was okay, Andy led the way to the same bench in the main hall's lobby that he and Mari had occupied yesterday afternoon. They sat down, Michael's every muscle stiff.

"What isn't fair? Damon more than broke the rules, he broke the law. Mr. Kirk isn't demanding a jail sentence, Michael, or even restitution. I think he's been more than fair. Damon will get a second chance when he gets back to Vreeley."

While Kirk's inclination had been to send Damon back to Kansas City immediately, he'd decided nobody could be spared to accompany him. With discontent roiling just under the surface as every boy formed his own opinion about yesterday's revelations, the director felt all the staff were needed here. Damon would return when camp ended next Friday. In the meantime, Kirk had relinquished his share of the activity program into the therapists' hands so he could devote his hours to supervising Damon. The boy was finishing the repairs on the cabins, which no longer required much skill beyond wielding a paintbrush.

"You think it's *fair* to keep Damon all shut up by himself? It's like—like *solitary* or something. He's got *rights*."

"What rights he has here, he forfeited when he took that crowbar to the cabins." The words were stark, but Andy kept his voice gentle. "Besides, you know there's no such thing as solitary confinement. This isn't Alcatraz. Mr. Kirk is with him day and night."

Michael snorted. "If that's all the company he gets, solitary would be better."

Leaving Damon alone was the last thing Kirk would do. Damon had grown completely uncommunicative; his last display of emotion was the punch he'd thrown at Malloy. He refused to speak to Dr. Everheart and even the false smile was gone. Kirk watched him like a mother hen, and Andy knew by the director's grim face that he was worried. Everyone was hoping that when Damon returned to the intensive therapy dorm at Vreeley, he'd finally have the breakthrough they'd hoped for. He was tough. But he couldn't be tough forever.

"You know Damon can't be left alone."

"Why not? Malloy and I get 'periods of reflection.'" Michael mimicked Kirk's voice. With typical teenager logic, he didn't even realize he'd reversed his argument. "So why can't Damon?"

Andy backtracked, understanding from Michael's question that even in the close quarters at camp, Damon had managed to hide—or explain away—his scars. "It just wouldn't be good for him," he said, knowing the excuse sounded lame. He steered the conversation to Michael. Damon wasn't the only one whose defenses hadn't been breached this summer. Mari's nephew had come a long way from the surly youth who had arrived at camp, and his parents were pleased with his progress. But the staff still felt he hadn't faced the roots of his troubles—hell, he hadn't even admitted them—and he was still too easily led. "How are you feeling about all this? Your friend tried to get you to take the blame for his actions."

Michael's tone turned defensive. "Only because he knew they'd send him back to that—that jail at Vreeley."

"Relax—the intensive therapy dorm isn't a jail."

"He said it's a *shithole*. I would have gotten off easy—I *wanted* to take the blame so he didn't end up there. It's not like he made me." The words were forceful, but Michael's expression was troubled.

"And that's it? That's all you think?" Andy wished Kirk or Dr. Everheart or another counselor would stumble by. He was roaming out of his depth.

"I wish people would stop asking me what I think!" Michael stood up, his movements jerky. "Everything is just so . . . so *fucked-up*."

The outer door opened and they both looked over, Andy hoping to see one of the counselors. Instead, Mari stepped inside and Michael's expression changed to disgust. Although he tried to school his features, Andy was afraid the same expression was reflected on his own face.

But Mari wasn't looking at him. She reached out a hand toward Michael, but let it drop when he turned his back. Expression bleak, she spoke to Andy. "Yesterday . . . I was upset . . . I mean, I left my bag," she faltered. "In Kirk's office, and I need you to let me in so I can—" She darted another look at Michael and took a few tentative steps toward him. "Michael, *please* listen to me. I didn't want to get anyone in trouble, but I couldn't let you take the blame; you know I couldn't. I like Damon, but I love you." She touched his arm.

He shrugged away. "Sure you do." When he turned around, his face was flushed, his eyes wary. "You're lying. If you cared, you wouldn't have left me here alone."

"You're *not* alone." Mari's glance brushed Andy. "And I explained why I couldn't stay."

"Whatever. Lil told me you were leaving for Chicago in a few weeks. You're just like everyone else." He shoved his hands in his pockets, looked down at his feet. "Better places to go than sticking anywhere around me."

"Oh, Michael, I'm not leaving *you*, I'm leaving . . ." Again, a glance at Andy. "I mean, I've just decided to go back to school."

In Chicago? Andy's gut suddenly felt hollow, but he forced his attention away from Mari. This was about Michael. Not her. Not them. "What do you mean, Mari's like everyone else?"

"Like my dad!" Michael burst out, the tips of his ears going red. "He couldn't wait to get out after I was born."

Feeling smug that he was right about Jon Van Castle, Andy glanced at Mari.

The look she returned made him ashamed. "You're not the reason he left, Michael. Your dad—"

Michael didn't let her finish. "And Melanie went away to college when she could have gone somewhere close and been home a lot. Then my—my mom . . ." He broke off. "And now Aunt Mari. Everyone *leaves*. Everyone always leaves!"

Andy expected an *oh, puh-lease* and an eye roll from Mari at Michael's belief he was the center of everyone's universe. Face still burning from that look she'd given him that said he was petty, he prepared to intervene and redeem at least his professional authority. Michael's conviction was untrue, of course, but typical and not to be scoffed at, since it caused him pain. But while an impatient look did pop out on Mari's face, to his surprise, she only tried to gather Michael into her arms. Andy deflated. Sycamore had changed her, made her less centered on herself. He stifled the softening of his heart—unfortunately, it hadn't happened soon enough.

"Don't touch me!" Michael backed away. "You screwed things up between me and one of my only friends. Now Damon hates me!" His face crumpled and he ran for the door, banging it closed behind him.

Mari would have followed, but Andy grabbed her arm. "He doesn't need you—"

She opened her mouth to protest.

"—*or* me," he said firmly. "Dr. Everheart's in the cafeteria. You find him. I'll make sure Michael doesn't go very far."

Her eyes were wide in a pale face, but she didn't object, surprising him for the second time this morning. She turned and barreled through the door into the cafeteria. He watched her go, his emotions churning. Chicago . . . He started after Michael. She was leaving, and he'd bet this time she'd never come back. He shouldn't care. But he knew he did.

Twenty minutes later, Michael was ensconced with Dr. Everheart in Kirk's office. The psychologist had assured Andy and Mari that they didn't need to stick around, but, of course, Mari wouldn't budge until she'd seen with her own eyes that Michael was fine. She paced a few turns around the main hall, then banged out the door and onto the porch.

Andy followed, wincing as he hit air so thick and hot it felt like he could wear it. Leaning his backside against a railing, he watched Mari stalk from one end of the porch to the other until she finally tired and sprawled on a bench. A frown arrowed between her eyes.

He should reassure her, but Michael wasn't uppermost in his thoughts. "Chicago, huh?"

"The University of Illinois at Campus Circle to be precise." Not even glancing at him, she plunged her hands into her pockets and stared at her feet. "You should be proud. I'm taking a page from your book and returning to school for a master's in art therapy, full-time next fall, if they accept me."

Art therapy? He blinked. He'd hoped Mari would turn aside her dreams of fame and fortune—for him. He'd never guessed she'd do it for herself. He felt a measure of pride, followed by a stir of irritation. "Still running away from everything." He kept his voice mild.

"I'm *not* running away! I'll get a job, take the undergrad courses I need, get to know the city . . . I'm moving toward something worthwhile."

"But far away from here to someplace where you think the grass is greener. And you're sure not letting any grow under your feet. What's the rush?"

"I want to close this chapter, get on with the next." Her eyes flashed. "Is that so hard to understand? I mean, tell me, what's the point of sticking around? You won't even talk to me unless you're forced to."

"But—" He stopped. Why was he trying to talk her out of Chicago? What difference would it make to him? He looked away from her piercing gaze, afraid of what she might see. Unable to face it himself. "There's your family," he said lamely. "Have you ever thought that maybe they need you—and you, them?"

Bracing himself for the second emotional storm of the day, he was surprised once more when the exasperation in her face faded and was replaced by only a faintly troubled expression.

"Believe it or not, I have." She stood up. "But none of that is your concern, Andy Eppelwaite. Not anymore." Turning her nose up, she marched back inside.

Andy straightened, shrugged, and tugged down his cap. Setting off toward the greenhouse, he told himself forgiveness was out of the question; someone had to be accountable for Anna's death. He hadn't recognized the depth of his sister's pain while she was alive, but he could at least honor her pain now. If he didn't, who would? Gran had fed that drug reaction story to so many people for so long, she'd almost swallowed it herself. Sean Reynolds had moved on. And Anna could no longer speak on her own behalf. As for Mari . . .

He stumbled, swept by a feeling of loss so severe his knees nearly buckled.

And he suddenly realized he wasn't thinking about Anna.

Chapter 25

Nor was he thinking of Anna when he sought refuge in his grandmother's kitchen just over a week later. Mari was on his mind, just like she'd been ever since he'd learned about her plans to move to Chicago.

Rubbing his thumb back and forth over a chip of linoleum peeling off the table, he watched Tansy serve up slices of the pie she'd brought home from the diner after work. Her bustle and the rattle of a window fan soothed him, dulling the ever-present echo of what Mari had said. *None of that is your concern, Andy Eppelwaite.* Mari was right. What she did now wasn't his business. But that fact hadn't prevented eight days and nights of wrestling with his memories, memories he'd almost managed to bury under his work and his articles and his plans until she'd unearthed them again with her news.

"How about ice cream, too?" Tansy opened the icebox and rummaged around. "Never mind. Don't got any." She threw a glance over her shoulder, eyes hard as marbles and sharp as arrows. Nothing much got past her. "Would have picked some up if I'da known you'd be around. I got coffee though. Just take me a minute to make some fresh."

She didn't wait for a response, just shifted to reach for a tin. Even though she hadn't mentioned it, he knew she knew something was wrong. After all, he'd driven up here on a Thursday night without notice. He would have given her some, but when he'd hopped in his truck earlier this evening, he hadn't known where he was headed. Just away from yet another evening with only himself or Finney for company. Right now he and Finney had only had a pale version of their former camaraderie. The role she'd played in his confrontation with Mari was innocent, but it had made them uncomfortable around each other. He supposed as time passed, they'd slip back into their old friendship, but it hadn't happened yet. He was no fun to be around anyway . . .

Because he still hadn't gotten over Mari.

He ran a hand across his face. Would he *ever* get over Mari? If his reaction this evening was any indication, it would take some doing. Recently Finney had resumed the old routine of suppers at the O'Malley cabin, but he'd decided facing Mari across the table was unnecessary torture. Tonight, just like every night, he'd made some feeble excuse as Finney had readied to leave, and then once she'd gone, had spooned soup out of a can.

After he'd finished eating, just before he'd settled in with a red pen and his latest article, congratulating himself on an hour passed with only fifty thoughts of Mari instead of a hundred, he'd made the mistake of looking out the window. Through the trees and down the hill, he'd caught the reflection of her hair, turned to flame by the setting sun, as she walked along the water's edge with Finney. He'd started to turn away when she'd tipped back her head, laughing at something Finney had said. In a flash, in his imagination, he heard the warm depth of her laughter, saw the blue dance of her eyes, felt the touch of her fingers on his cheek . . .

And he'd thrown down his pen in disgust and headed out the door.

Tansy flipped a switch against the gathering darkness, flooding the kitchen with fluorescent light and startling him out of his reverie. His grandmother turned toward the coffeepot, hand pressed to her lower back. Her movements were no longer sharp as they'd once been, blurred now by age and the fatigue of standing at the grill all day. He resisted the urge to help, though, knowing she'd stand him down with a frown.

"Gran, you still doing okay by yourself?"

Tansy looked indignant. "Why wouldn't I be? Been doin' fine here all along."

"I know, but—"

"You say anything about me gettin' old, and I'll dump this pie on your noggin."

Andy gave her a grin, but felt a pang. Gran wasn't *getting* old; she *was* old. Used to be she'd head home from the diner, fix enough supper to feed a platoon, then spend the evening doing something relaxing— like painting the front porch. Now the porch was peeled down to bare wood, and the minute she got home, she sank into her chair with *The National Enquirer* on her lap, leftovers from the diner on a tray, and *Wheel of Fortune* on the tube.

He eyed the pie she'd lofted. "Since my aim is to have that pie in me and not on me, I won't say a word." Grunting, Gran lowered the pie, turned her back, and he added, "But when I come back here in a couple of weeks, you have to promise to let me paint that porch."

"A couple of weeks?" He could see a frown in the set of her shoulders.

"Being around this summer, I realized I've missed, uh, Cordelia. After camp ends and I go back to Vreeley, I thought I'd still mosey on down here once a month or so."

"And keep an eye on me?" She twisted part way around, shook a fork at him. "Boy, I'm fine, and you have plenty to do with your weekends without fussing around here." Turning back, she dropped the fork in the sink and poured two mismatched mugs full of coffee. "You have your work, and soon you'll be back in school. And then there's that O'Malley girl to spoon with."

Resisting a jab of pain, Andy didn't respond. He leaned back in his chair, its front legs lifting off the floor. Even without the ghost of Anna between them, he and Mari would never have worked. She wanted to get as far away from her origins as possible; he wanted to stick close to home. She'd never see that the flash of city lights didn't hold a candle to the warm glow of the family hearth. Family . . . Ironic, since that was what kept them apart. He righted himself with a thump. As usual, his thoughts ran in circles.

Tansy set a mug in front of him. "Where's that gal at tonight anyways? She's full of vinegar, and I liked chitchatting with her that last time—at least till she busted up some of my best china."

"Mari couldn't come. She's . . ." He got a pointed look and sighed. "Okay, okay. We're having—had—problems."

Tansy took the pie off the counter, pushed a plateful in front of him, then took a chair across the table. "What kinda problems?"

"We're—" He forked a peach chunk into his mouth so he could think over what he wanted to say. Shit. Why was he quibbling? They were through. . . .

Weren't they?

God.

Before he'd arrived at Gran's, he'd stopped at the Rooster, hoping Seamus might help clear out the confusion still muddling his brain. Instead they'd argued. Andy tried to explain his thoughts; Seamus insisted the tenth step held no room for exceptions. Sometimes Andy thought he'd explode trying to figure things out.

Every time he got a grasp on what he thought was right, it slid through his fingertips like a handful of water.

"Truth is, Gran, we're not together anymore."

Her face fell. "Sorry to hear that. I kinda got used to the idea of maybe having some great-grandbabies around the place. Been a long time since you and Anna were young 'uns."

He knew that look. Knew she was about to dip back into happy memories of when his dad and mom were alive. So he was surprised when she said, "Things were always so hard when you were young. My Andrew sure wasn't no picnic."

"Dad?" He wanted to be sure he'd heard right. In later years, he'd seen his old man for what he was, good and bad, but he'd never heard Tansy utter a word against her son.

"Oh, Andrew was the life of the party and a big-hearted man to boot. And don't we all got warts? But his were big ones. He was a ne'er-do-well. He led your mama on a merry dance . . . right into a bridge." Her faded eyes filmed with tears. "I never did blame your mama's folks for wantin' to have nothing to do with us. Leastways, with me. I shoulda booted Andrew in the behind when he headed the direction he did, but after his daddy ran off when he was a youngster, I didn't have the energy." She paused. "Just like I didn't have the energy to kick you in the pants when you started acting up. I'm truly sorry."

"*You're* sorry?" He put down his fork and reached across the table for her hand. "*I'm* the one who's sorry, and I'm the one who *should* be sorry, not you. I'm just glad you gave me a chance to make it up to you."

"That wasn't no big whoop on my part. You were young, too young to know much better. It was easy to give you a second chance—everybody deserves one, after all."

Her words echoed through his mind. Mari's face surfaced, but he pushed the image away.

Gran continued, "Now me, I've got a mite to answer for where you're concerned."

"No, you don't. You did the best for me that you could."

"No, boy. I saw what way you was going, and I shoulda got you some help before you ended up in jail time and again. But I just kept tellin' myself it'd all pass. And, truth be known, I was so wrapped up in getting through each day, I didn't look too much at the future." She squeezed his hand and let go. "It always struck me funny—you wanting to take all the blame for the drunk you turned into. Things ain't usually that cut and dried. Look close, and you'll see there's always plenty of blame to go around." Tansy shrugged and picked up her fork. "Eh, listen to me. Nattering on like the old woman I am. And here we've got us a nice slice of pie and each other for company." She stabbed her fork in the pie and twinkled at him. "Look close, and you also see there's plenty of good to go around, too. And at my age, peach pie's better than sex."

"Gran!" Picking up his fork, he laughed, although his mind was churning through her earlier words. Mari's voice echoed, too. *The world isn't painted in black and white. There are a lot of shades of gray.* He stopped with the fork halfway to his mouth. "Gran."

She looked up, eyes bright beads.

"With Anna . . . Did anyone ever mention anything about mental illness?"

"Mental illness? You mean did anyone ever say Anna was crazy?"

He nodded.

"Don't know why you'd think that, but no, not so's I remember." She shook her head. "Her other grandmother, though—now that was a woman who was severely tetched."

Surely if Anna had harbored serious mental problems, Gran would have known something. Then again, after Anna had graduated from high school, she'd rarely returned to Cordelia, so why would Tansy know anything?

He finished his pie in two bites and threw down his napkin. "I'm sorry, but I've gotta run. I just remembered there's someone I said I'd meet."

He was lying through his teeth, but he had to do this before he lost his nerve. Much as he hated the idea, he had to see Sean. Sean was the one person who could answer his questions.

As he headed out the door and down the walk, he heard the phone ring behind him. But what he didn't hear, after he'd revved up his truck and pointed it toward Kansas City, was Tansy hollering at him from her front porch.

"Andy! Phone! Something's wrong with one of your boys!"

That same evening, garbed in her navy swimsuit, Mari sat on the dock, her feet dangling in the water. From the radio beside her, Alabama pounded out a beat. Their music was jarring, at odds with the dusk that had spread a coverlet of pink silk over the lake. She flipped the radio off and silence settled over the cove, broken only by a few awakening cicadas. No breeze stirred the trees.

Behind her, her easel stood abandoned. But this time not because she'd failed to capture that elusive light. This time because she'd finally nailed it. Probably because her plans were finally set, probably because she'd finally seen what she needed to see.

For the first three days after she'd encountered Andy and Michael at Sycamore, caught up in a frenzy to take action, any action, she'd trolled the Internet, looking for just the right digs and just the right job for her life in Chicago. She'd mapped out a mid-

August trip, lined up appointments for apartment hunting and job interviews, and made list after list of things she needed to do, from forwarding her mail to getting a U-Haul.

But then, exhausted, mind feeling like it was tethered to one of those hamster wheels, she'd run out of steam. So for the last four days, she'd turned inward—a novel experience.

She wandered among the perfume of her mother's roses and imagined instead sidewalks scented by the tang of Lake Michigan winds and the bouquet of a hundred different cuisines floating through restaurant doors. She watched bumblebees wind lazy figure eights over wildflowers and thought about traffic that punched through freeways with serious intent. She stared at clouds fluffed like meringue and pictured a canyon of skyscrapers. She stared at vistas softened by woods whispering with the breeze and imagined the electrified bustle within every building.

Once in Chicago, she'd again grow accustomed to concrete under her Manolo Blahnik stilettos instead of the ground beneath her bare feet, to the cursory glances of strangers rushing along the sidewalks instead of Lil's soft gaze, Alcea's sharp looks, and her mother's penetrating stare. At night, she'd fall asleep to a lullaby of taxi horns and diesel brakes, hip-hop music skipping down hallways, and jazz spilling into the streets instead of the song of cicadas and the murmur of the lake lapping along the shore.

You've always thought something better lay outside your own backyard. Her mother's voice whispered through her daydreams and hummed to her in her sleep.

She wiggled her toes, and the water rippled out in an ever-widening circle. Andy's words had forced an issue to the forefront of her mind that she could no longer ignore. What did she owe her family? What did she owe herself? What did she want—*really*?

Yesterday, she'd finally headed back to the Internet. Yesterday, she'd made even more lists of plans. Because by yesterday, she thought she finally had all the answers. All the ones that counted anyway. And this morning she'd finally awakened at peace with herself, her mother's voice stilled. No wonder that when she'd taken out her paints this evening, she'd finally caught the illusive spectrum of twilight on her canvas. Less is more. . . .

The dock creaked, and she glanced over her shoulder. Raking a hand through her short-cropped blond hair, which, like her own, had corkscrewed in the relentless humidity, Lil walked toward her. "Whew. I thought it might be cooler down here, but it's not." She kicked off her shoes, eased down beside Mari, and swung her feet into the water. She squinted toward the sky. "Clouds disappeared again, I see." Each evening this week, thunderheads had stretched along the western horizon, but the rain that could snap the tension in the atmosphere hadn't arrived.

Mari nodded. "Everything okay up at the cabin?"

"The macaroni salad you made is in the fridge, Pop fetched hamburger, and I've cut up carrots and celery." Lil ticked off items. "Alcea will bring a cake when she comes tomorrow—and Patsy Lee said something about a green salad. When I left them, Jon was on the phone with a music company in Nashville, Pop was in front of the TV, and Mother was finally making sounds about going to bed. Good thing—she wore herself out."

"I know—somebody should leash her." Mari smiled sadly. "There was a time when she'd run rings around all of us, but . . ."

Lil patted her hand. "She'll still be around a long time, Mari."

"We hope."

Lil nodded. For a moment they stared across the cove, through the shadows cast by sunset.

Finally Lil stirred and sighed. "I did tell her we
didn't want a party tomorrow, but you know how she
gets. She invited everyone for Michael's homecoming." She slid a sideways glance at Mari. "I'm afraid
that includes Finney and Andy, too. Finney said she
couldn't come."

"I know. She was headed back to Vreeley this afternoon with Steve and a few of the boys; the last group
returns by bus tomorrow. As for Andy—" Mari
snorted. "The way he feels—"

"Mother said Andy told her he'd come."

Mari's closed her eyes, counted to ten. "If Mom is
still trying to play matchmaker between Andy and me,
it's a lost cause."

"Mother's never heard of a lost cause."

"I guess she'll find out there's a first time for everything." Mari opened her eyes and shook her head.
"What a thrill. Under the gun of Andy's moral judgment again."

Lil bit her lip.

"Oh, don't worry. I'll put on a happy face and
play nice."

"I didn't think you wouldn't. It's just—"

"I'm not exactly known for discretion?"

Lil's grin was brief. "No, it's not you. It's just—I'm
not sure there's reason to celebrate. At least, not yet.
I can hardly wait to pick up Michael from camp tomorrow morning, but . . ." She looked down at her
hands, folded like white linen in her lap. "Well, Dr.
Everheart tells us that even though Michael has made
progress in facing the things that really bother him,
there's something big that still lurks under the
surface."

Mari recalled Michael's words. "Something about
abandonment?" She still felt bad he thought she was
someone who would leave him high and dry. She'd
talk with him tomorrow, whether he wanted to or not.

"Dr. Everheart says buried anger, so that would

make sense. . . ." Lil's shoulder lifted and dropped. "Michael says he understands now that everyone messes up once in a while, and that when people make decisions, it might affect him, but that doesn't mean it's all about *him*. He knows Jon loves him—knows Jon gave up his touring career to make a home for him and Melanie as soon as he knew about Belinda's abuse. And he also knows his sister didn't choose a college to get away from him. Like Mel would do such a thing even if it crossed her mind." Lil raised her hands palm up, then let them fall. "But even though he says he *knows* these things, I'm not sure he *believes* them. And those things weren't such big problems for Michael before Belinda died. There's something *else* there. Something Michael still won't talk about."

"Well, wouldn't he see Belinda's drug overdose as the ultimate abandonment? Wouldn't that have set him off?"

"I know that must be part of it, even though Belinda didn't overdose intentionally. But I don't think that's the entire explanation for his behavior since then."

Nah, Belinda sure wouldn't have bowed out intentionally. She may have led a self-destructive life, but she'd taken too much joy out of kicking up shit and keeping everyone else's life miserable to have left the world of her own accord. Still, in a kid's eyes . . .

A lightbulb went on, and Mari straightened. And what about in an *adult's* eyes? At some level, some irrational level where everything was juiced solely by emotion, was that how Andy felt about Anna? Angry that she'd *intentionally* deserted him by cutting short her own life? Made sense to her.

She frowned, also wondering if, just like Michael, Andy had directed that anger elsewhere, unable to face that it was his sister's actions that had enraged him, not anyone else's. She kicked, splashing droplets all over and earning an elbow from Lil. Oh, who knew? Even if she understood it all, what good did it do her? He was determined to blame her entirely for what his sister had done.

Rubbing her side, she slowed her feet to a swirl. "There's one thing I don't understand. Why does Michael miss Belinda so much? Why would *her* death smack to him of abandonment? She was a real part of his life for only five years, and for those five years . . ." Mari let her voice trail off, not wanting to think about those scars on Michael's torso.

"And for those five years, Belinda hurt him." Lil's hands clenched. "Oh, how I wish I'd known how *much* she'd hurt him. I would have gotten him help years ago." Mari glanced at her sister. From the look on sweet, kind Lil's face, she wouldn't have just gotten Michael help, she would have hired a hit man to take out Belinda. "And Jon . . ." Her voice gentled when she uttered her husband's name. "Jon has wasted so much time beating himself up because he wasn't there."

"I take it trouble is over in paradise?"

"Yes." A soft smile played on Lil's mouth. "We've learned a lot—and remembered why we fell in love in the first place. Michael will come home to a new and improved household. And as for his issues over Belinda . . . Dr. Everheart says he needs some kind of closure, so we'll keep going to counseling and try to help him find it."

"Issues . . . closure . . ." Mari grimaced. "Psychobabble, but I suppose he's right. Like it or not, I've learned a lot of these folks do know something about what they're doing."

"Mari!" Finney's voice floated, high and thin, from somewhere up near the cabin.

Surprised, Mari twisted around. "Down here!" She exchanged a frown with Lil. "She should already be in Kansas City."

"Something must be wrong." Lil pushed to her feet.

Mari followed suit and slid her feet into her flip-flops. Finney was trotting down the hill, hair a floating banner behind her. They met her at the bottom of the slope.

Finney's face was a white orb in the deepening twilight. "Oh, Mari. We've all been so careful with him, but—"

Mari went cold. Beside her, Lil stiffened and sucked in a breath.

"Oh, no. I didn't mean—" She looked between them and drew a breath. "It's not Michael. It's Damon. He was in the first bus back to Vreeley, and when we stopped for gas, he said he needed to use the restroom. Steve went in first to check to make sure he'd be all right in there alone. There wasn't even a mirror, so he let Damon go by himself, and . . . and . . ." Finney's voice wobbled. "He was gone so long, Steve knew . . . We all knew. But we couldn't get the door open. There wasn't a spare key, and we had to break it down, and . . . he hurt himself. There was lots of blood." Tears welled in Finney's eyes. "And now we don't—we don't know if he'll live."

"Oh, God." Damon's handsome face and bright smile rose in Mari's mind, along with fear, sadness . . . and guilt. Damn guilt. Her constant companion. Without her, Damon wouldn't have been busted. But how could she have handled things differently? "Where is he?"

"At the hospital in Sedalia. They're doing everything they can. I came back to find Andy—he wasn't anywhere I called, and your line was busy. Kirk's trying to find him, too. With Kirk and Steve at the hospital, we need his help dealing with everyone else still at camp. Do you know where he is?"

Mari shook her head.

"How is Michael taking it?" Lil's face was pale. "Is he okay?"

"He doesn't know yet. We'll tell him separately from the others, since they were friends of a sort. And we'll help all the boys handle it this evening. But it probably wouldn't be a bad idea to get Michael in to Dr. Everheart right away."

Lil nodded and started up the hill toward the cabin.

"What can I do?" Mari asked, lingering behind with Finney.

"Nothing I can think of; I'll let you know if there is." Finney shook her head. "I just can't believe Damon found something to use on himself with all of us on the lookout."

"What did he use?" Mari asked before remembering that adage about cats and curiosity.

Finney dug in her pocket and pulled something out.

Mari stared at the object encrusted with blood in Finney's hand and wished she'd never asked. "You won't show the boys *that*, will you?"

"Of course not. God, what a setback this is. What a way for camp to end." Finney tucked the thing back in her pocket. "I've got to go—I've got to find Andy." She started up the hill.

Mari followed. "You might try Seamus Ryan at the Rooster Bar & Grill in Cordelia," she said to Finney's back. "Andy and him are friends. Or his grandmother, Tansy Eppelwaite."

Finney thanked her and hurried after Lil. Mari plodded more slowly, head down. She was relieved by Finney's assurance that she wouldn't tell the boys what Damon had used to hurt himself, but the information probably couldn't be kept from Michael forever. Nor could she keep what she knew from Andy. She'd have to bite the bullet and fess up to him tomorrow.

Because she needed Andy's advice. No telling how Michael would react if and when he found out Damon had cut himself up using Michael's Swiss Army knife.

And no telling how Andy would react when she told him she'd known Michael had possessed the damn thing the entire time he was at camp.

What a fun conversation *that* would be.

Chapter 26

What a fun conversation *this* would be.

A little over an hour after he'd left Gran's house, Andy had reached an upper-class neighborhood south of Kansas City where everyone had plenty of elbow room, despite houses that sprawled over a good chunk of their two-to-four-acre lots. He stood on the porch of his sister's former home, facing an ornately carved oak door, shuffling his feet on slate pavers, and working up the nerve to announce his presence. Halfway here, it had hit him that Reynolds might have moved, but when he'd pulled up to the end of the drive, he saw the name still elegantly lettered on the mailbox. He hadn't known whether to be glad or disappointed.

Wondering if the sweat pooling at the base of his spine was from nerves or the steamy weather, he jabbed the doorbell before he could change his mind. Inside, he heard a clamor of chimes, deep and sonorous. A minute ticked by and then the door swung open. Cool air rolled out. In stockinged feet and with the first few buttons undone on a white dress shirt, Sean Reynolds stood silhouetted in the light of the chandelier behind him that plummeted down from a three-story foyer. He held a book at his side, one finger marking a page.

Surprise mixed with fear flickered through Reynolds's eyes. He stepped back, one hand on the door.

Afraid the man would shut it in his face, Andy put a foot inside. "Relax. I just . . . We need to talk."

Sean studied him a minute, then his face relaxed. Without saying anything, he turned away and moved to a room at the right. Andy swung the door closed. Off to the left, a deep-piled living room in tasteful beige swept toward the back of the house. To the right was the library, oak-paneled and masculine. Ahead of him, a staircase curved gracefully up to a landing. Nothing had changed since he'd last been here when Anna was still alive. The walls were still filled with the wild abstracts she'd painted. The landing still frothed with the houseplants she'd tended.

He closed his eyes against sudden pain.

When he opened them, Reynolds was standing in front of him, holding out a cup of coffee. "You look like you could use it." Turning, he motioned Andy to follow him into the library, where a coffeepot sat on a small wet bar tucked between a fireplace and shelves heavy with hundreds of books. "Sit down."

Andy took one of two overstuffed red leather chairs, Sean the other. He sat slightly forward, as though poised to flee if the need arose. Andy couldn't blame him, considering the way things had always been between them.

"So, what is it?"

Andy set his untasted coffee on the small table beside him and shifted so he could see Reynolds's face. "Anna."

"I think we've said enough to each other on the subject of Jo—er, Anna—and Mari."

"I don't want to talk about Mari. Just Anna."

Sean sighed, rubbed a hand over his face. "What about her? She's gone, man. You've got to let it go." His voice wasn't unkind.

"I know . . ." Andy's eyes wandered the spines of the books, then came to rest on Sean. "You said Anna was mentally ill."

Sean's eyes sharpened, then he looked away. "I shouldn't have said that."

"No, you shouldn't. At least, not if it isn't true. Is it true?"

The silence stretched for so long that Andy wondered if Sean had even heard him. But finally Anna's husband blew out a breath. "It's true."

Andy's hands clenched on the chair arms. For a few heartbeats, he let it sink in. "What was wrong with her?" When Sean hesitated again, Andy frowned, wondering why he was so reluctant to discuss this. He *was* Anna's brother. "Well?"

"Bipolar disorder," Sean finally said.

Bipolar disorder. Manic depression. Oh, God. Poor Anna. "You're sure?"

"Oh, yeah. We were sure." Sean sounded weary. He stood up and moved to the wet bar, picked up the carafe, then put it back without adding anything to his cup. "She wasn't diagnosed accurately until after we were married." He stopped, shot a glance at Andy. "How much do you know about it?"

Andy cycled through what he'd read about bipolar disorder in his psych classes and what he'd learned working at Vreeley. "Not much. I know it usually appears sometime in adolescence—" He halted, remembering Mari's words—*crying practically all the time*—and his own defensive reaction—*so full of energy we could hardly keep up with her.* "It's often chalked up to teenage moodiness."

"And then"—Sean reached for a bottle of brandy, opened it—"it's usually wrongly diagnosed as ADHD." Attention deficit/hyperactivity disorder. "Or depression. And substance abuse can cloud the issue. All three things happened with your sister. To simplify, it's a problem with brain chemistry—and often involves a genetic predisposition."

Gran's voice sounded in Andy's head. *Now that was*

a woman who was severely tetched. "Her maternal grandmother."

"Her maternal grandmother." Adding a dollop of brandy to his cup, Sean nodded. "Take those two factors, add some tragic life circumstances to trigger events, and voilà . . . bipolar." Sean set the bottle down hard, took a large gulp from his cup, then pinned Andy with his eyes. "And almost twenty percent of cases commit suicide. An even larger percentage try."

"You know a lot about it."

"Not because I wanted to."

"Why didn't you tell me?"

Sean sat again, slid down in his chair, and laid his head back. Eyes closed, he held his cup loosely in his lap. "Do you know what it was like to live with her, Eppelwaite? Those kids you manage—are any of them bipolar?"

"A few, but they're medicated."

Sean smiled grimly. "And do they stay on their meds?"

"They're watched when meds are doled out. So, yes."

"Anna wouldn't stay on hers. She said her artwork sucked when she was doped up. She didn't like the side effects she sometimes experienced—weight gain, nausea. And her psychiatrist was switching them around all the time trying to find the right combo . . . anticonvulsants, mood stabilizers, antidepressants . . ."

Sean opened his eyes, tipped his cup Andy's direction. "It made quite a cocktail. Cheers." He took a drink. "But the biggest stumbling block to her mental health was Anna. She loved the highs without the drugs, at least the beginnings of those episodes—times when she was so euphoric she thought she could fly, so sensual she seemed like a goddess. She said ideas were like shooting stars, so bright and hard she could touch them. But then . . ."

"Then?"

"Things would change. She'd be without sleep for days, become agitated, pace. Get angry. And—"

"And what?"

"And—" Sean shrugged. "Pretty soon she'd sink into the other side of the spectrum. Despair, fatigue."

Andy's eyes narrowed. He didn't think that was what Sean had originally planned to say. "What about therapy?"

"Cognitive-behavioral, family, interpersonal . . ."

"So you tried everything."

"Everything." Sean waved a hand. "You see how I live. I could afford everything."

Andy dragged a hand through his hair, for the first time in a long time wishing he could drink. "How come I didn't see it? How could I have missed it?"

"You missed it because she wanted you to miss it. You missed it because she asked me to help her hide it. You were only here a few months. And while you were, she stayed on her meds."

"And that's why it seemed to me like half the life had been zapped out of her."

Eyes distant, Sean smiled. "And once upon a time, she was *so* full of life," he murmured. Then, seeming to recollect himself, he drained his cup and stood up. He looked down at Andy. "I'm telling you the truth when I say I loved her. I *really* loved her."

Andy felt his temper rise. "If that's the case, then why in the *hell* didn't you stand by her? Why did you take up with other women?" Thinking of how scared she'd been of losing him, his rage spilled over. "Reynolds, I should take you out and whip your hide until—"

So quickly Andy barely registered he'd moved, Sean zinged his cup across the room. It shattered against the fireplace. "Don't you take that self-righteous tone with me, Eppelwaite. You have *no clue* what it was like to live with your sister." He stalked back and forth. "I gave you the clean, clinical version. But when

Jo wasn't medicated and hit one of those highs . . . She went on shopping sprees, racked up thousands on our credit cards. She drank and trolled for drugs down on Independence Avenue. She sometimes got off on having sex with total strangers. Do you know how many times I picked her up from a police station? From some flea-bitten motel? From a hospital? How many times she had to be committed—sometimes a few days, sometimes a few weeks—after an episode . . . or after a suicide attempt?"

He stopped, breathing heavy, pressing his hands to his head. "And after those episodes passed, once she was calm again, she'd be in an agony of remorse. She'd vow to do what the doctor said, promise to take her meds, if only I wouldn't leave her . . . And I'd tell her I wouldn't. That what she'd done didn't matter. That I understood. And, of course, I'd stay and try to help her." He turned to Andy. His face was wet. "But it *did* matter. I *didn't* understand. I didn't *want* to stay. And *I couldn't help her.* It wasn't me that drove her to suicide. It wasn't Mari. It wasn't even Jo. It was the monster that lived in her head."

Horrified, still processing Sean's words, Andy couldn't speak.

Sean flopped back in his chair. "Ah, shit. I'm not that strong, Eppelwaite. I was all she had, and much as I wanted free of her, I loved her and I wanted to be there for her. But, God help me, I tried to find a life without her, too. That's why there were other women. That's why there was Mari."

Mari. "Why Mari?" *Oh, God. Why Mari?*

"Simple answer and one I'd never tell her." Sean squeezed his eyes shut. "Mari reminded me so much of Jo—only Mari was free of the monster."

Andy didn't hurry his trip back to Lake Kesibwi after taking his leave of Sean Reynolds shortly before midnight. Still shaken by what he'd heard, he took the drive slow, trying to sort out, to *understand*, everything Anna's husband had told him. The two men had talked for some time after Sean's outburst. Andy still had a lot of questions, and, after carrying his burden silently for so long, Sean let his words now flow freely. Sensing the profound relief Reynolds was experiencing, Andy had once again asked him why he'd never shared the weight of Anna's illness.

Sean had shrugged. "Neither her grandparents—nor you at that point in your life—would have been of any help. But, more than that, with the exception of her doctors, Anna didn't want anyone to know. Nobody. Not you. Not her other relatives. Not the few friends we had. She knew her grandparents here would freak. She didn't want to worry you or Tansy. And mental illness—like it or not—still carries a stigma. She didn't want people to look at her and see her illness. She wanted them to see *her*. So I promised I'd keep her secret."

Andy had raised his eyebrows at that. Reynolds had already betrayed Anna in other ways—why not this one, too?

Seeing his skepticism, Sean had shaken his head. "It probably sounds stupid. I couldn't stay faithful to her. I couldn't give her mental health. I couldn't protect her from her disease. But I could damn well keep that promise. I never told anyone. Until now."

Following his headlights along the darkened highway winding through the Ozark mountains, Andy shook his head now, too. He couldn't approve of some of the choices Sean had made, but the torment he'd lived with would have tried the strength of any man. He could now see why Anna had refused to hear a word against her husband. He'd been all that had stood between her and an institution. Sean Reynolds had handled things to the best of his capabilities. He'd come through in many ways. And in some, he'd fallen short. He supposed most people did.

And Mari . . .

Andy sighed, his feelings tangling again. His long-held convictions were bending, breaking, trying to re-shape. But he was running on emotional overload and could no longer think clearly. Tomorrow was soon enough to take on thoughts of Mari.

Turning into the O'Malleys' drive, he was surprised to see lights on in the guesthouse. Nobody should be inside; Finney should be in Kansas City by now. Frowning, he eased out of the truck.

Before he'd taken more than a few steps, the door flew open and Finney hurried toward him. He felt a sudden chill despite the sticky heat and glanced up at the sky.

The night was cloudless, but he could feel a storm gathering muscle.

Chapter 27

Despite cloudless skies on Friday, the atmosphere had still pressed hard from all sides, driving Michael's homecoming party indoors. Swimming had provided no escape, since the lake was about as refreshing as warm tea. The men had cut short their fishing expedition because even the fish couldn't drum up any enthusiasm. Some celebration. While they'd done their best, and Michael had been welcomed home with as much fanfare as the Prodigal Son, the mood had been decidedly dismal, infected as it was by Michael's gloom. Even those who didn't know Damon had spent the day anxiously awaiting word from the hospital.

Which still hadn't come by evening, when towering clouds knotted into fists and punched the sunset aside. Now thunder rumbled, rattling the windows.

Washing dishes from the cookout that had climaxed with one of Alcea's chocolate cakes an hour ago, Lil handed off a plate to Andy and anxiously peered outside. "I hope they get back soon." Michael and his cousin Rose had left for a walk a half an hour ago.

"They'll be okay," Andy said absently. He dried the plate and set it on the counter.

Off in the family room he could hear the slap of cards from a game of Spades, but no talk, arguments, or laughter, a very strange situation given all the O'Malley family were gathered in one place. Even Alcea's daughter, Kathleen, fresh from her internship and almost ready to head off with her cousins for their sophomore year in college, had joined them this time. Low conversation floated from a bedroom down the hall where she was huddled with Daisy and Melanie to talk about whatever college coeds talked about. Kathleen had inherited her mother's beauty—Alcea's willowy figure, the same blond hair—but Andy had been more impressed by her air of confidence, unusual in a young woman her age. It was the same poise her mother carried, as well as her Aunt Lil, and—he glanced over his shoulder—now her Aunt Mari. Andy frowned. He didn't remember a time when Mari had seemed more self-assured than she did today. Ironic, since he couldn't remember a time when he'd felt this uncertain.

At the kitchen table, back to him, Mari sprawled with her bare feet out and ankles locked, cradling the phone between ear and shoulder. She'd been on hold with the hospital for the last ten minutes. He hadn't needed to look to know she was there; he'd known exactly where she was at every minute all day long although he hadn't talked to her beyond a few courtesies intended to set everyone else at ease.

For the thousandth time, he wondered why he'd accepted this invitation. To wrap up loose ends? Or—pain tugged at his heart—to see Mari for what might be the last time?

He realized Lil had spoken. "Sorry—what?"

"How did things go at Sycamore last night after the boys found out about Damon?"

He took another plate from her hands. "Fine."

Yeah, fine. It had been a nightmare: belligerent, even tearful, entreaties for explanations the therapists and YCPs hardly understood themselves; acting out—some boys growing sullen, others flaring in anger. Even the kids who hadn't been close to Damon—even those who hadn't liked him at all—had been distressed. The staff had worked hard to soothe the situation, and it had finally eased. But bemused over his own reaction, Andy didn't want to talk about it. He ached for Damon but also realized he was just downright mad. His reaction—and the strength of it—surprised him. Disappointment at Damon he could understand, but not this seething anger.

The last time he remembered feeling this way was the night he'd found out Anna was dead.

"It's a hell of a note to end camp on." He stacked the plate and reached for the next.

"That's the truth. I was glad Dr. Everheart agreed to see Michael first thing this morning. Bless him—he squeezed him in before his office was even open."

Seeing the continued strain on Michael's face today, Andy wasn't sure the psychologist had done much good.

Handing off the last dish, Lil dried her hands and echoed his thoughts. "I'm not sure talking helped though. I think what happened with Damon has set him back." She sighed. "Dr. Everheart agrees. We scheduled Michael for several more sessions this week."

"Good." Maybe Everheart could get Michael to talk it out. Ever since yesterday evening, Michael had been a walking sphinx—withdrawn, uncommunicative—and probably ready to blow.

Behind him, Mari clapped down the phone. "Good news! Damon did well all day and they think he'll come through with flying colors." She jumped up from her chair. "Where's Michael? He needs to know." She looked only at Lil.

Thunder barked again, and Lil again gave a worried glance at the window. "He and Rose went for a walk."

Mari hesitated a moment. "Then . . . then, Andy and I will go find them."

He was surprised. Not only at the suggestion—the pair could have gone in any direction—but because

Mari had dodged him all day with queenly determination. But right now she was looking at him full-on and with an odd appeal in her eyes.

"Let me get Jon and Dak," Lil said. "They can help you try—"

"No!" Mari turned pink. "I, um—"

Lil looked between Mari and him, and her brows rose a tad. "Oh, sure. Sure. You two go on ahead. We'll, um, we'll join the search if you aren't back in . . . twenty minutes enough time?"

Mari's flush deepened. "That sounds good."

She grabbed a slicker hanging on a hook near the door and headed toward the deck, but Andy didn't move. If she wanted to mend fences, and that's what it sounded like she intended . . . well, there just wasn't any way to repair this kind of damage. Besides, he wasn't ready. He hadn't sorted everything out. He didn't want—

Mari flung open the sliding door. "Are you coming or not?"

Of their own volition, his feet moved and he followed. "Mari, I don't think this is the right time for—"

"Oh, can it." Her voice was weary. "This isn't about you. *Or* me. Besides, I already know your opinion of me, and I don't want to hear it again, thanks very much." She moved toward the stairs that led to the path down to the dock. "C'mon."

He followed her again. Overhead, the clouds twisted in dirty ropes against the falling night. Lightning flickered. But still the rain didn't come.

They walked a short way from the cabin, stopping just short of the rise before the path dipped down to the lake. Mari glanced up at the deck, apparently to be sure nobody was there to overhear, then demanded, "Did you see the knife Damon used to hurt himself?"

"Yes. But what does that have to do with—"

"I told you: This isn't about *us*." Mari almost stamped her foot. "It's about Michael."

So sure she'd planned to try to convince him to give her another chance, he was disgusted to find he was actually disappointed that he'd misunderstood. "Okay. What does the knife have to do with *Michael*?"

"I recognized it. It was his. A Christmas present from his mother. Or at least he thought it was from his mother until I opened my big fat stupid mouth and told him it was from Lil. Which is why . . ." A lightbulb went on in Mari's expression. "Which is *why*," she continued more slowly, "he probably gave it to Damon. He was mad because it *wasn't* from his mother, and because Lil had fooled him, so he just decided to get rid of it. And since he was feeling guilty about Damon getting busted, he just—"

"Christ, Mari. Slow down. I'm not following."

"The short version?" Mari took a deep breath. "It was Michael's knife. He gave it to Damon."

He might have been slow on the uptake there for a moment, but the implications of *that* hit him right away. "Shit. Why didn't you tell me earlier?"

"I don't know, I—" Mari looked away, then back at him, her chin defiant. "All right. Because I didn't want to be in the same room with you, let alone *talk* to you, and—and because I knew you'd lecture me."

"Why would I lecture you?"

She looked down at her feet. "I knew he had it. I've known for a while, but I didn't think—"

Finding an outlet, his anger flared. He opened his mouth, but she held up a hand to stave him off.

"And when I *don't* think, you have a horrible habit of making me feel like I'm not fit to live." She glanced up. "Look. I'm *sorry* about this. I'm *sorry* about Anna. I'm *sorry* about everything I've done. But last I heard, nobody was perfect, and I don't know what more you want from me. I can't turn time back. I can't undo my mistakes. And it's a pretty far stretch to think I won't make any more." She kicked at a rock. "So, go ahead, give me another lecture."

He closed his mouth. He by God *had* opened it to give her another lecture. He was acting like a self-righteous prig. If he'd known Michael had a Swiss Army knife he was keeping as some kind of reminder of his mother, he would have taken it away, yes. But he wasn't so sure anymore that he would have busted Michael's chops for having it. Sometimes the rules lacked compassion. Sometimes what seemed right wasn't right. As for the rest . . . Enlightenment tried to bust through his brain, but his defenses warred it off. Still, he tried. "Mari, I'm sorry. Maybe the rules aren't always—"

At the mention of rules, her mouth tightened. "Forget it. None of that is important now. I need to know what to do. If Michael finds out Damon used that knife to hurt himself, then—"

"He'll blame himself." Andy ran a hand over his face, thinking. She was right. Michael needed to be their priority. Thunder boomed again, closer this time. A few raindrops splattered at their feet. A blast of wind hit and the treetops took a bow.

"So what do we do?" Mari persisted. "Just tell Lil and Jon? Dr. Everheart? Talk to Michael ourselves before he finds out from someone else? Somebody—"

"Somebody should lock me the *fuck* up!"

They both whirled around at the sound of Michael's voice. Coming up the path from the direction of the lake, Rose and Michael had emerged at the top, almost hidden in the growing darkness. Lightning flashed, revealing Michael's tortured expression.

Rose looked up at him in alarm. The wind gusted, blowing her blond hair across her face. "Michael . . ." She reached out a hand.

At her touch, he whirled to face her. "Don't you be nice to me, Rose. I almost killed you that day in the Bronco. You know I did. You yelled at me to stop, to slow down, but I wouldn't. And now Damon is hurt and that's all my fault, too. You, my mom, Damon—"

"Michael, listen to us . . ." Mari stepped a few paces toward him, but halted when Michael took an equal number back. His eyes were wild.

What did he mean, *my mom*? Andy held out his hand. "Let's go inside and talk." The rising wind nearly drowned his words.

"No! No more talking!" Michael continued to move backward. *"No. More. Talking."*

"Well." Face grim, Mari spoke in a low voice only Andy could hear as she slid a little further toward Michael. "Lil got her wish. Looks like he's finally taking responsibility for his actions, even when he shouldn't."

Suddenly, Michael spun around and took off down the path toward the lake. In the startled pause that followed, the rest of them stared at one another wide-eyed.

But the sudden sputter of the bass boat's motor underneath the crackle of thunder unleashed Mari's voice. "Oh, sh—I mean shoot. Pop must have left the keys in the boat. Go get Jon! And the Cobalt's keys. I'll try to stop him!" Dropping the slicker, she surged down the path and into the darkness.

The skies opened up. For a bare second, Andy vacillated, then heard the motor rev and realized he wouldn't get to the dock before Mari. With Rose on his heels, he ran for the cabin. Mari's ride to the rescue was careless, rash . . . everything she was. But he understood it, because he understood her. Not only did Michael think Damon's self-injury was his fault; Mari was taking on her share of guilt, too.

But, like Mari had said, Michael shouldn't accept all the blame. And neither should she. No matter the situation, no matter what other people did—real or imagined—individuals were responsible for their own choices.

Clarity burst through his brain and he stopped short. Rose bumped into his back.

She gave him a push. "Get going!"

Shelving the thought for later examination, he bounded up the deck stairs two at a time. Around them, lightning sizzled, and the hair rose on his arms.

Chapter 28

Her path lit by strobes of lightning, Mari ran pell-mell toward the dock, hitting it in a skid just as Michael knocked the gears of the bass boat into reverse. The boat was flat-bottomed and shallow, rising only about a foot above the surface of the lake. Barring a sliver gouging one of her bare feet, she should be able to make the jump between dock and boat onto the flat front deck without much problem—*should* being the operative word. Without giving it another thought, not wasting a breath on yelling, and just as the boat cleared the dock, she gathered her muscles, muttered "Come to Jesus," and launched herself over the gap.

She sprawled across the deck, her knee and shoulder scraping across the turf of the all-weather carpet, her head narrowly missing the pedestal fishing chair, her chin thunking onto a tackle box. Her right foot twisted beneath her. Her teeth bit tongue. A metallic taste flooded her mouth, and blackness fogged her vision. Shaking her head, she raised up on one hand and balanced there until her brains rattled back into place. At least she could count one blessing. She didn't have a fish hook in her ass.

She barely had time to register pain in her ankle before Michael punched the throttle. With her weight forward, she was momentarily afraid the boat would simply take a nosedive. Water did foam over the lip, but the boat surged forward and the bow drove up.

Rain blurring her vision, she slithered toward the driver's well on her elbows, afraid to straighten, afraid the buck of the boat would knock her into the deep. Michael sat in a low bucket seat. Rain combed his hair and battered his face, but he didn't acknowledge it, or her, by even a blink.

When she was within reach, she rapped her knuckles on the thumbnail of windshield in front of him. "Turn around!" she screamed.

He didn't respond. He stared straight ahead, hands locked on the wheel.

She rolled over on her back, lifting up on her elbows to see where he'd headed. The two sloping hills silhouetting the mouth of the cove with every blast of lightning yawned open onto the broader basin of the lake, a shade blacker than the tumultuous sky above them. Beyond that basin was the main channel, where the swaths of water grew wider, rougher. And the gently rising hills turned into unforgiving cliffs. The waves would be ferocious on a night like this. Not to mention a lightning bolt could crisp them in an instant.

She shivered and twisted back toward Michael. "Michael, turn around!"

"I killed them!" The wind whipped his words away. "I killed both of them!"

Both of them? "No, you didn't. Damon is okay!"

The boat stayed the course. He either couldn't hear or didn't believe her. Staying low, she crawled crablike to starboard. The lake roiled, and the boat shuddered. When she'd neared a point in front of Michael, she reached out and slapped the switch on a spotlight Pop had mounted just in front of the console. The light flooded on, and she glanced forward again. The beam hit the driving rain, raising a silver curtain between them and the darkness, improving visibility not a whit. But maybe whoever had followed them could now spot the bass boat. She knew *someone* was riding to the rescue. That's just the way things worked in her family.

Hoping to see the running lights of the Cobalt boat racing toward them, she looked back but saw only a faint glow up on the hill. Their cabin . . . growing smaller and smaller.

She had to do *something*. Afraid she'd lose her balance if she sat up to swing her legs into the well, she scooted again until she was close enough to reach around the console to the key on the dash. She reached out, pulled her hand back. If she turned the engine off, chances were the waves would swamp them. Then it'd be *Sorry, Charlie*.

She tried yelling again. "We have to go back!"

"I killed them. I deserve to die!"

Scared as she was, her eyes rolled up. *God*. Teenagers always had to be so damn dramatic. "Well, I *don't*!"

They had cleared the mouth of the cove, and if her sense of direction wasn't totally screwed up, they'd reach the main channel in another minute. It was now or never. Not knowing what else to do, she grabbed the wheel to alter their course. Whether she was turning them toward the shore or only in a different direction, she didn't care. Either way was better than a close-up with the cliffs.

But she hadn't reckoned on Michael wrestling for command. He shoved her hand off, yanked the wheel, and the boat spun out of control. She flew sideways, then forward, banging her forehead on the tackle box, sprawling onto her back. Stars sprouted in her vision against the opaque black of a hill that loomed too close. The engine screamed as Michael swerved the other direction, trying to miss the shore.

The boat whirled sideways and she tumbled like a rag doll. Up was down, and down was up. Her fingers clutched for purchase, but her limbs were leaden and wouldn't work. In what seemed like slow motion, she rolled. Toward the side. Past the pedestal seat. Over the lip of the bow. And into the lake. Above the roar of the wind, she heard Michael's yell.

Then the water closed over her head, and everything went silent.

Jon Van Castle at the wheel, the Cobalt raced through the tar-black night, the engine roaring as it shot out of the water with each wave. Trying to keep his butt in the passenger seat, Andy gripped the edge of the dash with one hand and raised binoculars to his eyes with the other, figuring the effort was futile. It was. He cursed and let them drop. Nobody could see or hear a damned thing in this chaos. Certainly not a small bass boat pitching across the surface of an unforgiving lake. Back at the cabin, he'd wasted precious minutes on explanations, and then they'd all wasted even more time tripping over one another in their search for the Cobalt's keys. By the time he and Van Castle had fired up the boat, Mari and Michael had disappeared.

Mari . . . Fear that he'd never see her again shot through his veins.

Despite the slicker Zinnia had shoved in his hands, water ran down his neck and soaked his shirt. The hood was no match against the wind. He raked his gaze side-to-side, still seeing nothing in the bursts of lightning. He willed himself not to think of a bolt hitting the water. Unlike the bass boat, the Cobalt had a bimini top, wipers, and two spotlights, one mounted on each side of the windshield. Fat lot of good they were doing. Against the wall of water, the spots were useless. The wipers worse than useless. And the bimini was designed for shade from the sun, not protection from storms. To emphasize the point, the frame of the canopy suddenly ripped from the boat, somersaulted, and disappeared into the wake.

In the bucket seat next to Andy, Van Castle didn't

even flinch. His silhouette was carved in the backwash of light from the spots, the cast of his face determined. Andy wondered what the man was feeling—even *if* he was feeling anything more than a gale of adrenaline as he battled the elements.

Suddenly, the dull gleam of a covered fishing dock loomed to starboard. Jon swerved to miss it. The twenty-footer hawed, the engine set up a squall, and Andy braced himself to prevent being thrown from his seat. Then the boat died. Just as quickly, the storm's fury relented. The slash of rain became a shower.

Van Castle cranked the starter. The engine set up a grind, but didn't catch. He tried again. Failed again. He snapped off the spotlight on his side to conserve battery power, then dropped his head back on his seat, his lips pressed tight. Annoyed, no doubt, that the boat hadn't obeyed him. Andy left his light on, training it toward the shore. The wind still gusted but with less ferocity, no longer threatening to smash them against it, but still rocking them that direction. Thunder sounded, yet further away.

"Sorry," Van Castle muttered, eyes closed. "Racing around was an idiot thing to do."

"It's all right," Andy replied, talking more to himself than Van Castle, who didn't seem to need reassurance. He tightened the slicker at his throat while images crowded his brain. . . . Mari and Michael hurled into the lake. Or their battered bodies tangled in a bass boat broken on the shore. Urgency rose up and claimed him. "Try it now." His voice was overly loud.

Van Castle rolled his head sideways and opened one eye. "Better if we wait. Feel around over there—there's an oar."

Andy resented the other man's calm, but groped in the storage well running along his side of the Cobalt until his hand wrapped around an aluminum handle.

While Van Castle sat still as stone, eyes again closed, Andy extended the retractable oar and kept watch, ready to push the boat off the shore if they rocked too close. The seconds crawled by. Finally, just at the point when Andy thought his nerves would snap, Van Castle sat up and reached for the ignition. "We'll tool along the shore on this end. If we don't see anything, we'll chance the main—" His voice, so matter-of-fact to this point, suddenly broke. He pressed the bridge of his nose between fingers that trembled violently. "Oh, *God*," he whispered. "Oh, *Michael.*"

Andy stared. Some psychologist he'd make. The man wasn't calm, wasn't cool. He was hanging on by a string. "They'll be okay." Lame, meaningless words, but the best he could do. "We'll find them. We'll—"

Jon's hand fell. "You don't get it. When he was five, Michael fell off a boat—in this very lake—and almost drowned. It scared the bejesus out of him. Swimming in the shallows is fine. Fooling around with his grandpop in the bass boat near the shore is fine. Anything deeper and he loses it. If he's so out of his head that he set off for the main channel in weather like this . . ." He fumbled for the keys, tried the engine again. Then again. It still wouldn't fire. "*Dammit.*" He clenched the wheel with his hands and his voice dropped to a harsh whisper. "He has so much anger. At life. At me. I didn't protect him. Not on the houseboat. Not with his mother. I've tried to make it up to him, but there's not a damn thing that *can* make up for missing those first years of his life, for all the crap he lived through." He looked at Andy. "That's what you've waited to hear from me, isn't it?"

Andy was glad the night hid his flush. His opinions of Jon shimmered, blurred. "Yes, I mean, no . . . I mean, well, sure any kid would be angry when his dad let him down, but . . ." His mind came to a dead halt.

When his dad let him down. Any kid would be angry.
Any kid . . .

One corner of Jon's mouth crooked. "That's what I figured you thought." The slight grin faded. "And now Everheart says Michael's dealing with even more anger over Belinda's overdose."

Andy's thoughts were busy rearranging themselves, jumping around like drops of water popping in hot grease. Everything seemed so simple all of the sudden. Everything so clear. It was Psychology 101.

"Yes," Andy said slowly. "Because when someone you love fails you by dying it feels like betrayal. It's the ultimate abandonment, so anger is a normal part of grieving. Especially if . . . whether it's an accident or on purpose, the death is self-inflicted." ·

This time Jon's glance was sharp. "Exactly like Everheart puts it. And since Michael doesn't understand his anger, he's turned it on everyone—including himself." He ran a hand through his hair. "But I'm not telling you anything new. You've probably seen this same thing a hundred times."

A beat passed before Andy replied. "No. Only twice." With his father. And with Anna. *Physician heal thyself.* He stared off into the darkness, then looked back at Jon. "You know, you shouldn't blame yourself for everything that's happened to Michael because . . . because everyone makes mistakes. Yours weren't intentional." His dad and grandmother rose in his mind. *Mari . . .* "Most people's aren't."

Jon was quiet, drumming fingers on the wheel. Then he blew out a breath. "I know that. Lil convinced me of it a long time ago. But sometimes I forget."

It was easy to do.

Jon turned the key again. This time the engine caught, and he pushed the throttle forward, leaving the Cobalt at just over idling speed. Andy panned his spotlight at land, where dark water met rain-soaked woods. Feeling utterly spent and heartsore, his thoughts circled in and out, touching on Anna, remembering his parents, thinking of Gran, then finally settling on Mari.

Suddenly he straightened, his heart bumping. "Wait! What was that?" He could have sworn a light had flickered. Jon slowed the boat further and Andy stared where he thought he'd seen a muted flash.

"There! I see it!" Jon twisted the wheel to bring the Cobalt closer to shore.

They'd found the bass boat. It was shoved onto land, tipped slightly to one side. While they stared, its spotlight fluttered bright, then dulled to a bare wisp of flame. But there was no other movement. No Michael. No Mari. Just the boat and a wall of brush and oak and hickories marching down the Ozark mountain to the water's edge.

As Andy strained to see anything that could offer him hope, the spotlight on the bass boat gave one last gasp of brilliance and died.

Chapter 29

Minutes later, with the Cobalt beached and corded to a tree, both men stood alongside the bass boat and aimed their flashlights inside. It was battered. Empty. Like a broken toy, the boat was tossed up on the narrow shore of gravel and clay bordering the woods. It hadn't landed gently.

Giving evidence to both their fears, Jon turned and skimmed his light across the water. Andy's gaze followed the beam. There was no sign of anything—he swallowed—or any*one*.

Finally Jon sucked in a breath. Shoulders slumping, he turned. "Let's look around." His voice was barely audible over the slap of the rain on the leaves of the trees that loomed in dark shadows around them.

Jon moved one direction, Andy another. Images broke through the paralysis that had gripped his brain—Mari laughing, Mari nagging, Mari drowsy from lovemaking, Mari . . . drowning. A moan escaped his lips, and he shook his head. He played his flashlight up the embankment and over the ground. She couldn't be gone. Not just like that. Not before . . .

He frowned and snapped his light back to where it had just been, then moved closer and studied the earth about twenty feet away from the bass boat. "Jon!"

Jon hurried toward him.

Andy pointed with the flashlight. "Look at this."

He'd almost missed the footprint pressed into the clay, half full of water and losing its shape. Still the swirls of an athletic shoe were unmistakable. Michael's? Maybe.

Hope surging between them, the men moved around, studying the earth. Where the bank disappeared into heavy woodland undergrowth, Andy found the blurred impression of a bare foot. Jon another.

Excitement mounting, Andy stared up the steep hillside. "Mari!"

"Mi-chael!" Jon's voice joined his, but their calls were lost in the rattle of rain.

Slipping and sliding, they scrambled up through the brush and into the woods.

Huddling at the base of a squat cliff halfway up the hill, its outcrop providing some protection from the rain, Mari leaned back against rock, tightened her arms around Michael, and rested her cheek on top of his head. Despite her sodden state, she felt the heat of his tears on her neck, although he'd been mute since he'd hauled her out of the drink.

Nobody was likely to find them tonight—it was too dark and too wet and the lake was too big. Still, they probably should have stayed with the boat anyway. But after she'd belched up an ocean of water on the shore, she just hadn't been in the mood for common sense. Only one goal had driven her: to put as much distance between herself and Lake Kesibwi as she could. So, despite a gimpy ankle, no shoes, and a pounding head, she had, heading straight up the hillside.

"Well." She aimed for jocularity and hit closer to shrill. "I'd be halfway to the Arkansas border by now if this cliff hadn't gotten in the way." When Michael didn't respond, she added, "So much for remaining calm and cool in a crisis."

He still didn't react.

Huge surprise. This wasn't exactly one big yuck-fest. When she'd rolled off the bass boat, she hadn't been so addled that she hadn't realized what was happening. But her limbs had refused to respond to her semi-conscious brain. Thinking of the bleakness she'd felt as the water had closed over her head, she shivered. Thinking of the fear Michael must have felt before he'd jumped in to save her, she gathered him closer.

"Hey," she said with complete sincerity, talking past the lump in her throat. "Thank you for saving my life."

At first he didn't answer, and she thought he hadn't heard her.

Then he shuddered. "B-big deal."

She snorted. "*I* certainly think it is."

When that didn't even get a chuckle, she drew back. It was too dark to see his face. Michael had scrounged a flashlight out of the wreckage of the bass boat, but since the battery was almost a goner, she'd switched it off when they'd stopped. "Do you want to talk about it?" She didn't know squat about squat when dealing with trauma, but unloading had to be good.

Her question acted like poking a pin in a balloon. His words rushed out. "You shouldn't thank me; you should hate me. I didn't care what happened to you because I was mad at you. If it weren't for me, you wouldn't have almost drowned."

She looked for the right words—for once—and finally decided a light note might diffuse the drama. "Let's see . . ." she mused. "You blame yourself for Rose nearly getting hurt—which she didn't, by the way. For Damon hurting himself—and he'll be fine, too. And now for my near-drowning—which you actually prevented, you know. Everyone's fine. Imagine that."

"Don't joke! It's the *truth*. It *is* my fault."

So much for that approach. "Oh, Michael. Think about it. Don't you see?" Since summer's start, she'd learned a lot. Recently, she'd also thought a lot.

"You're acting like someone made you God and everyone's choices are now up to you." Remembering all the times she'd joined Andy in some escapade, her voice turned dry. "Believe me, Rose knew what she was getting into when she climbed into the Bronco, just like I did when I jumped into the boat. As for Damon, there was no way you could have known what he'd do with your knife."

"I should have figured it out!"

"How? At Sycamore, they guard everyone's pasts like Fort Knox. You couldn't have known unless Damon told you."

"But I *did* know about my mom, I knew how she was, and I still—" He choked on his words. "And she *died*."

Mari frowned. "I don't get it. How can you think you are even remotely responsible for your mother's overdose?"

Michael pulled away. When lightning flickered, she saw he'd pushed the heels of his palms against his eyes. She rested her hand on his back.

"I gave her money," he said dully.

She remembered what Melanie had said. *I told him . . . she'd probably just use the money he gave her on dope.* Understanding surfaced. "And you think she used it to buy the drugs she overdosed with?"

"I don't *think* it. I *know* it. The last time I saw her, she said she was broke." He sucked in a breath. "Melanie said not to give her money, but I thought Dad had brainwashed her against Mom, so I did it anyway." He choked. "And the very next day she—she died."

"Oh, God." Knowing exactly how he'd felt lugging all that guilt around, tears pricked her eyes. She slid her hand up to his shoulder and pulled him back against her. He didn't resist, but he also didn't relax. "Listen to me. You're not—"

She broke off. Through the trees, a light flickered.

She stared intently at the spot. At the same time she saw it again, a yell sounded over the rain.

Andy's voice! Her heart leapt and the tears welled over. "Over here! We're over here!" She yelled back, but didn't rise. And when she felt Michael's muscles bunch, she gripped him harder so he couldn't either. Not only was she unsure if her swollen foot would support her again, she knew Michael needed to hear what she had to say. And he needed to hear it now.

There was rustling in the undergrowth. She called again and switched on what remained of their flashlight. Shifting, Michael tried to rise, but she hung on like a terrier.

"Aunt Mari! Let go!"

"Not until you listen."

A beam bounced over the rock and finally pinned them. "Jon! Over here!" Andy rushed forward and dropped to his knees in front of her, his face white in the reflected glow from his flashlight. He felt her face, her shoulders, patted Michael, patted her again. "Are you hurt? Is anyone hurt? Oh, God, Mari, I thought you'd—"

"Me, too. Me, too. I'm fine. He's fine." She snuffled, and they both babbled. She'd never been so glad to see anyone in her life, but when Michael pulled against her grip, she reached out and tenderly touched Andy's lips. "Now shut up."

He fell into a startled silence.

"Are they all right?" Jon called from somewhere nearby.

"They're fine!" Recovering his voice and standing up to wave his flashlight, Andy looked down and glowered at her. In a normal voice he added, "In fact, your sister-in-law is as bossy, stubborn, and confusing as ever."

Hope bloomed in her chest, bigger than her mother's cabbage roses. He couldn't fool her. She'd heard affection in the complaint.

Once more, Michael started to scramble up. This was getting old. She latched onto him and yanked him back down. "Wait a minute. Just listen." Locking his face between her hands when he would have resisted, she looked straight into his eyes. "*Listen*."

He finally stilled.

She took a deep breath. "Just like Rose, just like Damon, and just like me . . . Your mother made her own decisions, knowing the risks she took. *Nobody* caused your mother's death, except her. Her death. Wasn't. Your. Fault." She glanced up at Andy. *And Anna's wasn't mine.*

She saw him swallow hard, but his eyes stayed on hers. So help her God, if a bomb went off in this clearing, she couldn't have torn her gaze off of his.

"No," Andy finally said, after a long pause in which she'd died a thousand times over. "It wasn't your fault."

Thank God . . . She could finally breathe again. Although now there was a good chance her heart might burst in her chest.

Jon pushed into the clearing. "Michael—" He fell to his knees in front of his son, swept him up against his chest, and rocked him back and forth. "I love you, bud. I love you so much."

Michael went stiff . . . then melted. His arms snaked around his father's neck. He buried his face in Jon's shoulder. And then he burst into tears.

Oh, *criminy. More* tears. Just between you, me, and the bedpost, she'd be glad when everyone quit jerking her heartstrings. Mari dashed at her eyes and turned her face up toward Andy. "You'll have to help me out here. My ankle's the size of a blimp and I don't think I can walk."

"I should have figured. Nothing with you is ever easy." Andy leaned over, grasped her wrists, and hauled her up.

Before she could do more than sputter in response,

he'd stripped himself of his slicker (even though the rain had diminished to mist and she couldn't get any wetter), tossed it over her head, and then scooped her up as if she weighed no more than one of those bags of potting soil he tossed around. Damn those extra six inches (and the few added pounds) he had on her.

She started to protest the caveman act, but as his warmth penetrated to her wet skin, even through his slicker, she decided against it. And when he whispered, "Easy or not, Mari O'Malley, I'll follow you anywhere," she decided the role of helpless female might have something going for it. At least for the moment.

She looped her arms around his neck, cradled her face in the crook of his neck, heard the beat of his heart . . . and felt safe for the first time in hours.

No, years.

She held on tight as he started down the hill, trusting him even when he slid a few feet. There'd be time enough tomorrow to tell him he wouldn't have to follow her far. Time enough to say that where she'd once looked for bustle, noise, bright city lights, and Manolo Blahniks to provide her with purpose, she now realized passion for life started inside. With what you gave to it. And with what you received in return. She hadn't wanted to be needed in Cordelia. But it had finally hit her that being needed wasn't so bad—especially by the very people *she* needed, too. She wanted to be near her family. . . .

Murmuring to herself, she smiled and snuggled closer in Andy's arms and closed her eyes.

And she wanted to be with No-Account Andrew Eppelwaite.

"What did you say?" Andy asked.

She repeated herself, this time putting her mouth to his ear. "I said: Besides, everyone knows Dorothy ended up back in Kansas and home at last."

Abruptly, he stopped. He tucked his chin back to

try to see her face. "Mari, out on the bass boat . . . did you hit your head?"

"Mmm-hmm." She traced the furrow between his eyes. "But don't get smug thinking you've avoided the Magnificent Mile altogether. We're spending our first vacation in Chicago. And the second one in New York. Even if we have to take out more loans."

She felt his frown deepen under her fingers. Then he gathered her closer and picked up his pace. Voice urgent, he called to Jon and Michael who had moved ahead with the flashlights, "We'd better get her home as fast as we can."

Smiling, she nestled back on his shoulder.

That was exactly what she wanted to hear.

AUTHOR'S NOTE

In *Home at Last,* the twin organizations that help troubled youth, Vreeley Home and Camp Sycamore, grew out of the sometimes skewed world of my imagination. In reality, of course, a number of such facilities do exist.

In the course of my research, I was fortunate to visit one such place: Ozanam Home for Boys and Girls. Since the late 1940s, Ozanam has been helping emotionally wounded adolescents find their way to healthy futures. (See www.ozanam.org for more information.) I came away from the time I spent there filled with profound sadness at the invisible scars borne by many of our children, yet buoyed by tremendous hope—due to the people who dedicate their lives to helping them heal. The "Finney glow" described in this book is not a fictional aberration.

While I took dramatic license with what I learned during my research and undoubtedly stretched the boundaries of truth, I struggled not to trivialize the remarkable efforts of those working within these organizations. What they do is vital; our need for them, acute. They deserve respect and gratitude, and I hope that's conveyed here.

Dear Reader,

If you've enjoyed *Home at Last*, I know you'll love my next book about Patsy Lee O'Malley, the widowed sister-in-law of the trio of sisters featured in my first three books. While she's appeared in each one, this quiet mother of four has always faded into the background in the midst of her more colorful relations. But in my next book, you'll discover she's a woman who's been hiding her light under a bushel.

But not from everyone . . . I'm also excited to bring back Zeke Townley. I've loved him—his dry wit and his wonderful self-honesty—ever since I introduced him as a country music sensation in *Sing Me Home*. Soon, Patsy Lee will love him, too.

Please join me again in September 2006 as I bring these two lonely souls together for a happy ending all their own!

Wishing you happiness,
Jerri Corgiat

P.S. Titles and release dates often change. Check www.jerricorgiat.com for the latest information.

Sing Me Home

The story of the O'Malley sisters began with Sing Me Home. . . .

When country music star Jonathan Van Castle, escaping from a clutch of fans, bursts into Lil O'Malley's bookstore, the young widow has no idea who he is and is fairly certain she doesn't want to. But for Jon, that first look from her china blue eyes is magic, and he redoubles his efforts to impress her.

"And your name?"

A drumroll filled his head. "Jonathan Van Castle."

The bookstore lady's eyes rolled halfway up. "Is that with a capital V and C?"

He deflated. "Yes. Deliver the book to the front desk. They'll get it to me."

"$243.60?"

"I still have a problem."

"Which problem are we discussing?"

"I seem to have left my wallet in—" He backed toward a door he assumed led to a storeroom with a delivery door, and motioned toward the pile of books. "Just pack it all up. I'll be right back."

He turned, headed through the back room before

she could protest, and found the delivery door. Just as he'd thought, it led to an alley.

"We do have a front door. The one you came in." She'd paused in the doorway, arms crossed.

He peered up and down the alley, then looked at her over his shoulder. "My phobias."

"Oh, yes. Your phobias."

The thermostat in his face ratcheted up another notch. He turned and almost banged the nose *Country Dreaming* called "regal" into the jamb. Muttering a curse, he slipped out.

Dodging through the warren of alleys at full tilt, he wondered if he'd gone nuts. What difference did it make if he returned? From the tone of her voice to the slant of her eyebrows, it was obvious she thought he was a jerk. A few bucks wouldn't change anything, and it wouldn't matter even if it did.

He reached a copse of trees that bordered the back of the park. The bus slumbered in a clearing and hadn't gone undetected. He spotted an orange head among a few women leaping to try to see through the tinted windows, but most milled yards away around the park entrance. His bodyguard, Roy, stood at the closed bus doors, thick arms crossed. Only his eyes moved, sweeping the park and finally lighting on Jon. His chin, the edge of an anvil, moved up a notch in acknowledgement.

Taking a deep breath, Jon sprinted. He was on them in seconds. Before the women could squeak, Roy had shoved him in the bus and muscled in after him. The driver slammed the doors.

Roy flopped into the first available seat and mopped at his head with his bandanna. Jon patted thanks on his shoulder.

Zeke turned a page of his magazine. "Having an adventure, my man?"

Jon leaned down to give the driver directions, then shoved Zeke's feet off the couch and took their place.

Zeke gave him a look of mock annoyance and straightened the crease in his trousers.

"Just a slight detour," Jon said.

The driver shifted into gear. Zeke's eyebrows shifted higher. "She must really be something."

"She? I just found something I want—"

"I'll bet."

Jon frowned. "And I forgot my wallet."

"Mmm."

The driver eased up to Merry-Go-Read. The bus halted with a hydraulic wheeze. The bookstore lady couldn't help but notice.

Jon stood up, signaling Roy. The other security guards also stood, abandoning their cards, and got out. Sure she was watching, Jon bypassed his usual leap from the bus, gathered his dignity, ignored Zeke's eyebrows, and promenaded between his sentries the eight feet to her door.

Inside, everything was still in its place, including the bookstore lady. She stood behind the counter, her hands folded, and if she'd noticed his triumphant return, she didn't betray it by even a blink. "$243.60?"

Wilting, he approached. "I know. You told me." With one final flourish, he handed over a Platinum Visa with "Jonathan Van Castle" emblazoned across the front.

Now she would recognize him. She would finally put two and two together. He pasted a modest look alongside a grin, and waited for her hand to fly over her fluttering heart. But she only slid the card through the machine and waited for it to belch out a receipt.

His grin faded. He reached for the card, but she pulled it back, and slid the receipt in front of him. "Please sign."

Hell. He grabbed a pen, scrawled his John Henry, and when he was done, she by-God picked it up and compared it to the card. Satisfied—and she'd better be—she offered him the card and receipt. He snatched them from her.

"Thank you. Have a nice day." Polite words, no smile.

He'd have a nice day all right, no thanks to her. He grumbled his way to the door. As he reached for the handle, voices crescendoed outside.

The soft scent of honeysuckle tickled his nose. The bookstore lady had moved up behind him. "My goodness. Mari! What is she doing?"

"The redhead?"

"My little sister." Her tone was grim.

Roy held the redhead back as she and her friends tried to force their way to the bus. Apparently they thought he was in it. Jon turned to look at the bookstore lady.

For once, she was looking back. "Who are you?"

Finally. He let his slow smile surface, but didn't reply. Instead, he chucked her gently under the chin. Curiosity turned to a glare. He opened the door and stepped into his world. Squeals rose, hands reached, but his guards held firm. As he swung into the bus, his smile lingered.

Zeke glanced up. "Get what you wanted?"

"Oh, yeah."

"A phone number? A date?"

"Nope." He tossed his sack down, settled onto the sofa, and locked his hands behind his head.

Zeke raised an eyebrow.

"I got the last word." And he hadn't had to say a thing.

Follow Me Home

The story of the O'Malley sisters continues in Follow
Me Home. . . .

*Four years after her divorce from Stan Addams,
Alcea O'Malley has to face not only foreclosure on
her house but a difficult fourteen-year-old daughter,
an interfering family, daily run-ins with Stan's former
mistress, and no job prospects except schlepping eggs
at the local diner under the cantankerous eye of its
owner, Peg. But all that pales beside her surprise when
she encounters an old flame. Dakota Jones is back
in town. He has the same disarming smile, the same
chameleon eyes, a past he's hiding from . . . and a
trailer for rent. Living in a trailer has never been high
on Alcea's wish list, but after Dak gives her a tour
and invites her for coffee, she finds herself tempted,
despite her misgivings. . . .*

Dak handed her a mug, then settled himself beside
her, locking his ankles on top of an empty planter.
The sun was now well up over the horizon. For a
moment, they watched the Ozark hills in the distance
and the clouds scuttling across a sky as blue as the
cornflowers that grew in her mother's garden. She slid
a sideways look at him. He looked totally relaxed,

head tipped back, eyes half-closed, hair lifting off his forehead in a light breeze.

She picked up her coffee. "So, what have you been up to for the last twenty years?"

"Traveling. Writing."

She took a sip. She couldn't get rid of the odd tension in her body. But years at the country club had given her an ease with the social niceties, although—what a surprise—they'd never come naturally. "What do you write?" she asked.

"Stories, articles." One of his shoulders rose and fell.

"Do you—" She'd been about to ask if he made much money, but stopped to rephrase. "Do you sell many?"

A smile tickled his lips. "Enough. And I enjoy it, so what more could I ask?"

A lot more than this. Her gaze swept his "inheritance," the scraggly yard, the pink trailer, the narrow house. "Did you ever marry?" The words slipped out.

"Once. A long time ago. We were both still in college." He spoke easily. No artifice, no evasion. "It only lasted a few years. Nobody's fault. What about you? I know you married Stan. What happened?"

She squirmed, then responded with the same directness. "Stan's a shit."

His quick smile flashed. "That says it all."

She shrugged. "He was a serial adulterer. After Kathleen was born, he had an affair because I didn't pay enough attention to him. At least that was his excuse, and I forgave him that one. But not the twenty gazillion other ones that came after. He was discreet about it at first." She halted, surprised at herself. She wasn't one for the current rage of baring her soul. But, just like when she was sixteen, she was telling him things she usually kept to herself.

"At least he showed you that small courtesy." Dak's voice was dry.

She snorted and decided to forget discretion. "Oh,

it wasn't for me. If she'd gotten wind of his escapades, his mother would have killed him—or worse, changed her will. But after she died seven years ago, he was a tomcat in heat."

"But you stayed with him until, what, four years ago?"

"Call me a chump. Or call me a wimp. It seemed easier to stay. I didn't leave because I didn't know how I'd support Kathleen." She looked across at the trailer. She still didn't.

"I wouldn't call you either of those things," he said quietly.

She eyed him. He didn't look judgmental. She relaxed further. "I guess one day I'd just had enough. When Lil got married, and I saw how happy she was . . . Well. My pride had taken all it could take and I knew if I didn't get out, I'd . . . lose myself." She took another sip, then thunked the mug on the table. "I don't even know what I mean." Nor did she understand why his presence caused an alien to take over her mouth.

"I felt the same way about my marriage. And my career. There's no shame in making changes, you know. The shame only lies in continuing in the same rut if you're not happy."

"Yes. Well." She looked at the trailer again. "I guess I've dug a whole new rut."

"You never know what lies around the corner. Maybe you'll like this rut better."

"Maybe. Kathleen won't."

She stopped, startled again at her frankness. Obviously, she'd been way too long without friends.

"So Kathleen learned at school about the foreclosure."

On the verge of telling herself Dak wasn't exactly a friend, so she should shut up, instead she said, "And she's not exactly thrilled by the change in our circumstances."

"Gave you a hard time, huh?"

"Hard time doesn't begin to cover it. Screaming, throwing things, refusing to come out of her room. *That* begins to cover it. I can't blame only her, though. I spoiled her." Good God. Her self-admitted failings as a mother were a secret she didn't normally blab about.

"I don't know a thing about raising kids, but I hear they're pretty adaptable."

"You don't know Kathleen."

"She'll adjust."

"She won't."

They fell silent.

Alcea picked up her mug and studied her coffee. "Do you remember that night?"

The question felt normal, natural. And she wanted to know. For a short while, he'd had a profound effect on her, and she'd always wondered if it had all been one-sided.

He locked gazes with her. "Sure, I remember." He didn't pretend not to know what she was talking about.

She looked away. "Why wouldn't you take me to the senior dance? I practically put the invitation right in your mouth." And had embarrassed herself in front of the entire school population. He'd left her sitting alone in the middle of her classmates' muffled laughter, her eyes starry from barely-held tears.

She could feel his gaze resting on her. "We were young, Alcea." His voice was gentle. "And I wasn't very smooth in the way I handled everything. But you were barely sixteen, and I was about to leave for college. And . . . there were differences in what we wanted. I thought about you all the rest of that night, if that makes any difference, but there didn't seem to be a point."

"I guess not." She looked at him again. "But did you ever wonder, 'what if?' "

"No." This time *he* averted his gaze. For the first

time she wondered if was being honest. "What-if isn't very useful." A blink of a smile. " *'Do, or do not. There is no try.'* "

Ha. One she knew. Not like the Shakespeare he and Julius spouted at each other. "Yoda." She reached for her mug and took another sip. "So you live by doing. No holding back. Dam the torpedoes and full speed ahead?"

"Yes, I'd say I'm a little more self-assured than I was back then." His eyes hooked hers, and she sucked in a breath. "I know what I want. And I pretty much get it." His gaze dropped to her sandals. "You have very pretty feet."

The air suddenly radiated sex.